THE SHADOW BROKER

TINA CLOUGH

THE SHADOW BROKER

PAPERBACK ISBN 99780473599119

Disclaimer

Most locations in this book are real places, but details have been changed to avoid comparisons with real businesses and individuals. The characters are the author's invention and are not based on any particular persons.

Lightpool Publishing

www.lightpoolpublishing.com

Cover and book design by Andrene Low

A catalogue record for this 5x8" edition is available from the National Library of New Zealand.

To order print copies please contact: Publishers Distribution Limited orders@pubdist.co.nz

1

It is half past nine and she is finally alone, dementia-struck Brendan safely asleep and the day's work done, and this is her time. Her reward for giving up a research career and coming home to look after her widowed father, teaching science at a high school and putting her personal goals and ambitions on hold. There is no sound from upstairs, the nightly sleeping pill, always referred to as his vitamin pill, has done its job.

Minnie switches the kettle on, unlocks her phone and frowns in confusion. The usual swirly blue screen has been replaced by an analog clock face with an alert saying that she has unread text messages from someone called Broker, and the messages are strange and in some sort of shorthand. The contacts folder confirms her suspicion; this is not her phone despite the fact that she unlocked it with her usual PIN.

Her mind rewinds to early evening when she sat in her car and watched Jane sprint towards her across the school parking lot, dark ponytail swinging from side to side, waving something above her head.

'Sorry, Minnie – I forgot your phone!' She arrived panting and pushed a phone into Minnie's hand. 'I knew you wouldn't miss it for days – nobody else could lose their phone and not notice.'

'Where was it?'

'I picked it up in the bistro last night, after you left. It's been in my bag all day, sorry!'

'Are you coming with us for dinner?' Minnie slid the phone into her bag on the passenger seat.

'No, no – it's book club night at my place. I just stayed to watch them film the award ceremony.'

Now Minnie nods to herself and checks her bag again and her own phone is there, so Jane picked up someone else's phone.

Isn't that odd, she thinks, and looks at the phone in her hand – I knew that my PIN was simplistic in the extreme, but 2580 was so easy to enter and I could never forget it, just a straight line down the number pad, but someone else had exactly the same idea. And what are the chances that someone with that PIN would come across another phone with that same PIN? Or are there thousands? I should turn it off and hand it in at the bistro, but those messages seem so odd, and the contacts – not a single real name just nicknames and initials. I'll have another sneaky look.

Five minutes later her curiosity is at high pitch, and she picks up her own phone and calls Jane, but gets no reply, just 'Hi, it's Jane, please leave a message.'

'Hi, it's Minnie. Can you call me please? It's about that phone.'

She continues reading messages on the stranger's phone, occasionally pausing deep in thought, until Jane calls half an hour later.

'Jane, you won't believe it, that phone - it's someone else's. I had mine in my bag all along.'

'Oh, no! I was sure it was yours. You know where we sat on that curved seat? When you left, I slid along to make some more room at the far end and my hand touched the phone. It was sort of wedged in the crease between the seat and the backrest. It never occurred to me it wasn't yours – it looked the same.'

'It is the same - identical.'

'Never mind, I'll call in at the bistro and ask if someone has tried to locate it.'

'Either that or hand it in to the cops, I suppose.'

They talk about other things for a few minutes, but Minnie's mind is only half on the conversation. As soon as the call is finished, she picks up the found phone, enters the PIN and opens the message folder again.

These people are concealing their identities and using what looks like code in some places, she thinks, and they aren't kids and it's not an illicit love affair – it's something illegal or subversive, but exactly what? Acronyms and initials – some of them I recognize, this is very interesting.

Her researcher's mind is hooked, and she fetches a notebook and starts making notes. An hour later she puts the phone down and goes to make another cup of tea. Deep in thought and with a feeling of unreality, she leans against the kitchen bench and waits for the water to boil.

I'm not going to hand it in. I'll keep it for a while, try to figure out a bit more. Nobody will ever know that I managed to unlock it. I'm sure I know what it's about now, but what should I do next?

She opens her laptop and searches the internet for ways to save the text messages from the phone to her computer while her mug of tea goes cold beside her. What she eventually saves on her hard drive is a folder of a kind she has never seen before with the suffix ".smscom", and her attempts to open it fail.

This is crazy but totally fascinating, she thinks, this phone belongs to someone who is involved in illegal deals with officials. Who can I discuss this with? Only Rumble, really, because I must be careful – it is so easy to end up in trouble these days, suspected of subversive activities or being labelled as a security risk. The intelligence services have such incredible powers now, and I don't want to be put on that damn Watch List, because once on it, you stay there for life. The rumour is that there is a Kill List too where you end up after you've clocked up three so-called national security transgression and then they kill you, but could it possibly be true?

An hour later she has three pages of detailed notes and apprehension mixed with excitement building in her mind. When the phone in her hand vibrates silently, she jumps. A new message from the contact called Broker has appeared.

'Please respond asap. I want to know how the meeting went.'

She feels as if a stranger has got into the house and suddenly nervous, she turns the phone off, and after a moment's thought she takes out the SIM card.

Email to Rumble: Rumble, can you please come for lunch Saturday? I need help with a technical problem.

Minnie is deep in a dream where she wades through deep snow in an endless forest, pursued by a shapeless threat, when Brendan's urgent voice wakes her up.

'Minnie, wake up – we're going to be late for work.'

He is leaning over her with a shirt clasped in one hand, his face anxious. She checks the time; twenty-five past six and time to get up anyway.

'It's all right Dad - don't you remember? You have two weeks off. You can go back to bed if you like.'

Creating calming scenarios has become second nature since she moved back to live at home, and as usual a reasonable-sounding story helps him accept a confusing situation.

'Of course,' he says, pretending to remember. 'I forgot, how silly of me. I'll go back to bed and listen to the radio. Tell me when you're ready for breakfast and I'll join you.'

While she showers and dresses, Minnie starts planning a fifteen-minute test to surprise her Year 12 chemistry class and mentally maps out a dozen questions to go on the whiteboard, with a couple tricky ones to catch those who haven't paid attention since the start of this hot summer term. Downstairs she checks that Brendan's reminders are in place: laminated signs attached here and there with Velcro dots. "I am at work. Sharon will be here soon. Minnie". She has no idea if they comfort him; last week she found them neatly stacked in the bathroom cabinet.

When Brendan has made toast and the kettle has boiled, she quietly flicks the concealed circuit breaker for the stove and the kitchen power points when he isn't looking. Rumble calls while they are eating, and she walks into the hall with a piece of toast in her hand to talk to him out of Brendan's hearing.

'Hi, Petal, what's wrong? Something you need help with?'

'I'll tell you when I see you, it's too much to explain over the phone. Could you bring your laptop please – I think we'll need it.'

'Have you broken something?' He laughs his deep Rumble laugh. 'It might do me good to get out in daylight for a change – don't think I've seen the sun for a week. See you tomorrow.'

While she tidies the kitchen, she contemplates Rumble's awful lifestyle, which is that of a modern-day cave dweller who works through the night, orders fast food and drinks buckets of coffee.

Half an hour later, when she kisses Brendan goodbye and reminds him that Sharon will be there at half past nine or ten, he has an unexpected flashback to the past and says cheerfully, 'I think I'll sit down with old Herodotus' History today. It's been years since I read it. He was one of the very first people to write in prose, you know - possibly the very first. What we know about the Peloponnesian war is all thanks to him.'

At the end of Rawhiti Terrace the street is blocked by a minor accident involving a van and car, and while two men push the car to one side, she stares unseeingly at them and thinks about those text messages. The driver behind her toots impatiently and she manages to get around the van and turns left into Glasgow Street. As she drives through the city centre her mind reverts to Brendan talking about Greek history. These glimpses of her father's old self that appear without warning, like ghosts of the man he used to be, they unnerve her every time. And it triggers memories of him reading stories at bedtime, of creeping into Sander's bed when she woke in the night, because he was nearly like a parent, and seemed so much older. She can still imagine Sander's voice saying, 'it's ok Min-min, go back to sleep'. And then the accident changed it all, she thinks, and our lives never went back to that barely remembered normality. She takes a deep breath and shifts her focus to the day ahead.

At morning break Minnie is in the staff room putting papers away, when Jane appears beside her and drops her bag to the floor with a thump.

'God Minnie, I'm so sorry I've left you with that damn phone. It's not fair to give you the responsibility for it, so give it to me and I'll do something with it.'

And Minnie surprises herself with a top-quality spontaneous lie, not something she is usually good at. 'I dropped it at the bistro on my way to school.' After a moment's thought, she adds a detail she has noticed on one of her visits. 'They have a box with a little flap for mail on the door - it seemed secure enough. I just popped it in there with a note.'

'OK, that's all good then. What are you doing on Saturday morning? Want to meet for a coffee?'

'I can't – my friend Rumble is coming over. And Dad is a bit funny at the moment. We'd better have a quiet weekend at home, I think.'

'Rumble – is he that hacker guy you went to school with?'

'Yes – best friends from the word go. But he's a white hat hacker, Jane – not a bandit.'

'Yeah, you said that once before – but what does it mean? What's with the white hat?'

'It's like in the old cowboy movies, the good guy wears a white hat. Rumble tests the internet security for banks and big companies - if he finds a crack in their defenses, he tells them how to fix it.'

Jane grins. 'You must let us meet him sometime – Jordan would love it. He spends hours trying to work out how to make our computers do completely unnecessary things – turn the TV and the heat pump on while we're on our way home and whatever. I wish he would make up his mind to go back to university and finish that technology degree. The mail job's way too simple, there's no stimulation there at all and it's making him lazy.'

She makes a face, picks up some papers from her pigeonhole and leaves.

2

Rumble arrives, hot and sweaty in a black Metallica T-shirt. A hairy giant carrying a small backpack.

'God, it's nice to see you again,' says Minnie. 'It's been ages. You look hot.'

'Hot? Roasting is more like it. The bloody air con is on the blink again and the car was like an oven. What happened to cool and windy Wellington summers?'

She laughs and walks ahead of him to the kitchen. 'Dad, can you put up the sun umbrella on the deck please? There's beer in the fridge, Rumble, help yourself.'

'Nothing for you?'

'No, never, but you go ahead.' He says this every time, she thinks, like a security check in case someone is impersonating me.

They are very close, comfortable that they know each other's foibles and secrets and not concerned about the things they don't agree on. When Brendan settles down for an after-lunch snooze in his armchair, Rumble and Minnie sit side by side at the dining table with their laptops in front of them.

'Right,' says Rumble and waits.

'Right,' says Minnie. 'This is what happened. Jane found a cell phone at the bistro after I'd left the other night. It looked like mine and it was where I'd been sitting, so she picked it up. She gave it to me and when I turned it on, I found it wasn't mine. And it's got some weird stuff on it.'

He frowns. 'Wasn't it locked?'

'Yeah, it was, but I used my own PIN and it unlocked, so

whoever owns it uses the same PIN – cosmic coincidence. But it is a very simple PIN, stupidly simple.'

'And what do you need help with?'

She tells him about the code names and the messages, and how she managed to download them after several attempts.

'But I can't open that folder – it isn't like any folder I've seen before. And I don't want to turn the phone on again. '

'Why didn't you just hand it in?'

'It's those messages. I want you to read some, and then we'll talk about it.'

He gives her a searching glance, but all he says is, 'OK, let's do that.'

'I took the SIM card out – I didn't know if anyone could find me, if I left it in the phone even if it was turned off.'

'Both the SIM card and the phone itself leave traces every time you use it. Phones have ID numbers, and the networks record them. But if the SIM card is out, it's completely off-line.'

'OK, that's good.'

'Let's get on with it then - first we'll crack this folder. I'll shift it to my laptop so I can work on it.'

She watches as Rumble gets a memory stick out of his pocket and copies the folder to his own laptop. His big fingers tap away with incredible speed and the cursor moves so fast she never has time to see what he clicks on. One screen after another is opened, studied and discarded, while she sits silent beside him. After a few minutes he grunts. 'Got it!'

She leans over to see and there are the text messages, but not in neat paragraphs with the date and time on separate lines, just a dense mass of continuous text.

'Oh God, look at it – what a mess!'

'Yeah, I know - hard to read. When you saved the folder, did you get an option to open it or save it in another format?'

She thinks back and shakes her head. 'I don't think so – just a Save button.'

'OK, we can read them like this – we'll get used to it.'

'I want you to read quite a few, please – and not just messages to and from one person, try several. And then we'll talk about it.'

'OK, give me another beer and I'll do anything for you.'

He scrolls through the dense text with a look of intense concentration. At one point he looks up and stares into the distance with a frown, scrolls back and re-reads something. For ten minutes Minnie fidgets and tries to resist the urge to lean over to see what he is reading, then he looks up and runs his hands through his mass of tight curls.

'Shit, Minnie – this is weird.' His voice has a hard edge to it.

'Exactly - I made some notes. I'll show you the stuff that really freaks me out.'

She gets her notebook out and shows him the page where she jotted down acronyms and abbreviations. 'Does this suggest something to you?'

'Does it what! People hiding behind made-up names and those initials – this is about politics and money, a nasty mixture. Not to mention threats from higher up, whatever the hell that means.'

He up-ends the bottle and tips the last drops of beer into his mouth.

'When you seemed so worried about someone tracking down the phone, I thought you were being paranoid, but you were right. We'd better discuss where to next.'

'Let's park it for a day while you think about it. I want to sort out some of these acronyms and abbreviations – there are so many, and they are such a mixture of things, official ones and others that look more like personal shorthand, like some kind of private text-speak.'

'Really? Do you think you'll be able to work something out if you do that?'

Minnie studies the screen and says absently, 'Maybe – it's just a feeling I've got. That the combinations are significant. It might tell me something. I'll call you when I've got a handle on it and then we'll talk - one evening after Dad has gone to bed.'

'Let's do a search for this guy's number and see if it comes up somewhere,' says Rumble and she waits patiently without trying to see what he is doing, and after a few minutes he says, 'Nope – not a damn thing, but they'd use burner phones, of course. I just thought it might be worth a try. Do you still have the old laptop I told you to keep because it had a disc drive, in case you ever needed one – the blue one, years ago? OK – we'll save the folder on that and then I'll delete the file from this laptop and mine, set up a file shredding operation so there's no trace of it.'

A shiver runs down her back. 'Do you think they could trace it back to me?'

'This could be dynamite, Petal – I mean, who is this guy who owns the phone? And that talk about 'someone higher up' – a threat if I ever heard one. And they're going to a lot of trouble to stay anonymous – code names, initials and I bet they're using burner phones. This isn't your usual political influencers at work. Let's stay under the radar for now and make you untraceable. There might be a lot at stake, and these days it could turn to shit really easily.'

Once again, a current of unease runs through her. 'I know – I can't believe how fast things have changed,' she says, feeling sad and angry at the same time. 'Remember how we used to pride ourselves on being a good democracy, and we thought those things that happened in other countries would never spread to us – before Trump and Putin and the mega-rich who seem to sit outside the law. And now we too have a government full of rich people busy making themselves richer and all these draconian laws. I don't want to be accused of being subversive and end up on the Watch List – or the Kill List. Can they get into my hard drive and find the folder without having my actual laptop?'

'There's very little that they can't do - the world's a fucking mess. A couple of my mates have gone underground, they're sure they are on that Watch List, scared shitless they'll end up in prison on some crazy charge. So let's not take any chances. That ancient laptop of yours is the perfect option - it's not wifi capable and you don't carry it around. Just leave it safely at home. Now - let's put the SIM card back in one last time. They might have sent more messages since you took it out.'

As soon as the card is inserted, half a dozen messages arrive on the stranger's phone; increasingly urgent questions from people called Dustman and Broker about the whereabouts of its owner.

'Holy shit!' Rumble turns the phone off and takes the card out. 'They're getting very bothered about this guy and why he's not connected.'

Quarter of an hour later, with Minnie's old laptop plugged in and charging, Rumble transfers the message folder.

'Right,' he says. 'Now pay attention, Petal. The messages are now safely on that old laptop and deleted from your new one. I'm going to set up some processes on your current laptop – could you plug this one in to charge too?'

He connects her new laptop to his own with a double-ended USB cable. 'You know how you delete a file, but it's actually still there? It doesn't show up in the directory, but it stays on your hard drive until you overwrite that particular spot – which happens by chance and sometimes not for a long time. The software I'm using will do two things - first it defrags the disk, moves blocks of data to empty spaces in the sectors – consolidates it. A bit like tidying a cupboard to maximize the space.'

Minnie can't help laughing at the mental image of Rumble tidying his kitchen cupboards. 'Bet you've never done that!'

'Yeah, right - but I still understand the principle. Anyway, after the defragging, the file shredding software will go through and fill all the empty space with random digits, just nonsense, so your drive ends up full of junk, which you overwrite when you save new files. And it goes through this random data stuff a couple of times, it takes a while. It's like wrapping something in plastic and then putting it a box and then burying it in the garden. Makes it very hard to sniff anything out.'

She shakes her head at her own ignorance. 'I thought stuff was gone if I deleted it.'

'A lot of people do, but I must say I'm surprised you weren't aware. And it doesn't usually matter - I mean, who gives a shit if a deleted file is still on the hard drive? The rubbish bin is called the recycle bin because you can recycle things – unless they've been over-written. You can go into the recycle folder and delete things from there, but they can still be found. Very useful for the cops, when bad guys delete their incriminating files.'

'Lucky for me that I've got you.'

'We're both lucky, Petal.'

She very rarely hugs him, though she often wants to, but he's uncomfortable with people touching him and he has been since he was a boy. As far as she knows, he has never had a physical relationship with anyone. Mind you, she silently tells herself, you're a fine one to talk.

Rumble heaves his huge bulk out of the chair and looks at Brendan, who is sleeping peacefully with his mouth open.

'He is getting worse, isn't he?'

'Yes – in fits and starts. He sleeps a lot more too. And then sometimes he stuns me, like yesterday when he talked about some historian from ancient Greece - like having his old self back. But at least he's not done anything dangerous lately, thank God. And thank heaven for Sharon, too.'

3

When Rumble leaves Minnie returns to the kitchen and finds Brendan trying to tidy up after lunch.

'Where do these bottles go, Minnie?' He stands indecisive in front of the open fridge with two empty beer bottles in his hand.

'Just pop them in the green bin under the bench. They'll go out with the recycling on Monday.'

For the rest of the afternoon, she concentrates on Brendan; a walk around the block, a cup of tea and summer pruning the roses inside the front fence together. When finally, he sits absorbed in front of the TV after dinner, she sets up an Excel spreadsheet on her old laptop and begins analyzing text messages from the stranger's phone, so immersed in what she is doing that she jumps when the phone rings.

'Hi Minnie – Morgan here. Sorry to call you at home, but I wanted to check if it's OK to give your number to that TV guy? Luke what's-his-name. He called and said you two talked about a follow-up and he'd like to continue the discussion. He says he's talked to his producer, sounds genuine - but I think he's quite interested in you, as a person I mean.'

'That's OK – you can give him my number. He seemed nice enough, but I'm not looking for dates.'

God, here's another one that I quite like and now I must somehow move him from potential date to the friend zone, she thinks. It's a bit tedious, but I've done it before.

She puts the phone down and stares unseeingly at the TV,

thinking about how strangely her life has developed and wonders if she will ever date a man again.

When the science department went out for a drink after the award ceremony, Luke made a point of telling her and Morgan how impressed he was with the students.

'I can't remember ever feeling as if I was part of the faculty when I was at school,' he said. 'They seem to have taken ownership of this project, feel they're part of the team – I'm not surprised you got the award.'

'All due to Minnie's initiative,' said Morgan generously. 'I might be the head of the department, but this is all Minnie's work.'

He turned to talk to someone on his other side, and Minnie moved her chair so she could look at Luke without turning sideways. Was he pure Chinese or a mixture? Mixture probably, she thought, the best of both worlds. 'They've amazed us all – and probably themselves too.

'So, it wasn't part of the plan?'

'Oh no, the thing took on a life of its own – the seniors got engaged in the process of change and before we knew it, they'd made it a collective venture.'

'Maybe you've started a revolution.' His tone was light, but she could tell he was serious.

'More students opting for science is good, but the end goal is that more students go on to science degrees – at the moment, even the ones who are good at science often don't. Business and law attract far more students than science.'

He nodded in cynical agreement. 'Probably influenced by the potential for big salaries. Do you think the lack of science graduates puts a brake on research development in general? Would more science activity overall improve the percentage of the GDP we spend on research?'

She had under-estimated him and mentally apologized. There was no reason why a smooth presenter couldn't be intelligent and well-informed as well.

'I've thought about it a lot since I left my university job – high-school teaching has been a real eye-opener. It's vital that we inform the students of what science degrees can lead to in the way of career opportunities. Now we have industry and research people come to school for discussion groups with the students and mentoring them – and it inspires them, makes them think about science in a different way.'

He changed the subject. 'What sort of research were you doing?'

'I was working on commercially viable bioplastics, mainly to replace grade five.' She waited for him to ask why she left, but he pushed his chair back.

'Can I get you a glass of wine?'

'I'd like a tonic with lemon please.'

'Sure?'

'Yes, I don't drink alcohol.'

His face registered no reaction at all, which was unusual, most people did.

Now the phone buzzes again; she shakes her head and brings her mind back to the present. 'Hi, it's Luke Chan, from Up Close. I got your number from Morgan.'

'Hi, Luke.'

'We think a follow-up would be great. What you have initiated at your school sets an example and it deserves to be revisited in-depth. I've talked to Amanda, our producer - and she's very interested. She did a science degree before she got into TV productions and the subject is close to her heart. She's quite keen to film in installments, perhaps one per term and then edit them into a continuous update and add the conclusions - follow a small group of kids over time. It would be a full commercial hour devoted to your project. What do you think?'

She is surprised by how ambitious this is, a much bigger project than what she expected.

'What's a commercial hour?'

'Depends on the time of night it's broadcast, but it's about forty-four minutes – the rest is ad breaks.'

'It sounds great, but I need to think about the idea of doing it in segments. It would be pretty intrusive for the students - and the parents and the school would have to approve it of course. But let's talk about it.'

'Amanda wants a meeting soon, so we can start discussing it. If we are going to do it in stages, we have to start working on the proposal and a budget right away.'

'OK, let's do that, but I can't make it till Wednesday, late afternoon.'

Sharon can come and sit with Brendan nearly any time but letting them wait a couple of days seems like a good strategy, never seem too keen. They agree on Wednesday, on condition that Minnie can book Sharon.

4

Sundays are always the same with a morning trip to the supermarket and a walk or a drive along Oriental Bay to look at the sea, then home for lunch. Routines keep Brendan on an even keel, a comforting sameness that keep him grounded, the calming re-set position after incidents. Minnie is upstairs after lunch when she hears the front door slam, and she races down the stairs and out the front door to see Brendan striding purposefully down the sidewalk, nearly at the corner already. She runs to catch up, slows to his pace and takes his arm, matches her stride to his.

'Going for a walk, Dad?'

He shrugs her arm off, angry and frustrated. 'I'm running late, I don't know how I'll get there on time.'

'Where are you going?'

'It's that classics meeting, curriculum strategy – I'll miss my flight.'

Eventually she calms him, and they start back towards the house, but in Minnie's chest is a hard lump of worry, because this is a major incident, the worst for months. Now she must keep the front door locked even when she is home, and she must remember to warn Sharon. The lonely responsibility of creating a safe and happy life for Brendan is a constant balancing act. Her wish to give him as normal a life as possible must be weighed against risks, and she constantly re-evaluates things as his condition changes. When his dementia was first diagnosed the specialist suggested that he should live in a rest home, a secure facility where he could become familiar with a new environment before he deteriorated further.

But she has made her choice, and until he becomes a serious risk to himself, she will continue to look after him.

While Brendan snoozes over the newspaper, Minnie sits quietly thinking her way around the house where Rumble and a workman did the dad-proofing. The back garden is completely enclosed and the electrical appliances in the kitchen are linked to a couple of hidden circuit breakers. The front door has an electronic lock and there are window-locks on the ground floor windows, apart from those that overlook the back garden.

She sighs and re-reads a sequence of text messages she has already looked at twice; a short exchange full of implications, not all of which she understands.

Broker: 30k is too much – she is only a junior polad. Find someone else in mpi?

Stranger: Can try minad, new to us, might want more but more influence. Highly trusted. Have to find leverage to get him on board.

Broker: OK, top limit 20k.

Stranger: Give me a few days.

Stanger: Done. Minad accepts but only to push intensive format and land-use exception. Will def need local body push too. Mbie issue still on hold. Discharge exception needs direct pressure, different polad.

She is fully aware that if she is found out, the consequences would be serious, but her curiosity is intense, and she wants to continue despite the risk. That saying, "all it takes for evil to triumph, is for good men to do nothing" sums it up, she thinks, and what if I'm the only person aside from the corrupt players who knows anything about this? I can't ignore it. The Ministry of Business Innovation and Employment and the Ministry for Primary Industries are key ministries for everything related to business. Whatever those messages refer to it clearly involves bribery of state servants, furthering business interests by high-level shortcuts and being given special privileges. How far will these people go to protect their reputations and investments? Powerful people with big resources and little in the way of conscience; already involved in illegal activities. Would they pull strings to use the Government's extensive new powers, put me under surveillance, eavesdrop on my phone and emails? I must be very, very careful and consider every step. She turns to a new page in the notebook and writes a summary of her impressions.

The Stranger who owns the phone works for Broker, prob. not a partner, just someone he uses as a go-between.

Broker decides money.

Stranger messages many people not listed in Contacts, mentions others by initials only.

Dustman issued a threat to Stranger 'your performance with GL less than satisfactory' and then 'Broker can destroy your career'. Is Dustman the enforcer?

A lot of activity relates to agriculture, but not all, some to national parks, mining and exploration of some kind.

Abbreviations/acronyms - some are the old ones that have changed over the last couple of years. Does this mean they have been doing this for years and use old names out of habit?

WQ – parliament's Written Question?

PM – Prime Minister

MOE – ministry of the environment

MPI – ministry for primary industry

DOC – dept of conservation

MOED – ministry of economic development? Is it still called this? Check if it has been split in two.

EIR – environmental impact report?

Rescon – resource consent?

Cpros?

What does minad/polad mean?

When Brendan goes to bed that night, he is back to his normal state of mild confusion. She stays upstairs for a while and checks that he is asleep before she returns to the Excel spreadsheet. By the time she has worked through another forty messages her eyes are closing by themselves; it is slow going and requires total concentration. Even when the messages are transferred to individual cells in the spreadsheet, it's hard to resist the temptation to read the next one instead analyzing the current one. She adds several columns for details, so she can sort by different criteria, but it makes the spreadsheet wider, and now she has to scroll across the screen to see all the columns and progress is slower.

She takes the laptop upstairs and wants to put it somewhere safe, to feel certain that it can't be found. Apprehension hovers like a dark shadow and her mind constructs scenarios of being tracked down and – and what? She thinks of the draconian surveillance laws introduced a couple of years ago, the way the authorities can monitor your private life from all angles and the universal use of face recognition. And worst of all, the long prison sentences for dubious crimes where the evidence is never made public, that people whisper about. She shakes herself to dispel the mood and tells herself she is being paranoid.

Her eyes light on the free-standing oak wardrobe in her bedroom, that has a board across the back at hip-level that keeps it slightly clear of the wall; her childhood secret place to hide treasures. The laptop just fits between the back of the cupboard and the wall, and she fetches her grandfather's walking stick from the hall cupboard downstairs and pushes the laptop along the ledge until it's well in from the side. After making sure that she can hook it out again, she leans the stick in a corner and goes to bed, but sleep is slow coming.

5

After a disturbed night when Brendan got up twice to ask if he should get dressed, Minnie wakes to a warm and windy morning. Over breakfast Brendan seemed calm and content, and relieved Minnie backs out of the driveway, smiles at the neighbour's cat sunbathing on the stone wall and turns the air conditioning on.

On an impulse she turns left at the roundabout and continues along Kelburn Parade, around the steep right-hand bend into Salamanca Road and left into The Terrace. She has an urge to drive past Parliament, and there it is. When she stops at the lights at Bowen Street, the grey bulk of Parliament crouches like a brooding beast straight in front of her. And she imagines corrupt officials moving through the corridors of power, indistinguishable from respectable colleagues, their dishonesty and greed concealed behind smooth facades. If she had heard a rumour about serious corruption before she found that phone, she would have dismissed it as unlikely, despite the changed political climate since the Covid panic was over. But now she knows that an underworld of deceit lies behind that imposing façade and the knowledge skews her word view and makes her feel unsafe.

A message from Luke comes just as she drives into the school grounds to park, and she checks it before she turns her phone off for the day. Amanda has a late afternoon meeting on Wednesday, and he asks if they can meet at half past five, so Minnie says yes, hoping that Sharon will be available.

At school things have settled down after the excitement of the award ceremony and the TV interviews, and the day proceeds smoothly. Today Sharon is staying an extra couple of hours, so Minnie and Jane can go out for their Tuesday coffee date after school. Jane studies Minnie's face across the table. 'What's the matter? Is your dad being a problem?'

'He's a bit odd - on and off. I don't understand what's going on in his mind any longer. We've had one escape attempt and some confusion about night and day, but nothing too bad. I've just stayed up late the last few nights and I suppose it's catching up with me.'

'You aren't creating new lesson plans, are you? I thought you spent weeks setting up the perfect system last year.'

Minnie shakes her head and changes the subject. 'No, that's all good unless the curriculum changes. You know Up Close – the TV documentary program who filmed the award ceremony? The producer wants to follow up at intervals over a year - I just heard. But filming in installments! So much distraction for the students - and for the whole school.'

'God no! The Head would never approve it. Can't they just do a review after a year? It's not as if anything definitive would be obvious at short intervals anyway.'

Minnie smiles. 'Exactly – I won't even bother to put it to Morgan or the Head. It could easily develop into some sort of personality contest among the kids. A one-off is a different thing altogether. I suppose they could come and film one or two of the industry people when they come in to talk to the kids, that might be a good thing to include. I've got some great people lined up from really interesting industries this year – stuff that will intrigue the kids.'

'What are you working on in the evenings then - how to improve the project further, or what?'

'No, just reviewing an old research project of mine from the university job, just for fun. But you know how it is – you get carried away and before you know it hours have disappeared without a trace and it's way after midnight.'

Jane makes a face, laughs and shakes her head. 'No way, that would never happen to me. If I'm not in bed by half past ten, my eyes close by themselves and I fall off my chair – unless it's a party. I have to get my eight hours sleep. But going back to the parent problem, is Brendan still safe at home with the caregiver only there part-time?'

The implied doubt of her judgment stings Minnie, though she has recently wondered about this herself.

'It's a balancing act, Jane. I have to make a call about when it's no longer safe, but I want him to have a real home life as long as possible – he doesn't need a full-time minder quite yet.'

She feels obliged to explain her motivation, to make Jane understand her reluctance to act. 'It's because I'm worried about changing things. He's so easily unsettled and any change in his routine upsets him. Moving to one of those dementia units might tip him over the edge and change him for the worse. And the dementia path is a downward slope – there's none of that 'two steps forward and one back' stuff. He's only sixty-nine and he could live another twenty-five years.'

'It's so sad - he's far too young to be like this,' says Jane and then something else occurs to her. 'Hey, I forgot to tell you – I had a text message about that phone I picked up.'

Alarm bells ring in Minnie's head, and she tries to keep her voice and face calmer than she feels. 'What? How did they know how to get hold of you?'

'I don't know - it's freaky. I got a short message that just says, 'please reply to arrange returning the phone you found'. No name or anything, just a few words. But it felt really uncomfortable to think somebody had found out who I am. And I knew you had handed it in, so I texted back and said I had no idea what he was talking about.'

'Why did you say that?'

Jane shrugged. 'I couldn't be bothered explaining why I gave it to you and what you did with it. I mean, once you'd handed it in at the bistro it wasn't my responsibility - more as if I'd never picked it up in the first place.'

Minnie agrees, but she is worried now that an unknown hand is pulling strings from the shadows.

'And let's face it,' adds Jane, suddenly cheerfully. 'They can't *know* I found it – I didn't hold it up and exclaim or anything. I slid along the seat and felt it under my hand, instantly assumed it was yours and just popped it in my bag. I wouldn't think even those at our table noticed. Wonder if they managed to contact the other three?'

When they part outside the café Jane stops and turns back. 'Minnie! Wait a minute – Jordan and I are going to the Italian film festival tomorrow night. Do you want to come?'

'I can't - I'm meeting with that TV producer tomorrow.'

She says nothing about Luke. Jane only knows the most basic facts about her childhood and very few details of her adult life in Auckland. If she mentions a man, Jane will get excited about a possible date, as she has once or twice before, but the challenge of explaining why she will never have a man in her life again is too hard to contemplate.

6

The next evening, with Sharon keeping Brendan company, Minnie drives to the city centre thinking of Rumble's email message saying he is coming to see her on Saturday and wonders if he has discovered something.

Surprisingly she finds a car park only a couple of blocks from the Green Parrot Café and hardly notices her surroundings as she walks, mentally going over what she wants to say, and where she will draw the line depending on what comes up.

Amanda turns out to be youngish and glamorous with dead straight black hair cut like a helmet and scarlet lipstick.

'I'm so pleased to meet you, Minnie. I had planned to be at the award ceremony, but I had a migraine and spent two days on my bed with the blinds down.'

A waiter appears to take their order; Minnie says she wants a cup of tea, and Amanda hands Minnie a single sheet of paper, businesslike now and somehow impersonal.

'Let's get down to it right away. I've written a bit of a brief – just a short one and I'd like to hear what you think of it when you've had time to look it over. Luke already saw the first version earlier today and had some input, but I'm sure you'll want to comment.'

'Thank you.' Minnie reads the short list of bullet points and sits quietly thinking until their order arrives. She puts sugar in her tea and stirs it slowly until Luke breaks the silence.

'So, what do you think? Is it what you expected?'

She looks up and smiles across the table at their waiting faces.

'It looks interesting, but I need to consider what it would mean - for the school and the students.'

'Do you have any specific objections? Or is it the whole concept?'

She has no idea that her tone of voice says more than her words, thinks Minnie, she's not interested in my opinions, she just wants me to agree so she can get on with it and do it her way.

Aloud she says calmly, 'I haven't formed an opinion for or against, but one thing I would like to see included is a simple protocol. I mean 'protocol' as in a research context where we would set out the objectives – I would like a clear focus on what is being reported on.'

Amanda raises her glass of wine in a slightly mocking toast.

'I can see that we're going to have fun with this one. A protocol! It would be very unusual, perhaps limit our scope.' She smiles, but there is a sharp edge of irritation behind the words and her eyes are hard.

Luke looks from one to the other. 'Well, I knew you were going to have a plan Minnie, you made that clear when I called. And I get your point – we need to focus on the same issues throughout, so we get consistency.'

He glances sideways at Amanda. 'I think I told you that Minnie was a research chemist before she took up high school teaching.'

Amanda's smile is forced. Minnie catches a fleeting glint of amusement on Luke's face and speaks, as if she didn't hear his last comment or noticed the dynamics between the other two.

'I don't want the students put under a microscope and feeling exposed. And it could easily develop into some kind of personality contest if you only follow a small group.' She drinks some of her cooling tea to create a pause. 'The success of what we have achieved is not worth fifteen minutes of personal fame. It took a lot of effort to connect with the various industry professionals who now come in regularly and mentor the students - I don't want them to lose faith in us.'

She smiles at Amanda and Luke to make her statement appear less of an ultimatum, but she can see that they both understand that she has drawn a line in the sand. There is not much else to be said, and they agree to meet again to develop the idea further.

'I'll email my thoughts in more detail before we meet next time. And I'll talk to the Headmaster and the Head of the science faculty. We have to get their approval, not to mention the parents.'

Amanda has decided to be gracious, to demonstrate that she can deal with minor setbacks. She smiles. 'That's great, Minnie, I look forward to hearing from you soon. And meanwhile we can start putting together a budget and think about how to schedule the filming – we'll work on two alternative models.'

They talk about other things for a few minutes and Minnie is fascinated by how much she can read between the lines of what is said. Sitting across the table from the other two, she sees the expressions on both faces; the occasional flickers of amusement on Luke's face when Amanda speaks and the crease between Amanda's eyebrows when Luke makes a joke.

I wonder how long they have worked together. There's a tension here – I think he finds her a bit overbearing, and he is amused rather than daunted or irritated. And she's used to getting her own way by either charming or bullying people, but he's immune to both. Now and then she is quite dismissive of him, talks over him, probably a big mistake - more to him than meets the eye, I would think. Wonder if she doesn't see that? And isn't it funny – there is that old saying about the 'inscrutable Oriental' as Agatha Christie used to say, but I can read his face quite well.

7

They say goodbye outside and set off in different directions, but before long Minnie hears rapid footsteps behind her and Luke appears beside her.

'Minnie, have you got a minute? I'd like to talk to you without Amanda if you have time?'

She slows down and slants a sideways glance at him. 'All right - the minder isn't expecting me for another hour or so.'

He points at the Thai restaurant across the street. 'Shall we pop in there, out of the wind? It's a really nice place - we can just have a drink if you want, but the food is good.'

It is like a different world. Outside grey clouds scurry across the sky, but the room they enter glitters with ornaments and mirrors reflecting candle flames and coloured lights.

'This smells lovely,' says Minnie, suddenly famished. 'I might eat something, I think – my dad's having dinner with the minder.'

'And I didn't have lunch, so I'm starving.'

As soon as a waitress has taken their orders Minnie voices the question uppermost in her mind. 'What is it we need to talk about without Amanda?'

'I must say first up that I don't want to be disloyal to Amanda – she is my producer after all, but there's something you need to know.'

He hesitates for a short moment before he starts, and she presumes that what is coming needs a careful choice or words, but she tries to keep her expression neutral and waits.

'Amanda has told one of our people to research your background, look for personal stuff. I don't know what she came up with if anything - and I don't want to know. Believe me, if I want to know something personal, I'll ask directly. I always did when I was in the press gallery – you get a lot from how people look and sound when they answer.'

Apprehension fills her mind, and she hopes the tension doesn't show on her face. 'And did she find anything interesting?'

He shakes his head. 'I've no idea. The girl who worked on it mentioned it quite casually when we were chatting this afternoon. Amanda hadn't told me.'

'Why are you telling me?'

'If Amanda thinks something in your past has news value, or shock value, she might use it. I wouldn't put it past her to use a sensational tagline about your personal life to create traction and increase ratings. She's pretty ruthless - and I thought you should know. I haven't worked with her for very long, but I know she's done it before. In the industry she has a 'tabloid' reputation – takes risks to ramp up the interest.'

He is studying her closely now, looking for a reaction. Minnie sips her water and hopes she looks unconcerned.

'There's no scandal in my life, no crimes or dismissals. But there are personal things that I would prefer not to have used for publicity. Excuse me please, I've just realised I forgot something - I'll be back in a moment.'

Her heart is beating fast now, and she gets up before he can comment. She stands for some minutes vacantly looking at her image in the restroom mirror, thinking about what Amanda might find, and what the consequences would be if her life were to be laid bare in public. And why has he warned her, does he know something of her past?

She returns just as the waitress arrives with their plates. 'Sorry, I had to make a call – I forgot about it when we decided to come here.'

Luke smiles and makes a gesture to indicate that he isn't worried and tastes his green curry. 'Great curry - let's eat while it's hot.'

His calm acceptance of her excuse and the smile of reassurance make her feel she has known him for a long time. She pushes the feeling aside and for a few minutes neither of them speaks. Minnie runs ideas around in her head and tries to decide on a course of action that won't make him curious.

'But thank you,' she says casually. 'I'm glad you warned me about Amanda's tactics – I'll consider this before we meet again. Could you send me a message or call me if you hear anything more? It would be useful to know if I need to pull out before our next meeting – I don't want to waste everybody's time.'

She changes the subject before he starts wondering why she might pull out. 'But tell me, why did you give up your job in the press gallery? It must have been a fascinating job - provided you like politics.'

And then it strikes her, and she nearly laughs out loud, the coincidence! Here is someone who might know the answers to some of the riddles in those messages. But caution stops the thought before it becomes a temptation to act. It is too risky; her feeling that she knows him well means nothing, in reality she knows nothing about him.

'Oh yes, it's an interesting place, very intense and a bit addictive,' he smiles ironically. 'Probably a bit like working on a cruise ship or in a hospital – a self-contained world with its own rules and realities, quite insulated from the rest of the world. Swirling with rumours and intrigues – if you don't thrive on that sort of stuff, it wears you down. You might think that really hard-core scheming for political power went out with the Medici's centuries ago, but it is alive and well in Parliament – and these days it's overlaid by the Citizens Surveillance Act and all the implications of that. And I got tired of it, so when I was offered this chance, I thought documentaries would be a nice change.'

'But not quite so interesting?'

'No, not as interesting.' He laughs. 'Remember the anti-government riots around Parliament last year when they introduced that additional surveillance bill, the one relating to encrypted emails and VPN's – that was a bit more than interesting, very tense for us who were in the building. We couldn't leave, complete lock-down - and that huge crowd surrounding the place on all sides. The police said two or three thousand, but someone did some kind of video crowd count and said there were eight thousand at least. The authorities wanted to play down the numbers, make it seem less important. And the chanting going on and on - that was frightening. Like a huge animal roaring. We worried they would try to storm the building.'

She nods; nobody could forget the TV images from those two tense days, until the army was called in to back up the Special Police Unit and the last protestors were dispersed or arrested. Over two hundred were given prison sentences and untold numbers injured. It was rumoured that the organizers of the protest were in solitary confinement and incommunicado, that their families had been warned not to talk to media.

'And the discrepancies between what politicians say and what they think – that's sometimes hard to swallow. So, the change of jobs is probably better for my peace of mind.' He makes a wry face. 'That kind of job turns you into a cynic for life.'

'God, I can imagine – these days truth and honesty seem to be in short supply in public office. I'm sure we never know what really goes on anymore. Not like we used to.'

'You are so right – I'm always pleased to meet another cynic. But about Amanda, please don't get me wrong - she's a good producer and I'm not leaving this job unless she does something completely unacceptable. I'll see what I can find out and let you know.'

They part outside and Minnie is about to walk away when he stops her.

'Hey, would you like to go out again one evening?'

He is looking at her in a speculative way and again she wonders how much he knows about her.

'I don't mind going out now and then, but I want to be upfront from the start – I'm not interested in men in any romantic sense, just as friends.'

'OK, no problem - being friends is fine. I'll be in touch.'

He's very attractive, she thinks as she drives through town, and he could be useful, but I need to keep him at arm's length.

Sharon is watching an American forensic drama and Brendan is in bed when Minnie gets home. 'I'm sorry - late again. Everything seems to take longer than planned at the moment.'

'That's OK. Derek's working the late shift, so he's not home yet. I gave Brendan his vitamin pill and he went upstairs about half an hour ago. He kept nodding off, so I thought he might as well be in bed.'

'Thank you - he sleeps a lot more these days, just sitting down in that armchair acts like a sleeping pill.'

She writes Sharon's hours in the diary beside the phone and goes upstairs to get the laptop, mentally planning how to stamp her mark on the documentary and wondering how to cope with Amanda. Protecting her privacy is the most important thing in her life after Brendan, and the thought that it might be breached is intolerable. It would change her in the eyes of colleagues and new friends; it might even damage the credibility of the science project.

8

Rumble arrives in a cape-like garment dripping with rain. He wrestles himself out of it, throws it on the verandah rail and comes inside, irritated and overheated. 'Bloody stupid idea!' he mutters as he kicks his wet shoes off.

'Rumble!' Minnie tries to control her urge to laugh. 'You didn't walk? You never walk!'

'Yeah, I know – but I did. I'm supposed to get more exercise and I thought this was a good opportunity. I don't think I've walked up a hill in ten years. I didn't realise I would get so damn hot – I mean it's evening and raining.'

She grins. 'Never mind, at least you got a good work-out – and a free sauna. Come on in and have a beer. Where did you get the rain-cape? Haven't seen one in years.'

'Oh, that – it's not a cape. I mean, it wasn't a cape until I cut a hole in it. It's one of those nylon tarpaulin things you get to cover your sandpit or whatever. I got it ages ago to cover the car when someone smashed the side window.'

He tries to look cool, but their eyes meet, and they dissolve in helpless laughter.

'God, Rumble!' Minnie is laughing so hard she can hardly speak. 'I thought it was a small tent.'

Once again, they sit side by side at the dining table, Rumble with his laptop and Minnie with her old one, and Rumble says seriously, 'This thing is worse than I thought when I first looked at it – as if that wasn't bad enough. I'm sure there's a network of bribery – and God knows who's involved.'

'I know. Once I went through all those abbreviations and read a bit more, I knew it had to be. But I can't get my head around these guys, Broker and Dustman – the ones who issue instructions to the guy who owns the phone – I think of him as Stranger, just to give him a name too. I just kept reading, and though I don't know who all his correspondents are, there's one thing I'm sure of – the Stranger is an errand-boy, who just does what he's told.'

She turns her laptop towards him and shows him the list she has made. 'A lot of the acronyms are Government departments and NGOs, and some I can't identify. But if you correlate the text with the initials of who it was sent to, suddenly a few things start falling into place.'

'Like? Let's see if we've found the same things. Give me an example.'

'There's one message from Broker to the Stranger where Broker says, "Dustman is dealing with the CP now, cease contact". And it made me wonder why he said *the* CP – if it's a person's initials he'd just say CP. And then I remembered the list of notes I made, where I listed an abbreviation "cpros" and that could mean Crown Prosecutor - which would mean it's not just politicians and state servants involved, but the courts and the police as well.'

Rumble nods. 'Yep, we need to go through it in detail to get a better idea of who's involved. But say Broker is the boss, and maybe Dustman is his partner, or works with him anyway, and then they have this Stranger guy running around on their behalf. It's hard to work it out from these texts, but it could be that the two top guys issue orders and make the rules, but they never meet face-to-face with the people they deal with, keeping anonymous – and that's why they need a middleman like the guy who owns the phone.'

He rubs his face and scowls. 'And if this is what the country has come to in this shitty post-Trump post-Covid world, then it needs to be exposed. I know everyone seems resigned to letting big business run our so-called democracy, but this stuff – it's complete bloody dishonesty.'

'Have a look at this,' says Minnie and moves closer, so they can both see her screen. Sitting close to an overheated Rumble is like sharing a chair with a damp walrus; she tries to put the image out of her mind.

Rumble stares silently at the Excel spreadsheet, trying to make sense of what he is looking at. 'Jeez Minnie, what the hell is this?'

'This column on the left has the full text messages. I extract the date, the time, check which weekday that was and enter those details in separate columns. And then I extract codes, initials and abbreviations and enter them in a separate column – or two because some are quite complex, longer and seem different from the rest. If I want to see all the texts that mention a particular acronym, say a Government Department, I just sort the information like this ... and they show up in a group. And then I can see that particular issue in context – instead of having it mixed up with other topics. Or say I want to see all messages to and from on a certain date, I can just pull it up.'

She looks at Rumble expecting a flow of ideas, but he continues studying the screen and waits for her to continue.

'So - I've eliminated a few early assumptions and got some new ideas.'

Rumble remains silent, glancing from her to the screen and back again.

'I also had to keep in mind that there must be missing parts that we don't see. Conversations and comments made to and by others that are not on the Stranger's phone. Like exchanges between Broker and Dustman for example, or between Broker and those he bribes.'

'Holy crap, Minnie,' Rumble turns to stare at her. 'This is awesome. I didn't know Excel could do tricks like this, never used it, really. And what a lot of work!'

'I'll show you something interesting,' says Minnie, and hands him her notebook. 'These names are all in a message that Broker sent, saying "have ticked the boxes for these, no concerns". And I'm sure he sent them to the Stranger by mistake. Because the Stranger replied with a question mark, nothing else. And Broker said "sorry, wrong person". What do you think those names mean?'

She watches his face as he reads the names out loud. 'Digger, Driller, Electrician, Farmer, Miner.'

She takes the book and runs her finger down the list of names. 'I presume the names indicate specific industry interests. But are they part of a group – and in that case why would they have a group? Or are they just clients of Broker's? It mystifies me.'

Rumble wrestles a USB stick out of his pocket and plugs it in. 'Let's have a look at this – good news and bad.'

He looks so serious that Minnie feels a twinge of apprehension. 'What is it?'

'It's CCTV recordings from the bistro where Jane picked up the phone – about two days of footage.'

'How did you get that? Did you steal it?'

'Well, let's say I had to resort to a bit of borderline illegal activity – people sometimes have really simple passwords – or they stick with the manufacturer's password. And you can access things from anything connected to their Wi-Fi and from quite a radius - it's funny how some people think their Wi-Fi doesn't work any further than the outside walls. I went down there and sat in the car and hacked into their so-called security system and copied what I needed. Their password was 'password' – classic.'

She is on tenterhooks now. 'And?'

'Well, two things really – look at this.' He turns his laptop slightly towards her. 'They've got two cameras, one above the till at the bar and one that looks down the length of the room. There's your group – you're hidden by the high back of the banquette and by that chap leaning over to talk to someone at a table. That woman there must be Jane – right? She's a lot taller than you and a bit further around the curve.'

He slows the recording. 'This is the point when I think you've just left, because Jane slides along the seat to make more room at the far end. You're hidden behind that group of guys walking past - there. Now watch this - Jane kind of pauses and looks down to the left. Then she reaches over to the direction she has moved from – I bet she's pulling her bag along with her. Now she's looking down - she's picked up the phone and dropped it into her bag.'

Rumble stops the recording and rewinds a bit. 'There is one moment - here - when you walk through the crowd towards the camera and you're clearly visible, see? It's only for a moment, but anyone who studied the whole scene very carefully might be able to put two and two together. But overall, I think you're pretty anonymous. Jane and the rest stayed for another hour - and nobody sat in that booth after them.'

Minnie has watched intently, and Rumble is right; by following Jane's movements she can picture what she was doing, and so could anyone else.

Rumble's fingers move fast over the keyboard. 'And now for the really interesting stuff. We'll start four hours before you got there.'

He back-tracks to a place he must have marked earlier, his voice is full of suppressed excitement. 'Watch carefully now!'

She leans forward, intent on missing nothing.

It is the mid-afternoon quiet period with a few people are having coffee or a beer. A waiter slowly polishes glasses at the bar while watching TV. A man in shirtsleeves and carrying a jacket comes into the picture from the left, goes up to the bar and buys a beer. His face is clearly visible while he faces the camera. He takes a first sip and walks to the booth in the corner, where he sits down, half turned away from the camera. A few minutes later another man enters, looks around and walks to the booth without ordering. He slides along the seat until he is sitting close to the first man, and they talk for a few minutes, before the man who came in last leaves again.

'After this the first guy finished his beer and then he left too. Did you notice his jacket? He carried it in his left hand and the beer in his right when he walked away from the bar. He sat down and slid to the right. He must have put the jacket on the seat on his left. Then the other guy comes and slides along, quite close to number one - so what happened to the jacket? Did he push it along, scrunch it up - and the phone fell out of a pocket?'

'Show me again,' says Minnie. 'Do you know who those people are?'

Rumble runs the video again.

'I know one of them, but it took me a while. The one who came in last and left first is a top bureaucrat in the Ministry of Business Innovation and Employment, otherwise known as MBIE. It's quite easy to find people if you use the right software. I have no idea who the first guy is, the one who lost the phone, but I'm going to try some new face-recognition software with a link to Google images and YouTube clips and see if I can ID him. But he's your Stranger, for sure. And I'm pretty certain there's nothing else to identify you by. Jane is the weak link – the fact that she sits just where these two sat and seems to fiddle with whatever it is that we can't see. Because the bad news is that someone had been there ahead of me and copied the recordings.'

She stares at him and a shiver runs down her spine. 'What? Who did that? And how do you know?'

'Presumably someone from this group. Say they tried to work out when that guy last had the phone. They'd be able to figure out where he might have lost it if they knew where he had been. I don't really know - it's all guesswork. But the log on the CCTV hard drive shows that someone copied that entire day and the next – a couple of days before I did.'

They look at each other in silence for a moment.

'Minnie, these guys are bad news – corruption, could be big money involved and powerful people. You might be able to get something more from the analysis of those text messages, but for God's sake don't talk to anyone else about it. So far, you're invisible, and I've got the phone and the SIM card in my safe – let's not take any risks.'

She mentally goes through her actions since she first opened the phone, tries to pinpoint anything she has done that might expose her to danger. The thought of the intelligence services and their extensive new powers is always present in her mind.

'I won't tell anyone, and I was cautious right from the time I first saw how weird those messages are. But listen - Jane told me someone sent her a text message about the phone. That'll be how they knew how to contact her – they've tracked her through that security video and our group. The bistro people know us well.'

'Shit - already! What did she do?'

'She said that she had no idea what they were talking about. She said to me that she couldn't be bothered explaining the whole saga about how she thought it was mine, and my discovery that it wasn't - I had already told her that I handed it in at the bistro anyway.'

'I didn't know you'd told her that it wasn't your phone.'

'Well, I had to, kind of. I talked to her the night she'd given it to me and said, 'where exactly did you pick it up because it isn't mine'. And then she asked later if I'd handed it in to the police, and I lied and said I'd dropped in at the bistro on my way to work - just to put an end to the conversation. Because I wanted to hold on to it for a while and read more of those messages.'

'And did you tell her that you unlocked it?'

'God no - Jane has no idea that I got into it. I just said it wasn't mine. She replied to that message the way she did because it seemed to be the simplest way to get this person off her back. She thinks the phone was handed in at the bistro, so it's back where it was to start with. Only I didn't do that of course. But I'm really worried now that this might get her into trouble.'

'Now listen, Petal - this is important. Never Google anything or write an email to me or do anything else on your new laptop or your phone that relates to this – absolutely nothing. There's really evil spyware out there, like the one called Galileo and it's really hard to detect. It hacks your devices, and it can do tricks you wouldn't believe – turn on your microphone and listen to conversations in your home, turn the camera on and take pictures, check your GPS locations and lots of stuff – all of it bad. You won't know you've been hacked, and your antivirus won't find it. It's pure evil. It can be on your phone too. And then there's Pegasus and Grater and a couple of new ones that are even harder to find.'

The thought makes her shudder, but she realises that she knows very little and needs to understand more.

'How would it get it? Does it just creep in when I read stuff on some website? Or is it something I do – like click on a link to another site?'

'They've got untold bloody ways of getting in – infected wifi connections, email attachments, via your browser. You name it, they do it. So, keep everything strictly on this old banger of yours, OK?'

Standing on the doorstep in the rain, watching him shrug into his tarpaulin cape again, she has an idea. 'Hey, Rumble – I know someone who used to work in the press gallery in Parliament. And I think I trust him – we could ask him to come over and watch that recording. He might know who the other guy is.'

Rumble stops on the second step, a large round shape with his head poking out at the top. His arms under the cape move around as he adjusts the straps of his backpack, and she starts to laugh again. 'God, Rumble – you look weird with no arms showing and things moving around inside that awful cape. Like something's about to hatch out of a big black egg.'

He laughs too. 'Just as well that I'm fond of you, you rude little shrimp. But seriously, I'd rather nobody else knew about this, not yet. I'll print that guy's face and you can collect it tomorrow. I'll leave it in my letterbox in case I'm asleep when you come. And then you can show it to your friend. My box is in the downstairs foyer by the lifts, the number is the same as my flat. I'll leave it unlocked. I'll text the door code to you.'

9

The staff room is stirring with the end of the lunchbreak imminent when Minnie turns on her phone and finds a text message from Luke.

'Timing is everything,' she says, and Jane looks up. 'Timing? What's the context?'

'Sorry, just thinking out loud. I thought of someone as I was reaching for the phone and here's a message from him – just coincidence.'

Minnie reads the message and looks thoughtfully into the middle distance while Jane stares at her, openly curious.

'You look like you're trying to make up your mind about something?'

'It's from that TV guy, Luke. And I was just thinking of another thing I wanted to discuss with the producer and him, so it's perfect. Now I don't have to contact them - I'll be able to just hang it off the back of his text, great. It never pays to look too keen.'

The message from Luke is brief: 'Time for a coffee one day soon?'

'I have two free hours on Thu - 11 to 1pm if that suits you.' She presses Send and turns the phone off.

When she gets home late that afternoon after a department meeting, she hears the phone in the kitchen ringing when she opens the front door.

'Hi, Dad!' she calls up the stairs where she can hear Brendan moving around. 'I'll get the phone.'

'Hi, this is Minnie.'

'Luke here – how are you?'

'Fine, thanks. Can you make it on Thursday? I'm afraid it's the only free time I have this week in the daytime.'

'I'd rather meet somewhere private. Any chance that I could come over one evening, just for half an hour? I promise I won't stay long.'

'All right, I'll be in tonight, if you are free.'

It will be easier to gain his confidence in a private setting, she thinks, and if he comes here, I can set the scene and have more control over the situation. But I could have sounded a bit friendlier, I don't want to turn him off.

'I live with my father and he's often quite confused. I hope you don't mind?'

'No, of course not – I hope he doesn't get more confused if a stranger comes for a visit.'

'He won't mind at all – he's very sociable, and anyway he goes to bed early.'

She gives him the address and turns to find Brendan standing right behind her

'Minnie, come and have a look at what I've done. I started after Sharon left – it's a great improvement.'

Upstairs he opens the door to the linen cupboard with a flourish and Minnie chokes back a laugh. 'Wow, Dad! That's a big change.'

'Isn't it great?' he says with great satisfaction. 'I've never been able to keep my shoes tidy on the floor in my wardrobe. This is much better.'

The linen is piled high on the two top shelves and Brendan's shoes and boots are lined up neatly on the two lower shelves. She shakes her head and goes downstairs to prepare dinner.

Just after nine she lets Luke in and notices his surprised glance when she picks up the remote from the hall table and locks the front door.

'I have to keep it locked - Brendan is asleep upstairs and if we're in the living room with the door closed, I might not hear him if he tries to go outside.'

'Does he do that at night?'

'Not at night so far, but he's done some odd things lately– he's quite unpredictable. Would you like a cup of coffee or tea?'

'I'd sell my grandmother for a coffee, thanks – it's been a long day. I've never seen an electronic lock with a remote in a house before.'

She leads the way to the kitchen and reaches for the hidden circuit breaker in the cupboard under the bench.

'It's necessary I'm afraid – to keep him safe. And window locks and a couple of these secret switches for the power sockets. He can go out into the back garden, which is escape-proof - so he's not trapped inside.'

They sit opposite each other at the kitchen table with a plate of biscuits between them.

'I've found out a bit more, not much - but you ought to know. Louise, the researcher I told you about before – Amanda told her not to talk about her findings, but now those two have had a fight about something and she asked me to warn you.'

He reaches for a biscuit. 'I don't know the details, but she thinks Amanda might use something she called 'personal trauma stuff' to generate interest. God knows why she's started planning so early.'

Now she needs to think before she says anything. The various dramas of her life parade through her mind. What will Amanda regard as interesting? Or will she use everything she can find and build a picture of a tragic, flawed woman?

'Anything else? No details?'

'Some of it is about how your brother died - she started telling me, but I stopped her. I'm pretty sure Amanda would use anything she can find to increase the ratings, even if it's completely irrelevant. Ambition is her middle name.'

She must tell him a bare minimum; he has taken the trouble to warn her, and he can easily find it out for himself if he wants to.

'Thanks for warning me. It was in the news at the time – a long time ago. I'll tell you the basic facts, but it's not something I usually unload on everyone I meet. It had a huge impact on my life on more than one level.'

She takes a deep breath and feels sadness wrap itself around her shoulders like a grey cloak.

'My brother Sander - Alexander - killed himself when he was

thirteen. Your researcher probably found the report from the inquest.'

She drinks some of her tea and continues without looking directly at Luke. 'He had caused an accident a couple of years earlier, where I was badly injured, and it was probably frontpage news for a short while. It was some time before I recovered, and he never stopped feeling guilty. My parents didn't understand how badly he was coping, and then later they blamed themselves for not having paid enough attention to him. You see, for a long time they concentrated on me and my rehabilitation, and when he died, they felt it was their fault – that they could have saved him, if they had noticed how depressed he was.' She makes an effort to relax the tension in her shoulders and sits back in the chair.

'God, how awful for your parents. And the poor boy – what a tragedy.'

'Exactly – and I missed him so much. I was too young to understand what had happened to Sander and why. And later, when I understood things better, I felt guilty about having had all their attention and I suppose it's only after a long time you begin to get over it. My mother died of cancer a few years ago and I think she felt that it was a punishment for Sander's death in some cruel old-testament way. She never said it, but I think that was in her mind to the end.'

'How old were you when you had your accident?'

'I was four, nearly five, and Sander was eleven. I was six when he died. He was my hero and I adored him - he protected me from night monsters and ate my Brussel sprouts when my mother turned her back.'

Surprisingly, he asks nothing more. She has only told a few people over the years, and Rumble has always known and the teachers at school, of course. It's unlikely that any of her present friends and colleagues have heard about it. Talking about it brings back the sense of guilt she has carried with her since she was old enough to grasp the details of Sander's death and understand her parents' grief. It is always there in the background somewhere, the guilt, not rational, but still a lasting presence in her psyche. The term "survivor guilt" is probably a good description, she thinks, because however it played out, he died and I lived.

They are at a standstill now; Minnie is not prepared to tell him anything more and Luke is clearly reluctant to ask. After a few moments he clears his throat. 'Are you going to pull out? Obviously, you don't want a personal tragedy used for PR purposes - and without you there's no point in carrying on.'

She needs to come to a decision, so she reaches for his mug and weighs up the consequences while she puts their mugs on the bench.

'No, I think we should continue – it's worth it. But how can I prevent Amanda turning me into a freak show to make it more interesting? Will she use what she discovers when this year's documentary screens – and when is that?'

God knows what else they have found, she thinks, things that might interest Amanda even more.

'Any time in the next few weeks. It depends on how much topical stuff pops up in between – it might be pushed to the back of the list. The piece we filmed at the school the other day will just be a small part of the weekly program. I really don't know, but I guess she'll save whatever she finds about you for bigger impact next year.'

'Do you know how I could stop her?'

He shakes his head. 'There's a sort of consent form you might be asked to sign - it outlines what your involvement is and what sort of input you will have. But it's more to protect us than you. I'm not sure if anyone's tried to gag us on one particular aspect before. I haven't been with the company long enough to know that side of things.'

'Perhaps I just need to get the right legal terminology for a privacy clause, some kind of 'limitation of disclosure of personal information' clause with a penalty if it's breached.'

He smiles wryly. 'Amanda would break the contract without batting an eyelid and face the consequences, if she thought it was worth it. They say she does whatever she wants and then faces the music later – quite ruthless. The company lawyers have had a go at her once already, just in the short time I've been there.'

Minnie gets up again. 'OK, let me sleep on it and see what I come up with. But while you're here, there's something else, something I want to show you.'

10

She gets her bag from the hall table and pulls out the print Rumble gave her, puts it in front of him, unfolded with the photo the right way up and watches his face for a reaction.

'Have you seen this man before?'

He reaches for it and nods. 'Yeah, it's that guy Watson - Robert, Richard? He's a lobbyist, kind of like a gun for hire. All kinds of people hire him – he calls himself an influencer, but we all know it goes further than that. Where did you get this?'

He is alert and interested now, black eyes gleaming. Minnie tries to keep the excitement from reaching her face, but inside she is jubilant.

She replies without any particular emphasis. 'I have a friend who wants to know who this guy is, and I asked for a print because I thought you might know – what with your past life in the press gallery and all that.'

Having someone with Luke's experience to tap into is too good to pass up, and she must tell him something in return.

'My friend came across some information - let's say it's been leaked – and he wants to identify the people involved. But he had to pass on this one and I told him about you.'

'OK - so, he found something linking politics and business – and he's carrying out some sort of investigation? This photo looks like a video still. Security recording? Is he a journalist?'

Careless! she thinks. I forgot I'm talking to a clever and experienced journalist, not just a pleasant face on TV - this might be tricky.

She makes a strategic leap of faith and nods. 'No, he's not a journalist, he's just come across something he says is sensitive and I know it involves industry and lobbying – something a bit out of the ordinary.'

'How are you involved?'

'I'm just helping him, doing some research and correlating dates and times.'

She tries to sound casual, but his alertness is so intense that she feels slightly alarmed. He pushes his chair back and crosses his legs, his eyes fixed on hers. He's going to question me, she thinks. He's interested and he's going to interview me about it. I feel as if he's looking into my head.

'Watson's an interesting chap,' says Luke, watching her face for reactions. 'They say he has fingers in many pies, including foreign ones – quite a balancing act.'

'Who are the foreign interests?'

'He's the front man for a consortium of Chinese investors, who have already bought big tracts of agricultural land here - and want more. Something I came across just recently made me wonder if he's also acting for Taiwanese interests – which would be a risky combination. You know how it works - foreign investors want to by-pass the environmental laws and the red tape. They want to farm intensively, so called feed-lots among other things, factory farming, but still trade on our reputation for quality grass-fed beef for example. Their motive is big profits, of course, which means taking shortcuts with the resource management regulations and things like water rights. They negotiate concessions from Ministers and Departments – so they manage to do things that individual farmers would never get permission to do.'

'You mean more liberal effluent discharge permits? Or not having to abide by the rules for wetlands management and threatened species protection - stuff like that?'

'Yes, all of those –and being allowed to draw gigantic volumes of water from rivers and aquifers for irrigation. And then there's the additional aspect of what you might call the perversion of democracy – not that anyone in power seems to worry very much about that these days.' His voice is hard, nearly angry.

She tries to evaluate what her options are, because the connection between this and the text messages is obvious, and once this occasion is over it might be hard to get him talking again. But she must be very careful and not give away too much. Feeling that he's trustworthy means nothing, she must watch her step.

'But can a lobbyist achieve anything apart from presenting a good case? Can he really influence how decisions are made?'

'There was a culture change a few years ago – new tactics that are now used extensively. Lobbyists representing some industries are run openly as agents of foreign powers, they're in the employ of and under the total control of their governments. Sometimes those governments use a combination of approaches, their agents issue veiled threats about consequences for New Zealand exports for example, like tariffs being imposed if demands aren't met - it carries a lot of weight. So, yes - they can do more than present a case, far more.'

She watches his face, sees the simmering anger under the smooth façade and knows she has pressed the right button and must keep him talking.

'Does that particular guy actually bribe people? Does money change hands?' She tries to sound casually interested, as if the question is theoretical and not important. 'And if he does, who is it? I mean, who single-handedly has enough clout to change things like environmental laws or fast-track things through Parliament? But I suppose nearly everything is for sale these days?'

His eyes lock on hers, as if he is willing her to believe what he is about to tell her. 'We've always known that some interest groups manage to achieve special status – tax incentives granted by the Government or changes to the trust laws for example. There's an expression in politics for those special Government arrangements that favour big business, it's called 'corporate welfare' – and it predates the so-called Trump Effect by decades. Ostensibly this corporate welfare is justified by the idea that there's a flow-on value for the country, like an increased tax take or a trade deal, but a lot of the time it only makes already wealthy people richer and does very little for the country. The trickle-down effect is a proven fallacy. The profits usually go overseas and there is little tax paid here, if any. I am sure that huge sums of money change hands behind the scenes.'

She hears the cynicism in his voice and is about to respond, but he hasn't finished; he is opening up now and venting deep frustration and anger.

'There have always been lobbyists and attempts to sway the law makers - nothing new about that. But in the years since what we call the Trump Effect spread out from the US there's been a sea-change right through the so-called democratic world. A kind of brazen acceptance that big business is part of policy decisions, that they can influence everything - from defense spending to foreign policy. It has spread like a virus, it's probably unstoppable now.' He shakes his head in disgust.

'But the rewards, if we can call them that, have changed from just gifts and holidays to money – and as I said, I think it's big money. God knows how much you need to spend to bribe a cabinet minister - the current front bench is the wealthiest ever. It is cheaper to bribe top state servants and policy advisors and try to influence the lawmakers through them. Not as effective or as fast, but I imagine it works well.'

He pauses and hesitates for a moment before he continues, and she can sense the pent-up outrage like a charge of electricity, she feels the hair on her arms stand on end. This is turning out to be unexpectedly exciting.

'Ten-fifteen years ago, the incentive might be as simple as a donation to a political party in return for policies being changed to suit foreign business – or rewards for Government ministers who exerted their powers to give people residency or citizenship. Say someone was rejected by Immigration because they didn't fit the criteria for a residence permit or citizenship – perhaps they were accused of something criminal in another country. And then a Government minister intervened, and there it was, mission accomplished. And then later came the donation to the party or a more personal reward. And that still goes on, of course – a lot, but it's probably mostly harmless.'

She listens without interrupting, intent on keeping him talking.

'But it has ramped up. I've invested time and effort into the likes of Watson for some time – and those he influences. I told you I left the press gallery because I was tired of trying to find the truth behind the press releases, listening to the gossip - that sort of frustration. Well, the truth is that I left because my life would have become professionally impossible if I stayed. I asked a few questions that went too deep, and I was warned off - threatened. So, I backed off and had a change of career.'

He doesn't expect me to believe this, thinks Minnie. Look at his stance, he's ready to leave – and now he worries that he told me too much. This is such a windfall, but if I probe, he might become suspicious of my motives. I haven't told him enough - I must make him trust me.

'I'll tell you a bit more about what my friend has found, but you must promise to keep it strictly to yourself.' She leans forward and speaks quietly, her eyes on his. 'You can't use it in your job, not in any way at all. And in return, perhaps you might tell me a bit more about what it was you asked that caused your problems? I have a feeling that we might be interested in the same thing.'

He gets to his feet, hesitating and reluctant to tell her more, but curious about what information she has. She can read the conflict in his mind, and she tries to clinch the deal by adding a layer of friendliness which she knows she might regret later. A change of scene might be useful.

11

Having made a quick decision Minne says briskly, 'Let's sit down in the living room, and I'll tell you some of what we have found out first, so you know you can trust me.'

She leads the way without looking back and turns on the lamps on the little tables at each end of the sofa, motions for him to take a seat.

'Would you like a beer or wine? I have both, the beer is cold.'

'I thought you said you don't drink?'

'I don't, but Brendan likes wine and I have friends who like beer.'

'I'm fine for now, thanks. Let's just talk.'

He sits down, but not as if he expects to sit there for long, so now she has only a few minutes to gain his trust, or the opportunity will be lost. She sits in the armchair across from him and makes a lightning-fast decision about how much she will reveal and how she will phrase it.

'My friend has some material that makes him think there's a group of people who are involved in just the kind of thing that you talked about - influencing the lawmakers by bribery, buying them or perhaps more or less owning them. But it's like hunting shadows - they hide behind aliases, there is nothing to get a grip on. And these days you don't expose yourself to suspicion just anyhow, so we're being very careful.'

She pauses, but he makes no comment. 'And you got it completely right,' she smiles into his watchful face. 'He has a video clip that seems to be important. That print I showed you is from the video.'

She wants to keep up the impression that she is removed from direct involvement. The likelihood of Luke identifying Rumble is remote; neither she nor Rumble use social media.

Luke leans forward slightly, something she said has decided him.

'OK, that's interesting. I came across random and rather strange connections between people and asked questions – and it ended in trouble. It was about a high-ranking state servant in the Ministry of Business and a man connected to the US oil industry – a guy who's not been here before, not to my knowledge anyway. They were seen together in a very unusual place, and I wondered what was going on. There's no saying he wasn't here on a normal errand, just unusual nothing had surfaced about it. And what was he doing meeting with a state servant in a place neither of them would normally be seen at? And then a mate of mine told me some gossip about another state servant and that got me really interested. I asked a few questions too many and pretty soon I was getting warnings, first veiled and then direct threats – serious stuff.'

'But who was warning you? That in itself is an indication of guilt – you don't warn people off asking questions, unless you have something to hide.'

That wry smile surfaces again. 'True. But you can't trace a text message from an anonymous cell phone. I had three messages from the same guy, two while I was still digging and then, when I was considering my next move, a final one – openly threatening. It left me in no doubt.'

She is about to ask why he didn't go to the police, when he starts talking again.

'They told me in no uncertain terms what would happen if I went to the police or any other authority. And as you said, when you're hunting shadows, you don't know who you're dealing with – you see the shadow, but you never see the actual person, you have nothing to go on.'

He hesitates for a moment and then he says abruptly, 'They put a bullet through my windscreen.'

'What! Were you in the car?'

'No, it was parked at the back of my apartment building. They sent a text message late at night that said, 'lucky you weren't in the driver's seat'. I went down to check the car - the bullet had gone through pretty much exactly where my head would have been. As I was standing there staring at the car, I got another message and the feeling of imminent threat, knowing that someone was watching me as I read the message - I'll never forget it.'

'Did you report it?'

'God, no! That last message told me what would happen, if I went to the police – and I took it seriously.'

Minnie is on the edge of her seat now. This is amazing, and her mind is buzzing with half-formed questions, theories and mental notes for later, things to tell Rumble.

'Which phone company did the texts come from?'

He looks surprised, considers for a moment. 'I think it was a 022 number. Why?'

The temptation to carry on and reveal more is nearly irresistible, but she wants to consult with Rumble. 'I need to check with my friend before I tell you more. I'll let him know what you told me, and then we can talk again.'

He frowns briefly and then his face relaxes.

'OK, if you trust me, I'll trust you. But they're probably still watching me, they made that very clear – that I can't hide, they'll be keeping an eye on me. And there are many ways of doing that. It's always in the back of my mind.'

'I promise we won't do anything to draw attention to you. My friend is a bit of a loner and because of his job his security measures are extreme – things most people have never heard of. His online life is like a fortress - he says he has built a 'wall of silence' around himself.'

Luke looks as if he has another question on the tip of his tongue, but he pulls back. 'OK, but make sure he understands that I don't want it getting out, not to anyone at all. I've kept it very close to my chest until now, literally told nobody. And because I had just received that offer to move into documentaries, I didn't have to explain why I left the press gallery job.'

He is trying to gauge if she is taking him seriously and how far he can trust her, and she knows that she must reassure him.

'Of course! We're working very quietly on this, just us two – we won't take any risks. I'll get back to you.'

'Don't use the number you already have - that's my own phone and I have one that belongs to the company. But I have a third number you can use.'

He sees her look of enquiry and smiles, but without joy.

'I know it sounds paranoid - like some over the top TV drama. But when I got that final threat, I bought a burner phone – I don't even top up the balance online with my credit card, I just buy top-up cards from the supermarket.'

He reaches for the pen on the coffee table and writes the number in the margin of the newspaper. 'That's the anonymous one, so if you use it, don't mention my name – or yours. These days I try to keep my private life as untraceable as possible. And I have the GPS function on my phones turned off.'

She wonders if he is still investigating, despite having been warned off, becasue his caution seems extreme. 'What did they threaten to do to you?'

'Something along the lines of 'we can wipe you out, you can't hide from us' - and I believed them.'

I'm right to be scared, she thinks, it's not paranoia, this is very dangerous. Aloud she says, 'I'll be in touch soon.'

'Thanks for being frank about what your friend is doing – it was good to be able to talk about it.'

'Thank you too - for telling me what Amanda is up to. I need to do some thinking before I meet her again.'

Before going to bed she sends an email to Rumble: 'Can you come over tomorrow night, need to talk urgently.'

His reply arrives in her Inbox within seconds. 'OK, see you tomorrow.'

She lies awake for a long time wondering about Luke, very aware that when she is with him, her instinct is to trust him, but also aware of how deceptive instincts can be.

What if he's putting a spin on why those threats were made? I'm sure the threats were real, but what's really behind them? Maybe he was involved in something shady himself and fell out with someone dangerous and powerful? What if he just wants to find out what we know to pass it on as a token of goodwill, to get that dangerous person off his back? I'll ask Rumble to check him out – he'll know how to probe his background.

12

Minnie leans forward over the kitchen table and tells Rumble about the conversation with Luke. She tries to remember every word, tells it blow by blow and when she gets to the end he starts laughing. 'Hot shit! What's the odds of coming across this guy just now? Awesome coincidence!'

'Isn't it?'

She gets another beer out of the fridge and hands it to him. 'I got goosebumps all down my arms when he told me, it was uncanny. The chance of coming across someone so useful hadn't entered my mind, but there he was - as large as life. Serendipity hardly covers it. Mind you, I could be wrong – perhaps he just made up the story about being told to back off?'

'But would he have been so helpful if that was the case? He told you things you didn't know and if he's involved himself - God knows!'

Rumble reaches for his backpack and wrestles his laptop out of it. 'Luke Wong - so I guess he's Chinese, or New Zealand Chinese? Let's see what we can find. We need to check him out.'

She tells him what she knows about Luke and goes upstairs to check on Brendan, who is tucked into bed fully dressed and asleep with the light on. She stands in the doorway gazing at him, thinking that this is another step down on the dementia slope; he's never done this before. If she wakes him now, he'll not go back to sleep, and she needs time with Rumble. She closes the door and returns to the kitchen, where Rumble is frowning at his laptop screen.

'What is it with this guy? I've tried everything, can't find a bloody thing. There are a couple of guys called Luke Wong who clearly aren't him. All I get is the official blurb from when he was in the press gallery and some new stuff from the documentary company. He has no personal presence anywhere apart from on LinkedIn – he went to school here in Wellington and he's got a degree from Victoria University.'

Minnie smiles at his frustration. 'I think that's exactly how he likes it, remember his off-contract phone and the paranoid way he pays for top-ups. He said he hasn't mentioned those warnings to anyone at all - he's as secretive as you are. What's the degree?'

'Political science major and then post grad journalism school. And I'm not secretive, I'm just very, very careful. This guy is exactly what we need – if we can trust him. What he knows about people and goings-on at Parliament would be very hard to find out any other way. I'll do some proper research on him later – we've got to know he's on the level before we tell him anything sensitive.'

She nods. 'I don't know anybody else who knows that sort of thing. It's not just the facts, like who's in what role, but the parliamentary corporate knowledge, if you can call it that - and the background gossip.'

'Be careful, if you talk to him again - don't tell him too much until I've done some research. I'll get a burner phone for you – I've had one for years. I'll pop it in your letterbox, and you can use it to send a text message to Luke or to call him. Keep your name out of it. Make a date for one evening as soon as he can make it and I'll come along.'

'OK, thanks. Shall we meet here?'

'Yeah - for now anyway. If he's already attracted the attention of the dark forces, we probably need to be a bit careful if we see him more than once or twice.'

When he is leaves, he stops on the doorstep. 'And what's Luke like, apart from useful? You obviously got along with him.'

'Nice enough. But I'll reserve judgment until you've done your research.'

She goes upstairs deep in thought. Did she reveal a bit too much when she told him about Luke's visit? It might have been her tone of voice when she spoke about him. It's hard to hide anything from Rumble; he knows her too well. Once or twice in her adult life she has fallen in love with someone, but she has trained herself not to show it. Luke is the first man she has lied to about her sexual orientation, and she wonders why she never thought of it before. Thinking about it brings back a host of memories from long ago and dreams of shame and self-loathing disturb her sleep. She wakes at intervals and gets little rest.

13

At morning break the following day Minnie shares a table in the staff room with Jane and two others and tries to stay interested in an animated discussion about flu vaccinations.

'I don't give a damn what you say!' Jane is getting upset and her voice is rising as it always does then she encounters opposition. 'I don't care if the stuff's 'dead' or 'inactive' or whatever. I got sick last year when I had the flu shot and I'm not having it again. I'll keep up my multi-covid shots because I don't want to die, but that's all.'

'For God's sake,' says Pete, physics and biology, looking exasperated. 'Could you try to look at it from a rational point of view? If you vaccinate one hundred people against flu in autumn the odds are that two or three are already incubating an infection - and when it breaks out, they blame the flu shot. It's just statistical reality. You're cutting off your nose to spite your face, Jane.'

'Minnie!' demands Jane hotly, cheeks flushed now and about to lose her temper. 'Didn't you get sick after the flu vaccination two years ago when you had just come here? I'm sure I remember you being here for a few days and then you got sick.'

'Yes, but it was nothing to do with the flu shot,' says Minnie. 'I'd been feeling achy and tired for a day or two before the vaccination - I remember debating with myself if I should postpone it, and I probably should have. But never mind, I survived, and I'm going to have it again and of course I'm having the multi-covid shot too. Anti-vaccination la-la land is not my country, Jane.' Her thoughts return to the text messages on the stranger's phone, and she stops listening.

Back in front of a Year 12 chemistry class, Minnie makes an effort to concentrate on a student trying to explain why an experiment went horribly wrong, while her mind speculates about what they might learn from Luke and how far to trust him.

'Martin, that explanation tells us only one thing,' she says patiently. 'You have no idea why it happened, but it demonstrates why we use safety goggles in the lab. You and Grace can clean up the mess now - broken glass in the glass bin please - the rest of you start writing up your results. I want Martin and Grace to write a report for me, try to analyze what might have caused this, and how you could have prevented it - hand it in on Monday please.'

She looks out over the faces gathered around the lab benches and smiles at Martin and Grace, who still look discouraged. 'Listen guys, lots of experiments go wrong or don't yield a useful result – I have made plenty of messes in labs in my time. The main thing is to go back over the disaster and identify all the things that contributed to it, because you might retrieve something valuable from the wreckage.'

Minnie balances a bundle of books and lab reports with one hand and picks up a bag from the letterbox, adds it to the pile and keeps it in place with her chin while she fishes out the front door remote. Sharon is waiting in the hall, in a hurry to keep a dentist appointment, but she pauses when she sees Minnie's burden.

'Goodness, you're loaded down.' She takes the bag from the top of the pile and puts it on the hall table. 'And be careful what you say about the linen cupboard, he's very cross – I've really put my foot in it. Sorry, I must run.'

Minnie goes quietly upstairs and opens the linen cupboard. Brendan has taken over an additional shelf. Tidy stacks of folded sweaters and shirts and some ornaments from the living room in a neat row, and in the corner, the phone from his bedroom. Bath towels and pillowcases are piled on the floor below the bottom shelf.

Brendan is in the kitchen listening to the radio and she greets him cheerfully, 'Let's have a cup of tea, Dad. We had a disaster in the lab today – just wait till I tell you.'

'I wonder if we have any biscuits,' he says vaguely and starts rummaging in the pantry. 'I think Sharon and I had some this morning, those chocolate ones with coconut inside.'

Their late afternoon carries on calmly with preparations for dinner. Brendan sits at the kitchen table, and she tells him about her day at school. She glances at him now and then; he is more mentally absent than his normal state of passive interest and says little. She could say anything at all, but he's not taking it in; he just likes to hear her talking.

While Brendan is setting the table, she un-wraps the new cellphone and smiles. It's just like the phone she already has, but with a white back cover. There is a note in the bag: 'Battery charged, $50 credit, my number in Contacts as Friend 1. GPS turned off'.

She sends him a message straight away: 'Thanks for the phone, lovely'. She enters Luke's number as Friend 2 and messages him and Rumble: 'When can we meet?'

Half an hour later she has two replies. Luke says: 'any evening this week apart from tomorrow', and Rumble: 'really busy this week how about tonight?' After a couple of messages back and forth it's settled; they'll come to her place at half past nine. She sends a final message to Rumble: 'Our new friend thinks I'm gay, please confirm if asked. Did you find anything about him?' There is no reply.

14

The men arrive together, and Minnie leads the way to the kitchen. Uneasily aware that she still has no idea what Rumble has found out about Luke, she thinks that she should have called him. Suddenly she doubts the wisdom of this meeting, but it's too late now to change anything and all she can do is take her cues from Rumble.

'We met at the gate, good timing.' Rumble starts wrestling his laptop out of his backpack. It gets stuck as it always does, and he jerks and tears at the top of the pack while Minnie watches in amused disbelief.

'For God's sake, Rumble! Why don't you get a new backpack? One you can get the laptop out of, instead of nearly ripping it apart.'

He looks at her with an expression that clearly says that he has no idea what the issue is. 'I've had this backpack for years, it's still perfectly good.'

She laughs and Rumble pulls his jersey off and throws it on the floor. 'I can't believe how warm it is in the evenings this year – no idea why I put a jersey on. Minnie, why don't you tell Luke how this started and what we've done so far. You'll do it much better than I would.'

Help, she thinks, he really means it, how weird - and how unlike Rumble. He must have done some serious background checking; I wish I knew what he discovered. Maybe he hacked into Luke's emails. God knows he's perfectly capable of doing that and more.

'Oh rubbish, Rumble – you just don't like talking.' She turns to face Luke. 'I was out with some people from school at a bistro and after I left, my friend Jane found a phone just like mine where I had been sitting. She put it in her bag and took it home and gave it to me the next day, and that night I discovered that I had two identical phones in my bag.'

She pauses and considers how best to tell the story without wasting time.

'I thought the first one I put my hand on in my bag was mine, used my own PIN and it unlocked - incredible. That phone belonged to someone who had used the same PIN – but it was a very simple one, stupid of me. I read some of the messages and got intrigued, so I asked Rumble to have a look.'

'Rumble,' says Luke, 'what exactly is it that you do?'

'I'm in IT security, like a consultant, I do penetration testing. You know the phrase?'

'No, please tell me.'

'Not as potentially rude as it sounds,' says Minnie and laughs at Rumble's expression.

'Say you're a bank and you have new software that you want to integrate with your existing systems,' says Rumble. 'Or perhaps a troll is threatening to create some kind of IT havoc. You ask an outsider like me to check everything, use every trick I know to see if your defenses are good enough, or if they can be penetrated. And you pay me a hefty fee for writing a report telling your in-house IT guys where the hole is, so they can fix it. Sometimes they ask me to write the code to fix it - which costs them even more.'

Luke looks across the table at Minnie. 'What a useful friend.'

Minnie smiles at Rumble. 'I know – everyone should have a friendly neighbourhood hacker. But because of what we've discovered, we feel apprehensive now, just like you do - and it might be for the same reasons.'

She watches Luke's face carefully, not wanting to miss any warning signals. He looks thoughtful but says nothing. Time for a challenge, she thinks, he needs to pay his dues.

'Luke, I think you should tell us the background to those threats that made you change jobs.'

Luke shakes his head, as if he still can't believe what has happened to him. 'It was unbelievable how it escalated. It started with a coincidence - I heard some gossip about a top state servant. A press gallery colleague told me about this guy's extravagant life.

Two weeks at a luxury golf resort in the Bahamas with his wife and three sons, Christmas in a top Swiss ski resort so expensive it makes your eyes water - and a Mother's Day weekend at Huka Lodge – that sort of stuff, lots of it. They never seemed to do anything that didn't have a huge price tag. I checked a few prices and calculated that as a family they spent way more than he earns in a year on holidays and things I could track – but all based on hearsay and estimates, of course. And he has two boys at an expensive boarding school and one studying abroad, not on a scholarship. Oh, and a second-hand Ferrari F12 which he keeps in his garage and never drives – I mean, never, not been out on the road one single time since he got it. He and his wife drive the most expensive model Tesla, as does their oldest son living at home – not to mention the extravagant restoration of his house. Plenty of unexplained spending money.'

Rumble and Minnie sit silent, fascinated and Luke smiles grimly at their expressions of disbelief mixed with excitement.

'I asked my friend how he knew all these details and he said his niece knows their maid; they went to school together - not that I knew people had maids these days. And they don't just have a maid, they also have a cleaner, a gardener and a man who comes to valet their cars. The story is that they inherited a lot of money three years ago – that's what the maid told his niece. I made some enquiries and as far as I could find out there's nobody this couple could have inherited big money from. The wife comes from a very modest background and he's just a guy who climbed up the state service ladder. And now he's pretty much at the top, but there's no way he earns enough to cater for the expensive tastes that he's developed over the last couple years.'

'Lotto?' says Minnie.

'But why would you pretend it was an inheritance if you win a fortune?' He pauses to collect his thoughts. 'Anyway, a short while later, somebody else mentioned that they'd seen this particular guy with a US oil industry man. It was just coincidence that the person who told me recognized the oil guy – because the American was a front person in the news over the Gulf oil-well disaster and my friend is into ecology, and he had watched every second of the Gulf TV coverage. And I've since found that this oil guy now works for an international oil drilling consortium that's interested in getting the rights to the Great South Basin expanded acreage – for which there's huge competition and some serious controversy about whether it should be developed or not – again - but this time I'm sure it will be. There's still money to be made from petroleum products. My mate thought it was unusual to have someone of that calibre here without a press release or anybody talking about it – not a whisper in the media.'

'But he might have been here on private business or on holiday - maybe a bit of trout fishing or something?'

I'll just keep on testing the waters, putting little objections in here and there, thinks Minnie. Rumble seems to have decided he's genuine, but I want to see how he deals with things, it might tell me something – he seems kosher, but there's no harm in being a bit irritating and checking his reactions.

Luke shakes head. 'No, I don't think it was a vacation. Ivan, my mate, says the oil guy was in a suit and carried a briefcase and a heavy overcoat, like he'd just flown in from some cold climate or was leaving for one. What made him suspicious was where he saw them – the kind of place they would never normally go, a little fast-food joint in Adelaide Road. Not their sort of place unless they live around there. Ivan lives just by the hospital and he was picking up dinner on his way home. I went to have a look while I was digging for facts – it's a scruffy little place and the windows aren't clean. Mainly take-aways, just two tiny tables where people sit and wait for their orders.'

'How did you friend know who the state servant was?'

'He was a reporter on The Dominion for a while, that's how I know him – he's a student nurse now. He told me, because he thought I'd be interested in the fact that those two guys met in such an unlikely place.'

Two beers and one cup of tea later, Rumble turns his laptop towards Luke. 'Here it is - check out these two guys at the bistro where Minnie's friend picked up the phone.'

Luke watches the CCTV video to then end in silence. 'Can you show me that full face shot again?' Rumble rewinds and pauses on the Stranger's face, and Luke nods.

'It's Watson, no doubt about it. What an amazingly careless thing to do if they're up to no good. A top state servant going out to meet Watson like that during work hours - and in a place where he could easily be seen.'

'Post-Trump era fucking arrogance,' says Rumble cynically. 'Some people think they're entitled to do anything they like.'

'Rumble blames everything on Trump. Holds him personally

responsible for everything bad that's happened in the last several years, everything that he doesn't like.' Minnie puts her old laptop on the table and opens the Excel file. 'I want to check a few things before I do any more work on this thing - it's becoming a monster. It's been useful so far, but there are still things I want to find out. Sorry, just going up to check on Brendan.'

15

Minnie returns and picks up where she left off. 'This spreadsheet has taken on a life of its own, and I'm still expanding it. Just yesterday I tried to correlate the abbreviation WQ with known events and still can't make up my mind. And I have a few abbreviations that I haven't identified – and lots of initials.'

'What's with the WQ abbreviation?' asks Luke. 'And what are the unknown things?'

'WQ appears a few times in texts between Broker and the Stranger, I mean Watson. I thought it might mean Written Question and wanted to see if I could correlate the topic of the texts that had WQ in them with what came up in Parliament later. But it's hard to be certain because of the time lag. They seem to, but in a delayed reaction kind of way, so I can't tell if they're really connected. You know - if a topic in a text message is submitted as a written question and replied to by a Minister a bit later - is it just chance or did the message trigger it?'

Suddenly Luke looks very alert. 'Tell me what it was about.'

'The first topic was effluent discharge regulations – and we know how controversial this is already, particularly in regard to those feed-lots with thousands of cattle crammed into a small space. So, if they made an exception to the rules that govern resource consent for discharge of dirty water into waterways, say for an intensive farming investor, the media might latch on to it and the Government would look bad. All of this is hinted at with lots of abbreviations in a thread of messages between Broker and

Watson – or that's what it seems like. Then two weeks after the last message about this, a government MP submits a written question about exactly this, which creates a platform for the Minister to reply with complete confidence that it's been looked into, it's not an issue, will cause no harm or is of no great consequence and consultations have taken place – blah, blah - and that the Department of Conservation is happy with it. Thank goodness all those records of what's been said in Parliament are online or I'd never have known. It's like using written questions to advertise how good you are. Like a pre-emptive PR strike before anyone starts discussing it.'

Luke grins. 'Ah, yes - it's a well-known device. In the press gallery we call it show time, all the parties use it when they're in power. As you say, it's a simple way of creating your own PR. Can I have a quick look at the spreadsheet?'

Minnie pushes the laptop over, and he studies the screen, first with a frown and then with gradually dawning understanding.

'Wow! You've separated out all the acronyms and abbreviations, what a job. I'd like to look at this more closely some time.'

'You can look at it here,' says Rumble, 'but everything stays on this laptop and the laptop stays here for now. It's an old one that she never connects to the internet, no Wi-Fi function. I want everything to do with this to stay offline. I've got a copy of this stuff on a flash drive in my safe along with the phone itself. I'm bloody sure this material is toxic and the more we poke around the greater the danger.'

Minnie nods. 'Me too. Paranoia is my new best friend – we hang out all the time.'

She turns back to Luke. 'Rumble told me how to keep this stuff safe and he cleaned up my other laptop, the new one – nobody can find any traces of it now. I had no idea how ignorant I was. And I've turned off the GPS on my regular phone too.'

'That reminds me,' says Rumble. 'I forgot to say – last night I hacked another CCTV setup just down the road from the bistro – a place that has an outside camera. Just checking the street scene, thought I might see something interesting from the few days after Jane took the phone.'

He rubs his hands over his face and yawns. 'But there was nothing there that told me anything. And while I was there, I took the opportunity to hack into the bistro's CCTV hard drive again – thought I'd grab everything they recorded since that day. You know, hoping to see someone come in and ask about the phone, search the seat where he sat.'

'Yes?' says Minnie. 'And what did you find?'

'Nothing, not a fucking thing. Someone has wiped all old history - everything right up to two days ago is gone, not just the last three weeks, everything.'

'Broker making sure nobody works out who lost the phone?' suggests Luke. 'And maybe it is or was a place where they often met? Would they be able to tell that you had already downloaded stuff?'

'If they checked the log, they would. It takes a bit of know-how, but if they did, they know now that someone else has the evidence of that meeting. It ramps things up a bit.'

Luke thinks for a moment. 'If they check that other camera down the street, would they see your car? I mean, are you at risk now?'

Rumble yawns again. 'Sorry! No, I was parked at the back of the bistro – next to their loading area, approached from the back street. I checked for cameras, but there didn't seem to be any.

'OK, that's good. No need to expose yourself any more than you have to. Perhaps I could come over a couple of times and go over that spreadsheet data and make some notes, Minnie?'

'Of course - but Paranoia says perhaps my life shouldn't suddenly be full of male visitors at all hours of the day and night. What do you think Rumble?'

'If Broker and Dustman are keeping an eye on Luke, we should probably be careful. We don't want to make them suspicious. But we could meet at my second flat - it's empty at the moment.'

'What do you mean, second flat? Have you got two flats now?'

'Well, yes and no - I have three. I live in the first one I bought because I can't be bothered moving all my gear – cables everywhere. That's the smallest one. Then I bought a second one, nice little place, seemed like a good investment. The tenants just left after two years, and I haven't done anything about it yet. I bought a third one last year, right in the CBD, very flash - which I rent out for a humungous sum of money to a Spanish guy, some game industry coder here on a temporary work visa for a year.'

Minnie starts laughing. 'Oh my God – I don't believe this! That's the sort of thing most people tell each other because it's interesting, but you keep buying investment apartments and nobody knows. I hope you have a lawyer and a will and all that stuff - your life is a mystery.'

'Yeah, of course I do, made a will years ago. I'm leaving everything to you – my mum's dead and I have no brothers or sisters.'

Her laughter dies abruptly. 'That's crazy, Rumble - why me?'

'Why not you? We've been best friends forever and I like you, and if I died, you'd have something to play with. I thought you'd be pleased. I'm not leaving a cent to my bloody cousins, who despise me because my mum was an unmarried office cleaner. Hadn't planned to tell you, Minnie, I was keeping it as a nice surprise. Luke, if I die tomorrow, you'll have to make sure it's investigated properly in case she knocks me off.'

Minnie feels tears coming to her eyes and Rumble protests, embarrassed at this display of emotion. 'For Christ's sake, Petal, don't start bloody crying about it. I have to leave it to someone.'

'So where is the second flat?' asks Luke and lowers the level of emotion. 'Is it a safe place?'

'Perfect probably - it's in Berhampore, about sixty apartments in a huge U-shaped building with three or four entrances. Lots of people coming and going. I think a lot of the flats are rentals, so the population probably changes regularly. I'll give you each a key. No phone, but the power is on and I can organize a broadband connection. The tenants only moved out at the end of last month - I was going to engage one of those rental management companies, but I haven't got around to it yet.'

Minnie picks up her notepad and checks her list of notes. 'Luke, what was the phone number those threats came from – in case it's one of our guys.'

While he searches through his phone messages, she makes mugs of tea and Rumble waits patiently.

16

Luke studies the message for a moment with a frown. "Here's the one that persuaded me to resign, and I left the press gallery a month later and went to the documentary job. It says "Stop asking questions or we ruin your career and wipe you out. You can't hide from us and we will be watching you. You will never feel safe again." That was followed by the bullet through my windscreen, so I took it seriously.'

He reaches across to pull the notepad towards him and Minnie hands him a pen.

'Here's the phone number. And as I said, all the messages telling me to back off came from the same number.'

He pushes the pad back across the table and watches Minnie check it against her notes. 'It's from the guy called Dustman, so maybe there's a weird kind of logic to his alias too. Perhaps he's the one who cleans up when there's trouble?'

She hands over the list of names from the message Broker mistakenly sent to Stranger for Luke to see.

'These are the names from that message I told you about earlier. We presume they relate to specific fields of interest. Driller would be oil - Miner could be gold or coal?'

Luke runs his finger down the list. 'And there's a Digger too - maybe the precious metals interest is separate from coal? And the Electrician might be something to do with power, dam construction or whatever – someone who wants to bypass the regulations to make the most profit? The government is just about to make radical exceptions to the national parks legislation to allow mining in the national parks – it started out with some good safe-guards a couple of years ago, but now it will probably be "when justified" as they say, which could mean anything at all. There's a rumour that they're going to allow dams in protected rivers too – and in effect unprotect them.'

'Those code names - they cover just about every sector I can think of where people might want to use corruption to get what they want,' says Rumble. 'And that Broker guy is the spider in the middle of the web. But why a group at all? They can't be working together - it doesn't make sense.'

'Perhaps it's not a group as such,' says Minnie. 'I have been thinking that each lobbyist or influencer or whatever they are called probably thinks Broker works only for him. Broker gets the results and charges a commission for his – or her - services.'

'That makes sense - and then he really is a broker in the real meaning of the word,' says Luke. 'He's the middleman who takes a cut. And probably those industry guys don't know who Broker is. And let's not forget that MPs are targets for bribery too – remember a few years ago when the intelligence services made it known that foreign powers were bribing Members of Parliament, back when we had a real democracy? I remember the outrage when that was made public – but it happens all the time now, it's a new normal. The Russians or the Chinese, for example, go shopping for a suitable MP and buy them for a particular issue. So, Broker's business might reach further than just the top dogs.'

Rumble nods. 'I bet he knows how to stay safe. If he's built up such a large base of clients, he must have lots of people he can bribe – he's probably been building this business for years - an empire of corruption.'

Minnie writes "MPs?" on her pad and underlines it. 'If I were Broker, I would never reveal my identity. Nobody would know me - not Dustman, not the officials or the politicians, and certainly not the industry players.'

She lifts her mug, discovers that she has drunk her tea without noticing and puts it down again. 'Broker has probably got an off-contract phone for each group he deals with, one for ministers of the crown, one for state servants and so on.'

'God yes, that's what I would do,' says Luke. 'I'd want to keep things separate, have several untraceable phones. Say that Broker is the brains and Dustman is his partner or assistant - he wouldn't want Dustman to know too much either in case he tries a take-over bid. The old silo concept again.'

'Exactly!' Minnie is getting excited, and despite her apprehension when she thinks of the consequences, she is enjoying herself. 'Broker could be *anyone* - a Government Minister or a top official or a journalist. He starts with one industry lobbyist, offers to facilitate something under the table and uses something bad he knows about a contact to exert pressure on that person. At arm's length of course, so neither side of the deal knows the other – everyone is kept in separate compartments. After a few deals Broker can put the squeeze on all his contacts by blackmail – now he owns them.'

'Yeah, that fits,' Rumble says slowly. 'And when he uses blackmail alone, he doesn't tell the industry client it cost him nothing, he just keeps all the money for himself.' He thought for a moment. 'But he couldn't do that too often – he'd have to keep his contacts sweet. If the pressure got too heavy some of them might resign or change jobs to get out of his reach. But - and it's big but - how does Broker get the lobbyists to trust him, if they don't know who he is?'

They look blankly at each other; why would people trust an anonymous man with big sums of money?

'And we haven't even got to that guy they refer to as the "cpro" - if it really stands for Crown Prosecutor that's another whole level of involvement. But now it's time for a reality check,' says Rumble and yawns again. 'Do you think we should back off now while we're safe? These people probably think nothing of hiring a hitman – and I'm not joking. We'd be playing in the big league if we go any further.'

'God no, we can't stop now!' Luke's response is instant. 'Not when we have all this evidence. When I was threatened, I had nothing concrete at all, just rumours and suppositions, but you've got the messages and the video from the bistro – and that changes everything. I think between us we can work out how to stay safe. And all the data on Minnie's laptop is safe.'

'Just a thought, Minnie,' says Rumble. 'Where do you keep it?'

'My friend Paranoia told me to hide it. It's behind that old wardrobe in my room, do you remember it Rumble? The thing is so heavy it takes two men to even budge it. There's a board screwed across the back of it, and I poke the laptop along the little ledge with a walking stick, it just fits. You can only see it if you put your cheek against the wall and look in sideways.'

Both their faces register surprise mixed with amusement, and she grins. 'I know! Totally over the top - but it makes me feel good.'

Rumble turns to Luke. 'How about yours, Luke? Laptop I mean. Perhaps I should check it out and make sure it's safe.'

'It's in the car. Do you want me to get it?'

'No, don't bother now. You can follow me home and we'll do it there – might take a while. Minnie, we'll be in touch, I'll just write the apartment address for you both.'

He reaches for the notepad. 'This is it - the street is on the right off Adelaide Road after you go over the crest of the hill and down a bit, halfway to Island Bay.' He draws a sketchy map with Luke watching over his shoulder. 'It's called Palm Grove – and yes, there is a bloody great palm in the courtyard. Don't park in the lot that belongs to the apartment block – just park on a street somewhere nearby. I'll have keys cut and delivered to you in a couple of days and then well arrange a time to meet.'

On the doorstep he turns and grins. 'I wasn't seriously asking if we should stop, just wanted to make sure nobody wanted to opt out. See you soon, Petal.'

17

Minnie closes the door behind them and stands against the wall doing her 'tall and flat' exercise, but for once it doesn't work. Her scars are pulling at her back muscles from leaning forward over the kitchen table for so long; thick, ridged scars from the burns that cover the left side of her back and ribcage. She takes the laptop upstairs and runs a very hot bath.

As soon as she gets out of the bath, she can sense that something is wrong and quickly wrapping a towel around herself, she goes dripping into the hall. The light is on in Brendan's bedroom, and a cool draught comes up the stairs. She runs halfway down, looks in horror at the open front door and races back up to fling on clothes and shoes. There is no sign of him at either end of the block, so leaving the door unlocked and the lights on she searches the streets sloping down towards the city, driving in figures of eight in case she has missed him at a corner. An hour later she is back at the house, but nothing had changed. The door is closed and unlocked, and Brendan has not returned. She dials 111 and asks for the police and feels like a failure when she can't even describe what he might be wearing.

It is a long and nervous night with worry and guilt at not having set the electronic lock churning through her mind. While patrol cars keep an eye out for Brendan, she waits helpless at home, imagining newspaper headlines about Brendan having been found drowned or being endlessly searched for but never found.

Just as dawn begins to dilute the darkness, the phone buzzes, and a calm and reassuring voice says, 'We've found Brendan. He seems to be OK, but he's very cold – he's only wearing pyjama pants and a pair of slippers. He'll be back with you in about ten minutes.'

She runs upstairs and gets his fleecy dressing gown and waits in the hall. As soon as the police leave, she ushers Brendan into the kitchen and starts making a hot drink.

'Dad, where were you going? In your PJ pants and slippers!' She knows it is pointless to ask him, but she can't stop herself. 'Never mind, have a nice hot cup of tea and then we'll both go to bed.'

His confusion is obvious and overlaid with fear, and she tries to imagine what it feels like to know that your mind is going and that there's nothing you can do about it.

'I was going to work, Min, but I couldn't find the right street. I don't know why I haven't got any clothes on – I got so cold.'

She sets the electronic lock and helps him put a jersey on over his cold white chest, before he gets into bed.

At half past seven she leaves a message at the school to say she can't come in and then she calls Sharon asking her to come in later, after she and Brendan have rested for a few hours. By the end of the day, she is light-headed from lack of sleep, Brendan is on the waiting list for a secure dementia unit at a rest home, and Sharon has agreed to come and spend full days with him for the time being.

Jane calls after school. 'What's wrong Minnie? Did you get that tummy bug?'

'God, you can't imagine the drama we had last night. Awful - I'm kicking myself for being so careless. I had a very late bath, and Dad got up and left the house - I'd forgotten to set the electronic lock on the front door when I went upstairs. I drove around for a while, but I couldn't see him, so I had to call the police and then I just sat here waiting. They didn't find him until just before dawn, way across town - dressed only in PJ pants and slippers, frozen.'

'Oh, the poor old thing! Is he OK?'

'He's had a sleep and he's pottering around upstairs now. I don't know if he remembers and I'm not going to remind him. He said he was going to work! I've sorted out a place in a residential facility – I just can't keep him safe here any longer.'

'What an ordeal! But listen, Jordan applied for a new job a while ago – he's had two interviews and a security check, and we just heard yesterday that he got it. So, we're having a little celebration dinner on Saturday next week, just a few people. But, of course, what we really want to do is show off the new kitchen. I hope you can come.'

'I'd love to – I'll check if Sharon is available first and let you know. What's the job?'

'He's going to be a parliamentary messenger – a bit different from the post office.'

Minnie blinks in tired amazement. It feels as if someone has eavesdropped on her life and said, "let's change the script and give her another connection to that place". The coincidence leaves her speechless for a moment, but she makes an effort to sound casually pleased for Jordan.

'Good for him – I bet it's an interesting place to work, better than being a postman.'

Jane snorts. 'Yeah, so long as it's not too interesting, or he'll never go back and finish his degree. He needs a challenge instead of coasting along doing simple jobs with lousy pay.'

'I didn't know they had messengers – do they run around and give people memos and deliver things?'

'I don't really know, but I guess it's probably pretty basic' says Jane indifferently. 'I'm sure you'll hear all about it next Saturday. He's only on a casual contract at the post office, so he's leaving at the end of this week. They want him to start the new job as soon as possible – which is Monday. By next weekend he'll be an expert – you know what he's like, sucks up information like a vacuum cleaner.'

18

The keys to Rumble's empty flat arrive by courier the next day with a note about three alternative entrances and the apartment number, and the following day Luke sends a message asking for a meeting.

The apartment complex is a large U-shaped, four-storied building surrounded by older houses. Minnie enters through a side entrance and takes the stairs to the second floor. The long corridors are quiet; just an occasional child's voice and in one spot a delicious smell of Asian spices from behind a silent door. The flat she is looking for is nearly at the end of one wing, and she stops outside the door, suddenly struck by apprehension, and listens for a moment before she puts the key in the lock. Luke is standing by the window looking towards the door and she closes it quickly behind her. The open-plan room is empty apart from a brown paper carrier bag and a small bar fridge humming on the kitchen counter.

'Rumble has provided refreshments – there's beer in the fridge and packets of biscuits and unhealthy nibbles in the bag.'

She smiles at the thought of Rumble bringing a fridge so he can have cold beer.

'He's always been keen on having a spare supply of food – used to come to school with his pockets full.'

Luke's phone buzzes. 'Yeah, we are. Which entrance? OK, I'll be right there.' He heads for the door. 'Rumble is downstairs - he wants me to help him carry something.'

'Hold the door, will you Minnie?' pants Rumble five minutes

later, coming in backwards, pulling a handcart with three large boxes on it, followed by Luke carrying two more.

'Are you moving in?'

Rumble's big face is bright red and shining with sweat. 'Just the basics so we have a table and something to sit on. And some emergency gear.'

He rips a box open and starts pulling things out, handing them to Luke and Minnie.

'Just unfold this stuff and put it somewhere, will you?'

Out of the first boxes come folding chairs and a small table, extension cords and multi-plug boards, an electric jug, and plates, mugs and glasses. Another box has supermarket bags full of various snack foods, chocolate bars and salted nuts. The biggest and heaviest box is wheeled into the bigger bedroom and left unopened.

'Look at that,' says Luke fifteen minutes later and sets the table upright after screwing the legs on. 'We could practically live here now.'

'Don't even think about it, mate, just pray we never need to.' Rumble opens the little fridge and looks inside. 'Time for a well-earned beer. Minnie, there's stuff to make coffee and tea in that bag and juice in the fridge, and milk. Oh, and teaspoons and stuff – I think that's in there too.'

He pauses and looks closely at her. 'You're looking tired, Petal.'

'I haven't slept well the last few nights – Dad's been escaping, going to work dressed in his PJs in the middle of the night.' She tries to sound casual. 'He's on a waiting list for a secure dementia place.'

'Poor old chap,' says Rumble and shakes his head. 'Now let's sit down on our new chairs and hear what Luke wants to discuss.'

'I'm not sure if I'm confessing or bragging.' Luke looks at Rumble with a faint smile. 'I went to that fast food place in Adelaide Road and pretended to be a salesman for a CCTV installation company - took a couple of glossy brochures about cameras and recorders and stuff. They said they already have a surveillance camera, so I said, but listen - we could set up a recorder with a big hard drive so you could have months of stuff in case you needed to look back - and the guy said they have a pretty big hard drive already. I was hoping they'd show me what they have in case it turns out to be useful for you to hack into it, but no such luck.'

Rumble looks surprised, as if he hadn't expected such enterprise. 'Cool - where did you get the brochures?'

Minnie smiles inwardly; here is another one who has underestimated Luke. She has a feeling that this happens regularly. Perhaps his intriguing mix of laid-back calm and personal reserve make people feel a bit superior, as if he is an intellectual lightweight or has no ambition. She plays with the idea in her mind, wonders if those he interviews sometimes walk unsuspecting into deep trouble, when they fail to see where he is leading them. He might devise a line of questions that leaves them trapped in a place where they had never planned to go, with no idea how they came to be there. A chilling thought intrudes; what if she has underestimated him too? She never asked Rumble how he found out enough about Luke to trust him.

Her mind re-focuses on the present and Luke is in the middle of telling Rumble what he did. '... but anyway, I thought it would be great if we could get some real evidence of the meeting between that bureaucrat and the oil guy.'

'Yeah, I can - if they haven't got a good password. I'll go there tonight after they close and check it out – I don't need to know what kind of system they have. Do you know when it was?'

'Not the exact date, but it must have been a couple of months before Christmas. I hope they have recordings from that far back.'

'I hope the camera isn't just aimed at the till.' Minnie thinks about the cameras she spots in shops. 'If those two sat at a table they might not have been in camera range.'

'I couldn't tell what the camera is aimed at - it's in a grey Perspex dome. There are two little tables up against the window by the door – it's mainly a take-away place. Let's see what you can get Rumble, fingers crossed.'

'It will be movement activated, I'm sure. They could have months of recordings.'

'While we're talking about security,' says Minnie, 'how was Luke's laptop?'

'Fucking awful, don't remind me.' Rumble digs his hands into his mop of hair and groans. 'Useless - his antivirus was total crap for a start. Some medium unpleasant things had got in, but it's all fixed now, cleaned out and set up with proper protection.'

'Very embarrassing,' says Luke, not looking in the least embarrassed. 'Rumble found all sorts of evil things. Every time I log on now, little notices pop up telling me that something's been quarantined or archived or updated. Yesterday, out of the blue, a scary woman whispered that she had locked something dangerous in a vault – very creepy.'

Minnie drives home on autopilot, deep in thought about what is developing. It's crazy, she thinks. When I found that phone it was like a theoretical puzzle, trying to figure out what was going on and who these shadowy people were. There was a feeling of danger attached, yes - but now it feels like real menace, and it grows with each step further we take. Look at what we're doing now, deliberately tracking down evidence, identifying people by stealing video recordings – we're playing with fire.

She tries to imagine what kind of retribution Broker might launch if he knew they what they were doing, and shudders at the ideas her mind produces. A man like him might have the keepers of the Watch List and the Kill List at his beck and call. Not that she knows for sure that the Kill List is real, but there are persistent rumours. A list of people who could get picked up with no warning on some trumped-up charge, possibly never to be seen again. But how could it happen, she thinks, it can't be true. I know they can legally keep people incommunicado now, but killing them – or is that what "incommunicado" is code for?

19

Later that evening the phone rings when she sits at the dining table reading Year 12 lab reports. The caller display shows an unfamiliar Auckland number and her new awareness of risk, boosted by her thoughts on the way home, makes her hesitate before she presses the Talk button.

'Hi Minnie - it's me, Andy.'

Her spirits lift when she hears his voice and she sees him in her mind, dark and solid, vivid blue eyes smiling.

'Andy! How are you and the family?'

Andy is the only cousin she is always more or less in touch with. His father and her mother were siblings, and Andy's family was part of every childhood Christmas.

'We're all fine, thanks. Alex is just about to start school and the baby is due next month – Cara looks like a pumpkin. How are you and Uncle Brendan?'

She feels happy and connected just hearing his voice. Apart from Rumble and Brendan he is the most important person in her life.

'We're OK. What about your job? You said you were looking for something new. Are you still with the police?'

'No, I left last week. We're thinking of moving south and buying some kind of business to run together. I think I've used up a couple of my nine lives and the city is getting impossible – the traffic is worse than ever. We'd rather bring the kids up in a smaller place.'

He laughs and she hears someone's voice in the background.

'Is that Cara agreeing with you?'

'She reckons we're down to six lives between us. We're looking forward to a change of scene and a quiet life.'

'What kind of business are you looking for?'

'Don't know yet – something touristy perhaps, like a lodge or maybe some kind of produce business. We're thinking of Hawke's Bay or Wairarapa. You must come up for a visit soon – I've hardy seen you since you went back to live with Uncle Brendan. How is he coping?'

'Not so good, gradually more confused and lost. He's getting a bit dangerous too - he escaped the other night, but the police found him. He was wandering around the city for hours dressed in his PJ pants, so now he's on a waiting list for a secure unit in a rest home.'

'God, isn't it sad? Such a brilliant mind just slipping away, and far too early. But listen Minnie – I had a strange call today from some woman asking about you. It didn't feel right, so I thought I'd better tell you.'

Her heart skips a beat; it must be Amanda's researcher. But tracking down her cousin to ask questions, that's going too far, it is a serious invasion of her privacy. 'What was her name? And what did she ask?'

'She said her name was Gloria and she knew you years ago, wanted to get in touch and she was very chatty. And she did know stuff that made it sound quite plausible. But then she said something that made me wonder if she really knew. I couldn't figure out it out, so I went along with it, tried to trip her up and suddenly she just put the phone down – so I knew it was some kind of scam.'

'I know what it is, Andy. My school got a science teaching prize and the award ceremony will be screened on TV soon. The producer wants to do a documentary to follow up next year, and I was tipped off that they had a researcher looking into my background - I've been wondering what they'd come up with.'

'Why the hell would they do that?'

'It's a trick of the producer's – apparently, she does this in case there's some controversial stuff she can use to increase the ratings. She might portray me as dysfunctional - or perhaps even unsuitable to be a teacher.'

She stops and draws a deep breath, counts to ten; just talking about it makes her anxious.

'What a fucking bitch! Do you want me to come down and deal with them?'

She can imagine him using his size and his police sergeant manner to great effect and smiles at the thought.

'You're a treasure - but no thanks. I have a plan of sorts. I was warned about it and now I'm prepared for her when we have our next meeting.'

'Listen, Minnie,' says Andy, still concerned. 'If you think there's the slightest chance that you're going to be persecuted by that high-octane bitch, just let me know and I'll be on the next flight. The way you've coped and pulled yourself together by sheer will-power is amazing - you don't deserve anyone tripping you up like that.'

She reassures him and changes the subject, asks after his three sisters and his many nieces and nephews. When they end the call, she sits with the phone in her hand, staring at the blank TV screen without focus, deep in thought. By the time she goes to bed, her mind is made up. Much as she hates being vindictive, she must get this right and with surprise on her side, she can stop Amanda in her tracks. She recalls the saying that revenge is a dish best served cold and knows that she is lucky to have been forewarned.

20

Two days later Minnie arrives deliberately early at the same café as before for the second meeting with Amanda and chooses a table where she can see the door. Her plan is clear in her mind, but she has refused to tell Luke what she has decided.

'No, I'm not telling you. We must give a good performance of two people who haven't seen each other since that first meeting. I want you to react as if you hear it for the first time, without any prior knowledge.'

'OK, I'll display a bit of doubt about whatever you say, so it looks as if I'm not on your side.'

You might well discover that you don't have to pretend not to be on my side, she thinks with grim amusement, but all she says is, 'That sounds good.'

Now she quietly runs her script through her head. Andy's call forced her to consider the impact of having her private life exposed to the entire country, and she knows it would be beyond her to cope with the fall-out. She imagined Brendan in a resthome and the staff looking at her and whispering together when she visited, and the staffroom at school swirling with rumours and gossip.

Five minutes later, Amanda and Luke arrive together. Minnie raises her arm in greeting, and they head her way, Amanda in the lead with a warm and friendly smile. 'Hi Minnie, have you ordered?'

'No, I just arrived.'

Luke nods a greeting. 'Hi Minnie, what will you have?'

'A grapefruit juice, thanks.'

She smiles politely at Luke, and he goes to order while Amanda sits down opposite Minnie, just like last time. Today she is wearing an emerald-green dress and shiny red lipstick. Her thick dark hair sits like stiff brackets around her face and it reminds Minnie of the detachable hair on her childhood Lego figures. She imagines Amanda looking at her and thinking 'what a timid little creature and look at those red curls and how pale she is, she needs someone to show her how to make the best of herself'. She smiles at the thought and Amanda smiles back, and then Luke returns and sits down beside Amanda.

'They'll bring our drinks over. How are you, Minnie?'

She gives him a neutral smile and says politely, 'I'm fine, thank you.'

Amanda launches straight into it, eager to come to an agreement.

'You emailed me your thoughts, so let's start with that. I know you don't want to go any further until we agree on a strategy.'

Minnie looks straight into her eyes and speaks calmly, without preamble or emphasis, exactly the way she rehearsed in the car on the way here.

'I've only come today to tell you in person that there's no need to discuss it - I no longer want to go ahead with the documentary.'

Amanda stares at her for a long moment, an angry flush rises up her neck like a red tide and she snaps out an outraged, 'Why?'

Minnie keeps her face calm and tries to sound as detached as possible, nearly casual. 'When I found out what you were up to, I decided it's not in my best interests to have anything to do with you. And I was concerned about the students too - in case you extended your devious research to them or their families.'

She can imagine that Luke must be wondering if she has cast caution to the wind, if she's going to reveal what he told her.

Amanda is unable to contain her temper, and her voice grows hard. 'I have no idea what you're talking about!'

Her eyes are shooting darts of fury across the table, the very air is vibrating with her anger. Minnie deliberately lets the silence last more than a few seconds, looks straight into Amanda's eyes and mentally wills Luke to stay out of it. She is in control now and wants to do this her own way.

'I had a call from a detective sergeant in Auckland yesterday – he's actually my cousin. He said someone has been asking around for information about me, pretending they knew me years ago and had lost touch.'

She pauses, but Amanda says nothing, so Minnie continues, making an effort to sound calm and objective, though she knows this could end with a confrontation.

'We discussed what your motivation might be, and he said that he can have the number traced. He also told me that I should tell you in front of a witness that I'm not going to be involved and that I'm aware of what you are doing and why. He also suggested that you should think twice about using any information about me that you have dug up.'

She gets up and stands looking down at Amanda, suddenly feeling cheerful and light-hearted; she has won and there will be no public scene. 'Well, there you are – that's all I wanted to say.'

She walks away down the long room, past the counter and out the door, not fast and not slow. On her way out she meets the waiter with her grapefruit juice and two wine glasses on a tray and smiles to herself. She resists glancing sideways as she walks past the big window and wonders what Amanda is saying and how Luke will respond.

Luke calls an hour later. 'Jesus - what a performance! You socked her right in the solar plexus – she was so furious she couldn't piece a complete sentence together for five minutes. She thought you were a shy little academic and you totally floored her.'

He is laughing, and Minnie can think of nothing to say, but he continues, enjoying the memory of how she took Amanda by surprise.

'She's so used to dominating people - she just couldn't believe you took control like that. I had a really hard time not to laugh out loud. And the way you walked out – classic. Rumble will love it.'

She smiles at his enthusiasm. 'You're right, he will. He's always on my side, doesn't matter what it is.'

'So, the cousin is real? I mean the person they called to ask about you, is he your cousin?'

'Oh yes, he really is my cousin. Andy's a year older than I am – we used to hang out in the Christmas holidays each year, because Sander and Andy's sisters were a few years older. But I did tell a lie – he left the police a week ago, but I didn't think Amanda needed to know that.'

'Brilliant - quoting a police officer certainly added an extra dimension.'

'Do you remember a police drama in Hawke's Bay a few years ago? Some drug heavies were after a girl they thought had stolen their money or drugs or whatever and she and an undercover detective got shot at and ended up under a goods train in the middle of the night. Well, that was Andy and Cara – they've been together ever since. He offered to come down and deal with 'the high-octane bitch' – that's what he called Amanda.'

'Of course, I remember it - one of my best friends is with TV One and she was up there for a couple of days. She used to talk about it, said it was total drama, like a movie script.'

21

By Friday, the students are in early weekend mode and test her patience to the limit and the lunch break is a welcome relief. When Minnie checks her phone there is a voice message from the dementia unit saying that they have a room available and would she please call them.

'That was quick - I thought we would be waiting for weeks,' she says to the nurse at the resthome.

'Sometimes things change very quickly here. One of the residents has been moved to our hospital wing and her room is free. It's a nice room, sunny and quite close to the main lounge and the dining room.'

'Should I bring him over to have a look?'

'It's up to you, but I think you should just bring him, talk to him on the day, while you pack his things. The less anticipation the better - in most cases. The admission process takes about an hour – come after morning tea. Tell him that he's going to stay in a nice place and bring his clothes and whatever you think he'd like to have around him, pictures and books, radio – that sort of thing. And arrange for his favourite armchair to be brought over. It's helpful to have a familiar piece of furniture to make the room feel right.'

Minnie's feelings are a tangle of guilt and sadness, and she goes to find Jane.

'God Jane, it's awful. I always knew it would happen one day, but now I feel like a traitor, like I let him down. What if they're not kind to him when he gets muddled and confused?'

And Jane puts an arm around Minnie's shoulders and leans her head against Minnie's. 'I can imagine - I think. I know it sounds corny, but when I was fourteen and my dog had to have surgery, I was awake all night after we left him at the vet clinic. Just sat in my bed worrying that he was unhappy or scared with me not there to comfort him.'

They both laugh at the comparison, but Minnie knows Jane understands. They eat their lunch together and talk about other things.

'Don't forget dinner tomorrow night at our place. It will be just what you need after leaving Brendan at that place – better than being at home all on your own.'

But when Saturday morning dawns her fears come to nothing. Her mind has conjured up emotional scenarios where Brendan refuses to go or clings to her wanting to go home, but none of it happens. They are met by a chubby nurse in pale blue, who links arms with Brendan and tells him they have been looking forward to him coming, and he enjoys her banter. By the time Minnie leaves she feels better, but the nurse warns her that things will not always be so easy.

'Most likely he'll beg you to take him home one of these days - nearly everyone does. Or he might accuse you having 'locked him up' to get at his money. It's quite common that dementia makes people a bit paranoid.' She pats Minnie's arm. 'If you keep away for a week or two it will help him to get familiar with the routine here before he sees you again. If you visit too soon, he'll still be unsure of things and then it's hard to get away without a scene. Hard for him and even harder for you.'

'OK, I'll leave it for a week and then call before I come. But you'll let me know, if anything goes wrong, won't you?'

'Yes, of course. You mustn't worry – he'll soon settle in.'

Minnie drives home with a feeling of slight unreality. I feel guilty, she thinks, as if I haven't tried hard enough. Everything happened too fast and there hasn't been enough time to adjust to the idea.

When she walks through the front door, the house feels different, the quality that made it a family home is no longer there, and she stands in the doorway to Brendan's room and tries to come to grips with the fact that he will probably never sleep there again. He lived in the house for more than forty years, and her mother died in this bedroom. Grief and loss, she thinks, that's what it is, even though he's still alive.

The evening at Jane's starts out well. Minnie knows none of the other guests, but the noisy discussion about renovations is easy enough to take part in. Jordan jokes about the many times when they wondered if they had bitten off more than they could chew and despaired of ever getting it finished.

'I'll tell you what,' he says, as if he is sharing a meaningful personal secret. 'Don't worry about tiling, it's dead easy. The thing that drove us crazy was how slow we were getting the painting finished so the floor guy could come. Our planning was way out of whack. We gave up at eleven o'clock one night and rang a painter the next day.'

Everyone has a story about a renovation job gone wrong or tradesmen leaving a job half-finished and not coming back for a couple of weeks. They ceremoniously toast the new kitchen and sit down to dinner, and a couple of hours later while Jane makes coffee, Jordan's friend Bryce, slightly drunk and getting aggressive, turns to Minnie.

'For God's sake have a drink and stop being so bloody uptight!' he says, loud and challenging, and the conversation around the table stops as if someone has flicked a switch. 'Sitting there all night with a glass of water in front of you, it's bloody depressing for the rest of us – you should learn to live a bit.'

Minnie smiles and says quietly, 'No thanks, I don't drink alcohol.'

'Why? Are you some kind of religious fanatic? Can't do you any harm to try - have a go! You'll never get a man if you can't have fun.'

Over the next few minutes, the veneer of normal behavior is discarded and he gets louder and more insistent; her refusal to argue only makes him more aggressive.

'We shouldn't push Minnie to drink,' says Jane firmly and puts a bowl of chocolates on the table with a bang. 'She doesn't drink, Bryce, and it's none of our business, so please stop going on about it!'

Minnie glances at Bryce, anticipating another attack, but

Jordan steps in too. 'I reckon it would do us all a world of good to drink a bit less. I'm seriously overdue for a week's abstinence.'

Bryce tries to persist, but the idea of an alcohol-free week, or even month, is picked up by the others and he is drowned out in a discussion about Say Nay in May, Dry July and Sober October and who is planning to join in. Minnie listens without taking part, distracted by memories that still have the power to make her flinch. She is tired and wants to go home but leaving too soon will look like a flight, and she refuses to give Bryce the satisfaction. After half an hour without further attacks, she gets up and says a general goodbye to the whole party and Jane goes with her to the front door. Unexpectedly Bryce's wife joins them and tries to apologize on his behalf.

'God, I'm so sorry about that Minnie – Bryce never used to drink so much, but this last year ... I don't know what to do!'

Minnie looks at her troubled face and makes a snap decision to be frank, though aware that she might regret it later.

'I was a bit like Bryce at one stage when I was younger. I very nearly became an alcoholic – or maybe I was one. Something happened to me, a thing I found very hard to cope with, and I started going home at night and drinking too much because it made me feel better - until it became a habit and made me feel worse.'

The woman, whose name she can't remember, looks at her with an expression somewhere between fascination and hope. 'Oh please, would you talk to Bryce?'

'God, no! No way can I talk to him about it! I only told you, so you would understand that I know about drinking too much. I will never ever drink alcohol again as long as I live, because I know I'm at risk if I do. But you can tell him what I said, if you like.'

Minnie speaks quietly, not excluding Jane, but trying to make it a personal exchange with Bryce's wife.

'If I were you, I wouldn't talk about it when he's drunk or hung over. Wait for a good moment when he's relaxed and don't lecture him. Not that I'm an expert, but I remember how I reacted when friends tried to help me. It's really hard to face the fact that you are drinking too much, and that people are worried and only want what's best for you, that they're not just criticizing.'

She opens the door and says goodbye, intent on leaving before the conversation goes any further. Behind the composed façade she is uneasy about having told someone she hardly knows. It was an impulse triggered by the woman's distress, but now Jane knows too, and Minnie hopes she won't talk about it at school. Having nearly lost her job and very nearly ruined her career is something she would like to confine to the past.

Years ago, when she hauled herself back from the brink of alcoholism by sheer willpower and self-discipline, she never allowed anyone to discuss it with her. She shut the topic away and let nobody near it, neither those who wanted to lecture or advise her, nor those who just wanted to check on her progress. She could only cope if she did it alone in her own way, and as time moved on, she developed new friendships and people just accepted her as a non-drinker and only rarely someone would become insistent about it, like Bryce had. Those who urged her to drink were usually people who drank to excess themselves and she wondered if they resented her self-discipline.

Driving home, she thinks back to the time when she decided to give up alcohol altogether. To start with she avoided social gatherings, turned down invitations and isolated herself. But then she experienced one of those 'on the road to Damascus' moments, a flash of insight, and realised that the only way to achieve control was to expose herself to temptation and resist it. From then on, she would come home after evenings out, sober and triumphant and inwardly celebrating her achievement.

The house is dark and silent, and she doesn't feel like going to bed. She pulls the curtains across the windows and turns a light on here and there, feeling unsettled. The spreadsheet analysis fails to engage her interest, and her thoughts alternate between Brendan and the evening's events.

When her new phone buzzes at one in the morning, she jumps. A message from Rumble: 'Got fast food video. Tomorrow at 12?' and minutes later a response from Luke: 'ok with me'. She replies and says she will be there, and then on an impulse she calls Rumble, who is obviously awake.

'I keep forgetting to ask you how and what you found out about Luke? That first time you met him at my place you seemed to trust him totally, no suspicions at all. I was really surprised.'

'I did it the old-fashioned way. Bugger ... I've dropped the mouse, never mind. I knew from LinkedIn when and where he got his degree and I put out a call to some guys I know and asked them to find people who studied with him. Got hold of three, no four in the end, pretended I was writing an article about student politics now and twenty years ago. I managed to bring his name into it, kind of sideways. Turns out he was well-known back then too, very active – left of liberal, green, a strong advocate for free speech and civil liberties and so on. He not only took part in demonstrations, but he organized them as well. And he was very forceful in debates; they all said more or less the same things.'

She remembers Luke's anger about those who bend the environmental rules, and the way bribes get results and nods to herself. 'Yeah, that fits with what I've seen of him. If you are satisfied, we'll leave it at that.'

She lies awake a long time listening to the old wooden villa creaking as the night air cools and wakes in the morning feeling as if she has had no sleep. The phone she thinks of as her normal phone has a text message from late last night.

'Hi Minnie, hope you remember me, I met you a few weeks ago with Jane. Do you want to meet for a drink? Dave'

She has never met anyone called Dave with Jane. There is no doubt in her mind; it is either Broker or Dustman. But how did they know her name and phone number? With little currents of unease running down her spine, she dresses quickly and calls Jane.

'That was a lovely dinner last night, thank you, and the kitchen looks amazing. Did the others stay late?'

'No, we were in bed before midnight. Bryce got stroppy again after you left, and everyone got very uncomfortable.'

'I'm sorry. Maybe if I'd stayed longer things would have gone back to normal.'

Jane snorts. 'Oh no, not with Bryce in that state. He continued bitching about 'purists' and 'people who think they are better than others' until his wife dragged him home. I honestly don't know how she puts up with him. We hadn't seen them for a few months and he's a lot worse than he used to be. I think he was half loaded when they arrived.'

'Hey, I forgot to ask you what that guy said about the phone you found. You told me he'd sent another message and then we got interrupted.'

'It was quite nasty – he kind of implied that he had some information from somewhere and knew I had the phone. I don't think he can possibly know that I found it. I said I hadn't seen it or taken it, and if he doesn't stop bothering me, I'll go to the police and give them his number.'

'That's exactly what you should do, Jane, he's a menace.'

'I know,' says Jane, 'It's a bit weird and I have no idea why it's so damn important to him. He's obsessive – I hope he's going to leave me alone now or I'll have to change my number.'

22

This time she parks in a street off the far side of Adelaide Road and walks across to the apartment and coming from this direction, she gets a different feel for the area. There are far more old, wooden villas than she had realised, some in the process of being renovated. Generation change, she thinks, young couples buying older houses and improving them before moving on. Or maybe staying, happy to have a small footprint rather than aiming for large and lavish. She walks through the central courtyard to the main entrance, says a casual 'hi' to three dark-skinned young men in jeans and bright-coloured sweatshirts and takes the lift to the second floor. Walking down the long corridor to the end of the western wing, she once again notices the unearthly quiet, but possibly it's different at night when everyone is home. Rumble and Luke are standing by the balcony door with a beer each and turn when they hear her key in the door.

'Finally!' says Luke. 'I'm on tenterhooks.'

Rumble takes a swig of beer and goes through the usual struggle getting his laptop out of the backpack while Minnie watches impatiently and wonders why he didn't get it out while he was waiting for her to arrive.

'They've got the camera mounted above the cash register,' he says and opens the laptop, 'and it looks down the length of the counter, so you see half the distance from the counter to the door on the left and to the wall behind the counter to the right. Anyone who stands at the counter faces the camera when they pay. I think I've picked out the guys your friend saw, Luke, I've bookmarked the place. The camera is movement activated and they have weeks and weeks of recordings – lucky for us someone really had sold them a decent sized hard drive. I grabbed the lot just in case it's a regular meeting place.'

'My God, how long did that take?'

'Not long at all – I've got ways and means. OK guys, here it is. The oil guy is unmistakable, totally out of place. Looks American, you can always tell - their suits look different. And when he leaves you can see he's carrying a bag and a thick overcoat – quite different from their usual clientele. It certainly looks like he's on his way to catch a plane to a colder climate. Here we are.'

He pushes the laptop into the middle of the table and the other two lean forward to watch. The shot covers the counter and a couple of meters either side. A boy with a skateboard buys a burger and chips and leaves. The man behind the counter speaks to someone out of view and another two customers come and go. Then a man wearing a white shirt with the sleeves rolled up comes into view from where the street door is and another man dressed in a suit appears seemingly from under the camera. He says something to the man behind the counter, and the man in the white shirt pulls a wallet out of his back pocket and pays. Both men disappear out of view and the counter man takes two Cokes out of a chiller behind him, picks up a couple of glasses, walks around the end of the counter and disappears out of view.

'OK, that's it.' Rumble hits the pause button. 'From here nothing of interest happens until nine and a half minutes later, when your friend comes in to pick up his dinner.'

He fast forwards and pauses the recording again. 'Is this your mate? OK, thought so - he picks up something he has pre-ordered and he's obviously taking a good look at those two guys at a table beside the door. And then here - a few minutes after he left, you can just see those two guys walk towards the door from their table, which we can't see. But now the oil guy is carrying his coat and the briefcase.'

'Play it again,' says Luke. 'And can you pause just where the guy in the suit comes up to the counter and says something – where we can see his face?'

He leans closer and watches intently as the video plays again and then he smiles.

'Yep, I think that's him. Well, I'm sure it is –Kelvin was right. We can find a photo of him and check. That deep dimple in his chin that he misses when he shaves, I remember it from all those years ago when we saw him on TV. He's older, but it's him, all right.'

Minnie is trying to make sense of what she saw. 'Rumble, could you see the oil guy come in? I mean, when did he arrive – how long before the other one was it?'

'Nope, no sign of him until he comes up to the counter - but earlier we saw the guy at the counter speak to someone and make a sort of 'ok' gesture. Unless he was talking to someone behind the scenes, I think the oil man came in and stepped to the side where the table is, without coming closer to the counter - so the camera didn't pick him up. Perhaps he says something like 'is it ok if I sit here and wait for my ride?' and the guy behind the counter says 'ok' and then a bit later the man in the white shirt turns up. Good thing the guy who works there triggers the camera all the time or we would have missed that bit.'

Rumble stops talking and looks without focus at the window, deep in thought and the other two watch him, expecting him to continue, but the seconds tick by and he says nothing. Finally, Luke voices the question that is also in Minnie's head.

'So, what comes next? Being seen in a down-market fast-food place isn't proof of anything subversive. We need more substantial evidence, but how can we get it? Any ideas, Minnie?'

'I don't know - where would we even start? So far we have the text messages and we've more or less tripped over things - and Rumble has stolen useful video.'

Luke gets up, rotates his shoulders and stretches. 'That table is a torture device. What puzzles me is that Broker lets them get together like that. I mean, if he's the middleman for the deals, why would he let them meet at all? They might do some private trades and cut him out. I would have thought his entire brokerage operation depends on complete separation between his clients and his sources.'

'That's what I thought too,' says Minnie. 'But perhaps there are times when an industry guy insists on meeting someone face to face to make sure Broker isn't lying about his contacts. Like a safety check. Someone gets suspicious and thinks Broker is making it all up, particularly if the result isn't quite as good as expected. I wish we had Broker's phone instead of Watson's.'

Now, Rumble's focus is back on the others and stretching his arms above his head, he groans. 'This damn table is breaking me, too - we need a full height one, and a bit bigger. And about Broker letting both sides meet – perhaps he knows they won't do private deals because he's their safe middleman, the buffer zone, so there's no direct link between industry and the person accepting the bribe. He sanitizes the money, uses his influencer guy as a liaison and gets someone to organize the flights or pay for the cars or whatever the reward is. He probably has trusts and shell companies so he can launder money for the big payments – or he does it with bitcoin or one of the other crypto currencies. If you two can get hold of the addresses for the state servants and the ministers we're interested in, I'll do a raid one night and check if any of them has insecure devices. Someone might have a teenager who took the password off for some dumb-ass teenage reason, or they have a hacker-friendly password.'

'What would you do if we found one?'

'I would copy their hard drive, emails, documents, porn videos – the lot.'

Really?' says Minnie. 'Can you actually get into someone's computer that easily, and copy everything?'

'Yeah, provided it's turned on, of course. You just need to know what you're doing. It's just like those CCTV hard drives that are linked to the camera via wifi that I hacked into at that bar. If people do the right thing and put a good password on, then I can't get in, or not easily.'

Luke shakes his head and laughs. 'Christ, Rumble, you're a menace to society.'

'More or less – yeah, I suppose I am, but in a good cause. Nothing is totally safe, you can try as hard as you like – not even my gear, not a hundred percent. Which is why I have a second laptop that never goes online or connects via Wi-Fi, and when I want to move data to it, I use a flash drive or an external drive. No direct connection to anything.'

'Is there any way of hacking into the cell phone companies?' asks Luke. 'Could you get hold of messages and phone calls?'

'I've never tried, but I don't think it can be done – they have a DMZ around their servers. You know, a Demilitarized Zone, just jargon to say that you can't get in, better than a moat full of crocodiles. But some clever bastard toiled through the night and worked out how to grab phone calls and text messages without doing it via the phone company's server – a clever little device that intercepts microwave signals – but you've got to be within "line of sight". I haven't got one, but it might be useful.'

'But the rumour is that the government agencies *can* listen to your calls,' says Minnie. 'Remember that story in social media last year – the woman who claimed they had people listening to her making dates with people. She kept seeing the same men observing her when she went out.'

'Yeah, they can. Just about the only thing they can't do is pick up historical calls, unless they have some way of intercepting a number and recording them. Shit, I don't know - everything becomes possible sooner or later, and I'm not familiar with the latest, phones aren't really my thing. With that microwave interceptor I talked about earlier, they have to follow you around and listen. But those that have access to military technology can get right into iPhones, for example, and listen to both calls and conversations in a room via the phone mike – and turn the camera on and take photos.'

'Privacy is an outdated concept, and we might as well get used to it,' says Minnie and sighs. 'Perhaps we should turn everything off when we come here, stay offline. At least Broker isn't part of the intelligence services – or I hope he's not, but perhaps he has his tentacles there as well or works for them. But yes - I can list the Departments that are mentioned in the messages and see how many of the key people I can find addresses for. And we haven't even started looking at that guy called the CP to see if they have infiltrated the justice system as well - and the police.'

'And what if we're caught?' says Luke. 'Rumble's credibility would be ruined - his clients might never trust him again and his livelihood could be wiped out. Not to mention that the GCSB or intelligence services would have him in jail in five minutes for subversion or endangering our national security. And we would all be under surveillance till the day we die.'

'No, no, we can't stop now!' exclaims Minnie. 'These guys are corrupting our democracy. Broker's clients just want to grab our resources and generally create mayhem and then take off with the profits. And those who accept bribes are liars and thieves. You know what they say – all it takes for evil to triumph is for good men to do nothing.'

'I can probably do it without leaving footprints. I'm pretty good at covering my tracks.' Rumble closes his laptop. 'I think this justifies a bit of criminal activity. If I get caught before we find out what this is all about, it could be bad for my reputation, I suppose – or it might be good PR, who knows? But if we can expose them, really out them in public, then I think hacking into people's computers would be overlooked. Tell you what, Luke – I'm more concerned about my physical safety than my reputation. And I mean that – I'm not normally into conspiracy theories and all that stuff, but with this lot ...'

'Earlier on I was thinking that maybe we could pull together some evidence and document what we have found and hand it over to the police,' says Minnie and shakes her head at her naïvety. 'Or to the GCSB or whoever. But then my friend Paranoia asked what would happen if Broker had contacts there that report to him, or what if there's a corrupt boss, or a boss who reports to someone corrupt – a bribe-taking Minister for example? Our evidence might go nowhere, but we would be exposed - and God knows what they would be prepared to do to shut us up.'

'I totally agree.' Rumble reaches for his backpack. 'We need enough hard facts to make it impossible for the world to ignore it before we go public – the full-on mega sized whistle-blower job. Don't know how, but in some way that makes a huge bloody impact.'

Luke nods. 'If we plan it right, we can release the information and sit back and watch it become a public scandal that can't be explained away, it's PR tactics.'

'Of course – I took that for granted.' Minnie picks up the electric kettle. 'And then we can enjoy what follows from our prison cells. Coffee?'

'Yes please. And how Broker would react is anyone's guess. Talking of surveillance – did you read about those files someone from the GCSB sent out by mistake? About ordinary people, whose every phone call and email had been logged for years, details about their friends, their vehicles, social media activity, extra-marital affairs, everything - which is why anonymous phones are such a good idea.'

23

Rumble puts the backpack on the kitchen counter and starts pulling things out. 'I brought some stuff in case this took a while. The sandwiches are a bit squashed, never mind, it's still food – and let's see, chocolate bars, bags of nuts, chips.'

Minnie laughs at the sight of it. 'Oh my God, look at it - there's more chocolate and chips than anything else.'

'Yeah, but it is all nourishment, Petal.'

'OK - but listen, Jane had a call from that guy who sent her the text message about the phone. He implied he knows for a fact she picked it up. She denied it again and said she'd tell the police if he continues to harass her – I'm going to get the number off her this week if I can, but I'm sure it's Dustman.'

'Bound to be,' says Luke. 'Or Broker, but he probably doesn't issue threats himself. What can we do to protect Jane?'

'But wait, there's more. Last night I got a text message from someone I've never heard of.' She gets her phone out and reads the message out and both men start talking at once.

'No, hang on a bit,' says Minnie, using her classroom voice. 'Let me finish. It's from a phone that leaves no number, just says 'number withheld' or whatever - but I'm sure it's Dustman. Too much of a coincidence otherwise and I haven't met a Dave for years. How does he know my name and my number? What's he trying to achieve? I can't figure it out and it makes me feel very anxious, both for Jane and for myself.'

She is trying to keep her cool but talking about it brings back that shiver of fear, the feeling of being watched from the shadows by someone she can't put a face to.

Rumble says slowly, 'Remember when you first told me about the phone – I think you said you called Jane that night to ask where she found it? Did you leave her a message about the phone at some stage – then or later?'

Minnie thinks back to the evening when she found the two identical phones in her bag.

'I called her, but she didn't answer. I just left a voice message ...' Her voice dies away. 'I see - he tracked Jane via the bistro, somehow he got her cell phone number and he's hacked her voice mail and heard my message. I think I said 'hi, it's Minnie, call me about that phone you found' or something like it.'

'Yep – that could be it. And somehow, he got your number from her phone – not sure how he would do that, probably hacked her contacts folder. But listen – it must mean he has no clue about who you are, or that you work with Jane. Or that you ever had the phone. He's got your name, he knows you heard Jane talking about the found phone, and now he's fishing for a conversation with you because of that voice message.'

'Should I try and set up a date with him so we can have a look at him?'

'Shit no - no way!' says Rumble. 'You must stay safely out of sight. My guess is that he's trying to find out more about Jane, thinks she might have told you something. So long that you didn't indicate you got into the phone, when you left her that message.'

'I don't think I did – but heaven knows, it's hard to remember now, no I'm sure I didn't. But I have to protect Jane – what if he puts more pressure on her? She's not involved in this, and I've already lied to her, I said I dropped the phone in the bistro's newspaper slot with a note. I must get Jane to tell the cops she's being harassed - and then she must tell Dustman that she's done that if he contacts her again. But that's not enough, is it?'

'No, it's not enough. We must give her a safe way out of this,' says Luke,' or it might all turn to custard. Could you sit down and talk her through a scenario that keeps her safe, and make sure she does what you tell her?'

Minnie hesitates for a moment, does a quick mental survey of Jane's stroppy personality and how she might be able to direct her without meeting opposition.

'Yes, I think I can. I'll have to persuade her to call Dustman and have a conversation with him. She could say "yes, I did actually pick it up, and I gave it to a friend, but she knew straight away it wasn't hers, so she dropped it in the newspaper slot at the bistro the next morning". That might be enough to stop bothering her.'

'It could work, but what if he wants to talk to you? He might even want to meet you.'

'She could say that I'm just about to go off on a holiday overseas and give him my number, tell him to call me, before I leave – what do you think? He has my number already – I'm sure that message about a drink was from him – so giving it to him makes no difference.'

'And you can't let on that you know he's actually Dave, who asked you out,' says Luke, who seems to regret that he can't be directly involved in orchestrating this. 'Make sure Jane understands that you don't want to meet this guy any more than she does, but you think you can convince him that you returned the phone, and it will get him off her back. That should encourage her to make that call, however reluctant she feels.'

They spend a few minutes debating the details, until they agree it seems good enough to protect Minnie and keep Jane out of harm's way.

'But now I've had another nasty thought.' Rumble looks at Luke. 'Obviously Broker knows what car you drive – I mean, he sent Dustman to put a bullet through the windscreen. Have you noticed anyone following you around? We don't want him to find this place. He threatened to keep an eye on you, didn't he?'

'Yeah, but the car I'm driving now isn't mine. I swapped with a mate about a month ago – not because of the bullet, another reason altogether. And I don't use my parking space outside the apartment any longer, I rent a space in a parking building and walk from there.'

'Doesn't that make things dangerous for your mate?'

'Well, no – they live in Rotorua and never come to Wellington, so they should be safe.'

'Clever move,' says Rumble approvingly. 'Much safer for you. And great that they let you take their car."

Luke smiles. 'They couldn't wait to lay their hands on my car - they had a baby and bought one of those oversized buggies, you know, the cross-country type and it wouldn't fit in the boot of their car. And they couldn't afford to get a bigger car right away, so I said they could have my SUV for a few months while they save up. I drove up there and came back in a different car that's never been parked near my apartment.'

The casual way he tells them reminds Minnie about her previous thoughts about Luke; how he doesn't seem to need to prove things to people. Very unusual, she thinks, most people would make a bit of a production out of their generosity and expect praise, but he just skates over it. It's like a form of extreme self-confidence - he has no need for the world's approval.

Over lunch they try to talk about other things, but the conversation keeps swerving back to the earlier discussion. Luke gets up and puts his hand out to take Minnie's cup.

'I am going to call you Minli from now on– sounds much like Minnie, but I think it describes you better after your performance with Amanda.'

'What does it mean?' asks Rumble. 'Is it Chinese?'

'Two Chinese words – min means clever or sharp and li means strong, I just put the two words together. Li is often used as a man's name, but I think in combination with Min it makes a nice name. What do you think, Minli?'

Rumble laughs at the look on her face. 'Just accept the compliment and enjoy it, Minli – it's a good name and so close to Minnie it doesn't even matter. And nobody apart from Brendan ever called you Minerva anyway. And what ...'

She interrupts him to sidetrack the conversation. 'You're right about this table – it's a torture device. I'll bring the folding table I sometimes use on the terrace. It is regular table height and a bigger than this.'

'Will it fit in your car?'

'I think so – the legs fold, so I can probably shove it in behind the front seats.'

They're ready to leave when Rumble suddenly remembers. 'Hey, Luke - what happened with Amanda? What did Minnie do?'

Luke shoots Minnie a sideways glance and grins. 'I'll give you the whole thing blow by blow. You're going to love it – it was an awesome performance.'

'OK guys, I'm leaving now.' Hearing Luke tell the story will embarrass her as much as Rumble will love it.

She walks to her car deep in thought. Perhaps it was a good

thing that Brendan ran off that night, at least he's in a safe place now. And it's a blessing that his memory is getting worse all the time – soon he won't remember who I am, and then he'll not miss me if something happens. She shakes her head to dispel her gloomy thoughts and drives back to the empty house.

24

Minnie and Jane always go out for coffee after school on Tuesdays and have recently discussed trying to find a café they like, where parking is easier,

'Let's take my car and I'll drop you here after, so we don't both have to find somewhere to park,' says Jane, as they walk across the school parking lot. Jane is rummaging through her bag as she walks. 'Damn! I left my keys in my cubbyhole. Hold this please and I'll run back.'

She thrusts her bag at Minnie and runs back across the half-empty parking lot. Minnie sticks her hand into the bag and pulls out Jane's phone. It's a moment's work to unlock it, she has watched Jane do it a hundred times. Standing on the far side of the car she opens the text folder and scrolls quickly down the messages. There! A text message from a 022 number with no name next to it, but it's not the number Dustman used to message Farmer. She memorizes it, reads the message and lets the phone slide back into the bag as Jane comes running back towards her.

'Don't turn your head and make it obvious,' says Jane and starts the car, and now her voice has an edge of tension. 'Check out the guy standing by the 'give way' sign. Take a sideways look as I drive past.'

She loops around the one-way circuit towards the exit. A tall man in a brown leather jacket is facing in their direction, but it's impossible to see if he is actually looking at them from behind his sunglasses.

'OK - I had a good look. Why?'

'I think he's stalking me – I'm not joking. This is the second time I've seen him, he was here yesterday too. And he's not making any effort to make it look accidental, is he? Yesterday he didn't have sunglasses on and he just stared at me, and I looked in the rearview mirror when I had passed him and he had turned around, still looking at my car. I went around the block and when I passed again, he'd gone.'

'And he didn't try to talk to you?'

'I think he's that obsessive guy who's been nagging me about the phone. But I've been really consistent and firm and told him I never picked it up. It's scary, Minnie. Perhaps he's a head case - do you think I should report him?'

Minnie thinks fast and decides to risk a suggestion that might pay dividends. The idea terrifies her, but it is a one-off opportunity.

'Do you think we should take a photo of him? We could go back right now and ask what he's doing. Turn around and go back! I'll talk to him and you can take a photo while I do it.'

'God no, I'm not going anywhere near him!'

Minnie feels guilty about how relieved she is that Jane has turned down her offer. Their café date, which is normally happy and relaxed, feels tense and strained. Jane is upset about the man in the parking lot, so Minnie uses the opportunity to put her scheme forward and Jane listens with a dubious frown.

'I suppose I could call him,' she says reluctantly. 'But then he'll pester you instead - are you sure you want to talk to him? He's quite scary really, finding out my number and being so persistent.'

Minnie knows this is her best chance to make amends for involving Jane in danger, she must persuade her to call Dustman or things might get out of hand, and there might never be another opportunity as good as this one.

'Never mind, just give him my number! I really don't mind – let's face it, there's not much he can do to me, is there? Just tell him that I'm about to go to Fiji on holiday on Saturday and to call me before the weekend. Once he's talked to me, he won't keep on bothering you, because I'll confirm that I was the last person to have the phone. I'm sure I can make him see reason.'

Jane nods, and seems about to start the discussion all over, so Minnie changes the subject. 'And don't forget that we're going to that panel discussion tonight at the museum. Do you want me to pick you up?'

Jane shakes her head and makes a face.

'No, I'll have to meet you there - we're having dinner at the in-laws' place. I'll go back there and pick Jordan up after the museum thing. I'll be pleased to get away, his mum is relentless about this damn baby thing – she keeps banging on about it every time she sees me. Tales about other people's grandchildren, on and on and on. I'll only rate in that family if I produce a grandchild.'

When they return to the school car park Dustman has left and Minnie drives home trying to think of other ways to avert unpleasantness for Jane. Now that she has seen him, her sense of threat has escalated, he is a real person, not just a shadowy threat. Now he inhabits her imagination in a more menacing way, and she can imagine him as an actual person coming after her and maybe harming her.

Why is the phone so important? The messages on it are sensitive, but there are no names and anyway, wouldn't they assume it was safe because it was locked? Perhaps it's Broker's obsession with secrecy combines with his silo mentality – nothing must be left to chance, no loose ends? What if Broker has contacts in the intelligence services, or works there himself - maybe he could get her put under surveillance for no reason and how would she know if he has?

She sends a message to Luke and Rumble and tells them that she thinks she has seen Dustman. Their replies are more or less the same; 'at least one of us knows what he looks like, hope he didn't notice you'. She makes no mention of her offer to confront him on Jane's behalf.

Five minutes after event has started, the foyer at Te Papa Museum is empty, and apart from an elderly couple and a boy on a scooter, the forecourt is deserted. Minnie decides that Jane will have to find her in the lecture hall and heads up, but halfway up the big staircase her phone signals a message: 'In ED, dislocated thumb. Sorry.'

Nearly two hours later she moves slowly with the surprisingly big crowd down the wide stairs and out through the big glass doors.

What a boring evening – and nothing was really debated anyway, everyone just politely agreed, she thinks. So now I know that there are times when museums should repatriate objects to their country of origin – so what? I knew that already. Political correctness is turning people into intellectual cowards, nobody has the guts to be the devil's advocate and create a good debate these days.

'Minnie - wait!'

She turns and sees an arm wave frantically some meters behind her, so she stops to let the woman catch up with her, but even when she gets a good look at her, she has no idea who it is. Good grief, who is she? About my age, maybe someone from high school or even primary school?

'Bet you don't remember me! Do you?' She is tall and dark haired and wears glasses with a bright red frame.

'Sorry – I don't. You'll have to help me out.'

To her surprise the woman seems delighted with her response.

'I'm Mathilde,' she says triumphantly. 'I went out with your cousin Andy a few times years ago. He was at the Police Training College, and you and I were in our last year at high school and he used to stay with your family in the weekends. I saw your photo in the paper when you got that teaching award – what a great effort, congratulations!'

'You've changed a lot – no wonder I didn't recognize you. You look wonderful!'

'Yeah, I know, isn't it great? I was always such a fatty, but a few years ago I got sick of it, so I worked off a third of my body weight - and then I got carried away with being nice-looking and took up being fashionable as well.'

She grins; delighted with her own achievement. 'But you're exactly the same Minnie. I can't believe it - you haven't changed at all, amazing. You must give my regards to Andy, I read about his heroics under that train in Hawke's Bay some years ago - what a drama!'

'Thank you, I will. What are you doing these days?'

They spend fifteen minutes catching up on news of old classmates and teachers, and when they part company, the forecourt is empty again.

'I walked here, I live in in a loft in Taranaki Street,' says Mathilde. 'Which way are you going?'

'I'm in that parking lot off Barnett Street, the opposite direction.'

'Lovely to catch up,' says Mathilde, 'and don't forget to tell Andy that we met.'

25

It is tempting to postpone going back to the empty house, and on an impulse Minnie turns and walks slowly along the quay towards the Rowing Club Basin instead of heading for her car. The wind has dropped and the hills, festooned with garlands of street-lights, are reflected in the still, dark water. She stops and thinks she might take a photo of the view, when suddenly a man is right beside her. He takes a firm grip on her upper arm before she has time to react, and something hard pushes into her ribs.

'Just keep walking. Don't scream. I have a pistol in my hand.'

He pulls her close to his side, still with the tight grip on her upper arm, and adjusts his stride to her shorter steps.

'What *are* you doing? Let go of me!' She hopes she sounds as if she's just annoyed at being accosted, but she knows she's in serious trouble. His fingers close more tightly around her arm, her heart beats faster and a bubble of panic rises in her throat.

It's him! He's going to force me to tell him about the phone. How did he know where to find me? I must keep calm, deep slow breaths – I can't let him see how scared I am.

Fear makes her stomach clench and her instincts urge her to tear free and run. But he's tall and strong and he would catch her in no time, so maybe the best thing is to wait for someone to come along and then scream for help. Collapse, she thinks, just drop to the ground and scream.

They continue along the edge of the quay, with his fingers digging into her arm just below the shoulder and his off-side arm across his middle with the gun pushed hard against her ribs.

'Let's go for a walk. I know you're a friend of Jane's – I saw you in her car, you teach at the same school. I knew Jane was going to be here, but I couldn't see her - and now I've found you instead. I want to know who Minnie is.'

He doesn't know I'm Minnie - he just followed me because of the school connection! I have to play this right, persuade him that I'm of no interest.

She scans the area in front of them and as far to the sides as she can without turning her head, but she sees nobody. Will he really shoot her if she screams? She tilts her head sideways, looks down and tries to see if it really is a gun, and he jerks her arm hard, and his voice is calm and full of menace. 'Don't try anything. It's loaded, and I'll kill you if you cause problems – they'll find your body in the water in the morning. Do you know Jane's friend Minnie? Is she a teacher too?'

'I have no idea,' says Minnie. She feels slightly more confident now. If all he knows is that she is at the same school as Jane, perhaps she has a chance to talk her way out of this. 'Of course, I know Jane, but I don't know anyone called Minnie. Why don't you ask Jane yourself?'

'What's your name?'

'Wendy,' she says. 'Wendy Gordon. What's all this about anyway?'

Wendy Gordon was a fellow lecturer at Auckland University, and she has no idea how the name popped into her mind just in time to avoid an awkward hesitation.

'Jane found a phone in a bar – did you hear about that? Do you know what she did with it?'

'She was talking about it a few days ago in the staff room.' Minnie tries to sound as if he is irritating rather than frightening. 'She just said that she'd had messages from someone who thought she had found a phone somewhere. I don't know why they thought she had found it – she didn't say.'

'Do you believe her?' His voice is quiet and controlled, his grip on her arm as tight as ever and the pressure of the gun is constant.

'Yes, of course I do. Why would she lie? I mean, it's not as if it's that important, is it?'

She hopes she sounds reasonable and a bit naïve. Her mind whispers, 'Be very careful, stay calm, be brave'. Her heartbeat has slowed. Now that she has come up with a credible angle, she feels less frightened. She prepares her voice to sound steady and innocent.

'And what's so special about this phone anyway? I mean, can't you just get a new phone and claim it on insurance or something? I just don't get it. This is ridiculous – would you please let go of my arm?'

He pushes the pistol harder against her ribs and shakes her. He is strong and she is helpless in his grip. 'No, we'll talk some more and then I might let you go.'

Might, she thinks, and what's the alternative to might? Her mind conjures up images of what a man so much bigger than she could do to her. They are close to the edge of the wharf, and she wonders if she could topple them both into the water, but what would happen if she did? Dustman would probably drop his gun. And even if he held on to it, would it work if it got wet? Should she pretend to stumble and fall, throw herself into the water?

Running footsteps approach from the landward side. Minnie can't see past Dustman, but someone is closing in fast. Dustman turns his head, and his grip on her arm loosens slightly. She jerks her arm free and takes a step backwards as he swings around to face a man, who is now only a couple of meters away.

'Leave her alone, you bastard!'

My God, it's Luke- what is he doing here? And what can he achieve against a man who's armed?

Dustman says firmly, 'It's nothing to do with you. We're on our way home.'

'I don't believe you. Let her speak for herself – I don't think you even know her.'

He is trying to give the impression he doesn't know me. God, I hope Dustman doesn't shoot him. Could I grab the gun now that he's looking at Luke and not at me?

Dustman is getting angry. 'Fuck off! It's not your business.'

Luke bends his knees and leaps, fast and high. He turns as he rises in the air, his right leg lifts and with incredible speed and force the side of his foot connects with Dustman's head. Dustman staggers sideways, nearly rights himself and crashes to the ground, just missing Minnie, and the gun clatters along the concrete wharf. Luke glances briefly at Minnie and turns to face Dustman who is scrambling to his feet, swaying and turning his head from side to side looking for the gun. Luke takes three short steps to the right and kicks the gun hard; it shoots out over the dark water and disappears. Dustman makes a forward rush and Luke leaps again. This time his foot lands square in the middle of Dustman's chest, and he staggers backwards, trips and falls on the edge of the wharf. Minnie watches in frozen horror as Luke flings himself at Dustman; they roll first one way and then the other as Dustman tries to dislodge Luke, but suddenly the struggle stops and a shrill scream of pain cuts through the heavy breathing. Luke leaps to his feet, bends down and rolls Dustman over the edge; there is a splash followed by silence, then coughing and more splashing.

'Let's go.'

'What if he can't swim? He could drown.'

'Let him drown!'

His voice is calm and uncompromising, but before he can stop her, she walks to the edge of the quay and looks cautiously down. Dustman is swimming clumsily towards one of the concrete supports, hampered by his leather jacket, which is like a balloon full of air, slowing him down. There is no doubt he will make it, though she has no idea how he will get up on the quay; the water is a long way down.

She turns and her foot strikes something light that skitters a short distance over the ground and she bends to pick it up, 'Let's go – quickly!'

Now she is frantic to get away, walking fast towards the museum. 'It's a phone,' she says in a low voice, as if Dustman might hear her. 'I just picked up a phone! It might be his!'

'Christ - let's get away from here.'

'My car is in the parking lot on the far side of the museum.'

'I know – I was there, waiting for you to come out. I had to park in Tory Street, but I got worried when other people left and you didn't turn up. We'll get your car first and then mine.'

'That was Dustman.' Now she has to hurry to keep up, high heels not helping. 'Or at least it's the same guy who was in the school parking lot. How did you know where I was? Have you been following me around?'

'Rumble told me you were going out with Jane tonight. I've followed you a couple of times, just in case.'

She is unsure how she feels about having a self-appointed bodyguard without being aware of it, but grateful that he was there, and now is not the time to consider it, so she changes the subject. 'I've never seen anyone do that sort of power kick, or whatever it's called, before.'

He makes no comment; glancing up at him she sees a slight smile, and it seems to her that the smile is not one of pleasure or pride, but of amusement.

It's like when Amanda was dismissive of him in that first meeting, and I caught that little smile. I'm totally right about him - he finds it funny when people underestimate him. So self-assured that he doesn't need to prove they are wrong.

26

Minnie drives through the city with Luke following close behind. She has locked the doors around her and all she wants now is to get home and feel safe.

She parks on the driveway, as she always does, because Brendan's car is still in the garage, and with Luke following she leads the way inside, unsure of what will happen next, but grateful that he is there.

In the living room, she turns on the light and pulls the curtains; her entire focus on shielding herself from the outside world.

'Would you like a drink? I think you deserve one after that.'

'No, thanks. Do you mind if I look around?'

She stares at him in surprise; his dark eyes are steady and serious.

'You didn't expect to be caught and attacked in a public place and we have no idea how much he knows about you – I think we need to be very careful.'

He leaves the room, and she stands rooted to the spot, overwhelmed by the realization that she is really no safer at home than she is anywhere else. She takes the phone out of her pocket and rubs the scratched screen, wonders if Rumble will be able to get into it and what they might find out if he can. What if it were to ring now? she thinks and drops it on the table as if it burnt her hand.

Luke returns from his tour of the house. 'I've checked all the windows on both floors. Is that his phone?'

'We have to talk to Rumble – he might be able to get into it.'

She calls Rumble but gets no reply. 'I'll send him a message – sometimes when he's working, he closes off the outside world. Are you sure you don't want a drink?'

Luke picks the phone up and turns it off.

'OK, thanks – a cup of coffee would be good. What did he say to you? I can't believe how calm you look. Didn't you realise he had a gun?'

She stares at him in disbelief and nearly laughs. 'For heaven's sake, Luke, of course I knew he had a gun – it was pressed against my ribs.'

She remembers how she briefly considered falling into the water. Now she has no idea why she thought it might save her, seeing she cannot swim. The memory of people looking at her scarred body the only time her mother took her to swimming class, the cringing embarrassment of pretending not to notice and then climbing out of the pool crying; she never learnt to swim. What a stupid idea, she thinks, I would have drowned. Just shows you how badly your mind works when you are desperate.

'Well, you certainly kept your cool. If that was Dustman, I won't recognize him again. I could hardly make out his face under that cap.'

'And that goes for you too. He can't have seen your face – not with the hood up and the light behind you. I only knew it was you by your voice.'

'So, what did he say?'

'He said he knew Jane was going to Te Papa and he couldn't see her, and then he spotted me staying behind to talk to an old friend. You see, Jane couldn't come after all - and he remembered me from when he saw me in Jane's car this afternoon. He asked if I knew someone called Minnie, and if I'd heard about Jane finding a phone. And by the way, I talked to Jane about making that call today, and she promised she will do it. We went through the whole scenario, and I think she's relieved to pass the ball back to me. I'll check tomorrow that she really did call him.'

'OK, but what did you tell Dustman?'

'Well, I said my name was Wendy and I said, that Jane had talked about it in the staff room, that someone sent her a message about a phone, but she had no idea what it was about. And then I thought my best bet would be to act a bit more naïve. So, I said things like 'why don't you just buy a new phone' and 'surely it isn't that important'. You know, as if I just thought it was slightly over the top to turn up with a gun to ask questions about it - just trying to make him be a bit more reasonable. So, he'd think there was no need to shoot me.'

Fear runs an icy finger down her spine when she remembers the feeling of the pistol pressed against her ribs.

Luke moves his head very slowly from side to side but makes no comment.

'And then he shook me really hard and said we had to talk a bit more, and then you turned up and saved me.'

Luke says, with quiet emphasis, 'You are the coolest customer I've ever met. At least now he thinks your name is Wendy, and he doesn't connect you with the phone. And when he speaks to the woman called Minnie on the phone, he'll think he's talking to a different person.'

They look at each other in silence, thinking the same thing but reluctant to voice it: What will he do if he finds out that she is Minnie? In the end Luke says, in a way that takes her agreement for granted, 'I'm camping on the sofa tonight – I can go home and tidy up for work when you go to school.'

'There's a guest room just across the hall that would be far more comfortable.'

He shakes his head. 'No thanks, I want to be where I have a direct line of sight to the stairs.'

They check the locks, leave the outside lights on and go to bed. Minnie lies awake for a long time, thinking about what happened.

How can she possibly protect herself from him, if he decides he wants to question her again - or if he finds out that she is Minnie? Could he trick the school into giving him information? Ring up and describe her? Check if there is a teacher called Wendy? She must ask the office staff at school to confirm they have a teacher called Wendy and saying that she has a stalker would probably work. And thank God that documentary hasn't screened yet.

When she finally sleeps, she dreams she is standing in the school parking lot and a man in dripping wet clothes is coming towards her. He has a gun in his hand, and he is going to kill her.

It is twenty to seven in the morning and the living room is suffused with light filtering through the curtains. Standing beside the sofa she contemplates Luke, who is asleep with a large carving knife upright in the hand that rests on the edge of the sofa. How will she wake him without one of them accidentally getting stabbed?

Very slowly she says his name and reaches out to touch his shoulder. His free hand shoots out and grabs her wrist at the same time as his legs swing to the floor. 'Oh, it's you – sorry!'

She jumps back. 'God, you gave me a fright! I thought you were asleep, and I was so worried you'd hurt yourself if I woke you and you didn't remember you had the knife in your hand.'

He puts the knife on the arm of the sofa. 'I was asleep.' He yawns and rubs his face. 'But I knew I had the knife in my hand, and I let go of you as soon as I realised it was you.'

'God knows why I worried about you – complete waste of time,' she says, and adds, on a sudden impulse, 'Could you teach me how to defend myself? Just some simple tricks. I know that stuff you do takes years to learn, but there must be something I can do to defend myself?'

'I can teach you how to find a nerve point and hurt someone very badly with one finger, but that takes a bit of time to learn. Self-defense courses teach people some quite good tricks. Not martial arts, but definitely better than nothing.'

She remembers the scream of pain when Luke struggled with Dustman. 'Is that what you did last night – when he screamed?'

'Yeah, I didn't think it would work, finding the right spot while he was moving like that, but I must have.' He smiles. 'I just managed to get my finger in behind his collarbone – it hurts like nothing else, impossible to move for a few moments.'

He gets to his feet. 'But back to your question, screaming and running is supposed to be the best thing you can do. If I grab hold of your arm, like this, just like Dustman did, and you're going to surprise me, so you can pull free and run for your life – what would you do?'

She swings around and hits him as hard as she can on the side of the jaw with her fist. He laughs in surprise and rubs his face.

'I wasn't expecting that. A good hit, but that wasn't a real punch. When you hit with a closed fist you must lead with the knuckles – then it really hurts.'

She nods, it makes sense. She clenches her fist. 'Do you want me to try again?'

'God, no - next time you'll probably do some real damage. That one was quite enough this early in the morning. I never expected you to go for the face – I thought you'd hit me in the chest or the arm.'

She doesn't even consider apologizing. 'And? What else could be useful?'

'Screaming very loudly. Don't laugh – apparently a lot of people, men and women, don't scream loudly when someone attacks them, so maybe put that at the front of your mind. The only other thing I can think of is to use whatever is at hand as a weapon – if you feel insecure, say when you walk across a dark parking lot. Hold your keys in your first with the points of the keys sticking out between your fingers. Or a pen or a nail file or whatever you have. Then when you punch someone it's not only your knuckles that make contact, but something hard and sharp that really hurts. If you don't know how to fight it's all about surprise and the chance to get away.'

She nods, thinking of how effective this would be. Luke hesitates, starts to say something and stops.

'Yes? What?'

'It's a revolting idea, but I'll tell you anyway. If you could condition yourself to do this, you would win before the fight had even started. Keep your forefinger and middle finger rigid and fold the other fingers. And then you prod straight into someone's eye – and you've disabled the attacker completely.'

He takes in her expression of revulsion. 'Sorry, I did warn you. But it's probably the most effective way a small person can disable a stronger attacker. They'll be blinded by tears and screaming in agony.'

Over breakfast they call Rumble with Minnie's phone on speaker so they can have a three-way conversation.

'I only went to bed a couple of hours ago.' They hear him yawn. 'Sorry, I worked all night. Is it important?'

When they tell him about what happened outside Te Papa and about Dustman's phone he instantly revives.

'Bloody awesome luck! You two get to have all the fun while I slave over a hot computer. And what is it with you and phones, Petal - is it some new kind of gravitational force?' He yawns again. 'Can you drop it off on your way to work? I'll see what I can do and then we can meet at the flat tonight. Don't know if I can get into it, but I'll try.'

Luke offers to drive her to school and to pick her up afterwards, but she can see no reason to break their self-imposed rules.

'No, I'll take my car. Imagine if Dustman is in the school parking lot and recognizes you from the press gallery – he'll put two and two together and then we're in real trouble.'

Luke takes Dustman's phone and sets off to deliver it to Rumble, and Minnie sets the alarm and leaves for school.

27

Locking the door behind her, she stands for a moment listening to the empty house. Since the Te Papa incident her awareness of potential danger has increased to a level that is becoming obsessive and now affects every aspect of her life. Today the added worry about the phone call she expects from Dustman makes her feel even more on edge. Jane has done her bit, though she baulked at actually talking to him and sent a long text message instead, saying she couldn't keep calm if she had to speak to him.

To divert her anxiety, she calls Sharon. 'The rest home left a message today - Brendan is fine. He seems to have settled in quite well, and the nurse told me he's found someone to do crosswords with.'

'Oh, that's nice,' says Sharon. 'Such a relief. I think about him every day and wonder how he is. Are we allowed to visit yet?'

'They said not to visit until next week. I'll let you know how he is when I've visited him the first time.'

A message arrives from Rumble: 'Will be at the flat at 7. I will bring dinner. Pls bring laptops.'

Cryptic, thinks Minnie, and unexpected, but I won't ask any questions now. I'll go out and water the roses in the front garden instead of thinking about it. She stands absentmindedly holding the hose and wonders if she should start parking the car way down the street when she gets home, so she can quietly walk up to the house and check if it looks OK. Would it be safer? And Brendan's car must be sold, and how useful it is that she got Power of Attorney last year. And the Easter break is coming up, so it's time to give all her classes some short tests to check they're up to speed and with Brendan not at home, she will have so much time to mark papers over the break.

Her thoughts revert to security; perhaps she should call the people who installed the alarm and find out how to arm the ground floor separately, when she is upstairs at night. She has never tried it and she can't remember what they told her. Or maybe she should have a bolt on her bedroom door.

Back inside she locks the front door again and tests the handle to make sure it is secure. Dustman has demonstrated how powerless she is; short and light and her range of movement on one side restricted; his grip high up on her arm gave him complete control. If he had gripped lower down, she might have had a chance to pull away, but he would still have out-run her.

To stop herself thinking about Dustman, she opens Brendan's big old roll-top desk in the dining room. Every drawer is crammed full of papers and before long she is deep in a sorting project of mammoth proportions. Letters and photos lie in untidy piles on the dining table and the wastepaper basket overflows. Two hours later she fetches cardboard boxes from the garage and starts tidying up. There is a treasure trove of photos from family weddings and picnics, from Christmas parties and holidays, one pile of papers to keep and some to investigate further at a later date.

Her phone buzzes, an unknown number and she steels herself to be calm.

'Hi, this is Minnie.'

'Hi Minnie, I think you have a phone that belongs to me. Jane sent a message.'

That voice, she would know it anywhere, neither loud nor aggressive, but low and very even and somehow more threatening than if he raised his voice.

'Yeah, I did have it, but I don't have it now,' she says, trying to sound breezy and unconcerned and a bit more high-pitched than normal, hoping he won't recognize her voice. 'Didn't Jane tell you? I took it back to the bistro on my way to work the morning after she gave it to me.'

'They say they've never seen it. Who did you give it to?'

'Nobody – there wasn't anybody there, it was early in the morning. They have this kind of box with a slot – you know the sort that snaps shut with a spring? For mail and things. So, I popped it in there.'

'Are you sure it was the right place?'

'For God's sake - of course it was the right place!' She allows a note of irritation to creep into her voice. 'It's where we went for drinks. And I put a note with it – just saying someone had picked it up thinking it was mine, but it wasn't mine after all.'

She stops talking and there is silence for a long moment before he speaks again. 'I'd like to talk to you in person if you don't mind. Can we meet somewhere – just for a quick chat?'

'I'm going away tomorrow – off to Fiji with my parents. And today I'm busy, I'm having to work late to catch up. And there's nothing else I can tell you anyway. I knew straight away the phone wasn't mine because I couldn't unlock it. And then I found mine in the bottom of my bag – they're exactly the same.'

'OK, thanks.'

When she ends the call, she is trembling. His voice has triggered an intense sense of threat, as real and physical as when he had her in that strong hold on the quayside.

The thought that there would be nobody else to be interested in the photos she had found only strikes her on the way to the flat and it makes her acutely aware of her own mortality. Sander is dead and she will have no children; there will be no next generation to treasure those mementoes of past lives, to study the faces to find a likeness. And who will sort things out when she dies? It makes her feel very alone. She parks the car and remains in the driver's seat for a few minutes, folding her sadness into a tight bundle in the back of her mind, to be kept separate from her meeting with Rumble and Luke.

28

Minnie closes the door behind her and smiles at the sight that greets her. 'Hi guys, you look very comfortable. Any left for me?'

'Come and sit down. There's a small pizza of the kind you like, with anchovies, and I got you some grapefruit juice. That phone was a great score.'

She picks up a piece of pizza and Luke raises his beer bottle in a toast. 'Here's to Rumble, who spent nearly the whole day working on that phone and only got three hours sleep. It's the phone Dustman used to communicate with clients or whatever we should call them. I've only had a quick look - but Rumble hasn't found the messages Dustman sent to Jane and her replies – so you were right, he's got several phones.'

Rumble interrupts with a slice of pizza halfway to his mouth. 'It is two and a half years' worth of messages. We'll start sorting them as soon as we've finished eating. I had to talk to a guy I know in Germany to find out how to get into the bloody thing.'

He takes a huge bite of pizza and chews frantically before he continues. 'This German guy specializes in forensic stuff, and he's developed a great kit that he sells to police labs all over the world. You know how they say what goes around, comes around? I did him a favour last year. Something quite simple, but he needed someone who was physically in New Zealand to do it. So now he told me how to break into the phone.'

'Ah yes, of course - IT karma. I've suspected it existed for a long time,' says Minnie. 'I felt certain there must be some kind of belief system in your world of hard drives and binary code.'

Rumble reaches for another piece of pizza. 'When I called this guy, the first thing he said was "is it in a Faraday bag?" and of course it was by then, but that was so many hours after you picked it up, it didn't even matter – could have been too late.'

'A Faraday bag? It must be a bag version of a Faraday cage – is there really such a thing?'

'Shit, yes – they've been around for years. Some people use them to keep credit cards safe from being hacked. The cops use them to prevent criminals from wiping everything off a device remotely when they've got hold of it. They even make briefcase linings so nobody can hack the devices inside.'

He picks up another slice of pizza. 'Anyway – all the data from the phone is on an external hard drive now, so it doesn't matter what happens to the phone. I disabled the GPS so he can't check where it is. They probably think it's at the bottom of the sea – there were a couple of messages that came in after Dustman went for his swim and then a few irritated questions from Broker about where the hell he is.'

'I can't wait,' says Luke and starts clearing the table.

'Here you are, one flash drive each,' says Rumble. 'I've copied about a third of the messages for each of us. But you'll be pleased to hear that I've converted the download file into a Word document, so we can work with it. The original will stay on my SSD. What I think we should do first off is just read them all and mark everything that might give us a clue to an identity. What do you think?'

'We could highlight identity clues, and we should convert all those lowercase acronyms and abbreviations to upper case – maybe Bold them too,' says Minnie. 'It's really hard to pick things out otherwise and I bet we'll want to go through them more than once. And what is an SSD?'

'Solid state drive – super safe, can't be wiped accidentally by magnetism, totally encrypted, very fast.' He takes another bite and points the remains of his pizza slice at Luke. 'Luke - don't get offended, but I have to check. Do you know how to save stuff to the flash drive instead of on your hard drive? Minnie's OK, she can save it on that old machine of hers, but you must keep it on the flash drive. I've disconnected the modem here while we work on this.'

Half an hour later Rumble interrupts their concentration. 'Let's compare notes on what we've found so far, and then I must go home and do some work and get a proper sleep. I can hardly keep my eyes open. Can we meet tomorrow after you two finish work? What time can you be here, Minnie?'

'I can come straight after my last class. No meetings tomorrow, so I'd be here by four.'

'Luke?'

'Half past five - if I'm lucky.'

They leave a few minutes apart as they always do. Minnie after Luke, leaving Rumble to turn the lights off. When she drives off, a car pulls out from a few spaces behind her and her heart skips a beat, her new awareness of danger flashes a warning. She keeps checking the rearview mirror and at the next traffic lights she looks at the reflections in the shop windows and sees that the car behind her is Luke's. She raises her hand in a wave and he blinks his headlights.

When she parks on the driveway, a car comes slowly down the street and stops two houses away. She looks over her shoulder as she goes up the steps to the front door, but once again it is Luke. He has followed her home and come around the block from the opposite direction. Like a bodyguard, she thinks. I must thank him - and I must remember to tell them that I had that call from Dustman.

'There are a couple of things we should discuss,' says Luke the next evening, with his pen spinning like a propeller between his fingers. He is studying his notes from the previous evening and frowning. 'There's very little talk between Dustman and Broker on this phone, apart from those last few messages. I think Dustman has a phone that's only for communicating with Broker, and that one drowned, so Broker then sent those few messages you talked about to the phone we picked up – not realizing that this one was no longer available to Dustman either. And the text Broker sent when he got no response from Dustman's Broker-phone is very interesting. It's about giving someone referred to as no5 a warning - Broker realised one phone was out of action and sent it to this one instead.'

'I bet Rumble was right,' says Minnie, 'and they think this phone that we picked up is at the bottom of the harbour. Dustman can't possibly have seen that it fell out of his pocket before he went into the water– he was flying through the air at the time.'

Luke ticks an item on his notepad and the pen starts spinning again. 'I wish we knew that for sure. I don't want Dustman coming after you because he thinks you have the phone. Thank God he doesn't know that cell phones gravitate toward you as if by magic. But as you said before – imagine if we had the phone Dustman uses with Broker. I'd give a fortune to find out which policy advisors and ministerial advisors they bribe – I know quite a few of them.'

Something clicks into place in Minnie's mind. 'Ha! Rumble, do you remember we wondered about those abbreviations? At the very start – minad and polad? Luke just said it – that's what they mean, ministerial advisor and policy advisor.'

Without a word Rumble pushes his chair back and disappears at speed into the bathroom. When he re-appears a few minutes later, he is pale and perspiring.

'Don't use the bathroom for at least five minutes – I left the fan on. I feel bloody awful - have to go home. I felt funny earlier today and it got a lot worse suddenly. Sorry guys, we'll continue tomorrow.'

They make commiserating noises and let him leave, and Minnie turns to Luke. 'I'm happy to continue working on this now if that's all right with you.'

'I'm fine, no worries. So, where did we get to with no5?'

'I was just saying that maybe they didn't always call him no5. They might have changed from initials to no5 recently for some reason. There might be some message just before the one about the threat that indicates who he is. I mean what his initials are.'

Their search for clues about no5 brings up nothing.

'Let's stop now – it's getting late.' While Minnie gets up and puts their coffee mugs into the dishwater, Luke picks up Dustman's phone and turns it on. 'Come on Luke – turn that off so we can go home.'

'Look at this!' Luke holds the phone out for her to see. 'I don't know what the hell I did, but that last message from Broker about no5 – it's got a whole previous exchange, a thread of messages that don't show in the material Rumble downloaded.'

He frowns. 'But how can I see it on this phone then? Aha, maybe this dialog was between Broker's phone and Dustman's other phone and then Broker picked up on the last reply from

Dustman and sent his next comment to Dustman's lobbyist phone – would the whole thread kind of tag along? Like when you forward an email?'

Minnie leans over his shoulder to look and shakes her head. 'Don't ask me – I know nothing about stuff like that. Let's write it all down in case it disappears again. I'm not trusting anything these days.'

She sits down at her laptop again. 'OK, you read them out, from the earliest in that thread to the last and I'll do the typing. And then can you please turn that horrible phone off and put it back in the bag – it gives me the willies.'

"Summary of text messages between Broker and Dustman re threat to no5 starting with the earliest message in the thread.

Broker: I need to give no5 a scare and pull him into line before he talks. He's a risk.

Dustman: Threaten his wife or his kids?

Broker: Violence is the last resort.

One day later - Dustman: Deliver something to his wife? Scare them both. Promise more if he won't obey?

Broker: I want a parcel delivered to him in a public space in Parliament. Something threatening that he can't explain away, make him worry about his career. I want him trembling, when he wonders what we will do next.

Dustman: OK

Four days later - Broker: Update on no5 pls.

Dustman: Slow progress. Two ways to avoid security and get something to him in Parliament. Checking which is best.

Two days later - Broker: Update on no5?

Dustman: Working on it.

Next day - Dustman: Two options. One effective & embarrassing, very public. Shall we talk?

Broker: No.

Dustman: 1– bypass delivery screening, bribe messenger to take parcel in and put in internal delivery system, will be delivered to Ministerial office and opened by his secretary. 2 – get it into the debating chamber but this needs someone to pose as secretary w ID card or find genuine secretary to bribe.

Broker: Option 2. Find someone from outside to act the part. Offer max 3k in cash.

Dustman: I'll start on it now.

Broker: OK. Get it sorted, you have one week.

Final messages in this thread sent to Dustman after the Te Papa incident when Dustman's Broker-phone had drowned:

Broker: Can't get you on your other phone.

Broker: Where are you? Pls reply.

Broker: Where the hell are you? I want action re delivery to no5. This must happen soon or he might talk.

NB: We presume that Broker tried to send messages to Dustman's 'Broker phone' which had drowned and when he got no response, he used the existing thread of messages on this topic but directed the last three to Dustman's other phone which we have. The whole thread does not show in the downloaded text messages, only on the phone itself."

29

First thing the next morning Minnie walks through every room in the house checking doors and windows, telling herself that she is being ridiculous, but unable to start her day until it's done. Over breakfast, messages from Rumble and Luke arrive and she replies to both saying she will be at the flat about five. Despite feeling apprehensive nearly constantly now, she cannot opt out now; this is the most important thing she has ever been involved in.

On her way to the staff room at the lunch break, she catches up with Jane in the large quad, where Jane makes a quick detour to tell a Year 9 student to stop kicking holes in the grass and returns to Minnie's side. 'Sorry, what were you saying?'

'I was just asking how Jordan likes the new job.'

Jane is lukewarm. 'I think it'll turn out to be a good move in one way. You know, more responsibility and better pay. Mind you, he still sorts a lot of mail, and he seems to get around a lot – delivers things all over the place. But at least he won't be out in the rain delivering mail in the winter, which is a good thing, I suppose.'

'You don't sound totally enthusiastic?'

Jane pushes the door to the administration block open and says over her shoulder, 'God, no - I'm not. I'd rather he had a totally boring job and got fed up and went back to university. Now the risk is that he'll think this new job is fine, not too boring, a bit more money and so on. And then he'll never get going again. What if we have a baby? He couldn't go back to his studies then. And he still earns peanuts, really.'

'He could be the home-dad and bring up the baby and do all the housework and save you heaps on crèche fees. And cook!'

'Sure, that *would* be great. I hadn't thought of that angle. I'll start priming him now, so he thinks it's his idea later on.'

At five that evening the apartment is stifling hot and Minnie opens the balcony door and a couple of windows and spots Rumble walking towards the main entrance, but before he arrives, Luke comes in. He puts two supermarket bags on the kitchen bench and drops his laptop case on a chair.

'I bought some more supplies. We've been spending so much time here - we must have eaten just about everything.'

Rumble comes in as they are putting things away in the little fridge. 'Aha – fruit. Minnie's been shopping.'

'No, Luke's been shopping. Buying healthy food isn't extreme, Rumble – it's normal.' And then she surveys the shopping and laughs. 'Well, mostly healthy – if you don't count potato chips, chocolate biscuits and beer.'

Rumble starts his usual wrestling match with his backpack to get the laptop out and Luke laughs and shakes his head. 'Try not to look,' he says to Minnie. 'I find I can pretend it's not happening if I don't actually watch him doing it.'

Rumble ignores the comment. 'Can't wait to see what you found. What a surprise and just what we needed by the sound of it. Broker must have forwarded the whole string from his phone instead of just sending a new message – not that I knew you could do that, but I've never looked into it – phones aren't really my thing. And I was getting bloody frustrated thinking of Dustman having a separate phone for Broker and how we'd never find out anything that goes on between those two.'

Minnie finds the file, opens it and swings her laptop around for Rumble to read. 'Here it is, not much but it sounds interesting. At least we know something really scary is about to happen to that no5 guy.'

'I can't see any more messages from Broker on Dustman's phone,' says Luke. 'And to go off-topic for a moment, Minli - I think it would be a good idea to leave some lights on when you go out in the evening, so it looks like someone's there, even when your car isn't outside.'

'But I have the alarm on, and I turn the lights on as soon as I get in.'

His dark eyes are serious. 'I know you do, but you walk into a dark house, like I saw you do last night and the night before. I just think it would be a good idea.'

Their eyes meet and she is about to tell him to mind his own business, when it strikes her how ungrateful she is. He spends a lot of time making sure she is safe, and he has rescued her once already, so she smiles and says, 'You're right - of course it would be much safer.'

He has noticed her hesitation and shoots her an amused look before he changes the subject. 'So, what are we going to do about this threat to number five - or maybe it isn't a number, maybe he's called no5 for some other reason? We could warn security at Parliament about it, but we have nothing concrete to tell them. What do you think?'

Rumble reads the thread of messages again before he replies.

'No, let them do it, whatever the hell it is - they're not planning to kill the guy. They just want to ruffle his feathers a bit and make him do what Broker wants him to do. I'd love to know how they hope to get something into Parliament via one of these messengers. You're used to the place, Luke - do you know how it works?'

Luke shakes his head and Minnie watches the pen spinning rapidly between his fingers, fascinated by the speed, and wonders if she will have time to duck, if it comes spinning across the table like a projectile.

'No, I only know what applies to members of the press gallery, no idea how they process deliveries and mail.'

'Jordan will know,' says Minnie.

She has recovered her poise after backing down on the home security issue and looks across at Luke as if the little incident never happened.

'He's just had a couple of weeks in a new job as a messenger in Parliament and he's like a sponge - Jane says he absorbs information by osmosis.'

Rumble stares at her. 'Who the hell is Jordan? Jane's brother or husband or something?'

'Husband or partner – I'm not sure if they're married. He's very bright and utterly unambitious. He dropped out of university years ago, worked as a mailman when I first got to know them. I asked Jane today what he actually does at Parliament and she said he delivers things and runs errands – it sounds as if he would know how things work.'

'There you go - it's who you know and not what you know that matters. How do we find out more?'

Luke gets up and fills the electric kettle. 'I don't suppose we can call him and start asking questions. Minli, could you go for a visit and get into a conversation about his new job or something?'

'Not something we'll find on the Internet,' says Rumble. 'They wouldn't put stuff like that out in the public domain.'

'How would it be if I say we're going to a Chinese restaurant Luke has recommended – and ask Jane and Jordan to join us? And then we get Jordan to chat about his new job. He loves telling people things.'

She takes the mug of tea Luke holds out. 'Thank you. We just need to nominate one of us to keep Jane busy.'

'I'm obviously missing the sub-text here,' says Luke and glances at Rumble, who shakes his head.

Minnie grins. 'Sorry, I forget you two don't know them. Any question directed at Jordan is likely to be intercepted by Jane – she'll answer for him and he'll just sit there with a smile on his face. He's so used to it he thinks it's normal.'

'Aha,' says Luke without commenting.

'Jane has heard me mention Rumble a few times - she's dying to meet you, so she can find out about your exotic job.' She grins at his disgusted expression.

'You're kidding, right?'

'No, it's true. She's asked a couple of times if she's ever going to meet you, so it's perfect. The fact that you look a bit like Hagrid from the Harry Potter movies will make you even more appealing. I'm sure she's never met anyone like you before.'

Rumble is unsure if he should be flattered or offended and says nothing. Minnie smiles affectionately at him and waits.

'OK then, I'm in – haven't had Chinese food for a long time. Luke, you'll have to pick a good one.'

'They won't come if there's a late sitting at Parliament,' Minnie says, 'because then Jordan works really late. Why don't we suggest tomorrow? They might be free even at this short notice.'

She sends a message to Jane, and they continue reading Dustman's messages. Within half an hour there is an enthusiastic response from Jane and Minnie holds her phone up. 'Was I right or was I right? She's very keen to meet you Luke and can't wait to have a chat with Rumble. Where are we going Luke? I'll tell her now.'

'Let's go to Wang's Wall, tell her it's a couple of blocks past the hospital. Best Chinese food in town after my mother's. I don't think it's likely they know it. I'll book for seven.'

'Oh, I forgot to tell you,' says Minnie suddenly. 'You know how I was going to list key people's addresses to you could try to hack into their computers? Well, you won't be able to – I can't find anybody's address, not anybody who matters, anyway. They seem to keep things confidential. Some state servants, yes, but not the top ones and not a single minister.'

30

The restaurant is tiny, with overly bright lights and uncomfortable chairs, and until Jane and Jordan arrive, Minnie and Rumble are the only guests who aren't Chinese. Jane homes in on Rumble like a heat-seeking missile, after a quick up and down appraisal of Luke.

'I've been dying to meet you, Rumble. I'll sit beside you so you can tell me about your amazing job – Minnie never tells me any details, but it sounds like something out of a spy movie.'

Minnie shakes her head and says to nobody in particular, 'Please note that I never said anything of the kind. That's the trouble with English teachers – they read too much fiction.'

Five minutes later Luke and Jordan are exchanging change-of-job stories. Jordan is delighted to find that Luke knows all about Parliament and before long he is in full flight and Luke only needs to fit in the odd comment here and there to keep the flow going.

'What's the plan, Jordan?' asks Minnie. 'Is there another step after this? Can you be promoted to another level?'

'I'd really like to be a C&G Officer, instead of delivering stuff all over these huge buildings – miles of corridors. The C&G guys are the messengers who act as ushers in the Debating Chamber and they kind of guard the public gallery. The others say it's a boring job, but it looks great to me – you stand around outside the door to the Chamber in case someone comes along and wants something delivered to someone inside.'

Minnie makes a face. 'God, that sounds incredibly boring - just standing around doing nothing.'

Jordan leaps on the opportunity to explain. 'Yeah, but I think these guys get to deliver quite a lot of stuff, like a Minister's reading glasses that he left in his office or some message. The secretary goes to the door of the Chamber and gives whatever it is to the usher standing outside and only he can open the door and give it to the guy standing inside. Nobody else can go in, no other staff. That's why there are two at all times, so that door is never unattended.'

'But won't it take forever to learn to recognize all the secretaries? There must be dozens.'

Minnie knows they are on the right track now. So long as they keep the questions minimal, and Jordan doesn't feel interrogated, the facts will gradually emerge.

'Well, you can't know them all, of course– there must hordes of them. But they all wear ID cards with a photo and over time I'll learn most of them.'

'I can imagine the volumes of mail coming in,' says Luke. 'What happens if someone mails something nasty – who would find it?'

Brilliant, thinks Minnie, such an innocent observation. I'm really enjoying this – it's a match made in heaven; a man who is used to getting information out of people and a man who loves telling people things.

'The mail system seems pretty robust from what I've seen so far,' says Jordan. 'Mail and deliveries go to the secure delivery room and get x-rayed and whatever they do, and then the stuff comes to the mail distribution room - which is where I work. We sort it into pigeon-holes – there's a whole wall of them. And then we deliver it to all the offices from there. But you know what ...'

He pauses; thoughtful now, and Luke and Minnie wait silently.

'If I wanted to bypass the system – shit, I've just realised, it could be done. Provided it's reasonably flat or not too big I could bring a packet in through the staff entrance, inside my jacket say. I'm not going to be x-rayed or anything like that - all I have to do is swipe my card. And then, while we're all walking up and down along that wall of pigeonholes with our arms full of items from the trolleys, I'll just slip the illegal packet into the right slot. Nobody would notice. It's very busy, people moving around, back and forth.'

Luke steers the conversation to internet scams and other forms of fraud and no more is said about Jordan's job. It's late when they leave the restaurant, and the street is quiet.

As Minnie loops around the Basin reserve to drop the men off at their respective flats, she realises something. 'This is the first time we've been seen in public together. After all this time of meeting and sharing information and working together. Amazing!'

'And we won't do it again – let's go back to our usual cozy state of paranoia,' says Rumble. 'So now we know the plan for no5 is realistic – do we agree that we won't warn anyone that parliamentary security is about to be breached?'

Luke's voice from the backseat is full of conviction. 'Christ, no! We've got to let it happen. And how would we go about warning them anyway? We'd have to hand over all our evidence to convince them - and then explain how we got it. We can't even tell them who the prospective victim is. It's too flimsy.'

'And don't forget,' says Minnie, 'if they beef up security at parliament, Broker will just do it some other way. He just wants to give that guy a fright and pull him into line. They're not going to blow him up or anything. Let it go ahead - one more piece of evidence for the files.'

She drops them off and makes a detour around Oriental Bay before heading home. Her head is full of speculations about how Broker's threat will be carried out and when.

It is a surreal situation, she thinks. What we do next could dramatically change things for people who don't even know we exist. It could ruin lives, break up marriages, wipe careers off the board. We're working behind the scenes, invisible and insignificant, towards a conclusion that we can't even guess at ourselves. A lot of people with influence are going to be furious, hell-bent on revenge. And if we're discovered before we make things public our lives will be wrecked.

The phone in the kitchen is ringing when she unlocks the front door and she runs for it, hoping nothing has happened to Brendan, but it's Luke.

'Just checking that you got home safely - I called you a couple of times, but you were off-line. Is everything OK?'

She fishes the cell phone out of her bag and walks back to the open front door.

'Hang on, I'll just check, maybe the sound is off. I went for a little drive along Oriental Parade and the bays - I've only just walked in the door.'

It is a clear night, and the stars seem very close. She sits down on the top step with the front door open behind her.

'The battery's flat. But thank you, everything is fine – I'm sitting on the front step enjoying the view and the stars, lovely.'

'That sounds nice. And it went well tonight – Jordan is a great source of information, isn't he?'

Minnie laughs. 'Yeah, he kind of interviews himself. Press the button and out it comes. But what I really want to know is who Dustman is – he's our best link to Broker and the whole setup. But all I know is what he looks like.'

'Do you think you'd recognize him again? I never got a good look at his face.'

'I know, but don't forget that I had already seen him in the school parking lot before he grabbed me at Te Papa. I tried to not look directly at him, and Jane wasn't turning her head either, so he probably doesn't realise we noticed him. But I'd know him again for sure. If we got more on Dustman, we could get Broker too.'

'Let's hope you never see him again.'

They say goodnight, and she goes inside, locks the door and goes straight upstairs. When she pulls the curtains in her bedroom, she hears a car start up further down the street. Once again fear runs a cold finger down her spine.

31

Minnie is back at the roll-top desk on Sunday morning, going through the last drawer; an occasional treasure, but a lot of old receipts and invoices from twenty years ago. When the phone rings it is a welcome break.

'Sharon, hi! How are you?'

'I'm fine. I wondered if you have seen Brendan yet. How is he?'

'I'm going this afternoon. I'll call you when I get back.'

She has just settled down again when Mr. Yeoman from across the street knocks on the door.

'I don't know if I'm being silly, Minnie.' He looks embarrassed and shifts his weight from one foot to the other. 'But I think you should know, just in case. You never know these days. I thought I'd better tell you.'

Minnie smiles encouragement, she knows she must be patient and wait for him to reach the point. He has never been one to rush headlong into a conversation or even get to the point in less than three minutes.

'I think it was Friday, or maybe it was Thursday – no it was Friday, I remember now. A bloke turned up while you were at school. I saw him trying the tall gate to your back garden, but I knew you keep that locked, and then he walked around the other corner of the house - where you keep the rubbish bin.'

He stops again and thinks for a long moment while Minnie tries to look patient and her nerves twang like guywires in a high wind.

'Yes, that's what he did. So, I went across the street and I said, "are you looking for someone", and he said a friend of his used to live here, but she might have moved away.'

He stops and looks expectantly at her, and she asks, 'Did he mention my name?'

'Oh no, he just said a friend. But I asked what the name was, and he said it didn't matter and he'd come back another time - and then he left. A chubby bloke, not very tall – young. Had those jeans with rips in them, like a tramp.'

'Did you see his car?'

'He didn't come by car, he walked.'

'Well, no harm done - and thanks for looking out for me. I don't know who it could have been, but if it's important I'm sure he'll come back.'

The old man leaves, and she remains standing just inside the front door, trying to figure out what this might mean. Not Dustman, she thinks, he's way above average height and nobody would describe him as chubby. Someone doing an errand for him? But would he invite an outsider into Broker's shadowy world? Perhaps it really was someone who had the wrong address. And I must tell the guys, just in case.

By midday she is finished and eats her lunch on the deck, which seems more enjoyable than anything she has done at home for some time. The summer is coming to an end and the light is less intense, the heat of this extraordinary summer has mellowed. The shadow of the big elm falls much further across the deck than it did on that day a few weeks ago, when Rumble came to see what she had found on the stranger's phone.

I worried about the messages from the start, I knew it was bad, but I never thought it would change my whole world view. I used to take for granted that you should always report crime to the authorities. Now I fear that going to the police might not be safe – and that those in power, the very people elected to safeguard a just society, might be corrupt and a threat to law-abiding citizens. And I worry about the security services being at Broker's bidding, that thought never leaves me now, it scares me more than anything else. Would I have continued with this, if I had realised how dangerous it would turn out to be? Rumble did warn me at the outset, but I didn't quite believe it.

It is deeply unsettling that her guidelines for right and wrong are shifting in unexpected ways, that she now doubts the integrity of the authorities and feels justified to illegally obtain emails and video recordings. Despite the draconian changes to the legal system over the last few years and the eroded right to personal privacy, she has somehow retained her belief in overall justice, if things were to go wrong. But now her caution, not only in regard to Broker, but also in regard to the authorities, seeps into the most mundane activities and the shadow of threat hovers just beyond conscious thought every waking moment.

I think of myself as quiet and not very brave. Luke thinks I am cool because I kept my head when Dustman grabbed me. But that wasn't courage, I just used my brain. I was very frightened - that gun barrel pressed against me made my skin crawl. I wish I was brave and didn't fear anything or anyone. I wonder if Luke is ever frightened.

She is lost in thought when she hears her phone buzz inside. Reluctantly she gets up and takes her plate and glass inside. A message from Rumble: 'Tonight at 6?'

She replies 'yes' and goes to pack up the papers and photos she is keeping. She has found the registrations papers for Brendan's car in the same envelope as a fourteen-year-old quote for roof repairs, and insurance policies for the house and the car. She has also found an unopened letter from a life insurance company advising that the pay-out value has gone up by three percent and reminding Brendan that the premium is paid by direct debit from his bank account. The letter is dated September the previous year. I never knew about this, she thinks as she carries another box to the hall, why does he still have life insurance? What a waste, not as if it's needed.

She takes the recycling boxes to the garage and leaves the two she is keeping beside the hall table, until she decides if they should go upstairs or into the spare room wardrobe.

When she gets to the rest-home Brendan's room is empty and she finds him in the lounge. He comes across the room to greet her, relaxed and pleased to see her and shows her to a bay off a wide hallway with armchairs arranged around a small aquarium.

'I like this,' he says. 'I sit here a lot.'

He isn't really interested in talking. His gaze is fixed on the bright orange fishes and he smiles contentedly but says very little. After a while she stops talking, studies him and thinks that he has changed again, he's slower, much more passive and less agitated. But perhaps that is a good thing, so long as he is happy.

When she leaves, she is simultaneously relieved to be going and feeling guilty. She misses the father he was and seeing him in his new environment makes her realise that she has truly lost him. He will retreat further and further into some unknown country of the mind that she can't even imagine.

Driving home she remembers the concealed drawer in Brendan's desk; seeing him has triggered the memory of being allowed to open the little hidden drawer when she was a child. She tries it as soon as she is inside the house, opens the little door between the small drawers at the back of the writing surface, feels the end of the lever under her fingertips and presses. The hidden drawer springs open with a sharp click. Here is her mother's wedding ring, Sander's swimming badge and his last term report neatly folded into a square just big enough to fit into the little drawer, and a snipped-off lock of black hair folded in paper. Her mother's or Sander's? And stuck in the bottom of the drawer, a copy of Sander's death certificate, also folded small and a photo, upside down with a date in pencil on the back. She has never seen it before. In it her parents stand side by side, and Sander and Minnie sit on the grass in front of them, dressed up and smiling. She turns the photo over and looks at the date; two weeks before the accident in the little garden shed. The cataclysmic day when Sander's new rocket-plane came crashing inside trailing a comet tail of sparks, knocking over the bottle of fuel he had left open and creating an inferno between her and door. Even now she can relive the feeling of agony and mindless panic as she ran towards the door with her dress on fire.

32

When Minnie arrives at the flat, the men are standing just outside the open balcony door with their backs to her and bottles of beer in their hands, deep in a heated argument.

'Oh, for fuck's sake Rumble, of course it won't work.' Luke sounds as if he has already said this several times, he is exasperated. 'We either give them everything at once or we live in hiding for a long time. You can't have it both ways, it's too bloody dangerous. Giving them the lot is the only way we can stay safe.'

Rumble's voice is louder than usual, dismissive and impatient. 'Fuck that - we'd be throwing away an opportunity we'll never have again. If we portion it out strategically, we can trick them into betraying themselves – think of being able to ID Broker or Dustman! We still have no clue who those bastards are.'

Neither has heard her come in. so she stands quietly with her hand on the door waiting for them to notice her.

'No, definitely not! Dustman knows what she looks like and if he finds out she's involved nobody can keep her safe, nobody. He could find out any minute now, and you'll never stop blaming yourself, if something happens to her.'

Minnie closes the door with a little bang and walks towards them with a smile, hoping to give the impression that she has just that moment come in. 'Hi guys, want an ice cream?'

She opens the insulated bag and hands them an ice cream each, notes their cautious faces, knows that they wonder what she heard.

'What are you discussing?' She peels the wrapper off her ice cream and folds it, looking at Rumble for an answer.

'Ah well, you know – just debating a point,' he says evasively and turns to Luke. 'Why don't we sit down and discuss it with Minnie now she's here.'

Luke's face is expressionless, but she knows how angry he is under the surface. She must defuse the tension that still vibrates between them, or they might not be able to continue working together.

'Let me ask you something first,' she says and sits down in her usual chair. She bites the tip off her ice cream and points it at the men. 'Are we recording the TV broadcast from parliament each day? What I mean is, I hope one of you is recording it. We never sorted out who would do it.'

'I'm doing it, but you can go back and find it online too,' says Rumble and Luke breaks in, wanting to get to the real agenda. 'Rumble and I have different ideas about how to proceed. What we should do with all the evidence, how to present it – and to whom.'

He stops and bites a piece off his ice cream. 'One idea is to give it out in portions, to all the media and to do it in such a way that Broker is provoked to reveal himself – to bait him. The other idea is to release everything to everyone at the same time, so the whole world knows the same stuff that we do, and there's no point in harassing us for more details.'

He stops suddenly, black eyes searching her face. 'Was that a little smile I saw just then? And if it was, what did it mean?'

Rumble looks from one to the other, bemused. 'Why would she smile? Did you smile?'

Minnie reflects that licking an ice cream and keeping up the feeling of resentment from an argument is hard to do; they both look more relaxed.

'I think it was a fleeting look of satisfaction – because this is exactly what I've been debating with myself for a while.'

She pauses to lick the side of the ice cream that is threatening to drip on her hand. Rumble keeps his eyes on her face, and she knows that she is about to cast the deciding vote.

I must present my case carefully. These two are so different, at times they come from opposite ends of the spectrum. I expected serious fireworks over something before now, there must be no outright winner here.

They are both watching her now, waiting, and she quickly eats the last bit of the ice cream before it drops off the stick, tilting her head back to stop it dribbling down her chin.

'I think there are only two things that matter. Broker must be stopped, and we must be safe. We don't know which authority we can safely approach. We can't risk giving it to some branch of the authorities where a top guy suppresses it - or worse, comes after us in some way, or alerts Broker to deal with us. And if we hand it over anonymously and it gets suppressed, then we can't follow up and we might still be at risk.'

She stops to see if either of them will comment, but they say nothing. 'Baiting Broker sounds like a recipe for potential disaster to me. The only thing that satisfies both my points is to make it public - every single piece of evidence, at the same time and to everyone. To media, government departments, the Prime Minister, police, intelligence services and so on.'

Rumble and Luke exchange a glance, but neither comments, so Minnie continues, 'We started talking about this once before, but we never finished the conversation. Maybe we could release the evidence in some permanent form, like on a USB stick or something, with everything indexed, in sections. The CCTV clips and the text messages and that database – the lot. And a description of how everything happened, finding the phone, Dustman grabbing me – everything.'

She licks both sides of the ice cream stick and catches the look on Luke's face. Well, let him be amused, she thinks, I always do it, I love that last taste of the melted ice cream on the wooden stick.

Rumble looks thoughtfully at her. 'And have you thought of how we might do that?'

'Luke will know, I'm sure – more his department than mine. Maybe we send out an invitation to a press conference at some big venue? And then front up and tell them how we got involved and hand out the USB sticks when they leave.'

She holds out her hand for their wrappers and sticks and gets up to put them in the sink.

'But a press conference at a big venue?' Rumble looks doubtful. 'Why not just a press release, send it out with the flash drive? Is there any need for personal appearances?'

'Of course, there is! We want maximum noise, right?' Minnie looks at Rumble as if she can't believe he is questioning this. 'We want the biggest event ever staged by non-politicians or the queen, as big as we can possibly make it. And the way to do that is to say that only the press who turn up at the venue will get the USB stick or flash drive or whatever the thing is called. Make sure they turn up and create an event that nobody can ignore!'

Luke nods and Rumble looks from one to the other. 'You really mean it? Like us three on a stage or whatever - telling our story?'

'Yes! Where else could we make a strong statement about it and get reported in all forms of media – that we know nothing more, it's all on the flash drive. That's how we stay safe. Killing us would be pointless.' Unless someone kills us for revenge, she thinks, but there's no protection against that, but that thought gives her another idea.

'And we have security guards and CCTV cameras very visible inside and outside the venue – spell it out that this is dangerous for us and important. Max impact on all fronts we can possibly thing of.'

The men look at each other for a moment and she knows a truce had been invisibly signed off. I wonder what else they have argued about, she thinks, they are both so self-contained – I would never have known about this, if I hadn't walked in on them.

Luke speaks first. 'I think you're right – you've covered the main points and I agree. Some kind of unprecedented media conference would do the trick – ramp it up and get far more attention than a press release emailed out. The more media hype about this right from the start, the harder it will be for anyone to try to defuse the issue. The details can be decided later. And some things should be marked as non-negotiable – publicly and at the outset.'

Rumble nods, only a trace of reluctance in his voice. 'OK – let's run with that. And non-negotiable? Do you mean we should dictate terms - like having witnesses at all interviews for example?'

'That kind of thing, yes. We could have a list of things like 'we will never be interviewed singly' and 'every interview or conversation with anyone in authority will be video recorded by our own equipment as well as theirs' or 'our lawyers will sit in on all interviews'. And it could be very effective to have a couple of things worked out with selected media ahead of time, like a teaser, to ramp up the interest.'

Minnie smiles. 'Well, you're the media expert and I'm sure you already know who would be most effective. Cartwell perhaps and some Radio NZ or TV current affairs show? And social media of course – unless they shut us down. Maybe we should have responses rehearsed in advanced, so we all respond the same way to any questions.'

'Right,' says Rumble, 'that's important. If we say different things, people might doubt our evidence. We must be on the same page all the time.'

As they continue tracking topics through the messages from Dustman's phone, his role becomes more clearly defined. Minnie is reading something on her screen and raises her head to look at Luke. 'What did you say a minute ago? I was concentrating and didn't listen. Someone was told to back off?'

'Yes, I think Dustman overstepped the line in his dealings with Digger. I suspect there was an interchange between him and Broker on his other phone, because his next text to Digger retracts something he said earlier, very carefully phrased – November last year.'

Rumble consults his own notes. 'Yeah, and a similar thing earlier when he was organizing something, not with a known industry contact, someone with a nameless phone number or maybe a brand-new contact. But just the same – he said something quite definitive to this guy and then he back-tracks a couple of days later. I think you're right - Broker pulls the reins tighter when Dustman makes independent decisions.'

Minnie points her pen at him. 'And isn't it interesting that he, Broker I mean, said 'no meeting' or 'no talking' or whatever it was in that thread of messages we found. So, we might be right about Broker working in a silo – solo in a silo, haha – and Dustman is his assistant, but even they never talk. Perhaps Dustman has no idea who Broker is, never met him face to face - complete separation?'

Luke grins. 'Imagine how they feel, those poor bastards who have given in to corruption or blackmail - when they move in the political circles in town or meet top businesspeople. They must look around them and wonder who Broker is. I'd be neurotic in five minutes.'

'Is there anything to be gained from texting or calling Broker?' asks Minnie. 'If we call and he answers, we'd at least know if it's a man or a woman – we might even recognize the voice.'

'I'm sure Broker is too risk averse to answer if an unknown number calls him. What do you think about texting him, Rumble?'

Rumble shakes his head and smiles regretfully. 'Christ no! It would alert him - he'd know for sure that someone had found one of the two lost phones and managed to unlock it. And so far, he doesn't know that. The disadvantage with using only messages is that they can be accessed by the authorities – but that's a risk he has to take.'

'And his phones are anonymous anyway, how would they prove who the phone belongs to?' says Luke. 'Sometimes I wonder if I met him or interviewed him when I was in the press gallery - I might know him. If I could talk to him just once, I might be able to identify him.'

'It might be you,' says Minnie, dispassionately studying him across the table. 'Maybe you're a master of double-dealing and you're cleverly playing both sides of the table.'

She shifts her gaze to Rumble and adds, 'You and I will discuss this later, in private.'

Rumble starts to say something and stops.

'Yes?' asks Minnie. 'You had an idea?'

'Bloody hell - for a split second I thought you were serious. You're very wicked, in your own quiet way, you know. We must finish reading this stuff so we can start on the next stage – whatever that is. The only thing I know for sure is we can't trust anyone, not anyone at all.'

33

The process of converting initials and acronyms into capital letters in all the messages is a slow and tedious process and tests their patience. After a short debate they decide to enter all last year's messages from Dustman's phone into the exhaustive database that Minnie started with the first phone. It was abandoned, but the value of being able to sort messages in groups, depending on key words has become apparent, so now Minnie will resume the work.

'But when it comes to releasing material to the media, we'll have to put both the edited messages and the originals on the flash drive,' says Minnie. 'And the database too. Not that this proves anything, but it will look good – proves we haven't deviously changed anything to fit our agenda - and it shows that we've been thorough.'

By the time they finish for the evening they are tired and bored, and in no mood to talk. They follow their usual routine of leaving the flat a few minutes apart. Minnie goes out through the main entrance into a cool evening with clouds scudding across the sky; suddenly it feels as if autumn is just around the corner. She drives home with her mind in neutral and no thought of Luke, until she notices a dark car parked outside the next-door house but one; there is someone in the driver's seat. Looking out from the kitchen without turning the light on she sees the car disappearing around the corner. Was it the same as Luke's or just similar?

She hesitates for a moment before texting Luke. The wording is a stumbling block; she wants to find out, but she is reluctant to make him feel that he is responsible for her. She puts a high value on her independence and prefers to not rely on others, but she needs to know. In the end she puts it as a question: 'Saw a dark car outside my house with someone in it, no lights. Didn't look quite like your car?'

His reply comes a few minutes later; he must have stopped on his way down the hill. 'I went around block the other way, parked at the far corner. Saw you go inside. What sort of car? What did it do?'

'Very like yours, don't know what make, drove off straight away.'

He replies, 'Must have passed me, I paid no attention, was watching your house, do you want me to come back?'

She thanks him and says she is fine, checks the locks and goes to bed.

The message she has waited for is on her phone when she returns to the staff room the following day after her last class. 'Listen to the news, will be in the flat at 5 with recording.'

She sits in the car a block away from the apartment and listens to the news before she goes in.

'In an extraordinary event in parliament today, a parcel with a pistol was delivered to the Minister for Primary and Rural Industries, John Heskett-White, who then appeared to suffer a stroke or a heart attack and collapsed. The Parliamentary TV broadcast went off air immediately and security staff evacuated the public gallery and the press gallery. We have been unable to get a comment from the Prime Minister or from the Leader of the Opposition, who were both in the House at the time. Both have said that no comments will be made until the matter is investigated further.'

They crowd around Rumble's laptop. 'This isn't available any longer on the Parliamentary website, by the way, they took it down, so it's good we started recording this. I'll start here - about two minutes before the parcel is delivered.'

First a long shot of the Speaker of the House, followed by a close-up of an opposition MP while he comments on a recent issue. The camera moves to the Minister who is about to reply and Rumble says, 'Watch the right-hand side.'

An usher appears from behind the Speaker's chair; he walks

down the central floor area along the front benches with something in the hand furthest from the camera. Heskett-White can be seen on the edge of the shot, seated next to the Minister who is speaking. The usher bends down and says something quietly to Heskett-White, hands him a flat parcel and leaves. The parcel is out of sight behind the desk in front of Heskett-White's seat, but it is obvious that he is opening it. His face turns scarlet, then white. He gets abruptly to his feet, and something falls to the floor. He looks down, his face a mask of fear, and collapses into the aisle. A handgun is clearly visible under his leg. Chaos erupts and those near him stare in shock, a backbencher runs down and kneels beside him. The camera pulls back and shows people on both sides of the House standing up and then the screen goes black. After a short delay, a voice announces that due to an incident in the House the day's transmission from parliament has been terminated.

'Can we see it again, slower, so we can see the details? He might have died, he looked awful,' says Minnie, and Rumble reverses the recording to the point where the messenger appears and plays it in slow motion. They watch intently.

'Stop!' says Minnie. 'Back up a bit – there's something there, just as he starts to collapse.'

'Aha, look at that,' says Luke when Rumble pauses again. 'It's a piece of paper.'

As the Minister buckles at the knees, the gun falls, either out of his hand or out of the packet, and he collapses. A piece of paper floats gently to the left and lands out of view.

'OK, let's carry on slowly – we might see it again.'

They lean forward watching each frame until the recording ends, and Rumble straightens up. 'That guy who rushed down, was he reaching for it - just when they killed the camera?'

They watch it again, but it's impossible to tell if he is reaching for the paper or just putting out a hand to steady himself as he kneels beside Heskett-White.

Luke looks thoughtful. 'Very, very clever – they have given him a warning in a forum where it gets max exposure, and at the same time they've demonstrated that Parliament isn't secure. And possibly they have accidentally killed one of the geese that lay the golden eggs.'

Rumble smiles grimly. 'Right – and now they can use this as a warning, when some other poor bastard decides not to play ball.'

Minnie swivels in her chair to look at Luke. 'Do you know who that was - the guy who might have picked up the paper?'

'Jonathan something, starts with a B – it's his first term, he's a list MP. I don't know him, but I'll go and find some of my press gallery mates to see what I can find out. If he read it, they might have got it out of him – he won't be as savvy about resisting questions as the old hands.'

He gets up and reaches for his phone. 'I don't know how long this will take. I'll text you as soon as I know something, and if you're still here I'll come back.'

'I've got to go and do some work,' says Rumble. 'I have a report to write, due on Monday. Come on, Minli – go home and have an evening off.'

Driving up Salamanca Road she remembers that she never told Rumble or Luke about the man Mr. Yeoman saw in her garden. Must do that when I next see them, she thinks, not that anything else has happened, and I do set the alarm when I go out, but I should tell them.

She is preparing dinner and still thinking of the incident in Parliament and what it might lead to when the phone beeps with a message from Luke: 'The note said, "are you prepared to commit political suicide?" Printed, plain paper. They have all been told not to talk.'

Wow, she thinks, how simple and effective. A gun and a note, a threat and a demonstration of power – very neat. For someone not used to weapons, a handgun would be a shocking thing to find in a parcel, with or without that note.

The late TV news is full of the incident with more speculation than substance. That there was a gun is stated as a fact. The recorded broadcast had been removed from the website, but the rumor that a note has been found is mentioned more than once. There is a quote from an unnamed source, that a dark-haired woman with glasses was seen handing the parcel to a messenger outside the debating chamber. A press statement from the office of the Prime Minister says that Minister Heskett-White is in a serious condition after a heart attack, his family is at his bedside, and at the request of his wife there will be no further announcements.

Minnie checks her schedule for the following day which is a teachers' in-service training day. The wind has come up and it is raining, and it seems like the perfect evening to go to bed and read. She is about to turn the downstairs lights off when there is a knock on the door and through the mottled glass in the hall window, she sees a tall figure making a thumbs-up sign. It's Luke, she thinks, takes a step sideways and unlocks the door. The door is shoved open, and she stumbles backwards against the hall table which wobbles, things fall to the floor and Dustman is inside with a gun aimed at the middle of her chest before she has time to scream.

34

Friday

Minnie opens her eyes to darkness and confusion, aching and shivering. Her searching hands touch damp soil and crumbling leaves, a patch of moss. She is lying on a steep slope with her hip up against something hard. Her fingers recognize the distinctive texture of a mature cabbage tree trunk. No lights and no sounds apart from unseen branches moving in the wind. She closes her eyes. What happened? There must have been an accident; her mind refuses to cooperate, her memory yields nothing.

I went to see Dad, drove home, no wait, I was in Rumble's flat - and then what? What's happened to Luke and Rumble?

Her thoughts are disorganized and the harder she tries to remember, the less focus she has. She keeps her right hand on the cabbage tree trunk and drifts into sleep, half-waking now and then, reassured by the tree trunk holding her in place.

Chilled to the marrow of her bones, she wakes up to the sound of birds. The cold, grey light of early dawn seeps through the branches, surroundings gradually come into focus. She raises her shoulders, looks around and lies back nauseated. Her tree is an arm's length from a dizzying drop, a bush-clad ravine far below. Above and around her shrubs and trees lean up and in, clinging to the slope. The abyss beside her brings her to the brink of panic and she tries to force herself to calm down, to move away, but she is dizzy and in pain and stays where she is.

Gradually brighter light filters through, colours and details come to life. A trickle of water from higher up curves around a rock embedded in the clay and disappears under her thighs. She reaches out, touches the damp earth and licks her fingers, a musky taste of earth and decomposing vegetation. She does it again and again and feels a little better.

It must have rained; my clothes and hair are wet. And my arms and hands are covered in cuts and scratches. God, how my head hurts. I wish I could remember. I feel sick, maybe I'm concussed.

She takes stock, raises her head and looks down her body: dark grey linen trousers, white cotton shirt badly torn, no shoes, a handkerchief and a paper clip in one trouser pocket, nothing else. All limbs seem to work, but her left shoulder hurts. Bruises, scratches and cuts, a deep gouge crusted with blood and dirt on her right arm, but nothing serious. Anything she might have had with her is elsewhere, flung in a different direction or lost in some place she can't remember. The light gets stronger, but the sun won't reach her until much later in the morning; the steep slope is in total shade, but through the branches she sees the opposite side of the valley lit by morning sun. A hawk circles high above, its shape like a drawing on the pale canvas of the sky.

I'm facing west or northwest, very steep terrain, native plants only, deep ravine, no sounds. There must be a road higher up or how did I get here?

The headache is relentless, and waves of nausea wash over her when she moves; she closes her eyes.

She wakes again with a start in the middle of a dream where she is choking on water being poured into her mouth while hard fingers hold her nose closed. She is drowning, tries to raise her arms to defend herself, but her arms are tied. Her heart hammers in terror; she shuts her eyes, can't decide if it is a memory or a dream. Did someone really do that - to make me talk? Or to force me to drink something or to kill me?

Desperately she tries to break down the barrier that separates her from her memories, but it's useless. The disjointed dream might or might not be real and she struggles with the uncertainty – even terrifying and brutal reality would be better than no memory at all. Her mind whispers, 'be calm, you are strong, don't be afraid'. She drifts into uneasy sleep and wakes again, to warmth and bright light. She must move; nobody will find her here; she must get further up the slope. Carefully, she raises herself on one elbow, struggles to sit up, looks at the drop-off and feels sick. What if she is on an over-hang? Desperation swamps her; she must get away from that edge, now!

Painfully she turns over, inches around to face uphill. When she moves, she imagines that she feels the ground tremble and her mind conjures up an image of the shelf crashing down. Common sense tells her nothing has changed for decades, the cabbage tree has been there for a long time, but her mind screams 'move, quickly!' Panting she pulls herself upwards, clutching at manuka branches, using small tree trunks to anchor her feet, pushing her body up the slope. It is agonizingly slow and her bruised muscles tremble with effort and pain. Sweating and exhausted she pauses and looks back down and her heart sinks; she is only a few meters higher than the top of the cabbage tree.

She lies down to rest, head pointing uphill, one foot wedged against a small tree. The sun filters through the canopy and warms her aching back. Her mind's quiet voice whispers, 'be strong, be patient, help will come'. Gradually she makes progress, crawling and dragging herself upwards, resting between bursts of effort. Nausea comes and goes, and her head pulsates with pain, like she used to feel after a binge of heavy drinking, like a mega hangover.

She rests sitting with her heels dug in to anchor herself and sees through the trees a vast landscape of steep mountains folded into deep valleys. Native forest, no roads, and no sound apart from the birds and the wind. At the end of the afternoon, with the sun about to disappear behind the mountain on the far side of the ravine, she has made real progress. The perspective has changed; she is much higher and can see further. That diagonal crease in the forest on a distant hillside to her left; is it a road?

It must be the Remutaka mountain range, she thinks, where else would be so steep and covered in native bush? Did I drive off the road or did I get out of the car and fall down the slope? Why would I have come up here? Or did someone take me; did they throw me over the side?

Thoughts of Dustman and Broker hover in the back of her mind, but no memories surface. Soon it will be dark, she must get as far up the slope as she can. Thirst plagues her, she constantly thinks of water, but she has seen no moist ground since midday. She ignores her thirst and struggles on, cramps in her back slow her progress to a crawl.

Her feet are damaged from pushing against stones and hard ground. Using only her right hand to haul herself upwards is hard work, but the scar tissue over her left shoulder blade and down her side restricts reach and strength. The slope is not so steep here, trees and bushes are sparse, the ground dry and dusty. Sharp rocks protrude from the clay-like surface and provide footholds. Further up is a huge over-hang, a rock ledge jutting far out. She will have to go to one side to get around it, but in which direction?

She sits down and tries to steady her breathing. Dust covers her sweaty skin and its gritty texture is in her mouth and throat, thirst has become an obsession. In the near dark she studies her hands with a feeling of detachment, as if they belonged to somebody else. Blood from fresh lacerations mixed with dust, fingernails broken and filthy. The torn blouse is useless as a garment, one sleeve nearly completely ripped away, the other torn. She pulls it off and wipes her sweating forehead, hangs it like a towel around her neck, reluctant to abandon anything that could be useful. She curls up on the hard slope, a cluster of sturdy shrubs directly below, and closes her eyes. Her mind whispers 'your name is Minli, you are clever and strong, be brave'.

Saturday

She wakes at dawn, shivering, every part of her is hurting, but after the torment of the night she now feels calm. The despair she felt is gone, and her sense of balance restored, though she still struggles compulsively to remember what happened and finds nothing.

Something happened, that dream – is that it? Did someone force me to swallow some sort of drug? Must be Dustman, he must have taken me here, no reason why I would come here, but how did I get down this slope? Was I thrown down or did I run from him and fall? I'm sure it wasn't a dream – that awful feeling of drowning, how else would I know what that feels like? But I can't just have fallen from the road, I'm so far down and below lots of obstacles. And all these scrubby trees, no way, they would have stopped me. I must have gone over in the car, been thrown out, maybe to one side instead of straight down. No way of figuring out where the car would be, could be anywhere, perhaps it continued falling after I got thrown out?

Out of nowhere a fragment of memory returns; waiting for a green light at the Riddiford Street intersection after leaving the apartment, then nothing more.

What can I use? My blouse - make a flag to signal where I am.

Does anyone know I'm missing yet? What if someone comes looking and they see a pale flag in the bush? I wonder what day it is. When Rumble and Luke realise that I'm missing they won't know where to look. How long have I been here?

She tries to work it out and remembers parts of Thursday, and she should have been at the teacher training day on Friday, but she has no recall of that. If she was taken on Thursday night today would be Saturday, or was she unconscious for more than twenty-four hours? There is no way of working out a timeline, there are too many unknowns, and her mind refuses to fill the gaps. She banishes the thought that nobody might miss her until school is due back on Monday and tries to keep despair under control; she concentrates on the thought that she must find a tall tree to tie the flag to.

An hour later she comes across a runnel of water meandering down from the jutting rock shelf above. Suddenly desperate she kneels and uses a broken stick to scratch a hollow in the path of the trickle, presses her cupped hand into it and watches it fill with a spoonful of water, lifts it carefully to her mouth; it tastes of clay. She stays there, repeatedly filling her hand and drinking. The acute thirst dies down, but she continues drinking, knowing that dehydration is the real threat. She rubs her face and neck with wet hands, enjoys the coolness and feels cheered for a moment. The water eases the hunger pains and she sets out again feeling better.

By midday she despairs of further progress in the direction she has chosen. The slope is getting steeper, the overhang still blocks her from climbing upwards, and she hasn't found a suitable tree to tie a flag to. She sits down in the shade of a scrubby bush absently looking down the slope and sees the perfect tree, tall and skinny, nearly like a ladder with the upright in the centre. There is a clearing on one side, a few square meters of bare ground which makes the tree noticeable. She surveys the incline and hopes she can negotiate it safely. Moving back some distance in the direction she came from, she loses sight of the tree, but the slope is gentler here, safer. She tries to stay on an even diagonal line of descent, lowers herself gingerly, clutches at branches, feels for safe footholds with her bruised and scratched feet.

She must have missed it, gone too far along this trajectory. The thought of going back and starting again is agonizing. Dejected she leans against a tree and flexes her back and shoulders, looks down and realises the flag tree is nearly straight below her. She scrambles down; the tree is skinny, but taller than she thought.

Are those branches too thin to climb? Can I throw my flag up? I would have to weight it, and if I miss the branches, it could disappear down the slope and I'll never find it again.

She starts ripping the blouse, but tearing across seams is hard, she uses her teeth and still fails to get it into the shapes she wants. Not like in bodice-ripper novels, or when the heroine rips her petticoat into strips to bind the hero's wounds. Who would have thought it would be so tough?

She ties the strips of cloth into a long two-tongued pennant and adds the handkerchief to the end of one tongue. The blouse is grey with dirt, but the still white handkerchief will be a light exclamation mark against the dark canopy of the forest.

The thought of climbing daunts her. falling and breaking an arm or a leg is a frightening thought. She stands close to the trunk and reaches up as high as she can, grips two branches close to the trunk to minimize leverage. She bends her knees until her feet are off the ground and the branches hold her weight. She puts her feet on small branches low down, close to the trunk, transfers her weight to her legs, and nothing creaks or cracks.

Minutes later, trembling with exertion, she is three quarters up the height of the tree, when a branch suddenly cracks under her foot. For a heart-stopping moment she thinks she is falling but manages to hold on. With one foot safely on a branch, she leans her torso against the trunk and reaches around to tie the flag to a branch on the downhill side, uses both hands and ties a clumsy knot. Will it catch the breeze and attract attention? Now she wants to get down fast, but fear of falling slows her and her scars pull on the muscles across her shoulder. Back on firm ground she trembles with exhaustion and tension, but her achievement buoys her spirits. She did what she set out to do, something quite difficult, and now she must get out from under the overhang and go upwards instead of sideways.

She retraces her steps and struggles on. Dust coats her sweaty skin and cakes the fresh dribbles of blood from scratches. By mid-afternoon she reaches a dead end. The incline is too steep, the rock shelf above still blocks her, and every foothold is a gamble. Devastated, she decides to go back; the risk of moving across the steeper slope is too great. She pictures herself falling, lying broken, unable to move and beyond help. So, she must get back to that trickle of water. If she has water she will last; hunger will take a long time to kill her, but lack of water would do the job in a couple of days.

It takes longer to go back, her left arm has to do the gripping and pulling, pain stabs her as she moves sideways one foot at a time. Her energy is nearly depleted, and pain is a barrier to be conquered at every step. Her mind whispers encouragement and urges her on, 'Don't give up, keep calm, stay strong'.

Sunday

She half sleeps, hungry, cold and dispirited, hugging herself for warmth that doesn't materialize. It rains in the night, and she wakes long before dawn, chilled to the bone, with pain drilling into her back and shoulder, sits hugging herself to preserve some body heat, but the rain on her bare skin chills her fast. Holding her hands out she gathers rain and drinks, repeats the action a dozen times and knows she is safe from dehydration for the time being, but not from hypothermia. Daylight is muted by rain clouds and the birds are silent. She remains where she is, enveloped in a feeling of hopelessness with her arms around her knees, trying to make herself as compact as possible, exposing the least amount of skin. It's a lot colder than the previous day, and the wind drives the rain in under the overhang. She tries not to think of dying here, alone and cold, but she knows now that she might never be found. She will die, her body will slowly decay, nobody will see her bones.

She tries to discipline her mind, to block despair. She must go back to the tree with the flag, it's her only hope; she can't be seen under the overhang, and she must set out on the laborious trek for the third time.

In her mind the quiet whisper rises, more persistent than before, 'hang in there, don't give up, you can cope' and she whispers the phrases like a mantra, over and over: I can do it, I can cope, I won't give up, I'm strong. But she is at the end of her strength when she recognizes the right spot and settles down under the overhang with her eyes on the flag tree to wait for the rain to stop. From time to time the rain sweeps in and soaks her, but towards midday it lets up and she spots a moving dot, something moving from right to left. Not a bird, she thinks, it is moving very straight and slow. Could it be a helicopter far away? Hope surges through her; she scrambles down the slope, falls twice, something stabs hard into her thigh. Limping, she reaches the tree and looks up at the sky and sees nothing, it has gone, and hope goes with it. She stands beside the tree, bent over with one hand pressed hard against her thigh, and blood runs freely down her dirty trouser leg.

When she straightens and looks up into the sky a light rain falls into her wide-open eyes. And then she sees it again; a helicopter a long way off, doing a steep turn. But something is wrong, her mind says one thing and her eyes say another. Is it a full-sized helicopter far off or a tiny one very close? Her eyes are locked on it and she hardly notices how close it has come, and suddenly it's directly overhead. It circles three times above her and moves away. A drone, she thinks, that's what it is and it spotted my flag - someone has found me.

She sits down beside the flag tree, holding her hand against the wound in her thigh. Ignoring the intermittent rain, she wraps the other arm around her knees and waits. Her mind is an empty white space.

When the helicopter comes, Minnie is half unconscious and chilled to the marrow of her bones, her skin bluish white, her lips grey. She doesn't see the man being winched down and only vaguely feels the harness he fastens around her body. She opens her eyes briefly and sees the underbelly of the helicopter and somewhere in the fog of her exhausted mind a whisper: 'hold on, you're all right, don't give up now'.

She is pulled into the helicopter; two pairs of hands drag her further in and remove the harness before straightening her out. Through the noise of the engine, she hears Rumble's voice as from a long way away. 'Let's wrap her up, she's as cold as ice.' Hard hands turn her over and wrap things around her. Someone else says loudly 'everybody, sit down please, we're heading back now.'

The next time she comes to, she is in a car leaning against Rumble, wrapped up like a cocoon. The driver speaks over his shoulder, 'Is she still out?'

Rumble tightens his arm around her. 'Not sure – I think so.' She drifts off again.

35

She wakes up, too tired to open her eyes, hears men's voices talking quietly and drifts off to sleep again. The next time she wakes, she is face down, firm fingers push into sore muscles on her back, and someone is holding one of her feet. Without lifting her head, she speaks into the soft surface under her face, 'Is Rumble here?'

The hand holding her foot grips hard. 'Hi there, Petal, just lie still for now. We're nearly finished. You're covered in cuts and bruises - I've never seen such a mess.'

Minnie closes her eyes and drifts off, vaguely aware of voices, but unable to concentrate on the words. She opens her eyes when they roll her over and tuck a rug around her. She is on an air mattress on the floor in a bare room. The curtains are closed, and the ceiling light shines straight down on her. Rumble is kneeling on one side and Luke on the other. Instinctively her hands move under the fleecy blanket: no clothes, sticking plasters in places and a bandage round her thigh.

'You took my clothes off!' she says accusingly and then she laughs, but her laughter is close to tears, and Rumble puts a hand on her shoulder.

'God, Minnie, you've no idea how worried we've been. But I think you're OK. We've disinfected all the cuts and put plasters on the worst ones. There's a really deep wound in your thigh that should probably be stitched, but Luke cleaned it out and we've stuck it together with some kind of duct tape for wounds.'

Luke gets up. 'We couldn't take you to hospital – we just did what we could. I'll get you something to eat and drink. Do you think you can sit up?'

She clutches the blanket around her chest but sitting up is beyond her. Her body feels floppy, her muscles don't respond as they should.

'Gently,' says Rumble, still kneeling beside her. He reaches behind him and hands her a huge black T-shirt and squirming and twisting she manages to pull it on lying down.

'OK, try again.'

This time she makes it. Rumble pushes a pillow behind her and drapes a fleece blanket around her shoulders. Leaning against the wall, she feels as if she can barely hold herself up.

'I think we can turn that heater down a bit now,' says Rumble. 'This room is like a sauna. We thought we'd better keep you as warm as we could while we fixed you up.'

Luke returns balancing a mug of hot milk, a glass of water and an egg sandwich on a paper plate. 'Here you are – you can't have eaten for three days. How about we tell you things while you eat and then you can tell us your story. There's more food in the fridge, this is just a start.'

'I drank some water – from the ground,' she says. 'I think I'm all right. I was so cold and sore and tired. And I didn't know where I was.'

She considers this and adds, 'Or why.'

'Just hang on a minute,' says Rumble and fetches a chair from the living room, while Luke sits down cross-legged on the floor.

Minnie takes a sip of water and then drinks the whole glass, unable to stop once she starts.

'You start,' says Rumble to Luke. 'You're the one who went to the house.'

'OK – so quite late on Thursday night I called you three times and got no reply. I had a terrible feeling that something was wrong, so I drove up to your place to check. Your car wasn't there, but some lights were on. I got no answer when I rang the doorbell, so I tried the door – it was unlocked, and the house was empty. When I saw the scene in the living room, I knew you'd been abducted.'

Rumble interjects. 'Tell her what you found.'

'OK, I'm getting there. For a start there was an empty bottle of wine on its side on the bench in the kitchen. There was a glass with a little brandy in it on the table beside the small armchair in the living room and next to it a half-empty brandy bottle. And on the floor was a bottle of pills - one of those plastic cylinders, but with the label nearly gone. Your bag was on the floor in the hall, beside the table and the table had been pushed sideways. I went through your bag and everything I would have expected to find was there, apart from your two phones and the car keys, so I called Rumble and told him to come over right away.'

She stares at him, trying to take it in.

'I took photos of everything, so we have the evidence,' says Luke, and she sees him glance at Rumble. It's clear that they are holding something back, but what? Rumble pats her leg affectionately.

'I've never been so fucking scared in my life, Petal. Those pills were Tramadol. We checked the markings on the tablets that were left and looked it up on the Internet. I've never forgotten that time years ago, when you had those skin grafts under your arm, and I went to see you in hospital. What were we, about fourteen or so? You were really sick because you had reacted to Tramadol. So that whole scene had to be a set-up. I knew you'd never drink yourself into a stupor or take Tramadol.'

'But you have to admit it was a great scenario for a suicide or an accidental overdose,' says Luke. 'Staged to look as if you had taken strong painkillers and then had a drink too many. And we know, thanks to Dr Google, that Tramadol and alcohol don't go together – it's the perfect recipe for confusion and impaired coordination.'

He nods across her legs at Rumble. 'And this guy knew without any doubt at all, that you had not done these things voluntarily. No way! he said, someone has staged this, and we know who it is.'

She has finished the sandwiches and drunk both the milk and the water. 'Can I have some more water please? Have I been to the toilet since I got here?'

Rumble looks at Luke who shakes his head. 'Nope – do you want to go to the bathroom?'

She smiles weakly, feels a bit ridiculous. 'No, but I think I need to drink a lot. I haven't peed for two days, and I feel funny, like I'm about to short-circuit.'

Luke gets up, in one single move she notes with envy, and fills her glass of water.

'Thank you. How did you find me - and where was I?'

'OK, I have to make a confession now,' says Rumble. 'When I heard that someone had asked Jane about the phone and all the subsequent stuff, I got worried about your safety, so I put a GPS tracker on your car.' He hesitates and then says very fast, 'And one on Luke's car too, the one he drives at the moment.'

There is a moment of silence and then Luke explodes in laughter.

'You devious bugger! You told me you'd put one in Minnie's car, but you didn't say that you'd done mine as well.'

Rumble shrugs. 'Didn't seem necessary at the time, but I'm in confession mode now. The trackers talk to my computer and my phone at regular intervals, so I checked and saw that Minnie's car had gone up the Remutaka road that evening, Thursday. And I could see it was still there, so we drove up about midnight, but we couldn't find it. The tracker said the car was about thirty meters away, but there was just a huge drop-off into a deep gully covered in native bush – you know what that road is like, just one huge ravine after another and the road skirting the edges. We went back to town and returned at first light Friday morning.'

'I must admit I thought the tracker was malfunctioning, 'says Luke. 'Part of that road has metal barriers and other parts don't - like at the spot the GPS indicated. We parked in a parking-bay further up the road and walked about a kilometer in each direction from the GPS location inspecting every inch of roadside, but we found nothing, so we started again. And the second time around we found the place – they had pushed the car over the edge and scuffed the grass on the edge to conceal the tyre tracks. It looked OK, until you looked straight down and saw the broken branches way below. From a car you wouldn't notice a thing.'

Rumble smiles grimly. 'There was nothing to alert anyone - no brake marks, nothing. All we could see where those broken branches, but no sign of the car. And then Luke turned himself into a Jackie Chan clone and went down that bloody slope and found the car.'

Luke says mildly, without malice, 'Well, one of us had to do it.'

'Yeah, and it wasn't going to be me, that's for sure! Your car was a burnt-out wreck in very steep and difficult terrain. And admit it Luke – on the horizontal plane it was only thirty meters away. But no sign of you, Minnie.'

She listens in a trance, fascinated but detached, as if the story is about someone else. Every now and then a shiver runs through her, a reminder of fear and cold.

'It was too late to carry on without equipment and we decided not to ask for help. We hoped that if you were alive, we could get you out and then keep you safe from Dustman,' says Rumble. 'It was a huge risk – God knows what we would have done if we got you out and then you died! We went back early yesterday. Luke bought two coils of towrope from a petrol station on Friday night - in some places we looped the rope around the barrier supports along the road. I've never seen anything like it, he spent hours crawling around that bloody mountainside, looking for you and found nothing, no trace of you at all.'

He looks across Minnie's bed at Luke with a look of disbelief and shakes his head. 'And every time he came back up to the road he said, "I know she's alive, I can feel it. She's alive, I tell you!" By then I was certain you were dead, I had no doubts at all - but he was like a madman. In the end we drove back to town and went to see a mate of mine. He's into gadgets of all kinds and he's got a drone that I borrowed from him last year to see what it was like, when I was thinking of buying one. I knew he'd lend it to me again. It's a lovely piece of gear – four rotors, five hours of battery life, video camera, GPS and everything we needed including a spare battery pack. And I had the software on my laptop and on my phone already – from when I borrowed it last year. We drove back up to the top of that road again really early this morning and started flying the drone in a grid pattern up and down the ravine where the car was. The look-out at the highest point was the only one place where we could stand and see the gully where the car was in the distance, so we parked there, and I was watching what the drone saw on my phone. It's probably the only place on that road where you get cell phone reception too, very lucky.'

Minnie puts the empty glass on the floor beside her. 'And you saw my flag?'

'Finally, yes. We'd nearly given up by then, thought we'd have to call in the rescue people after all, but we flew around to have another look at that thing caught on a tree, and I spotted you on the ground.'

Suddenly it is all too real; she is overcome by emotion, acutely aware of how close she was to never be found. For a moment she is lost for words, determined not to cry she blinks tears away and swallows hard.

'What a team – thank you! But the helicopter, I mean the real one. How come they let you take me here instead of straight to hospital?'

Rumble laughs. 'Yeah, right - but if you hire a deer recovery guy who owns his own chopper and will do anything for cash – well, then you can do whatever you like.'

'You mean those guys who bring the deer back hanging in a net?' She laughs. 'Thank God you didn't do that to me! Lucky he was handy at the right time, I mean the helicopter guy.'

'That was Luke's idea - he said on Saturday night that we had to get a helicopter booked to lift you out when he found you. He knew those slopes really well by that stage, so he knew he'd never be able to bring you up to the road. And we didn't know how badly injured you were either – as I said he was certain you were alive. I know the guy who owns that chopper, got him and his mate on standby. Perfect for the job – has a winch and everything. When we had located you, we drove straight back to town and met them at the airport and flew up to get you.'

Luke breaks in, keen to complete the story but also, as she gradually realises, wanting to reassure her that she is safe.

'We brought you back from the airport in my car, nobody saw us. Rumble went out and bought all the stuff we needed to patch you up and lots of other things, and while he was out, I got this room super-heated and cleaned you up. Thank goodness for heat pumps. And yes, I saw the look on your face - I undressed you, not that you had a lot left on.'

He pauses, waits for her to comment, but she says nothing.

'As soon as I started washing you – with a tea towel and hot water, which was all I had till Rumble got back - I noticed that the muscles on the left side of your back were very tight, so I called Rumble and told him to get some massage oil, if the pharmacy had it, or else some cooking oil.'

She mentally squirms with embarrassment and self-loathing; this is a situation she has spent years avoiding.

'Don't be silly, Minnie,' says Rumble gruffly, reading her face. 'It's just us, nothing to worry about. I told Luke what happened to you, the accident and all that stuff. He's great at massage – learnt it from his mother and he got your back all sorted – I could literally see your muscles letting go, bit by bit.'

God, she thinks, they've both been looking at me, naked and unconscious between them. How much did Rumble tell Luke? Did he mention the guy who said I look like the horror movie lizard woman? She stares mutely at her hands, but reassuring thoughts appear from the back of her mind: don't worry, it doesn't matter, you're safe now. And commonsense kicks in, she relaxes and tucks her embarrassment into the far recesses of her mind. Looking from one to the other, she says, 'You guys are marvellous, it's like a miracle.'

Luke gets up. 'I'm going to heat up some food. We all need a proper meal and I want to hear what you have to tell us.'

He leaves the room and Minnie glances at tired-looking Rumble and thinks how lucky she is to have him.

'Rumble, I don't know what to say – you've saved my life. I can't thank you enough.'

She kneels, wobbling on the air mattress, and reaches over to hug him. For once he allows himself to be hugged without protest and hugs her back.

She sits down and tucks the fleece rug around her. She feels cold in a strange way, as if her skin is warm, but the core of her body is chilled and the comforting feeling of being tucked in is irresistible.

'But Rumble, I haven't got any clothes – apart from this T-shirt.'

'It doesn't matter, you can't go out anyway – it would be too dangerous. It's vital that Dustman continues to think he managed to kill you. I had that T-shirt in my backpack for some reason, it will have to do for now. I rang Jane and the rest home too and said you have measles and have to be in isolation for a fortnight.'

'Measles? Why measles?'

'Because I heard about it on the news the other day. It was one thing I could think of that was easy to explain, and everyone knows about this outbreak they're having in Australia – thanks to those bloody anti-vax nutters. And two weeks gives us a bit of time.'

'But I can't sit here without panties, wearing one of your T-shirt for two weeks. We must go back to my house and pick up some clothes.'

Luke breaks in from the living room. 'When we left your place on Thursday night, we took your bag – it was on the floor. Rumble noticed a couple of boxes in the hall and had a look and it looked like personal stuff that might be important, so we took those too and your laptop. I locked the door behind us with the remote. And as I said, I have your regular phone, so probably Dustman has the other one. We'll get new SIM cards to be safe, but we never thought of clothes.'

Rumble says loudly, 'What the hell are you doing out there? I bet Minnie is famished.'

They hear Luke say something under his breath and Rumble laughs and turns back to Minnie.

'Listen, there's no way we're going back to your house. We went up there on Friday morning before we drove up the Remutaka road again – just a quick look around in the dawn light. And we think he'd been back after they dumped you, after we had been and gone, because something's been done to the front door. We locked it when we left, but there were marks on the doorframe, new looking and big enough that we should have noticed them if they had been there earlier. We think he broke in, and what if he booby-trapped the house to kill anyone who came to look for you? Or maybe they're watching via a CCTV camera in the hall. There weren't any cameras visible outside, but maybe your house is on the official watch list now – how the hell would we know?'

Minnie tries to take in the consequences of what he just told her, but within a minute her mind takes her down another track and she starts worrying about what happened in the house that night.

'God, it's awful, it's driving me crazy! I can't remember what happened, Rumble – nothing! Even now, when I've heard what you found at the house, my mind is blank. It's really frightening – like someone removed part of my brain.'

'I'm sure it will come back, just give yourself time. Don't worry about it, just relax.' Looking slightly worried, he changes the subject. 'Tell you what - some hot food will do you good. You need to eat and stay warm and relax and stop trying to force your memory.'

A delicious smell of potato and leek soup is spreading through the flat and Rumble gets up. 'Got to see what he's fixing to eat. I feel like baked beans.'

36

With a bowl of baked beans on his knees and a piece of toast in his hand, Rumble reverts to the subject of clothes. 'Thank God I bought some more household stuff or we would have been reduced to chocolate and chips. But we can get new gear for you, don't worry about that either. Luke will do it - I bet he knows how to shop for girls.'

Luke shoots him a sardonic glance. 'Don't you?'

'God no – I can't do it,' says Rumble and starts laughing. 'Imagine me in amongst the bras and panties – they'd call the cops.'

'I'll do it, Minli – not that I ever did it before, but how hard can it be? I'll get you some clothes and whatever you need, toilet things and that sort of stuff – just make a list. We'll need towels too and more food. You can't hide forever, but we are close to the end now.'

'The end – how lovely that sounds. It can't come soon enough.'

'At least we know how dangerous these guys are now,' says Rumble and his face is troubled. 'If Broker is prepared to risk committing murder to avoid being exposed, we've got to act really smart until it's all out in the open. We joked about being paranoid at the start, but it's not funny anymore. And somehow, they found out how much you know, Petal. I don't think they have identified Luke or me, but we can't go to your place and risk being spotted. There's been no news of your disappearance, and the car hasn't been discovered.'

'So, Broker just decided I had to die,' says Minnie, her voice rising in outrage. 'Just like that! To him I'm as disposable as a paper cup. He's a monster!'

'We've tried to figure it out,' says Luke. 'Somehow Dustman found out where you live, and this is my theory - remember that evening when I called and you didn't answer my messages because your phone was on mute? You said you were sitting on the step outside the front door while we talked. I think that's the only time that Dustman could have found out anything about us and what we know, because you mentioned Broker's name and then you said something like "if only we knew who he is". And then you replied to something I said, and you said, "but I do know what Dustman looks like, from when he was in the school parking lot". I never thought of it at the time – you were at home and so was I, we thought we were having a private conversation.'

She nods, and thinks that might well be the link, and they were careless and gave Dustman exactly the information they didn't want him to have.

'Here's how it might have played out,' he continues. 'Let's presume that Dustman somehow found out where the mysterious Minnie lives, God know how, but one way or the other he did. And let's say he was hiding in your front garden that evening - waiting for you, maybe to frighten you a bit and make you talk, because he didn't quite believe you had returned that phone. And he hears your end of our conversation, and he knows two things. The first is that now he must do more than scare you, he must kill you, because it's clear you know enough to be very damaging to Broker's operation. The second thing is that he puts two and two together – that Minnie and the woman who tricked him at Te Papa is the same person. I'm sure you said to me that you knew what he looked like from when he was in the school parking lot. Which probably makes him furious. So, he goes away, tells Broker and they plan how to do it. And he knows from what he heard that somebody else is in on it too, so he must make you talk first and find out who you were talking to, and then he must get rid of you. Because you know what he looks like.'

He is right; she sat there having a leisurely conversation and revealed how much she knew. They look at each other and there is no need for further comment. And the man Mr. Yeoman saw, she thinks, maybe Dustman sent him to see what he could find out.

And then the unspoken implication strikes her and makes her skin crawl. 'But Luke – he took me away to kill me...' She shudders at what she has missed. 'He must have made me tell him about you when he broke in and drugged me - I must have told him who you are!'

She thinks of the dream she had of someone forcing water down her throat so fast that she thought she would drown. Was it real, was she tortured and told Dustman what he wanted to know? The agony of having betrayed her friends threatens to overwhelm her; this is the last straw after what she has been through, but she sees Rumble glance at Luke, and she can tell they have already thought of this.

Rumble replies, and his voice is calm and level. 'Very unlikely. We think that somehow – whatever Dustman did to you – you held out and didn't tell him. Otherwise, why have we still not heard from him? He's had time to track us down, we've both been back to our flats and nobody came near us – it's the only explanation, Petal. He tried to make you talk, but you didn't.'

Minnie sits silent in intense concentration, working through what they know for a fact and what they surmise, trying to assess if Rumble's conclusion is the right one. In the end she relaxes and feels her shoulder literally drop, satisfied that it seems reasonable to assume that Dustman doesn't know who Luke and Rumble are, and her heart lifts.

'But listen, Jane will call to find out how I am, and she'll wonder why I'm not at home, and so might some of the others at work. And I must check she is safe and that she told the cops about those messages, and the rest home might call about Brendan – and Sharon too.'

Suddenly a string of complications has materialized in her mind, things that must be dealt with.

'OK, don't get stressed. Let's start with Jane,' says Rumble. 'Dustman thinks you had the phone last, so Jane should be safe for now. She was just a middleman, not important. As for the rest, we've talked to everyone who needs to know. Luke's damn good at inventing things, so he thought up the details and I made the calls because I'm a better liar than he is.'

Luke shares a smile with Minnie. 'He's a very convincing liar. After we spotted you from the drone, we worked it out what we should do on the way back to town. By the time we were on the motorway, we had it sorted. I drove the car and talked, Rumble made notes and found phone numbers. He rang Jane with the measles story and asked her to inform the school and then he rang the rest-home. He told everyone he's your cousin and you're staying with him and his wife while you're in isolation, because they have no children. We thought the no-kids bit was a good touch. And he gave them no phone number, just said you'll be in touch when you feel a bit better. He made his voice higher pitched than normal, very effective – Jane would never have guessed who it was.'

'Did you do Mrs. Green, Rumble?' Minnie smiles at the thought. 'My God, that's so funny - I haven't heard you do that for years. Luke, we had a high school teacher called Mrs. Green, who was forever picking on Rumble for not paying attention, and he could imitate her voice perfectly. He'd do it out of the blue, just anywhere at school and everyone would jump – we were all scared of her, and it was so convincing.'

Rumble grins. 'Yeah, but these days I don't sound like a woman, just different from normal. Jane said she didn't know you had a cousin in Wellington, so I used Luke's script and said we hadn't been in touch for years and I only just found out you had moved back here and made contact with you again. I said I'd called around to pick up some books for Brendan, to take when I went to visit him, and I got to your house and found you burning with fever, really ill, so I bundled you up and took you home and called my doctor.'

'He's a brilliant liar,' says Luke admiringly. 'Totally convincing – he should have been a conman.'

'He was always very clever,' says Minnie and yawns twice, exhaustion is catching up.

'Write a quick list of what you need before you fall asleep,' says Luke. 'Everything, and don't forget sizes. I'll go and get the basic stuff now and then we'll sort out the rest tomorrow.'

He brings her pen and paper, and she makes a list of basic things, struggling to keep her eyes open.

'I can't think of anything else. If you feel embarrassed about buying panties just leave them out, just buy a pair of trousers or tights.'

'It would take a lot more than panties to embarrass me.'

Rumble picks up the plates. 'Go to sleep now, and I'll tidy up a bit and wait for Luke to come back. Just shout if you need me.'

He turns the light off, closes the door to a crack and leaves her alone. She hears him say something and then Luke's voice, cold and hard: 'I'll kill the bastard, when I find him.'

37

She wakes up with the wound in her thigh throbbing. The room is dimly visible in the light that seeps through the curtains, but she has no idea what time it is. She gets up slowly, puts a steadying hand against the wall and notices the outline of someone sleeping against the far wall. She pads quietly through the dark living room to the bathroom, closes the door and turns the light on, and sits on the toilet, half asleep and dreamy.

On the shelf beside the hand basin is a cluster of things: shampoo, soap, toothpaste and a toothbrush, a nail file. There are towels on the towel rail. Her tired body feels too heavy to stand; she stays where she is, drowsily studying the shelf. Is that a mascara wand? Really? And that bottle behind the shampoo – it looks like a bottle of liquid makeup.

She gets up to have a closer look, but her pale face reflected in the mirror distracts her. There is a large bruise on one side of her forehead curving down around her eye, nearly black, a cut on her cheek and several deep scratches. Her arms and hands are covered in bruises and cuts, her hair is tangled and filthy.

I must have a shower - right now, she thinks, disgusted. I can't stand this another moment. She drops the T-shirt on the floor and unwinds the elastic bandage from her thigh, slightly shocked at the sight of the taped-up wound with purple skin extending out from under the tape. When she finally turns off the shower, she feels a lot better; the plasters are still in place and so is the tape on her thigh. She dons the giant T-shirt again, runs her fingers though her wet hair and picks up the nailfile from the little shelf, before going back to the kitchen to turn the kettle on.

'Are you OK? What are you doing?' Luke has appeared in the bedroom door wearing a T-shirt and jeans; he seems to find the situation quite normal.

She smiles. 'Thank you for doing the shopping and all the extras – you're a great shopper. But what are you doing here?'

'We thought one of us should be here, and Rumble had to go back to check on something urgent for a client. Personally, I think he just can't stand the thought of sleeping on an air mattress. Ah, you found the nail file, good. I cut off a couple of tattered nails with the scissors on my Swiss army knife. But that's as far as it went, there were more serious things that needed doing at the time.'

'Do you want a cup of tea? I've just boiled the kettle.'

They sit at the table with only the little light over the stove on, and after a few silent minutes Minnie says, 'I can't believe you bought make-up - I hadn't expected that.'

'I can't take the credit for that. I got my sister, Isabella, to come with me – and they have everything in the supermarket. I told her a made-up story and swore her to silence, so now she thinks I have a lover who has run away from her violent husband - with no luggage.'

He smiles at her expression. 'She asked me about your colouring and got everything she thought you might need. I told her you don't dare go out, so you can't do your own shopping, so she's going to get clothes and shoes tomorrow morning. She totally rejected the idea of buying a pair of tracksuit pants from the supermarket, but I'll pick up you new clothes from her at lunch time. She gets Mondays off because she works on Saturdays.'

She doesn't reply and he looks searchingly at her. 'Are you OK with all this? You don't need to worry about Bella – she'll keep her mouth shut. The story about a dangerous husband had her totally hooked. She loves romantic drama - never reads anything that hasn't got a lurid picture on the cover of a female fleeing through the night or a bare chested muscle man. And she loves shopping.'

'I'm overwhelmed – all the trouble and effort, and now I'm safe. It's all so ...'

Unsettled and agitated, she gets up and stands by the bench with her back to him. She wraps her arms round herself, wincing slightly at the strain across her scratched and bruised back. 'I was so scared! I thought I would die there and never be found.'

And suddenly she cries. She has controlled her emotions and her fear right through her lonely ordeal, but now – when she is warm and safe –the dam bursts. Luke gets up, pulls a piece of paper towel off the roll on the bench and hands it to her.

'Come and lie down again. You're overtired and your body has taken a terrible beating – what you need is lots of rest and some good food. I'm pretty sure you went down with the car and got flung out - by the bruises on your forehead I'd say you're concussed. Give yourself a chance. It will take time to get over this.'

She stops crying, unceremoniously blows her nose and follows him to the bedroom. Face down on the mattress she stifles a groan of pain, and then Luke's hands move over her back, his fingertips searching for the areas of tension where the thick scar tissue joins unharmed skin. When she twitches and protests, he puts one hand on the back of her head and says 'shush' and continues, and she falls asleep nearly instantly.

38

It's early afternoon on Monday and Minnie is dressed in clean clothes from the supply Luke just picked up from Bella. With a pen spinning rapidly in his fingers, Luke looks steadily at Minnie, and she gets the feeling that he is expecting objections to whatever he's about to say.

'If Minli isn't officially reported as missing and if there's nothing in the papers and nobody finds the car - then Dustman will check with the school and they will say that you're on sick leave and he'll know you survived. I'm sure Broker is checking the papers for reports of a missing woman – or perhaps he knows how to find out directly from the police if you've been reported missing.'

'Shit, Luke, you're right!' Rumble runs his hands through his mass of curls and groans. 'I think my brain switched off when we found Minnie. We've got to think of something fast.'

Luke nods. 'We have to keep you safe until the media launch, Minli. You are the vulnerable one, the only one whose identity is known, and you're also their link to Rumble and me. But we can do it – we can make it public that you've left town after being found, then you actually leave, and then we sneak you back. So, Dustman won't look for you in Wellington and he might even go off on a wild goose chase to find you.'

'Yeah, right,' says Rumble ironically. 'And where would she go and how would she return? And the real crux, how the hell would we let Broker know?'

'The South Island,' says Minnie and then she pauses. 'I don't know why I said that - silly idea.'

'Well, it's funny that you say the South Island, because that's exactly what I'm about to suggest. It's a bit of a mission, but it would be worth it if we can divert Dustman's attention. I would feel a lot happier if he doesn't spend all his time trying to track you down here in Wellington.'

'OK,' says Minnie, 'but first he has to find out that I've gone and where - and then I have to get back in some invisible way.' She points at Luke. 'Aha, do I see a crack in the inscrutable façade? You've got it worked out already?'

'Well, I have an idea – it needs fine-tuning, but in the main it's pretty solid. The one thing that's doubtful is how to make Dustman and Broker aware that you've gone to the South Island. I know how to do it, but you might not like it.'

Rumble leans back in his chair, doubtful eyes on Luke's face. Luke ignores the look and continues without change of expression.

'We need to keep Rumble and me out of this loop – if he ID's us we can't operate in the open. But let's say my mother takes a couple of days off, buys a ticket to take her car on the Inter-Islander ferry to Picton and stays there one night. Minli buys a ticket as a walk-on passenger from Wellington to Picton - on the same ferry my mum is booked to come back on. So, Ling, that's my mum, drives onto the ferry in Picton and you haven't disembarked, Minli – you've kept out of sight onboard. All you have to do now is slightly change your appearance, come out of hiding when the ferry leaves Picton and mingle with the crowds. And then you go down to the car deck when the ferry approaches Wellington. My mum sends a message telling you how to find her car, you will already know what the car looks like and we'll find a way to make it obvious – a toy in the back window or something. And the car is unlocked, so it doesn't matter who gets there first. Ling drives off the ferry and drops you back here.'

Rumble starts to say something, but Minnie interrupts him.

'But where would I hide? I've never even been on the ferries.'

'Exactly – it would have to be a safe place, but how will she know?' Rumble asks. 'If she's found hiding onboard there will be publicity, and then she's worse off than ever.'

'I know, but Bella worked at the onboard information desk on one of the ferries last year. She was between travel agency jobs and thought it might be a fun job for the summer. She can tell you how to do it, but it's got to be the ferry she worked on, because they're all different.'

'Sounds OK,' Rumble is still doubtful. 'Then we must somehow let Broker know that she's gone – which sounds nearly impossible. And I suppose Bella will have to come here to brief her.'

Luke nods. 'Yeah, and she must continue to think that Minnie is on the run from a violent husband, as I've already told her - I'll tell her the truth later.'

Rumble and Minnie never take their eyes off Luke, who continues smoothly. 'Bella and Ling – we tell them both the same story provided you agree, Minli. I'll say that you moved here because it isn't safe at my flat, while your husband is looking for you, and now you want to make him think that you've moved to the South Island.'

'But won't they both think I'm completely mad? Such an elaborate scheme, so much trouble – it will seem crazy to people living normal lives.'

'You wouldn't say that if you heard the stories Ling could tell. She volunteers in the weekends for an organization that helps immigrant women keep safe after domestic abuse. Nothing you say could surprise her - she's heard it all. Afterwards I'll have to confess to Ling and Bella and explain why I had to tell them lies and ask them to forgive me.'

'Right,' says Rumble, looking marginally happier. 'It's a possibility, I suppose. What about Broker and Dustman then - how do we let them know she's gone?'

'I know,' says Minnie off the top of her head. 'Luke leaks a little story to one of his journalist mates, something along the lines of "a woman has been found, injured and nearly starved to death, after driving off the Remutaka road. She's going to the South Island to stay with friends while she recovers". And then we book the ferry ticket in my name and off I go.'

Luke raises his eyebrows. 'You've done it again. That was going to be my suggestion, but I was worried you wouldn't like it, but we won't mention your name or any details. Broker will know it's you, but your friends and the school won't – so no harm done.'

'It should be on the news or in the paper the day she leaves,' Rumble says. 'I'm sure Dustman or Broker will have some way of checking that you bought the ticket and actually boarded – they're so damn organized and they probably don't take anything at face value. Once they've checked that you really left, Broker might send Dustman to track you, or they might just write it off as a waste of time.'

Bella arrives straight from work, nearly as tall as Luke and very slender, with bright pink streaks in her hair. She studies Minnie with frank curiosity. 'Nice clothes!'

They both laugh and even Rumble smiles. 'So, it was you who did the shopping. I hope you got reimbursed for that?'

'I used Luke's credit card.' Bella grins at her brother. 'First time he's ever let me, it was fun.'

She turns back to Minnie. 'Did most of the clothes fit you? I've kept the receipts in case we need to change anything.'

'They're great, thank you for doing that. And I'm sorry Luke – I never even thought of it. I must pay you back. I think my brain is in slow mode.'

'We'll sort it out later, it's not urgent.'

They gather around the table and Bella points with a pen. 'These are the only plans I could find on the internet and there's not a lot of detail, but I'll be able to describe where to go and we can write notes in the margin. Foot passengers come onboard here and from this point on you can go to various places.'

She takes them through the options; the different levels that she refers to as decks, the cafeterias, viewing platforms and lounges.

'This café here is probably the best place. It's always full – backpackers charging cell phones and laptops, sitting on the floor with all their gear around them –it would be easy to disappear in the crowd.' She circles the café on the plan. 'You board wearing my old crew shirt with the logo and with a sweatshirt over it, perhaps bring another one for the return trip. When they broadcast the message for car passengers to go down to the car deck, you head down with the last trickle, behind everyone.'

'Why is that?'

'You don't want other passengers to see what you are going to do. Two decks down, there's a door that says Crew Only on the landing.'

She draws an X on the plan and writes 'Crew only door' in the margin.

'You pull off your sweatshirt when you start down the stairs and stuff it into your bag, so when you go through the crew door you look like a crew member. You'll be in a narrow passage and go past two doors on your left – I think it's two. The first door on the right is a crew toilet. Go into a cubicle and lock the door and stay there until the ship leaves Picton for the return trip an hour and a half later. Wait a few minutes after the ship starts moving and then come out and do the whole thing in reverse. Put a sweatshirt on before you get to the door to the stairs.'

'What if someone notices how long I'm in the toilet?'

'I don't think they would. If someone comes back and the same cubicle is occupied, they'll just assume a different person is in there.'

She looks around for questions and continues. 'Everyone is so busy – it should be fine. If you're discovered when you come back out the Crew Only door, you say you felt sick on the stairs and you ran through the crew door to find a toilet - say you panicked. They'll assume you boarded in Picton.'

'That sounds OK. I'll have to look different on the way back - maybe I should take a baseball cap, as well as a jacket.'

Rumble pats her head. 'Good idea – nobody forgets that hair.'

Bella clears her throat. 'Minli, I hope you won't mind me saying this, but these two might not think of it.' She gestures at Rumble and Luke. 'Being guys, you know? But you should use that make-up I bought for you, when you go on the ferry – the bruising is very noticeable, particularly the big one above your eye.'

She thinks my husband beat me up, thinks Minnie, it's the perfect cover. Aloud the says, 'Good idea! I will - I hadn't thought of that.'

39

Feeling unsettled and anxious has become the new normal for Minnie; the awareness that memories of what was done to her are locked away in her brain is like an itch that she can't scratch. Her concentration level is at rock bottom and trawling through the text messages looking for clues is beyond her. As a diversion she goes through the boxes Rumble rescued from her house, those precious boxes that are now in the second bedroom in the flat. When she asked why they took the boxes when they left her house that night, Rumble said, 'I don't know. It was the way they were sitting there, right beside where Luke found your bag in the hall, as if you were planning to take them with you the next day, so we took them.'

She thinks of Luke arriving and finding the dramatic scene in the house, calling Rumble and the two of them searching the place, taking photos and debating what to do. In her mind's eye she follows them out the front door, Rumble with the two boxes and Luke picking up her phone on the driveway, sees them get into their cars. She imagines the neighbours hearing cars arrive and leave that evening; first herself, then Dustman and his helper, then Luke and Rumble. Did they think she was having a party?

After carefully thinking through what Jane might ask and how she should respond to avoid complications, Minnie calls her. 'Hi Jane, how are you coping without me?'

'Minnie! You poor thing –measles of all things. How are you, feeling better?'

'Not a hundred percent,' she says truthfully. 'I'm very tired still.

And I have to keep away from people for a while, so I won't be back at school until after the Easter break.'

'Are you covered in rash?'

'My skin is a terrible mess, but it will get better. So long as there aren't any complications, I should be fine.'

Even lying by evasion makes her feel guilty; her skin is a mess, but not because of measles. I've never told so many lies in my whole life as I have recently, she thinks, I hope it doesn't become a habit.

'I looked it up on the Health Department website,' says Jane. 'It sounds very nasty. But why weren't you vaccinated as a child? Perhaps it didn't take. I don't suppose I can come and see you?'

'No, you certainly can't! What if you got it too? What if your vaccination has worn off or whatever happened with me? You don't want to be ill over the holidays, and it's a very unpleasant thing to have.'

They say goodbye and Minnie heaves a sigh of relief that Jane didn't ask for the address where she is staying. She calls the resthome and asks if she can talk to Brendan, but he is on an outing in their minibus. Last, she calls Sharon and leaves a message about having measles and says she is staying with friends. She puts the phone down and sighs; now she has lied to every single person who matters in her life apart from Andy, and for the hundredth time she thinks that she can't wait for this to be over.

The following morning Minnie gets out of the taxi at the ferry terminal feeling unexpectedly cheerful. Luke claims to have organized his mother and the tickets with lightning speed, but Minnie doesn't believe him and feels sure he set it all up in advance before even suggesting his plan, because she is beginning to understand that it's just the sort of thing he would do.

She carries a large canvas satchel borrowed from Bella and wears her new navy-blue sweatshirt over the polo shirt with the crew logo, and a cap and the jacket she will wear on the return journey are in the bag.

When the ferry moves away from the quay she goes outside and watches the familiar landscape from an angle that is new to her. They move through the wide channel to the open sea, and she marvels to think that she never did this before. The water is calm inside the harbour, but as soon as they leave the sheltering hills and turn south, the swell becomes noticeable. The café Bella pointed out is as crowded and noisy as she said it would be, all the tables taken and in a corner a man plays a guitar surrounded by a group of people. She sits and reads with a cup of tea in front of her until lunchtime, when she buys a sandwich and goes outside to stand by the rail and watch their slow progress through the calm waters of the Marlborough Sounds towards Picton.

When passengers are told to go down to the car decks, she heads inside, follows Bella's instructions to the letter and starts down the stairs behind the last straggle of passengers. The door on the second landing says Crew Only, and Minnie goes quickly back up one flight, checks that nobody is approaching and runs down again, pulling the sweatshirt off as she goes. She crams it into the satchel and pushes the heavy steel door open. The passage is bare and functional with numbered doors on the left and one on the right with a sign saying Crew Toilets. She slips inside, desperate now to get out of sight before someone turns up. Waiting in the cubicle is nerve-wracking. Crew members come and go, but eventually she hears the call for all passengers to leave the car deck, the vibrating thrum of the engines change pitch, and the ferry gets underway again.

Finally, the hour and a half that seemed more like a whole day is over. She puts on the jacket, zips it up to cover the logo on the polo-shirt and unlocks the cubicle. In front of the mirror, she puts the cap on and carefully tucks every stray curl under it before she cautiously opens the door to the passage. There is nobody in sight, and she draws a deep breath of relief when the door to the stairway clangs shut behind her.

She stands outside until the ferry leaves the Sounds and the wind becomes stronger, when she retreats inside and sits reading in the café with a glass of grapefruit juice and a ham sandwich beside her. The call for passengers to go to their cars takes her by surprise, but the ferry is in the entrance to Wellington harbor and just as she puts her book away, her phone pings with a text message: 'My car is on H deck, walk along the R wall. Second row from wall seven cars from front of ship. Red Honda Accord, white teddy in back window. I will go down now. Ling.'

Five minutes later Minnie gets into the red car and the woman in the driver's seat looks across and smiles, 'Hi, I'm Ling.'

As they drive away from the terminal Ling says, 'That worked well. Did you have any problems?'

'No, not at all – it was very straight-forward. And thank you for doing this. I hope you didn't have to take time off. I never thought of it till just now.'

'I cancelled some appointments when Luke asked me to do this. It's the first time in years he's asked me for anything, and it was obviously important.'

Minnie raises her hand to remove the cap and then remembers. 'Oh no, I must keep the cap on – I don't like wearing hats.'

Ling glances at her with a smile. 'I gather you are very recognizable without the cap. Luke says you have wonderful hair.'

They drive through the rush hour in stops and starts and inch slowly along the length of Cambridge Terrace towards the Basin Reserve.

'How did you get your name?' asks Ling after a long pause.

'My father is a classics scholar and he named me Minerva after the goddess, and then it got shortened to Minnie.'

'I thought your name was Minli?'

'Oh no, that's just Luke's little joke. And it's close enough to Minnie – I don't mind.'

There is a searching sideways glance from Ling. 'I suppose he told you what the two words mean?'

Time to change the subject, thinks Minnie, any minute now she'll ask why. 'Do you live in town?'

'I live at the town end of Northland Road – still in the house where Luke and Bella grew up. Very handy to work.'

'Do you have your massage studio at home?'

'Oh, I don't do massage as a job, just for family and friends. I learnt from my mother and Luke learnt it from me – he's very good at it. Bella isn't interested at all.'

'I'm sorry, my mistake - I thought Luke meant you do massage as a full-time job. What do you do?'

'I am a dentist, but I only work three days a week now. My husband and I were partners – we worked together ever since I qualified.'

Minnie points. 'Take the middle lane here and head up Adelaide Road.'

When they stop outside the apartment building, Ling gets out and comes around to the sidewalk.

'Thank you very much for doing this,' says Minnie. 'So much trouble for you. I'll reimburse Luke for your expenses – he says he paid, but you have given up your time and I'm very grateful.'

'I hope everything turns out all right for you. Luke seems to take it very seriously, but you look remarkably relaxed.'

'Oh no, I'm not really. I just seem to hide my fears better than most – not that I try to, it's just the way my face is arranged, I think.'

They smile at each other and Ling gets back into the car and drives away.

40

Walking into the apartment feels like coming home. How strange, she thinks, I feel as if I've shut out the big bad world and I'm in a safe cocoon again. Everything I've been through lately has made this place special – I didn't realise till now. If I can't go back to the house for a while, I'll be fine here.

Rumble calls half an hour later. 'Did it work out all right, finding Luke's mum's car and getting away?'

'It went like clockwork. You know what Rumble? It feels like coming home, being back here, just great. Thank you – it's as if you had this flat just waiting for us to make use of it.'

'I suppose you're just about to have a cup of tea?'

'I know you're being funny, but I've actually got a mug of tea in my hand.'

He laughs and she puts the phone down just as the door behind her opens, and she swings around, unprepared for someone to arrive, but it's Luke carrying a shopping bag.

'Welcome back. I heard from Ling that it went like clockwork.'

'The very phrase I used to describe it to Rumble just now. No hitches at all. It nearly felt like an anticlimax. I was really worried, while I was locked in that toilet - dreaming up scenarios that might cause real trouble, like being charged with being a stow-away and getting arrested. Why are you smiling? It wasn't funny – waiting in that toilet quite stressful.'

'Of course, it's not funny – I was smiling because that was the only thing I worried about too. I nearly brought it up this morning, and then I thought I was being neurotic, and I'd better not make you nervous too.'

'It was such an anti-climax, you know. The guy who checked my ticket didn't even glance at me, and then I sat in a nice departure lounge and watched promotion videos about the South Island until we boarded, and I'll be on CCTV recordings for sure. I saw at least three cameras, before I even got to the ferry itself. I'm not sure what I expected, but it was all very ordinary.' And then she realises it's far too early for him to have finished work for the day. 'Why aren't you at work – did you leave early?'

'I told them I urgently need to take a month off for a family emergency. I just couldn't see how this was going to work otherwise. After the launch one of us has to be the interface between us and the media and the authorities and it will probably be time-consuming. I decided it should be me, I just couldn't see Rumble in the role, and I knew you don't want to do it.'

It makes her laugh and she thinks she was so right about him; he just goes ahead and arranges things. 'Yeah - Rumble would run a mile and I wouldn't be far behind.'

'How did you get on with Ling?'

'Oh, she was lovely - and she asked no questions at all. I wasn't sure what you had told her – the details I mean, so I kept it minimal. It was so kind of her to cancel appointments to do this. I really owe her. You didn't tell me she's a dentist.'

He raises his eyebrows. 'Should I have? It didn't seem relevant.'

'I thought she was a masseuse, but she says it's more a family tradition.'

'It is, and very useful at times.'

'Brendan is fine,' says the nurse when Minnie calls the resthome. 'I'll tell him you called – he's sound asleep in an armchair by the fish tank, I can see him from my office. He had a visitor this afternoon, but he stayed a bit too long and I think he tired Brendan out.'

'A visitor? Do you know who it was? An older man, short?' Mr. Yeoman, she thinks, but how would he have known which rest home Brendan is at?

'No, a tall chap, about forty or forty-five, I guess. Very nice man - said he hadn't seen Brendan for some years. He brought a magazine and a box of chocolates.'

Suddenly alarmed, Minnie tries to keep her anxiety out of her voice. 'I can't imagine who that could have been – what did he look like?'

'Quite nice looking, tall as I said, with a buzz-cut, brown leather jacket. He asked after you, said he hadn't seen you for a while.'

She puts the phone down and turns to Luke. 'Dustman has found Brendan and visited him – he'll have tried to find out where I am. I wish I could have heard that conversation - probably total confusion. Maybe Dad thought he knew where I was and gave him some crazy information. Thank God he has no idea about this flat or anything else.'

The next day Rumble brings The Dominion newspaper for Minnie to see the article about her rescue. 'I thought you might like to cut it out and keep it,' he says and she hasn't got the heart to tell him that nothing could be further from her mind.

Luke's young journalist friend has managed to filter in a short story, without any reference to where it had come from, with the headline 'Woman found after Remutaka crash' and she reads it out aloud. 'A woman aged thirty-eight has been found lost in a stream gully in the Remutaka mountain range after a car accident that had gone unnoticed for an unknown number of days. Her rescuers contacted her friends, who came to collect her. She was bruised and hungry, but not seriously injured and declined an interview, only saying that she was going to stay with friends in the South Island to recover before the school term starts after Easter.'

'Bloody perfect,' says Rumble. 'You're very useful, Luke.'

'Very bossy is more like it,' Minnie says. 'I heard him on the phone – this article is exactly how he dictated it. That young chap just did what he was told.'

'The guy owes me. I've done him a couple of good turns in the past and I covered for him once when he stuffed up - gave him my notes and a recording when he was late for an important media announcement. And this isn't cheating. He got a phone call from a 'rescuer' – me, so that's true - and the basic facts are more or less true, and there's no harm in it. I told him he'll soon find out why. Now we hope Broker reads the paper and takes the bait.'

41

Minnie leans back in her chair and groans. 'I am so sick of this! It's like we've done nothing else for ever – I need another cup of tea. Once this is over, I might throw my laptop in the bin.'

Rumble looks up and sighs. 'Me too, bored stiff. Wish we had never started editing these bloody messages with bold text and whatever, it's so slow! If you give me a beer, I'll give you anything you like tomorrow.'

'Really? OK, then.'

Luke emerges from deep concentration. 'What was that? Something wrong?'

'Don't worry. I'll give you a beer too. I was just having a hissy fit about how boring it is working on the messages. We should have left them as continuous text and let others to struggle through it like we did.'

Half an hour later Luke looks up and says 'Hey, listen to this. I just got an email from a guy who is a political reporter – he says, "check out mysterious media release re MBIE and see what you make of it." Let's have a look at the RNZ website – it will be on their news page.'

Rumble and Minnie wait while Luke finds the item; his eyes scan the text before he reads it out.

'This is it: At midday today the New Zealand Internal Security Agency released a press statement. We quote the exact text: "It has recently become clear that political agitators are engaging in subversive activities that could cause serious harm to the New

Zealand economy. Staff at the department of Business Innovation and Employment have been approached by known agitators and offered money to supply information about matters that could be used for illegal purposes. Any activities that might be deemed to be against the best interests of the country, whether they involve foreign powers or not, are punishable with lengthy prison sentences under the 2025 Subversive and Anti-New Zealand Activities Act. There has been no indication of what caused the press release, and the Minister in question has declined to comment.'

Rumble says impatiently, 'What the fuck does it mean? Sounds like a mash-up of Broker's activities and what we're doing. And no mention of an investigation. What do you think Luke?'

Luke shrugs. 'Maybe someone else has put two and two together like I did. Heard a rumour about someone with a suspiciously extravagant lifestyle and started digging? Or has Broker sprung a leak? Or is the Minister trying to protect Broker? Maybe Broker asked for someone to apply some diversionary scare tactics against us? Seems to me like a shot in the dark – they don't know anything concrete, they're warning people off, and shaking the bag to see what might fall out. And it could fit nearly any kind of activity – either side of the table.'

'Yeah, I suppose. Someone high up is worried that inconvenient facts will come out, so they issue a vague public warning - or threat.'

Rumble glances at Minnie, but she shakes her head. 'God knows – but I can't think of what else it could be. And we might never find out.'

That night, for the first time since her abduction, Minnie wakes up in terror, dreaming that she is falling from the ledge where she first regained consciousness. She lies staring into the dark with her fists clenched, and her heart beating so fast it feels as if it will explode out of her chest. Did she cry out? Luke appears beside her, says 'hush' and rolls her on her front and starts rubbing her back. First with one hand on her shoulder to hold her still and then with both hands. Gradually her breathing and heart beat slow, and she falls asleep.

She wakes late in the morning to full daylight. Without looking she knows she is alone in the room and lies quietly trying to remember the details of the incident in the night. Luke appears in the doorway holding a mug of tea. 'Ready for tea?'

He puts the mug beside her mattress and turns to go, but Minnie sits up quickly.

'Luke? Wait a moment. I'm sorry I woke you and – and thank you for being here.'

'That's why I'm still in this room with you – we thought one of us should in case you get into some sort of post-traumatic stress situation.'

She is surprised, nothing like it has occurred to her. 'Really? Do you think that will happen?'

'We think it might. You still can't remember it – either due to the drugs or the trauma. It's sitting there somewhere in the back of your mind waiting to come out. But if it happens, you aren't going to be alone. Clearly something brutal and probably terrifying was done to you that night.'

'I dreamed I was on that ledge I told you about - and I fell down into the ravine.' She shudders. 'The sensation of falling, hitting branches and things, falling very fast – further and further down.'

He nods. 'And you would know what that feels like, from when you were thrown from the car, so maybe something is coming back.'

After a moment of silence Minnie says, 'Thank you – it's impossible to say how much.'

'It's a pleasure, madam.' He leaves the room, and she drinks her tea thinking that he will probably tell Rumble about it, but she feels strangely relaxed about them discussing her in her absence. Maybe being nude and unconscious in front of them has changed me? she thinks. Maybe I'm just a little bit braver, with two people at least?

42

Rumble turns up after lunch to find that they have just finished and the material is finalized and ready to be duplicated.

'Finally!' says Minnie and hands him the flash drive. 'It's all there, the text messages – both the original file and the tidied-up version, the database, the video clips, photos, the linking text we wrote to explain things – the lot. And Luke has saved it on another flash drive for you to put in your safe. And he's got the script for the press conference in draft form, so we can discuss it tomorrow – it's very good. Are you taking this straight to your friend who owns the machine - or do you want to have a final look at it?'

'No, I think we've discussed it often enough. My mate's going to set his gear going as soon as I get the material to him, and I'll pick up the drives tomorrow. Did you decide on the text for the label?'

'Yes, just 'The Broker Corruption Investigation'. We have two labels, one with the name and then one for the other side of the drive with Luke's new email address and our new phone numbers. They're very narrow - they'll be fiddly to put on even though you got those bigger flash drives.'

'Have you seen the duplicator working?' asks Luke, curious as always. 'How fast is it? I'd never heard of the thing before.'

Rumble shakes his head. 'I don't know. He says it clones thirty-one flash drives at a time, takes a couple of minutes, even with complex data and images. Technically it sounds like quite a simple thing - it pulls the information from a master file and writes it simultaneously on all the flash drives you have plugged into the little ports on the duplicator unit. I think plugging the flash drives in takes as long as cloning the data does. Very expensive gear - costs several thousand dollars. So, you print the labels and I'll come back with the flash drives and the courier bags first thing tomorrow morning. And I got the lanyards, they're in my backpack.'

He tucks the flash drive into his pocket and hands Luke the little recorder he brought.

'Now tell me about this meeting with the young guy from radio. Are you going to pretend that he doesn't know who it is he's interviewing? Why don't you just do it over the phone instead of going to all this trouble?'

'That's what I said too,' says Minnie. 'It seems a bit mad, like meeting a secret informer in a deserted warehouse or something – very TV drama stuff. We're meeting him so we can show him some printouts and pictures – just to look at. So, he can say to his producer that he has seen real evidence, we aren't pulling a stunt. But he won't be able to see us, so he can also honestly say that he isn't sure who we are. He'll take the recorder away, but he'll have nothing else.'

'OK, sounds good. See you tomorrow.'

'This will be a real scoop for Dougal,' says Luke, 'particularly at his age.'

'He's being very obedient,' Minnie points out.

'Oh no, he knows he's going to get bonus points for this – very good for his career.'

The next morning, they set up a production line with ninety-eight flash drives, sheets of narrow little printed labels and a pile of bright yellow lanyards.

'Right,' says Minnie. 'I sit on this side of the table and put the labels on the flash drives, you sit there, Rumble and click the lanyards on and Luke who has tidy handwriting writes the addresses on the courier bags.'

At half past eleven Luke writes the address on the final courier bag and drops it in the box at his feet. He shakes his right hand above his head and groans. 'I might never be able to hold a pen again.'

'God, I hope it hasn't ruined your pen-spinning ability,' says Minnie and picks up her notebook. 'Let's tick off the list - just for the satisfaction of it. Press conference venue and video equipment – done. Set up a meeting with Dougal and print sample evidence - done. Flash drives – done. Transport from the hotel – Luke's cousin booked. Helicopter and lodge booked, including equipment. Cartwell's team confirmed. New email account for media and new SIM cards – we're done, yay!'

It has been a long and tedious process with frequent debates and a few heated arguments, and she can hardly believe it's finally over. It feels strange to think that all the decisions and strategies they worked so hard to develop are now fixed in place and will soon be implemented.

'End of stage two,' says Luke.

'Soon all our secrets will be out in the open – apart from this address.' Rumble reaches for his backpack. 'I'll drop the bags at the courier company now and come back later. I must say it's a bit scary. I wonder if it's going to be a slow-burner or go off with a loud bang?'

Apprehensive, but not about to let the men see it, Minnie says, 'We'll hand the whole thing over to the authorities and the press and let them deal with it all. When Jane gave me that phone, I never thought it would change my entire life. I want my life back, but I have a strange feeling it won't be my life as it used to be.'

'I know,' says Rumble with his hand on the door handle. 'This must be what parents feel when their child leaves home. Is their baby going to survive, make the right decisions, prosper? Bloody terrifying.' And on that surprising note he leaves.

43

Luke and Minnie set out to meet Dougal after a final discussion about strategy. 'I'm sure it will be fine. I trust him and we're so well prepared – what could go wrong?' asks Luke and start the car, and Minnie laughs scornfully. Good God! What could go wrong? If I could do Jane's snort, I would do it now.'

Luke casts a sideways glance at her and she grins. 'She has a master's degree in Dismissive Snorts. Unfortunately, she mostly does her famous snort when someone says something about Jordan.'

'The poor guy! I know she's bossy, but Dismissive Snorts – it sounds awful.'

'I do love her, but she's very bossy. The next turn is that little street where we'll park,' says Minnie. 'Turn left here.'

Luke locks the car and looks at her across the roof. 'Ready?'

'Yes – here's hoping it's not an ambush.'

They walk down the alley between the panel beater and the picture framer's studio, which leads to the narrow strip of unused land they spotted on Google Earth, fenced on three sides with six-foot rusty corrugated metal panels fixed to rickety wooden posts. In the far corner they arrange the recorder in a small gap between the panels and wait for Dougal to come to the fence from the street on the other side. A few minutes later they hear rustling noises, and a hesitant voice says, 'Are you there?'

'Yes, we're here. The recorder is in the gap here - between the panels.' Minnie pushes her hand through and wiggles her fingers. 'We'll show you some of the evidence after the interview.

Remember what we agreed - you can broadcast the interview tonight, and you can mention the press conference. You can say that you've seen evidence of what we told you. You can't keep the prints we show you or imply that you know who we are - and you must not follow us or take pictures.'

Dougal sounds excited and nervous. 'Yeah, no, of course - not a problem. But when you called, you said that the whole thing was about the 'Broker Corruption' and I wondered if we can use that name? You said that Broker is a code name – will his real name be on the flash drive we're getting tomorrow?'

'You can use the name Broker – it's not our name for him, it's what he calls himself,' says Luke. 'And we genuinely don't know who he or she is.'

'OK, got it. Can we start now?'

It takes four and a half minutes. They have carefully composed the questions, rehearsed their responses, and decided who will reply to which question. All Dougal needs to do is read from the script.

After the interview Minnie tells Dougal to take the recorder, and Luke passes four pages of photos and text messages through the gap. Minnie walks a distance along the fence and stands looking back towards the corner. After a couple of minutes Dougal passes the papers back to Luke, thanks them and leaves.

'What were you looking at?'

'I noticed a bigger gap in a gap in the fence along there when we arrived – I was just checking he wasn't taking photos of those papers with his phone, but he only made some notes.'

Luke laughs. 'I certainly picked the right name for you.'

Minnie shivers and makes no reply. Back in the car she adjusts the side mirror on her side and keeps her eyes on it. Amused by the charade, Luke starts the car and grins. 'Did you notice he nearly called me Luke at one point? He recovered himself just in time. I know Rumble thinks it's mad, but it's important to me that Dougal can look his producer in the face and say he didn't see us.'

The question of who should get a flash drive and whether the contents should be passworded had created an intense debate. They finally agreed that the more authorities and media got the material, the harder it would be for the government to shut it down.

'Everyone must have it,' said Minnie. 'Everyone! Police, intelligence services, the military, the various political parties, key overseas media as well as our own - the further it goes, the better it is.'

Rumble argued that the password was an unnecessary complication and gave the release an aura of artificial secrecy. He changed his mind, when Minnie pointed out that a password would ensure that media and others turned up to hear them speak at the press conference.

'The mass email Luke's sending out – and the text messages – says that the password will be handed out at the press conference, so they'll all turn up, even if their flash drive has already been delivered. They don't know that others, who can't be there, will get the password by email after the press conference.'

'And tonight, they'll hear the recorded interview we did with Dougal,' said Luke. 'And that little teaser will spread like wildfire. It's all about ramping up interest.'

'I hope Dougal keeps his word,' says Minnie now, her eyes fixed on the side mirror. 'He might get tempted to mention you by name.'

'I'm not worried about him, but his producer is another matter. If he told her that he was meeting mystery people about something big, she might have set up someone to follow us. So, we'll stick to the return route we discussed this morning.'

Minnie scans the lane behind them. 'OK so far.'

They drive into the car park under the supermarket on the Adelaide Road corner.

'Right – we'll give it a couple of minutes.'

Minnie gets out and stands beside the car looking towards the entrance they came in through, and after a couple of minutes, she gets back in.

'Only five cars have come in after us and the drivers have all gone up to the shop - we're OK.'

They drive out, turn left onto Adelaide Road and then left again at the corner and Minnie points. 'And another left again - Hanson Street. It gets narrow towards the end where you come back onto Adelaide Road. Perfect place to spot anyone following us.'

A council rubbish truck is working its way up the slope and stops just where the street narrows and they come to a halt behind it. A minute later a bulky man in a high visibility vest emerges between parked cars with two rubbish sacks in each hand and throws them effortlessly into the gaping slot at the back. Without glancing at them he walks away along the side of the truck.

'I wonder if he parks here and walks up and down the whole block. I could back up and turn down that side street behind us.'

Luke is looking in the rearview mirror with his hand on the gear shift, when a man appears beside Minnie's door. His right hand holds a gun, and his left hand reaches for the door handle, and Minnie screams, 'Watch out!' She knows without thinking that it's Dustman, and he is going to kill them.

Now everything happens very fast. Luke leaps out of the car and Dustman starts pulling the passenger door open. Minnie swivels sideways in her seat and kicks the door hard with both feet and Dustman takes an out of balance step backwards. She expects him to reach for her or to simply shoot her, but his focus has changed. He pushes the door nearly closed, trapping her feet in the gap, and takes two long strides towards the front of the car.

Minnie pulls her feet in and swings forward. Luke is in front of the car now, Dustman jumps up on the hood and everything seems to slow to a snail's pace. Dustman's hand rises and his arm straightens infinitely slowly to point the pistol down at Luke, whose hands slowly grip Dustman's ankles and heave him sideways. The gun flies in a graceful arc like a black bird in flight as Dustman topples, hits the lip of the gaping mouth at the back of the rubbish truck and lies balanced on the edge for a moment. His arms flail in a vain attempt to find something to grab on to, then he rolls into the truck and disappears from view.

Everything returns to normal speed. Luke gets back in the car, clicks the central locking button and the rubbish truck starts moving forward. Minnie stares at the rear of the truck expecting Dustman to heave himself over the edge, but instead the large hydraulic compacting blade inside the truck swings down. She can hear the heavy mechanism from inside the car.

'Luke - stop!' She has one hand on the door handle, ready to jump out and run forward to somehow stop the truck.

'No.'

Just one word, but the way he says it makes it clear that he means it; he is not going to stop. In frozen horror she watches the blade come down and push forward, compressing the load. Her skin twitches in dismay as she pictures what is happening inside the truck. The blade pressing forward with relentless force, the smell of crushed rubbish sacks, Dustman's face pressed hard against plastic, his lungs sucking for air and his body brutally squeezed, bones breaking. Her hands clench into fists as she stares at the back of the truck.

By the time the truck turns left into Adelaide Road the blade is retracting. They wait in silence to turn right, with Minnie still rigid in her seat and not a word is spoken on the way back to the flat.

44

Rumble, who has returned before them, takes one look and raises his eyebrows. 'Something went wrong?'

Minnie replies bluntly, 'Dustman is dead - Luke chucked him in a rubbish truck, and he got compacted.'

Rumble erupts in a roar of helpless laughter. 'Fucking hell! Are you serious?'

'I am very serious,' says Minnie grimly. 'He can't possibly have survived. If he wasn't crushed to death by the hydraulic ram, he got asphyxiated. And Luke refused to stop so I could alert the driver.'

They remain standing in the middle of the room while Rumble teases the story out of them. Once he gets it, he starts laughing again.

'Sorry Petal, I can see you're upset, but you can't deny it's a bloody fitting end for a guy called Dustman – ending up dead in a rubbish truck. And it's not as if Luke knew he'd get compacted, is it? Who would have thought you'd be able to throw someone that far, Luke – or even hit the target?'

'But Luke wanted to kill him – I heard him tell you the day you rescued me, he meant it. And I can't bear to think we did nothing, just let him die. If we kill people, we're as bad as Dustman is - was.'

'Now hang on, Minnie,' says Rumble reasonably. 'Let's back up a bit. Don't forget that this is the second time Dustman has tried to kill you, no it's the third time – and this time he would have killed Luke too. That guy had used up his chances.'

Luke's face is calm and unapologetic. 'Listen Minli - I didn't know he would fall into the truck. I wasn't actually thinking of where he would end up - all I was trying to do was take him by surprise, tip him over – or he would have shot both of us. He would have shot me easily and then you too – he had a perfect vantage point standing on the hood. There's no way you would have got away. I don't know why he didn't shoot you right away.'

Minnie says nothing.

'I know I said I wanted to kill him for what he did to you, and I meant it – he left you to die on that bloody mountainside. He watched the car explode in flames way down the slope and thought you were inside it - and dusted his hands off and went home for a beer. When I tipped him over, I wasn't trying to kill him, but when I realised the compactor would probably kill him, I decided to do nothing – I wanted him dead.'

She says bleakly. 'You wanted him dead.'

'Yes – I wanted him dead.'

There is a strained silence. Minnie turns to get a glass of water and she can feel their eyes on her back.

Rumble is the first to speak. 'How did it go with Dougal? Do you think he had someone ready to follow you?'

'No, Minli checked every time we turned a corner, and we made the stop in the supermarket car park, but nobody followed us. And she had a sneaky peek at Dougal, when he looked at those printouts but he didn't take any photos.'

Minnie is shocked that Luke sounds so casual, when only a minute ago he said that he wanted someone dead. It confuses and frightens her, that someone she knows and likes, can say what he just said.

She puts the glass down and leans against the kitchen bench and makes an effort to sound normal. 'I wonder how Dustman knew where we were. How did he turn up right then? And where was his car?'

'Could he have followed us and seen us getting stuck behind the truck? Maybe he found a space to park and just ran up to our car? Or is his car still sitting in the middle of Hanson Street? Did you see where he came from?' Luke looks at Minnie who finds it hard to meet his eyes, but she shakes her head and says, 'No, the first I saw was his hand with a gun right by my window.'

Rumble looks thoughtful. 'And where is the gun now? You said it flew through the air - did you pick it up?'

'Christ no,' says Luke. 'All I was thinking of was getting away before someone got a photo of us – someone could have been watching the whole thing.'

'Let's go down there and try to find the gun - we don't want it lying around for some kid to pick up. We can pretend we just found it by chance and give it to the cops or dispose of it somehow. OK?'

'All right,' says Minnie. 'And when they tip that load out at the Happy Valley landfill and push it around, they'll find Dustman and then they'll backtrack and work it out, maybe find his car. Let's go right away and see if we can find it.'

Rumble turns to Luke with a frown. 'I'm worried about your car. What if that truck driver saw you behind him?'

'I doubt it. We were very close behind him, too close for him to be able to see us in his side mirrors. And he wouldn't know where exactly Dustman went into the back of his truck – it could have been anywhere on his round. We went in different directions at Adelaide Road.'

Minnie agrees. 'He would have been watching for a gap in the traffic to turn left. And earlier, when he came to the back of the truck - he just tossed the sacks in and turned around right away. I don't think he even glanced at us.'

'OK, let's go – we can walk along the greenbelt just down the road, it runs way down towards the city.'

'At least the world is a safer place without Dustman,' says Rumble as they walk along the edge of the reserve. 'I'm sorry you're upset Minli, but I agree with Luke – once he was in that truck I don't know if I would have worried either, not after what he did to you. Though it would have been good to hand him over to the police I suppose.'

Minnie makes no comment.

45

They walk along the greenbelt, over the crest of a slope and then down along the edge of Mt Cook. People are walking dogs and riding bikes on the paths; the scene is one of normality, which makes Minnie feel as if her life is dislocated from everyone else's.

As they emerge from the track through the trees, Luke points. 'There's that playground we saw just at the end of Hanson Street. Look at the crowd!'

A diverse crowd of onlookers has gathered on the grass along Hanson Street, and they stop beside an elderly man with a poodle. Minnie bends down to pat the dog and asks innocently, 'What's happened? Has there been an accident?'

'I've only been here a couple of minutes, but I talked to a chap who lives here. He'd come over to this side to get a better view. He says they blocked off the street, because someone found a gun on the grass just here and called the police. He saw one of them putting the gun in a plastic bag, just like they do in the movies.'

'Funny place to find a gun,' says Minnie.

'Yes, very strange,' says the man with the dog. 'And now they're knocking on doors and getting people to come out to show which car is theirs - it's interesting, isn't it?'

Downhill from where they got held up by the rubbish truck, two police officers stand beside a white car, and Minnie walks past the crowd and up a little rise behind the play equipment, from where she gets a better view of the car the police are looking at. It is parked between two others at an angle with its rear end jutting out into the street. Luke and Rumble join her, and they stare the car in silence for a moment.

'I bet that's his car, look at the driver's door - it's been left half open' says Minnie thoughtfully. 'He followed us, saw us trapped behind the truck, ditched his car any which way and ran up to confront us.'

Luke nods. 'That fits – but what a crazy thing to do. I suppose he made a snap decision to get us when he had the chance.'

'Heaven knows what he was thinking. Maybe Broker said he had to eliminate us fast – but how did he know where we were going to be?'

They watch the activity for another few minutes before they start back the way they came, and Rumble says, 'Once they find the body, they'll piece it together – it might take a day or two, but they'll make the connection eventually.'

Suddenly Minnie stops. 'God, I hope nobody took a photo of us! I don't want this to come back and hit us in the face. You're easily recognized, Luke. I mean the fact that you're Chinese and your face is known from TV.'

It's impossible to assess the risk of recognition, and all they can do is wait with uncertainty hovering over them; an additional element of stress in what is already a situation of tense nerves and apprehension. They return to the flat, make cups of coffee and talk about other things, in an attempt to create some normality between the three of them again.

'OK, then,' says Luke. 'Now we wait for all hell to break loose. They'll have the teaser story tonight on the evening news as agreed, and after the press conference tomorrow it will be wall-to-wall coverage. Did we hear from Cartwell, Rumble?'

'Yeah, I forgot to say – they got their advance flash drive, he sent a message while you were out. He says he's very excited.'

'So he should be,' says Minnie, 'being given the whole thing in advance of everyone else. I just hope we have everything sorted in our minds, so what we say in the interview comes out right. There's a huge difference between talking to people, who know the same things you do, and how others understand it when they hear it for the first time.'

'By morning Cartwell will know as much as we do,' says Luke comfortably. 'He'll be very keen to get this right. When you meet him, you'll find it hard to believe he's not been part of this from the start – and he's got an amazing team.'

Rumble looks with longing at the last of the cakes he had brought with him that morning. 'I wish I could have that one too - I love custard squares.' He pushes the plate away and sighs deeply.

'Well, eat it then. I don't like them and I'm sure Luke won't mind if you have two.'

Rumble shakes his head. 'I don't think I will – Bella says the trick is to never have seconds of anything apart from fruit.'

Minnie stares at Rumble with a speculative look on her face, but all she says is, 'Ah well, in that case you'd better not eat it.'

Her eyes meet Luke's; she suppresses a smile and hides behind her mug.

When Luke is cooking and Rumble is debating whether to stay for dinner or go home, Minnie comes out of the bathroom with a towel in one hand and a pair of scissors in the other.

'Do you mind if I give you a bit of a tidy-up Rumble? How long it is since you had a haircut?'

Luke looks up and laughs at Rumble's panic stricken face. 'She's right, mate. You are too big to have so much hair.'

Rumble hesitates, but when Minnie points to a chair he sits down. She drapes the towel over his shoulders and looks despairingly at the mass of tight curls and at the small first-aid scissors in her hand.

'Rumble! When did you brush your hair last?' She pushes her free hand into his hair and laughs. 'It's like some wild creature with a life of its own. I hope there aren't mice nesting in it.'

'Oh, don't be silly – of course I don't brush it! It's un-brushable. I wash it and then it dries and that's it. Impossible bloody stuff.'

'Have you never heard of conditioner? That's what you need – it kind of takes the tangles out. And what happens when you go for a haircut – do they run screaming, when they see you coming?'

'Never been for a haircut actually,' he says in a strangled voice. 'My mum used to cut it and now I cut it myself.'

Minnie breaks down in helpless laughter and stops cutting for a moment.

'That explains a lot!'

'You're not cutting it all off, are you? I can feel my head getting colder.'

'Oh, for goodness sakes, cutting your hair is like a comedy act. Of course, I'm not cutting it all off – just trimming it a bit.'

'There's an awful lot of hair on the floor,' says Rumble suspiciously few minutes later.

'Just trust me – it's nearly finished.'

She glances at Luke, who looks as if he is about to laugh and refuses to meet her eyes.

'OK, all done - go and have a look.'

Rumble disappears into the bathroom, and they wait with bated breath for the explosion. After a moment of silence, Minnie walks quietly to the door and watches Rumble standing before the mirror with her makeup mirror in his hand, looking at himself from all sides with a little smile on his big face.

'Yes?' says Minnie. 'Will you survive the change?'

'It's awesome – I didn't know I could look this nice.' He puts the mirror down. 'You're just too clever for words, you funny little shrimp.'

In all the years they had been friends she has never interfered in his life in such a personal way, but his pleasure is a reward for the risk she took.

Luke looks critically at Rumble when he emerges from the bathroom and gives him a thumbs-up. 'Yep, very nice – you're better looking than I realised. Good move.'

46

The RNZ news at six is exactly what they had hoped for. They listen to the live broadcast on Rumble's laptop and even Luke is impressed.

'Top marks to Dougal. He got it just right, all the relevant facts, the mystery about who we are and the fact that he never saw us – shades of the Watergate saga long ago. And very good PR for the press conference. They're sure to repeat it on every news-reading tonight and first thing in the morning - and they'll try to get comments from various Government and police people, and they in turn will try to minimize it. The PM will say it's fake news or something like it – or that we are agitators, enemies of the state. And then after the press conference the shit will hit the fan in a big way.'

The TV news has the discovery of a body found in a rubbish truck as the third lead item, but there is no mention of the gun or the car in Hanson Street.

'I wonder what they're up to,' says Minnie. 'Either they know there's a connection and they're keeping it quiet or maybe they still haven't figured it out. I wish we knew – this waiting game makes me twitchy.'

Luke nods. 'I know – it's so close to the final act it seems as if even one more day is too long to wait. I'm used to being in front of the camera, but this is different. We'll be exposed to the entire country while all these powerful people are seething with fury and hoping to get away without any damage to their reputations. And probably trying to think of ways to discredit us. Not to mention the

Anti-New Zealand Activities Agency and what someone high up might get them to do.'

'God, I hope they don't manage to shut it down.' Minnie has repeatedly reviewed their findings, tried to reassure herself that what they are about to make public is convincing and powerful enough.

Rumble rubs his hands over his face and groans. 'I hate attention at the best of times. We must make some decisions tonight – I mean about Dustman's death. We must agree on what we say, if we're asked about it. It's surely more a question of when than if. We need a story we all stick to.'

'I will just own up. I'll say yes, I was defending us, and he ended up in the truck by mistake.' Luke looks at Minnie as he speaks. 'I refused to prevent the blade crushing him and I am responsible for his death, because I did nothing to stop it - and I don't regret it. I'll tell the authorities the full story and that's it. No need for anyone to tell any lies.'

'OK, I suppose that's best - and then it's up to the cops.' Rumble frowns. 'I'm still wondering how that bastard found you - and why he attacked you in broad daylight. Why didn't he just follow you to see where you were going? Could he have known you were meeting Dougal and followed you from there - and then when you got trapped by the rubbish truck, he took the opportunity? Stupid thing to do, but maybe he was frustrated by his failures. Maybe Broker was putting pressure on him – who knows? But how the hell could he have known about Dougal?'

'I know this sounds so simple it's ridiculous, but I think it was pure chance,' says Minnie. 'That supermarket serves a big area, Newtown and Berhampore and more, because people shop on their way home. Maybe he was shopping and spotted me in the underground car park. I got out of the car while we stopped there - say he saw me, got into his car and follow us. I know he hadn't followed us in, because I was keeping an eye on the entrance. Perhaps he saw me from the escalator. He knows what I look like - and stupidly I took the cap off, so that might have caught his attention.'

'OK – maybe it was just opportunity and chance. It just seems too simple, doesn't it?' Rumble shakes his head. 'He must have thought Christmas had come early, the bastard.'

'It fits perfectly,' says Luke. 'The way that car had been ditched at a crazy angle with the driver's door half open - he made a snap decision to get us while we were blocked. We've evaded him and tricked him, and he just boiled over and wanted to get the job done.'

Minnie surprises them both by abruptly changing the conversation. 'I don't want you to tell the police, Luke.' She hesitates as they both stare at her. 'You've risked so much for this thing we're fighting for – let's call it democracy. You don't deserve to end up in prison or whatever would happen. I owe you my life three times over, and I'll trade in my principles and not mention that we saw the blade compacting the rubbish after he fell into the truck.'

Luke starts to say something, and Rumble takes a step towards her, but she holds up her hand, palm towards them.

'I'm not going to discuss it - I just wanted to say it. Now can we please get on with our plans for tomorrow?' Her face sends a clear message; the topic is closed.

They go through the arrangements for the next day one last time, all of them nervous and trying to conceal it from each other.

'We've got a huge advantage now, compared to when we started planning – we know that Dustman won't stand up in the crowd and shoot us,' says Luke. 'But I can't help wondering what Broker is thinking, if he listened to the news – he must be feeling panicky. Dustman once again not responding, his own code name in the news – what next?'

Rumble reaches for his backpack, forces his laptop into it and slings the pack over his shoulder.

'Right, see you tomorrow at nine. I hope we all get some sleep - and thanks for the haircut.'

When the door closes behind him, Luke turns to Minnie. 'Off to show his new haircut to someone else, do you think?'

'Maybe – he's being very close-lipped about it, but he must have seen her since she came here that day. That bit about not having second helpings! He never said a thing like that in his life before.'

'Wait and see – if it's serious we'll soon find out.'

47

While cleaning her teeth and contemplating the green and yellow shadows of her bruises in the bathroom mirror Minnie makes a snap decision; before tomorrow she must see the pictures that Luke took at the house the night she was abducted. Until now she has refused to look at them, but suddenly she knows that she must. In the living room, Luke is watching the late news and she sits down beside him. 'Anything new?'

'They've just tried to interview Dougal and he said he has no comment other than what he said in the broadcast earlier. And nothing new about Dustman or the gun. '

'Could you do something for me, please?' She is annoyed to find that she sounds nervous. 'Can you show me the photos that you put on the flash drive, the ones you took at my house? I know I've refused to look at them, but I've just realised that I must see them before tomorrow.'

'Is that a good idea? You said you had enough material for nightmares without seeing them. I'm sure what went on that night was terrifying - what if you suddenly remember all the details? Tomorrow, you have to feel strong enough to face the press.'

'I might not remember it even if I do look at the photos. But I keep thinking of how I will feel when they appear on TV and in the papers. I must see them first, so I'm prepared.'

His face is calm, but she knows him well now, and behind the façade he is worried, but she's not going to change her mind, she must see those photos.

'All right then.' He pulls the laptop towards him. 'I'll get them up for you.'

She pretends to be calm while she waits, but her mouth is dry. She has tried so hard to reach those memories and she wonders what the images might trigger in her mind.

'Here is it – The Abduction of Minerva Porter.'

Luke gets up and she takes his place in front of the laptop. She reads what he has written describing the circumstances, what he found at the house and his and Rumble's search for her. She has read this several times and it's factual and unemotional and somehow more shocking because of that. She presses Next and there is the first picture of one end of the living room with the brandy bottle beside the armchair, the pill container on the floor, and a book lying open on the table. For some ridiculous reason she wonders which book it was that Dustman chose for a prop. She continues through the close-up pictures of the empty wine bottle on the kitchen bench, her bag on the floor beside the hall table, then an image from the drone with her curled-up shape beside the bald tree with the rag tied near the top. And then two dramatic shots of her injuries; a close-up of her scratched and bruised unconscious face, and one of her lying on her back with a towel over her torso, arms and legs scratched and bruised, covered in blood and dirt, the injury to her thigh like a stab wound. The final pictures are of her car, upside down on a steep slope among scrub and trees, crushed and broken with two doors open and the interior blackened by fire. She goes back to the beginning and looks at every detail in every shot and it triggers nothing in her mind.

Luke stands behind her, looking at the pictures he took, reliving the story from his point of view.

'I took the car photos with my phone, when I was down that slope looking for you, I don't think I told you before. It's a horrendous sight - it's a miracle that you survived. You must have been tossed out before the car did its final flip and landed where you see it – otherwise you would have died.'

'Is that last shot the gear shift?'

'Yes - when I found the car, I noticed it was in neutral, which proved you hadn't driven it over the edge - you were pushed.'

She gets up. 'Thanks – I still remember nothing, but at least I know what it looked like. It's cleverly staged, and if you hadn't found me, most people would believe what they were meant to believe. I'm going to bed now.'

48

Sleep comes slowly and with it dreams, jumbled and disjointed. And then she is in a state of half sleep; aware of being asleep, but unable to wake up and her mind finally lets her see what happened the night Dustman came for her.

She is about to go upstairs when there is a knock on the door. She looks out to see who it is - the outside light is off, but she sees a thumbs-up signal, it's Luke. She unlocks the door and Dustman shoves it hard and points a gun at her. Her breath catches in her throat, she takes a step backwards and knocks into the hall table, things fall to the floor. Her eyes are fixed on the gun in his hand. He comes closer, his face shows no emotion, the gun points at the middle of her chest. He gestures at the living room door. 'After you.'

She walks ahead of him, her mind desperately searching for an escape route. Not the back garden, fenced all around and the side gate locked. She would never be quick enough anyway, and he might shoot her if she tries. 'Sit there.' He points at the small armchair and when she obeys, he steps behind her and throws a length of fabric, maybe a scarf, around her neck. He gives it a jerk; it tightens, pulls her head back and restricts her breathing. He ties it to something and comes around to face her. He takes hold of one of her flailing hands: 'Keep still.' He fastens a cord around one wrist and then the other and her arms are pulled together around the back of the chair. He leaves the noose tight around her neck and comes to stand in front of her again; his face is hard and angry. 'You little bitch! How do you know about Broker? Who was it you were talking to on the phone the other night? I want names – now!'

She shakes her head, lips pressed tight together. He hits her hard across the side of her face, she says nothing, and he does it again. Her eyes fill with tears of pain and she wonders if he will kill her if she doesn't answer. He hits her again, a vicious blow with his closed fist in the middle of the chest and she gasps for breath. Her heart misses a beat and images of people being beaten to death flash into her mind.

How much can she take? Can she hold out until she is unconscious and safe from his questions? She must focus all her mental strength on staying silent until she loses consciousness: moans and cries, yes, but no names. He hits her again and again and shouts questions at her. She groans, her breathing is laboured but she says nothing, her entire focus internal.

He disappears in the direction of the kitchen, and she hears him talking to someone, then he comes back with a glass of water and puts it on the table she can just see by looking sideways. He takes a white plastic cylinder out of his pocket, unscrews the blue lid and puts it beside the glass. Is he going to drug her, take her away? Or is he going to poison her and make it look like suicide? Don't swallow, she tells herself, keep your mouth shut – don't swallow!

He puts one hand over her face from above and pinches her nostrils together. She tries to bite him, but she can't twist her head far enough to reach. Abruptly he pushes her head right back until it's tilted over the back of the chair. Her heartbeats feel like thumps inside her chest. She tries to kick him, but he is standing beside the chair, out of reach. He says, 'now swallow these like a good girl' and puts two pills in her mouth, tilts the glass and floods her throat with water. She can't breathe – she is drowning, her nose is held shut and she tries to swallow, the pills stick and she gags, he pours more water down her throat.

He lets go of her nose and allows her to raise her head, reaches inside his jacket and brings out a flat bottle, takes the cap off. Her eyes are full of tears and she is coughing and gulping for air, but before she has time to recover, he does it again. His fingers hold her nose shut, her head forced back and the neck of the bottle is in her mouth – brandy! The drink that nearly brought her to ruin years ago.

She is devastated; her mind rebels – no! not alcohol after all this time! The seductive fumes of strong alcohol and the characteristic brandy smell flood her senses. She will drown if she doesn't swallow, so she swallows and then she swallows some more. And her brain is fuzzy and slipping sideways into a blissful state where she seems to float - and then nothing.

She comes to; it's cold, and she feels sick. A man's voice, 'no seatbelt, just close the door' and another man says, 'OK, now we push – bye, darling!'

She is tumbling and the world is breaking up in a cacophony of noise: metal crushing and snapping, glass breaking - and then darkness.

She tries to wake up but remains suspended between consciousness and sleep. The scene starts again, like a loop of film. She is desperate to wake up, but she can't.

... she is about to go upstairs when there's a knock on the door. Someone is holding her nose and her head is pushed right back and her throat is flooded with water and pills. She is drowning....

Someone holds her and talks insistently right beside her ear. 'It's all right - wake up, it's just a dream – it's OK now, you're safe.'

A comforting hand strokes her back and slowly, slowly her mind disentangles itself from the tentacles of terror, and she knows she is awake and safe. But now the knowledge of what happened that evening lies cold and heavy in her chest, and she is overwhelmed by despair.

'Brandy! He made me drink brandy - and I liked it! Now it's all ruined.'

His voice is calm and reasonable. 'That's OK, you're allowed to like it and you haven't done it since, have you? Have you?'

Reason slowly returns and she says weakly, 'No.'

'So that's all right then – if you haven't craved a drink since then, there's no need to worry.'

She feels mentally mangled, and her mind is slow to process the present reality.

'Sorry - I'm all right now.'

The arms remain tight around her. 'There is no need to be sorry. It's over and you're not alone, and if anyone harms you again, I will kill them with my bare hands.'

She drifts into a light sleep, halfway between reality and dream. Later she wakes again, and the memory of that evening is clear in her mind. His arm is holding her firmly from behind, and she lies very still, breathes slowly and goes through it over and over until she knows she has completely processed all she can remember, all the details are clear. Now she must tell him. She can't sleep until she has told someone every single detail of what happened that night.

'Luke, I have to tell you - now.'

He replies instantly, as if he wasn't asleep a moment earlier. 'All right, tell me.'

And she talks and talks, repeating herself and stumbling over words, until she has told him everything, until she is certain nothing has been left out and the brutality and terror of what happened is understood by someone else. When she finally runs out of words, he says nothing, just pulls her closer. Exhausted, she shuts her eyes and falls asleep.

49

When she wakes the grey light of early dawn is bleaching the darkness. She has turned over under his arm in her sleep and her right leg is hooked over his. He is deeply asleep, his breath warm and slow against her forehead. She kisses his shoulder and whispers 'thank you', and his hand starts slowly stroking her back, rubbing a lazy circle across scar tissue and undamaged skin, creating the illusion that her back is one continuous surface. Her breath catches in her throat, and she dares not move in case he stops. She feels his body respond and his hand moves lower, a smaller circular motion at the base of her spine. And then the movement stops, and she knows from his breathing that he's awake.

'I thought you said you're gay?' He sounds as if he has been awake for hours, straight to the point.

'I did.'

'But you like this – I can feel it.'

'Yes.'

'Do you want me to continue?'

'Yes, please.'

Smothered laughter. 'Such politeness!'

Much later, bodies cooling, side by side with shoulders touching on the mattress that is only slightly wider than a single, he turns his head and looks at her in the early morning light. 'So, you lied.'

'Yes.'

'I want to ask you two things and this time it would be really great to get more than a single word for an answer. Why did you lie?'

She only hesitates or a moment. 'Because then I wouldn't have to try to stall any advances from you, but I could continue seeing you.'

He is silent for a moment, thinking this over. 'You never had sex before? Was that the reason?'

'Yes – more or less.'

Now the silence lasts longer, and she can think of nothing to say. Finally, he moves his arm and covers her hand with his. 'Tell me why.'

She has never told anybody apart from Rumble, and even then, she was only able to talk about it when she was drunk. He had asked her to explain why she was drinking so much and what he could do to help.

'I was in love. It was the first year of my master's and I'd never been to bed with anyone, because of my ugly body - I had never dared take my clothes off in front of anyone. We were in my room - he was pulling my clothes off, and he turned me around to undo my bra.'

She stops, wishes she doesn't have to say it, but there is no going back.

'He backed away so fast he nearly fell over and ... and he said 'God, that's revolting - I can't touch it!' And picked up his things and left, nearly ran out the door.'

He says nothing, but his hand tightens round hers. As if to punish herself she decides to tell him the worst part, the bit that makes her cringe even now, and she continues, tries to sound unemotional. 'Later on, I overheard a conversation in the cafeteria, not mentioning my name, but it had to be about me – he had told someone the sight of me made him gag, that I looked like the lizard woman from some horror movie.'

He raises himself on his elbow and looks down at her. 'Minli, remember what I said – if anyone hurts you again, I kill them.'

She knows he means it and it fills her with foreboding and revulsion and love – a doom-laden combination of emotions, impossible to untangle.

Can any good come of this? Is it possible to have a relationship, long or short, with someone so fundamentally alien? He functions on a different level than anyone she has ever met; he is gentle and kind and intelligent, but he is also physical on an immediate and nearly primitive level.

She looks at the face so close to hers, so calm and serious, and thinks, he's an animal, beautiful and gentle looking, you want to reach out and touch him, but I think he really will kill, if he thinks he must. And his assessment of what is a 'must' is not something I can understand or accept.

50

They arrive at the hotel's staff entrance within minutes of each other, Luke and Minnie by taxi and Rumble on foot. It's raining and Minnie is hoping Rumble will turn up in his improvised rain cape; she is looking forward to Luke's expression when he sees it. But Rumble wears a new all-weather jacket and looks tidier than usual.

'I like the jacket, Rumble. Not quite as much as I like the rain cape, but nearly. And the haircut is nice, too.'

He grins. 'I caught sight of my reflection in a shop window on the way here and I didn't realise it was me.'

The functions manager is short and chubby and has a bad cold. He takes them to a small room behind the conference room on the second floor, furnished with a table, six chairs and a water cooler.

'After the event we'll escort you to the goods lift at the back of the building.' He makes a desperate grab for a handkerchief, sneezes twice and rubs his already red nose. 'The van will be in the basement delivery bay – nobody will be able to pester you.'

He sneezes again, blows his nose and dabs at his eyes. 'Please stay here while I go and check the room.'

He leaves the door open, and they hear him talking to someone, then he sneezes again. Luke looks at Rumble over Minnie's head. 'Thank God he's so short - you and I are probably out of the immediate spray zone.'

Before Minnie can comment, the manager returns, smiling now.

'Everything's in place. The first row of chairs is five meters back from the stage and we have three security guards on duty - two at the entrance and one on the stage, facing the room, just as you specified. He's been told to keep his eyes on the audience at all times.'

Rumble nods. 'Thank you - and the cameras?'

'Yes, one in each corner of the room so all angles are covered, as you requested. Anything else?'

'It sounds good - thank you. The balance of the money was paid last night.' He waits for the man to leave. 'Maybe the security is a bit over the top now that Dustman's gone - unless Broker has another heavy waiting in the wings. And by the time we go to bed tonight, the Cartwell interview will be over too. And then we wait for the reactions.'

'God, Rumble!' says Minnie. 'You haven't told me what all this is costing. I'll pay my share into your account if you tell me how much it is. And Luke, you too – those ferry tickets for Ling and me, and my clothes. God, I must owe you both a fortune! I can't believe I've left it so long, it's like I've been living in a vacuum.'

'Don't worry about it now,' says Rumble. 'I earn more money than I know what to do with, so it's not urgent and it's worth every cent. We'll sort it later.'

Luke opens the door a crack and peers through.

'Wow – a big crowd already.' He looked at his watch. 'And still ten minutes to go – this is going to be epic.'

Perhaps we should have decided to wear masks after all, thinks Minnie. They debated this issue back and forth over a couple of days the previous week and changed their minds more than once. Rumble provided the clinching argument when he said, 'If we haven't got the guts to stand up and show who we are, then we buy into this fucking sleaze mentality that seems to be spreading everywhere. We'd be like Broker, hiding in the shadows. I say we just front up.' And that had been the final word.

'This is the scariest bloody thing I've ever done,' says Rumble now, an anxious frown on his face, and they sit in silence until it's time to walk through the door and out onto the stage on the dot of nine. The room is full, camera crews are lined up along the sides and people stand in double rows at the back. It's hard to know where to look, so Minnie, seated between the men at the long table, fixes her gaze in the middle distance and tries to stop her eyes from roving.

Then Luke picks up the microphone and rises to his feet. Slowly the noise dies down, nobody moves, and the huge room looks like a video clip in freeze-frame mode. He says nothing for a long ten seconds, and then he speaks very quietly and there is not a sound to be heard apart from his voice.

'Thank you for coming. My name is Luke Wong, and I am here with Minerva Porter and Peter Smith. As we stated in the press release, we won't answer any questions today, but I will explain why you were invited. By the end of today, all of you should have received a flash drive by courier. The drive contains every piece of evidence we have found about the Broker Corruption. Identical flash drives will be delivered to the Prime Minister, Government Departments, legal bodies, international media and various authorities, including police and intelligence services.'

He pauses briefly and glances at Minnie and Rumble.

'We have discovered a network of corruption and dishonesty among the top tier of politicians and state servants that also stretches into the police and judicial systems. We organized this press conference for two reasons. We want to expose the corruption to the world and make it impossible for people in powerful positions to suppress the evidence. Our second reason is purely selfish – you are our life insurance. We have put absolutely everything we have found on the flash drive and by the end of today you will know all that we know. There is nothing further to be revealed, so there is nothing to be gained by trying to silence us, either through official channels or by illegal means. The evidence on the flash drive is diverse. Some of the material has come our way indirectly, some of it we have unearthed by research over a period of time, and some we have obtained from others who, willingly or unwittingly, gave us access to it. We won't be available for comments or questions until the day after tomorrow.'

He pauses as if he is thinking, but Minnie knows he wants to maximize the impact of what he is about to say.

'This is the first time we have come out in the open and made our identities public. If something unexpected happens to one of us I hope the world will insist on finding out what happened and who caused it. Corrupt officials could complicate or delay investigations, and attempts might be made to divert attention or shift blame, or someone might want to eliminate us.'

He pauses again and then he speaks louder. 'Those who masterminded this systematic corruption have already tried to silence us. Minerva was drugged, abducted and pushed over the edge of the Remutaka mountain road in her car – we found her and rescued her. She was attacked and threatened with a gun in central Wellington – that attack was averted by a bystander. And just recently a gunman tried to kill Minerva and myself in broad daylight. The incident in Parliament not long ago, when a gun was delivered to a Minister during a debate, also pertains to this story. Details of these incidents and why and how they happened are on the flash drive. This story starts with Minerva. She will tell you how it began, and what prompted her to start this dangerous investigation.'

He hands the microphone to Minnie and sits down. She is calm now; all her nervous tension has drained away during Luke's introduction. She gets up and walks around the table to the very edge of the stage and sees TV cameras tracking her as she moves. She looks out over the audience and every face is turned towards her, and the silence is like a physical presence.

'Some time ago I was handed a cell phone identical to my own that a friend thought I had dropped. I unlocked it using my own PIN and discovered it was somebody else's when I opened the message folder. What I found there was so startling that I decided to investigate further. Even at that initial stage it was clear that it involved people who had something serious to hide. I wasn't going to risk handing the phone over to someone who might deny that it had ever existed, because many of the acronyms and initials were clearly those of Government Departments, legal structures and global business interests. Before long I was certain that this involved some of those we have elected to positions of trust and that they were misusing their powers for personal gain.'

She turns to the table and smiles at Rumble. 'This investigation would never have happened without my friend Peter Smith, who dealt with the technical aspects and provided ideas and moral support. I had no idea how to find out where the messages had come from and who was involved, or whose phone it was. Peter made sure we left no traces of our inquiries and provided resources of many kinds. From the very beginning we realised that we might put ourselves in danger, but it was much more dangerous than we thought at the outset. As you heard, I was threatened by a gunman outside Te Papa and Luke saved me – he was the bystander who intervened.'

Ha, she thinks, Luke didn't know I was going to add that bit, but no way would I leave it out. 'My home was invaded, and I was beaten, drugged and abducted. They pushed me off a steep mountain road in my car, and they thought they had killed me. I didn't die, however, and thanks to Peter and Luke, I was rescued, and since then I have been in hiding. Only the other day Luke and I were confronted by a man with a gun and once again we escaped thanks to Luke's presence of mind. The person who masterminds the corruption calls him or herself Broker and that is exactly what he or she is – a broker who facilitates the contacts and the transfer of bribes and favours between big international business interests and New Zealand Government Ministers and top-level state servants and also foreign governments. This involves way more than the odd free holiday – this involves huge sums of money, so we presume Broker has an effective money laundering operation and charges a fee in proportion to each transaction. He has a helper code-named Dustman, who does his dirty work and a middleman, who does the legwork.'

Someone in the audience drops something with a clatter and she jumps, instantly alert, then continues.

'We don't know the identity of either of these men. We believe that Broker is not known to any of his contacts and never meets with them. We think that Dustman carries out Broker's practical tasks, acts as an enforcer and threatens those of Broker's victims, who no longer want to cooperate. When I say victims, I mean those he has blackmailed instead of bribing to achieve the results his foreign clients want. We won't answer questions today, but we're available from the day after tomorrow. Details of how to contact us are on a label on the flash drive and also in the first document you'll see when you log on with the password. We expect that the authorities will want to talk to us, but because we don't know which branches of security, police or defence might have been corrupted - or who reports to someone corrupt at a higher level - we demand that all our dealings with official bodies are independently video-recorded with our own equipment. We also reserve the right to make public all recordings of interviews and meetings, if our safety or integrity demands it.'

Minnie walks back to the table and stands behind her chair, Rumble and Luke both turn to look up at her. 'And finally, I want to say that the fallout from this scandal will inevitably hurt many innocent people, family members of corrupt politicians and officials, and perhaps those who work for them. I am truly sorry for the pain that awaits many who never did any harm themselves, but this story is too big to ignore. If democracy is to have a future, it's essential that we deal with this here and now, as openly as is possible. The password that opens the files on the flash drive is 'shame' – lower case letters. That's all we have to say today. Thank you for coming.'

The men rise. There are a few moments of silence as they walk across the stage and then, just before they disappear, the room erupts with loud voices and chairs being shoved aside in a hurry. The guard lets them through, closes the door behind them and remains on the other side.

51

The woman who is waiting for them gets up from her chair. 'Hi, I'm Emily. I'll take you down to the basement. Your driver arrived half an hour ago.'

They pick up their overnight bags and jackets and follow her down to the delivery area in the basement where Luke's cousin Conrad sits in the front seat of his work van reading the paper. When he sees them coming, he gets out and opens the sliding side door.

'One of you can sit in the front if you like - sorry there aren't any proper seats in the back, but I threw in the kids' beanbags for you.'

'Thanks, but we'll all sit in the back,' says Rumble. 'The whole point is that nobody spots us.'

Sitting on a beanbag in the otherwise empty van, Minnie looks out through the tinted rear windows as they drive up the ramp to street level.

'This must be what it's like to be a star, trying to avoid the press.'

'Or a criminal not wanting to be photographed on his way to court,' says Rumble. 'Hey - you guys did really well in there. Very clear and concise, and everything covered. I suppose it's the advantage being a TV person and a teacher - you're used to talking in front of a lot of people. I couldn't have said a word without tripping myself up. You make a good team.'

Images from the night appear uninvited in Minnie's head, she meets Luke's eyes and feels her face colour.

'I was so nervous, Rumble – really stressed out right up until I started talking. That's why I walked forward instead of staying at the table - it's what I do in class. I hadn't expected such a big crowd.'

Luke shakes his head in disbelief. 'I couldn't believe that you went to stand at the edge of the stage like that – I was only too pleased to stay where I was. I'm used to being in front of a camera, but not a crowd like that. I've never seen too many media people in one place before – I bet everyone we invited turned up, and then you add the camera and sound people. Possibly the largest collection of media I've seen in one place in my whole career. And now we're on dozens of phone cameras too. I bet some of them live-streamed it on the Internet.'

'Hey guys, are you comfortable?' Conrad looks over his shoulder. 'How are the kids' beanbags?'

'They're fine,' says Luke grimly, 'but thank God they don't slide around. The way you drive around corners, Conrad!'

Soon Minnie is feeling car sick, and Rumble shifts restlessly on his beanbag as if he is uncomfortable and calls out to Conrad, 'Where are we now?'

'Just coming up to the gates. I checked on the Internet this morning and I know where to go, but one of you guys will have to do the talking or they won't let me drive in.'

The helicopter pilot is waiting at the hangar; he smiles broadly when he sees Minnie.

'Well, hi there.' He takes her hand in both his. 'I'm really glad to see you looking better than you did last time I saw you.'

She grips his hands hard. 'I want to thank you for that, you saved my life! I've never been so glad to see anything in my life – not that I remember much.'

He pats her shoulder and says gruffly, 'I don't think you had a lot of time left in you when we found you, girl. I'm glad we made it in time.'

They land on an expanse of tussock in front of a country lodge, high on the volcanic plateau in the centre of the North Island, with small chalets scattered among wind-stunted trees. The pilot helps them lift their bags out, accepts an envelope from Rumble, shakes his hand and lifts off. Minnie looks at Rumble with raised eyebrows and he grins. 'Cash payment – he's a good guy.'

The lodge manager has heard the helicopter and comes out to escort them to their villa. 'Just come and find me when you have settled in.'

The picture window in the chalet's living room frames a spectacular view of the two snow-topped volcanoes outlined against the sky and draws Minnie irresistibly forward.

'My God – look at this view, guys. I didn't realise there would be snow so early in the year! Imagine seeing this every day instead of buildings.'

Rumble joins her at the window. 'A bit quiet for my taste - very nice view, but I like to know I'm in the middle of a city full of people, even if I never meet them.' And Minnie laughs and shakes her head at how he seems to suddenly surprise her after all the years they have known each other and wonders if it is the influence of Bella that is changing him.

In a biting wind, they walk along a stone-flagged path to the main building, and Rumble steers them towards a terrace with double glass doors.

'To the right inside this door - I checked the floor plan on the website.'

The room they enter is a large lounge with a stone fireplace big enough to stand up in, and groups of leather armchairs arranged to take in the view, but before they can head for the conference room the manager comes towards them from a door at the far side.

'Ah, there you are. The group in the other helicopter has just been in touch and said they're about forty minutes away. We can serve a late lunch as soon as they have settled in if that suits?'

He makes a sweeping gesture around the lounge. 'You're welcome to use any of the facilities as you wish, of course, but I hope you'll find everything you asked for in the conference room. Come with me and I will show you where it is.'

A couple of minutes later, he leaves them in a large room with a long table set for lunch at one end, a group of four small armchairs in a semi-circle in the centre and at the far end two tables with straight-backed chairs lined up along both sides and a gigantic TV screen.

Rumble stands in the middle of the room and studies the layout. 'Hm, it looks about right and I made sure they've used the USB ports on the TV and know that it works. But if all fails, I think we can chrome cast straight from your laptop, Luke – and I brought a bunch of cables just as insurance. What do you think about those chairs for the interview?'

'They're OK. Enough room for cameras on both sides.' He removes a couple of side tables and pushes three of the chairs into a tighter curve and one a bit further to the side. 'That's better – good clear line of sight for the cameras from both sides. You should sit in the middle, Minli, with Rumble and me on either side.'

'I can't get enough of this view,' says Minnie. 'Come over here and enjoy it while you can, guys. Soon we'll be too busy to notice.'

They discuss the coming interview standing side by side with their eyes fixed on the distant snow glistening in the intermittent sunshine.

'I'm sure he'll ask if we used any illegal methods like hacking - people are bound to speculate.' Luke's gaze shifts briefly from the view to Rumble. 'It's important for Cartwell's reputation that this isn't a soft interview – he's got to protect his credibility and ask the hard questions. So, let's have our answer ready.'

Rumble groans. 'I'm no good at talking – you guys will have to do most of it.'

'Don't worry – you'll be fine,' says Minnie, trying to be comforting and bracing at the same time. 'If we have our responses rehearsed - at least for the tough questions – we'll be fine. We should have done this earlier.'

She turns and leans against the windowsill, so she can look at both of them but mainly concerned about Rumble and his reluctance to be in the spotlight.

'When he asks if we used illegal methods, Luke could say something like "we had to use some doubtful methods, possibly illegal". A bit vague, forehead creased in concern – you know how to do that Luke. Make it sound like an ad hoc reply. And I can say, "but it was us or them, you know, there was no way we could unravel this without using whatever was available" and then Luke says, "we had nowhere to turn, there was no way we could be sure who was involved in various authorities, so we didn't dare go to the police or the intelligence service or anyone really". And then you can chip in with the clinching rationale Rumble – say something like "we were fully aware that if they had killed us, like they tried to, this might have gone undetected for ever". Which I think should be enough to shut everyone up, don't you?'

'You're bloody good at this, Minli,' says Rumble, marginally more cheerful. 'You always were, even as a little girl. I remember how you used to tell me the stories from the books you were reading, the whole plot - I used to love it. Let's do just what you just said, it sounds like the right mix of being honest and justifying what we did at the same time. Let's go through it again.'

52

The rest of the day is a continuum of discussions, note taking and occasional negotiations. Compromises must be reached about the best way to present some of the evidence, and Luke tries hard to make sure that each question is phrased to give them the best opportunity to reply in full. They constantly refer to the material from the flash drive displayed on the large TV screen, making sure that the facts and chronology covered in the interview will be accurate, and that nothing relevant is left out.

'You must have been up all night going through it – you seem to have it nearly by heart,' says Minnie. 'It's a lot of stuff to remember.'

The producer turns from the large whiteboard where she is making notes. 'My God, all those text messages! Material for weeks to come once we start deciphering more of it. We've already started researching the main players, the ones you've identified so far. And we found out a bit more that might interest you – to do with the court system, a couple of judges, mainly by checking cases relating to things mentioned in the messages and initials.' She shakes her head. 'Makes it sound so easy, but we've had a whole team working on this, getting a first hint and then drilling down. Well, nothing definite so far, but intriguing and lots more work to do. We'll tell you later, but we must get this interview done first. We'll be doing follow-up on this for a long, long time – it's no seven-day wonder.'

Cartwell raises his head from his notepad. 'You know what drives me crazy? That we can't get any kind of clue about this Broker guy. I mean, how the heck does he do it? He must know a lot of key people, but he's managed to stay anonymous. And somehow, he still convinced people to trust him, well not all of them – some he obviously blackmailed, but even so. He's got an impressive line-up of so-called assets at his disposal.'

Luke turns from the camera man he is talking to and joins them.

'Exactly – a while ago Rumble and I debated if we should try to winkle Broker out of his hole by releasing information piece by piece, but we decided not to try. It was too dangerous at the time, because even then we worried that Dustman would ID Minli. Now it's different, but we have nothing to bait him with. We could let it leak out that we're close to identifying him, I suppose. And then either someone will suddenly move to some country we don't have an extradition treaty with and take up a life of total luxury – which would be a bit of a give-away. Or else he'll come after us in a big way and try to kill us as punishment, now that he knows who we are.'

Minnie says quietly to Rumble, 'We keep calling Broker 'he', but it could be a woman, you know. Someone who is or was in Government or high up in the civil service – or someone who sees herself as the power behind the elected legislators, who has an agenda of her own. Maybe she sits on boards of directors, perhaps she wants to make this country a totally commercial enterprise with far less scrutiny and less democratic insight - and bigger profits for business? It has to be someone who knows everybody. I can think of two such women without even trying, possibly three.'

Luke hears her and nods agreement. 'So can I - three actually and maybe more.'

Cartwell laughs. 'Yeah, and I can guess who you're thinking of. And perhaps Broker isn't motivated by politics or profit, maybe it's all about manipulation and a sense of power – ego driven.'

By quarter past seven the interview is recorded, and they are ready for dinner. Lodge staff bring in a drinks trolley and set the table.

'Cheers! This is the most explosive material we've ever worked with,' says the producer and raises her glass of wine. 'Thanks for letting us get the first interview.'

Over dinner they watch replays of the evening news from various TV channels and Luke continually checks websites on his phone.

'That's pretty amazing,' says Cartwell after they have watched the final news reading. 'Obviously they would show clips from your media event, but that TV One screened the whole event! Incredible – that's a heck of a long item for the news. Great impact.'

'It's gone viral,' one of the cameramen looks up from his phone. 'It's all over all social media and spreading like wildfire. The YouTube video of your media conference has had eighty-nine thousand views in two hours - you're as popular as a medium famous rapper. No need for us to do anything.'

53

It is after eleven when they walk back to their chalet in the freezing high-altitude night with thick frost on the ground and blazing stars seeming impossibly close. They're exhausted, but too full of nervous energy to go to bed. Minnie goes to wash the TV make-up off her face and returns to the living room to find Rumble sprawled in an armchair with a beer and Luke at his laptop.

'I can't wait to see the papers tomorrow. God, I'm glad it's over.' Rumble holds up his bottle to the light and checks the contents.

'Why do you always do that?' asks Minnie. 'Are you worried that one day there will be something in the bottle, like a dead mouse or something?'

'Nah, I just want to make sure I know how much is left – contingency planning.'

'I'll bet you a hundred dollars that not a single top politician – and that includes the Prime Minister – will front up on the news tomorrow,' says Luke. 'They'll send out some sort of bland statement saying they are going to need time to look into things, and that's all we'll get for a couple of days.'

Minnie sinks down on the sofa and lets her head flop back; suddenly she has no energy left.

'Being here is like being in limbo.' She yawns. 'I hope the media can't find us.'

'I wouldn't think anyone can.' Rumble yawns in sympathy. 'I got Bella to book for us all including Cartwell's team – Luke told Cartwell we'd do that, so we got privacy. Bella used her own debit card and her name - we paid for the press conference venue the same way. She didn't mention who we were or what the context was. The conference venue asked a few questions and she said what I had told her to say - if they couldn't do it the way she wanted, she would go elsewhere. I transferred money to her account, so her name was the only one involved. But I'm pleased you feel safe, Petal - that's good, just what I wanted.'

He yawns again. 'I'm off to bed. We'll deal with emails tomorrow.'

Luke looks up from his screen. 'Are you going to bed too, Minli?'

'Yes, I think I will.'

He shuts his laptop and gets up. 'I'm glad today went so well. The real media circus will start tomorrow.'

She nods, slightly unsettled by this casual stance. 'I know – the end of seclusion and peace.'

Lying on her back in the huge bed she looks up at the dark ceiling and tries to sort out what she had expected and why she feels disappointed. Despite her conflicting feelings about him, she wanted Luke to come to her and had assumed he would, but he had seemed - what? Distant, not interested? Had she been a disappointment in bed, did he not enjoyed it as much as she did? But in her heart, she knows that the most likely explanation is that he is pulling back, that he can sense that something in his nature distresses and repels her.

It's laughable, she thinks, here I am, until very recently a thirty-eight-year-old virgin and now in a quandary about a sexual relationship. How ridiculous, I'll go to sleep and think about it tomorrow.

But sleep evades her, and she gets out of bed to stand in front of the bathroom mirror as if studying her face for clues, and then she does something she hasn't done in years. She pulls her sleep T-shirt over her head and taking her makeup mirror she turns around and looks at her back and side. It's exactly as bad as it was last time she looked. It isn't hurting just now, but she can feel the outline of pain in her mind when she looks at the thick slabs of ridged scar tissue. Perhaps it is too much to expect that anyone would be able to look at it and not feel an urge to look away. She turns slightly and raises her left arm to see the area where the scars cover a portion of the side of her breast and sees Luke reflected in the mirror, standing in the dark bedroom watching her. He makes no comment on what she is doing.

'Come to bed Minli, I want to make love to you.'

She puts the mirror down, turns the light off and walks towards him. 'How long have you been there? I didn't hear you come in. I thought you weren't coming.'

'I know,' he says, calmly matter of fact. 'I felt it. I would have liked you to come to me. But then I realised you were getting upset, and I thought you might be worrying about why I hadn't come to you.'

She hears the smile in his voice and sits down on the edge of the bed in the dark room, suddenly confused, nearly frightened. 'You knew what I was thinking?' Her hands are gripped tightly together and she makes an effort to relax.

'I often know what you are feeling, when you are upset or scared – not your actual thoughts, just the effect it has on you.'

He pauses for a moment, and when she makes no response he continues, sounds hesitant, as if he doesn't expect her to believe him.

'I know it sounds weird, but I sensed a lot of your feelings when Dustman got into your house. I didn't know why you were so terrified, but I knew you thought you would die. That's why I went tearing over to your place. And then everything was a blank for hours, nothing, no fear and no panic – I thought you were dead. But early the next morning I knew you were alive - I felt your fear and pain when you woke up. I couldn't tell Rumble - he would have thought I was crazy. He thought you were dead, quite convinced - he just wanted to find you.'

He gets into the bed from the far side. 'Are you going to sit on the edge of the bed all night?'

'No, but this is so weird - I can't believe that you can feel what I feel. I don't understand it. Why didn't you tell me earlier?'

She slides in under the covers and he puts an arm over her; their faces are nearly touching, but it's too dark to see his expression.

'How could I have told you? You said you were gay and that confused me. I couldn't understand why I could feel your reactions if there was no connection. I had some doubts about your gay status early on, but Rumble confirmed it, so I stepped back and tried to figure it out.'

The situation is surreal; she has never believed in ESP, but maybe she is wrong? It feels as if the earth is shifting under her feet, as if her reference points have moved, and her scientist persona demands proof.

'So, what was I feeling just before you came in?'

'I was in bed reading, wondering what you were doing. Then I felt your worry and then suddenly you were very upset - I had a flash of something intense, disgust or something like it, quite an angry feeling.'

His hand rubs gently across her back. 'And I knew without a doubt that you were either looking at your back or thinking of it and punishing yourself for being what you call 'ugly'. So, I got out of bed and came through to tell you that the rest of you is beautiful.'

Much later she continues the conversation. 'How many people are you mentally tuned into – if that's the expression?'

'Until I met you it was only Bella. It started when she was a tiny little thing. I had no idea that my parents didn't pick up her feelings the same way I did. I never thought of why it was only Bella's feelings that I sensed – well, I was a child - and it's been like that ever since. When she broke her toe a couple of years ago, I was at Ling's place, and I said I had to call Bella because she'd hurt herself, and there she was, in a friend's car on her way to the Emergency Department with a bad gash on her knee and a broken toe.' He laughs quietly. 'Ling thinks it's too spooky for words - she says she wishes I'd never told her, and she never wants to hear a word about it again.'

'What did you sense when I was lost in the mountains? Did you really feel my emotions from that far away?'

'I don't think distance has anything to do with it, but it might if it's really far away - I don't know. I knew you were alive, and I knew you were in pain and frightened. I felt it very strongly when you despaired of ever being found, when you thought you might not survive - not in so many words, but I got the gist of it and it drove me crazy.'

She hesitates, uncertain of how to tell him, but she knows that she must. He has been completely frank and told her things that she could have ridiculed and dismissed as nonsense and it would be unfair not to tell him.

She takes a deep breath: 'I heard you, your whisper.'

Telling him is admitting the reality of it, making it impossible to pretend that it was just her own thoughts taking the form of words in the back of her mind.

'What whisper – when?' He is genuinely surprised.

'Many times, in two or three different contexts. The first time was that night outside the museum - a whisper in my head that told me to be calm and not panic or something like that, when Dustman grabbed me. I thought it was my own common sense, like my mind talking to itself.'

She pauses and tries to decide how to explain the next part, but it's hard to describe.

'And then several times after they pushed me off the Remutaka road – when I was in pain or distressed, a voice in my head would whisper something encouraging. I wondered if it was stress, if I was no longer in control of my mind - or if I'd been given drugs. But it was your reactions to what I experienced – it makes total sense. The whisper was vague and far off somehow, but it didn't feel as if I was telling myself, it was like someone was telling me to be brave and not give in.'

She hears him draw a deep breath of surprise. 'Bella can't hear me, my whisper as you call it. Between her and me it's strictly one-way.'

He puts his hand on her cheek. 'I'm really glad you heard me when you were down that bloody mountainside– at least you got some comfort. I wish I had known then that I could reach you.'

Later she lies awake beside him as he sleeps, deeply disturbed by what he has told her and paradoxically also disturbed, not only by what she told him, but by the fact that she told him at all. None of it makes sense, but she can't deny that Luke has proved how accurate his perceptions are. She had felt as if the whisper was coming from outside her head, but she dismissed it as a reaction to an extreme situation. Telling him about it has acknowledged an undeniable bond, a slightly frightening new dimension that she suspects can't be broken by any conscious act from her side.

She has to accept that he feels some of her emotions, particularly those of fear and worry, and that he has no control over the experience. But how? He can't explain it – why only with Bella and with her? Is it love or some mental connection different from love? Will she be able to have a relationship with him or should she stop this now? And if she stops it, will he still be able to feel her emotions?

The way he said he would kill anyone who hurts her, that's the sort of thing people might say for effect or when they are out of control angry, but it's different with him. He actually means it, and it doesn't worry him to say it. He is simply stating a fact – he's prepared to kill someone as punishment for what they have done. It's astonishing, so primitive and without conscience, like someone from centuries ago.

Can she have even a casual sexual relationship with someone so different from what she thinks is acceptable? It's as if he's two people, one she can love deeply and one that repels her. And why is she not at all frightened of him, never has been? She has always trusted him completely, and she knows he would never harm her whatever changes between them. It's ridiculous, she can't know that, but she does. There are things about him that are so appealing, he's so physical - that attracted her from the start, that animal quality. But she doesn't know how to cope with his uncompromising revenge instinct - or is it more like a determination to punish those who would harm and kill and go unpunished themselves? She was brought up to consider the ethics of everything she does, and according to her belief system he has no morals in some respects. Or is there more than one code of ethics, another system of rating right and wrong, but equally valid, some older world order that he is part of?

Eventually sleep claims her and when she wakes in the morning, she is alone in the bed. She turns her head and looks at the pillow with the imprint of his head, reaches out and puts her hand on it. The contradictions in his character and her reservations about him disturb her deeply. And, she thinks, he probably feels those emotions right now and wonders what I am thinking. I will have to develop a technique to block him. She switches her mind to a practical focus and heads for the bathroom thinking of the day ahead and what to wear.

54

Conversation over breakfast is dominated by the media reactions. Cartwell's team receives continuous updates, the front pages of the papers are filled with quotes from the documents on the flash drive, photos and short articles of speculation. Conjecture is rife, mostly without names, but often worded to allow identification by those with inside knowledge. The Prime Minister has made a rather vague statement saying that he finds the information disturbing and will consult with Cabinet about what measures should be put in place to investigate.

'Well, that's what he would say, isn't it? At least he didn't say it's fake news like he usually does,' says the producer. 'God, how I despise that stupid Trump method of avoiding responding to criticism. He's got the material, and he knows damn well who's implicated - so far. I wonder how they'll investigate. It won't be easy – too many potentially corrupt people who can't be allowed anywhere near it.'

'It's bound to be a Royal Commission and I'll put a hundred bucks on a couple of retired judges,' says Luke. 'They're less likely to be tainted and they understand about evidence. And perhaps a professor from another Commonwealth country, maybe a constitutional law expert. And then the resignations will start – people trying to get out of the way fast. Not that it's going to help them, but it's what tends to happen when people know they've been exposed - or will be.'

He looks at Cartwell on the far side of the table. 'Do you agree?'

'Yeah totally, and you can chuck in a suicide or two – I'm sure you've already thought of that. It's nearly inevitable with people's reputations blown to pieces, not to mention what the justice system will do to them.'

'I'm glad you gave us an opportunity in the interview to explain why we've decided to name those we've identified – to put a name to the face shots from the video clips,' says Minnie. 'Like that state servant with the multi-million life-style. At least the media won't try to ID them and get it wrong at the start.'

She had insisted that they must make their motivation clear, not only to the media and the Government, but also to the public. 'I can't help thinking about the ghastly impact it will have on the families of those involved and the resulting tragedies - but we had to do it.'

Cartwell reaches for a piece of toast and contemplates the choices of spreads. 'I understand what you're saying, but Luke and Rumble are right – if it's all out there, it makes it useless for people to deny that they're involved. And once we start tugging on the loose threads, it will unravel pretty quickly, I think. The positions they hold make it obvious once you get the hang of the abbreviations and the context.'

He reaches for the bowl of apricot jam. 'Yum, I love this stuff, I never get it at home.'

'And don't forget,' says Rumble, who has hardly said a word since they got up, 'that the people who took bribes are already well paid by the taxpayer, by all the little guys who work hard to make ends meet and pay their taxes. These bastards working in the shadows are not only greedy and prepared to undermine democracy - they're as despicable as any common thief. The fact that they wear suits and eat in fine restaurants, doesn't make them any different from the guy who breaks into someone's house and steals the TV.'

'Brilliant!' says Cartwell. 'I love it – puts it in a perspective everyone can relate to. I've got jam on my fingers - can someone write that down please, exactly what he said. I want to use that in the intro tonight – perfect, a single quote that exactly sums it up.'

Minnie smiles and casts a sideways look at Rumble.

'If it hadn't been for Rumble, we wouldn't be here now.' She looks around the table. 'And I mean that - if he hadn't helped me right at the beginning, it would all have derailed pretty quickly, and those shadow men would still be playing their dirty games. And I would probably be dead.'

One of the researchers pushes a notepad across the table to Rumble. 'Check that I've got it right please.'

Rumble reads it and nods. 'Yeah, I think that's what I said. Get Minli to check, she's the one who's good with words.'

'Why do they sometimes call you Minli?' The researcher is curious, and Minnie notices that others have looked up. Trying to brush it off she says casually, 'Oh, it's just a name Luke made up, like a Chinese alternative to Minnie. The guys use it a lot and I don't even notice – it sounds practically the same.'

'Does it mean something, Luke?'

Luke smiles across the table, well aware that she is trying to avoid explaining.

'When Minli was grabbed by Dustman at Te Papa and had a gun pushed into her ribs, not only didn't she panic but she came up with a strategy to defuse the situation till help arrived or until she could get away – very cool. And then she spent three horrendous days on that damn mountain side, drugged and injured and without food or water - not knowing where she was or if she would ever be found. But she refused to give in. She used every resource she could lay her damaged little hands on, all her ingenuity and strength of mind. Minli is two words - min and li –they mean clever and strong.'

Minnie hides her embarrassment behind her mug of tea, tries to ignore the attention and waits for the conversation to change.

It's only when they 're packing to leave that she realises that she didn't tell either Brendan or the rest-home staff that there might be media interest coming up. She comes to a sudden stop halfway across the lounge and drops her bag on the floor with a thud.

'Bugger! How stupid!'

Rumble, who is sitting on the sofa reading emails on his phone, looks up.

'Minnie! What was that you just said? The girl who never swears?'

She sits down beside him, devastated. 'Oh Rumble – I completely forgot that I was going to call the resthome and speak to Brendan and tell him to expect that media might call – you know, before it got on the news and into the papers. And Andy, and Jane too.'

'Really? If you had rung Brendan and told him yesterday, he would probably have forgotten it by now – don't you think?'

He raises his voice in the direction of Luke's room. 'Hey, Luke – did you hear that?'

'Yep - makes no sense to me. Brendan would forget it and you couldn't have told the staff at that place. More likely Jane and your cousin in Auckland might feel they should have been told.'

Rumble smiles at Minnie who still has a worried crease between her eyebrows. 'See, two against one. We promised each other not to tell anyone and it's only official as of yesterday. I don't think it's too late to call them if you feel you should.'

Luke appears in the doorway. 'Let them call you - I'm sure they will. Did your cousin call you when he was run over by that train, or did you hear it on the news?'

She smiles and shakes her head, admitting defeat. 'OK, you're both right - just a moment of worry that I had been rude. Of course, Andy didn't call me after the train incident. I read it in the newspaper and called his parents.'

'Any second now you'll start worrying about all the lies I told Ling and Bella. But let me reassure you - I rang them after the little broadcast the night before last and told them what we're involved in. I had to warn them that they might get the media spotlight trained on them too, at least briefly – they wouldn't be hard to track down. I also apologized for lying about you, Minli, but I think they've forgiven me – reluctantly.'

She senses the concealed amusement behind the word 'reluctantly' and makes a mental note to ask him about it later; somehow, she feel certain that it pertains to her.

55

They are in the helicopter flying down the Kapiti coast, when Minnie has an idea. 'Hey, Rumble, we haven't got a car at the airport, but perhaps we can ask Bruce to land on the green belt - you know where we walked to Hanson Street that day? If we landed at the end closest to the apartment block, we'd be a few minutes' walk from the flat.'

'Don't know. Bruce, can we do that?'

'Now you're all so famous I'll put you down wherever you like. Anywhere so long as I don't spend more than two minutes on the ground,' says the pilot. 'Just tell me where this place is - and make sure you've got your bags ready to jump out.'

'I didn't know there was a two-minute rule – that's convenient.'

Bruce laughs until their earphones vibrate. 'I just invented it, mate. Let's see if we get away with it, eh?'

'He's a treasure that man. How did you get to know him, Rumble?' asks Minnie, as they walk over the grassy slope towards the apartment block.

'He knows one of my mates - I helped him track down his estranged son a couple of years ago. Had to hack a few FaceBook accounts and whatever. The guy was into drugs and all sorts, but Bruce has got him sorted out, which is good. I never had a reason to call on him for anything before, but he's been very useful lately. He's asked to be paid in cash and he only charges us about half the regular fee. He won't declare it as income, of course.'

'God, Rumble – this is terrible. We must sit down and work it out, so I can pay you guys back. I feel so guilty about all these expenses - I've been living like a kept woman for weeks.'

Rumble looks at Luke and shakes his head; she only just catches it out of the corner of her eye.

'Don't worry Petal, I've got crazy amounts of money in the bank and I never spend very much. I don't travel, I don't buy fancy clothes and I don't care about flash cars. Mostly I just buy tech gear and gadgets. And I can't keep on buying apartments – it's getting ridiculous, and I'll be a capitalist pig before you know it, and that's not what I want to be. People who hire my services pay big money and this thing's been perfect - something really worthwhile to do with it.' He looks down at her and laughs. 'Dead interesting actually, the best fun I have had for ages, despite being scared shitless on occasion. It's good when I come across some deserving causes to spend that dough on – like a redistribution of wealth, I suppose.'

'What other adventures have you funded?' asks Luke. 'Anything else as exciting as this?'

'Nah – just rescued some people. A couple of my mates had problems so I helped them out, and then I wanted to buy Bella a flat, hers is like a shoebox, you can hardly turn around and it's not in a safe street - but she won't let me. I might let her live in my other apartment when that Spanish guy leaves, it's nice and central.'

Minnie decides that the time for discretely ignoring casual little asides about Bella is over.

'Are you and Bella an item now?'

To her surprise he isn't embarrassed, just shocked that she could even think such a thing.

'Shit, no! Of course, not – are you crazy? She would never be interested in me – she's so smart and so pretty too – she needs someone just like her, not an old bear like me.'

'Well, what's all this about then, you must tell me. You can't have two of anything apart from apples and you load her debit card, so she can book things on your behalf, and now this thing about a flat.'

'We're just friends, Minnie – not like you and me because you're like my sister, but Bella wants to learn coding and work in the IT industry and she's a gamer too, so we've just become friends. She very bright – I'm having fun teaching her things.'

. . .

'Well, look at that!' As soon as they are back in the flat, Luke opens the new email account on his laptop and counts quickly. 'Now there are eighty-two unread emails waiting for answers.'

He scrolls down the list. 'And how about this? We have requests from the BBC, ABC, CNN and a raft of print media – listen to this, The Times, the Guardian, La Figaro and the New York Times.'

'Anything from the authorities or the Government?' asks Rumble and Luke reads silently for a few minutes. 'Nope, nothing yet. They're probably still reeling from the shock and trying to come up with a plan.'

What starts as a low-key discussion about how to prioritize interview requests, quickly evolves into a heated argument.

'No fucking way - New Zealand media have to come first,' says Rumble. 'The rest of the world can be spectators until we have time.'

'That's ridiculous – we might lose our best chance to maximize the impact. If international media pick it up, it puts much more pressure on the government here, and they'll be held accountable by the rest of the world.' Luke isn't about to budge an inch.

Minnie listens, initially amused and determined not to intervene, but after a few minutes of no progress, she says mildly, 'Why not alternate them - do a couple of local media and one international and then another couple of local ones. Best of both worlds?'

Half an hour later she takes the mug of tea that Rumble hands her and sums up. 'OK, so Luke will send out the new press release today with the replies we decided on. And he'll start setting up appointments for interviews and all that, but there will be more as soon as the Cartwell interview has screened tonight. How on earth are we going to keep track of it all? What we really need is a joint diary that all appointments go into, one we can all access. Why didn't we think of that?'

'Oh, Rumble already did,' says Luke. 'He's going to load the app for it on all our laptops and phones today, so we can all see whatever one of us enters. And by the way, I've been going to ask you - when did you put that GPS tracker on Minli's car and the 'find me' on her phone? I've been thinking about it and I can't imagine how you did it without her noticing.'

Well, there's another thing I didn't know about, thinks Minnie. I'm sure he never mentioned my phone before. What else? Is this what it's like being the President of the US, every step under surveillance?

'Oh, straight after the Te Papa incident – I was really worried he'd get hold of her again. I knew you were keeping an eye on the house. The car was easy – it was a bit harder to get the phone to myself for a few minutes.' He smiles at Minnie. 'I didn't tell you, Petal – didn't want to ramp up the level of worry for you, but I had to turn the GPS on to get it working. And short of implanting a GPS tracker under your skin, it was the best I could do.'

'And look how well it worked,' she says. 'When the worst happened, I was with the car - or not far away.'

And then a flashback hits her; the paralyzing despair she experienced when she thought that she would perish alone, that nobody would ever know what had happened to her, and if it hadn't been for that tracking device she would never have been found. For a moment she can't speak, her throat constricts and panic nearly overwhelms her. She meets Luke's eyes across the table and 'it's all right, it's over now, you're safe' whispers through her mind. She takes a deep breath.

'How long are we going to stay here? Not that I don't like it, but we seem to bring more and more clutter in, and we never take any out. The place is getting to be like a slum.'

'You sound like Ling,' says Luke. 'And we still don't know if your house is safe, so we must do something about that, and both the house and my flat would be impossible anyway because the press would come and camp on the doorstep, and we'd never get any peace again. Lucky Rumble – nobody knows where his cave is, he can go home and sleep in his own bed.'

Rumble shrugs. 'They'll find me any day now. It's not as if I've made a point of hiding – I just never had my address showing anywhere public. And Broker might have a reserve hit man, who knows? After all, who was the guy who helped Dustman on the Remutaka road? Was he a mate of Dustman's or a Broker employee? Maybe Broker is so angry about how we've ruined his empire that he's prepared to have a go himself, just to punish us.'

Luke nods, but he looks unconvinced. 'Possibly – but I think he's too careful to expose himself to risk. We'll just stay here for a while until things calm down, and then we'll talk about it.'

'When this is over, I'll sell Dad's house,' says Minnie, suddenly decisive. 'I'll start that process as soon as the police have finished with it. Maybe Broker sits at his place and watches video coverage of my front hall waiting for me to come in – I mean now he knows I'm not dead. And that reminds me – all my stuff is still in the house, and I can't go and get it. You two are going to groan, but I must get some more clothes. I'm forever washing what I have - or I run out. Thank God there's a washing machine built-in here and heated towel rails in the bathroom. If I can't go home to get a change of clothes, I simply have to go shopping.'

Luke looks up from his laptop. 'OK, let's go shopping, first thing in the morning before my Inbox fills up again.'

'And will I be able to go back to school next Monday? The holidays will be over and then what will happen to me if it's not safe to go back to work? And what about your job Luke, you must have used up your annual leave by now?'

It seemed as if nothing is certain any longer – has her life changed forever? Not being able to go back to the house for a while is a temporary inconvenience, but she must earn a living once her savings are used up. How long will it be before it's safe to resume her normal life?

Rumble frowns and looks uncomfortable, and there is a short pause before Luke replies. 'I resigned. I told Amanda and my boss I had to be away for at least a month, offered to take unpaid leave - the management threw a fit and said I had to front up as usual or I was in breach of my contract, so I resigned on the spot. I didn't tell you - there was so much else to worry about at the time.'

I've just let things drift, thinks Minnie, and I've lived in a bubble, so insulated from my normal reality that I just postponed thinking about it, and now I must make decisions. How could I have ignored the problem all this time? My school teaching was forced on me by my move to Wellington. The changes I initiated at the school have made me part of a strong team, and I want to continue. Will it be safe to go back to work now? How will I juggle the media commitments and the interviews with the authorities, or how would I support myself if I resigned, and how long will my savings last? And I owe these guys a lot of money too.

There is a long moment of silence, and then Rumble says, 'I'm lucky, I work for myself and by myself, and I can work any time of the night or day. I didn't realise you'd been forced to resign Luke, that's bad - I thought you were on leave. Are you all right for money, until you can get another job?'

'Yeah, I'll be fine for a while, I've always been great at saving – ever since Ling bought me a Chinese piggybank when I was four that swallowed my coins and wouldn't give them back. I'll concentrate on liaising with the media until the initial storm of interest dies down.'

'I wonder how long we're going to be tied up giving evidence and being questioned? What do you think, Luke, weeks?'

Luke nods slowly, as if he is thinking of something else.

'I don't know – months perhaps. It's going to be a complex investigation and it depends on how they structure it and how important we will be to the investigation and at what stage. I presume they'll want to interview us repeatedly, confirming everything we put on the flash drive and asking hundreds of questions we never thought of. God knows – it's anybody's guess.'

'But what the hell can they ask?' Rumble is irritated at the mere thought of having to interact with officialdom. 'I mean, all we know is on the flash drive. If they want to know more, they can ask the ones we identified and whoever else they find out about. Even that lawyer we hired, I forget his name – he was vague about what else we can contribute, apart from stating under oath that it's all true.'

'Paul Morris,' says Minnie. 'And I think he was vague in that special way lawyers have - they hedge their bets by being non-committal. I'm sure the authorities and the commission of enquiry, or whatever it turns out to be, will want to talk to us over and over again. And we must give them the Stranger's and Dustman's phones. God, I hope nobody tries to discredit us to cast doubt on the evidence! We would have to fight back if that happened. It might not be plain sailing.'

It is the first time she has voiced her fear of trouble on a personal level, but it has been on her mind for some time. 'The authorities have spin doctors – will they use them to cast doubt on us to hide their own problems?'

'I don't think that's very likely or if they do, it won't last,' says Luke. 'We've provided evidence that identifies certain people and it's out there for others to draw conclusions from. Once the authorities start investigating how people acquired valuable assets for example and take their devices to track what they've been involved in, our evidence won't be so important any longer. And those we have identified have probably had their devices confiscated already – it's the first thing they do these days even if you're up for a minor offence, so for a change all those new draconian laws will work for us, not against us.'

He picks up a pen, and Minnie watches it spin between his fingers as he continues. 'One thing they're sure to do is compare people's income with what they have spent over a period of time and say, "explain how you earned only x amount over the last ten years, but you spent six times that much". And then they'll start tracing where the money came from. And they'll link the bribes to what that particular industry sector gained through the political system.'

She hopes he is right, that having given the world the raw material others will now follow up and do the job. Aloud she says, 'I'm still worried that some of those we have implicated will come after us and try to ruin our reputations - to throw dust in the eyes of the investigators. And to protect their own reputation in front of family and friends.'

Rumble has been silent for a while, but now he smiles grimly.

'There's not much they can try in that line, is there? And what would it achieve? Facts are facts, you know. They might persuade a few friends and family to think they're blameless – for a short time. But in the end, it will all come out - or most of it.'

And then he starts to laugh. 'Shit, Luke – can't you imagine what's-her-name, your producer and the management, sitting in the office right now cursing themselves? You resigned because they wouldn't let you have a month's leave, and you could have been their biggest asset ever - it's that karma thing again. Serves them bloody right.'

56

Rumble goes out and buys a TV and they eat pizza and watch the Cartwell Tonight hour in comfort instead of huddled around a laptop. 'I'm so glad you bought proper furniture, Rumble,' says Minnie and sinks into one of the three armchairs that were mysteriously delivered a couple of weeks earlier. 'And that shelf unit – it's just like a proper home now.'

The Cartwell interview is an eye-opener in more ways than one. Rumble is so upset at how large he looks that he can hardly bear to watch and groans with embarrassment.

'But Rumble, you know that you tower over other people, and you're not built like a reed. I think you look good. And the haircut is great even if I have to say it myself.'

But he is inconsolable. 'I'm like some fucking giant freak, thank God you cut my hair – I wish I'd never watched this.'

Five minutes later Minnie hides her face in her hands. 'That's awful – I had no idea my head is always tilted to one side like that. Why am I not sitting straight like you two?'

'Everyone's like that at first,' says Luke, amused at their reaction. 'It's just that you've never seen yourself as others see you before. It changes your self-perception, but you get used to it.'

'Cartwell can be proud of that,' he says at the end. 'And the best thing is the way we came across as normal people. Not like fanatics or nutters with a political agenda or conspiracy theorists, just ordinary citizens - which makes the impact even greater. And our prepared answers worked well. That little three-way response when he asked if we had obtained any information by illegal means - that was excellent. Hopefully people will forgive us when they discover how we got hold of some of it.'

Rumble's forehead is creased with worry lines. 'But why did he go over that twice? I was surprised when he asked again - as if he didn't really believe us. Was he trying to trip us up?'

'God, no - not at all,' says Minnie. 'I think he went back to that because it's something people will speculate about. By re-phrasing the question, he let us reply again and it will really sink in – we didn't know who to turn to, anyone could have been involved et cetera. I think it was a good ploy.'

'I agree,' says Luke. 'He gave us an opportunity to put our side of it twice, quite generous.'

Rumble's phone buzzes. He picks it up and says 'hi' and listens silently, staring at nothing, until Minnie begins to worry.

Eventually he says 'Really?' followed by another long silence. Now Luke is watching him too.

'Did you?' says Rumble on a note of disbelief and listens again before he smiles and says, 'OK, thanks, see you.' He puts the phone on the table and makes no comment, but it is too much for Minnie.

'Rumble, who was that? Several minutes on the phone and you say five words!'

Rumble tries to look cool and unruffled. 'It was Bella, she says we were awesome, and it was a great interview.'

Much later lying on their two single airbeds, that threaten to slide apart despite a sheet tucked in crosswise, Minnie turns her head and speaks with her mouth touching Luke's cheek. 'Reluctantly? And?'

She knows he is smiling. 'I don't know what you're talking about.'

'Liar, I know you do. I saw that look of secret amusement this morning.'

'OK then – this is what happened. Ling said, "how disappointing, I was so pleased you had finally found someone so lovely and clever" and Bella said, "Luke, you fucking idiot, grab her quick before she escapes". Happy now?'

'Well, yes – very flattering, but I'm more interested in what you replied.'

'I said I'd work very hard to convince you that your life will never be complete without me.'

She licks his cheek. 'You taste salty - nice. OK, I'm yours forever.'

'Really?'

'Yes, really.'

The next couple of days are frantic and there is no time for shopping. Media emails pour in, and everyone wants them immediately, in person. Confirmations of interview times and dates, requests for changes and lists of questions continue to arrive. By ten o'clock the second evening Rumble calls a stop.

'I have to go home and do a bit of my own work and get some sleep. I'll be back tomorrow.'

He has his hand on the door handle when Luke's phone rings.

'Paul Morris,' he says in an aside and listens for a couple of minutes, increasingly thoughtful. 'OK, thanks Paul – I'll call you back in five.'

'An unidentified political aide has asked Paul to set up a meeting with us tomorrow. The words used were, an informal meeting in a private setting that would not be recorded by either side. Paul thinks it's possible that it's the Prime Minister – and if it is, the guy has lost his marbles. Not a thing any PM should ever risk doing, totally mad.'

'I don't care who the hell it is,' says Rumble grumpily. 'We're not meeting with anyone in some secret setting. And not having it recorded! What a stupid suggestion. And if it is the PM, he can go stuff himself – I don't trust that devious bugger.'

Minnie is outraged. 'God, no – no way can we do that! And if it really is the PM, it only confirms what I always thought, the guy has an unrealistic sense of entitlement, he always did.'

Luke laughs. 'Yep, it's one of his major character traits. And once we start making exceptions, we've lost it - our integrity is toast. Doesn't matter who it is, the PM or some Minister. I'll tell Paul to say that our terms are unconditional - we don't meet anyone informally and every meeting is recorded.'

Rumble and Minnie talk quietly while Luke makes the call to Paul, and Minnie repeats that she still wants to go shopping.

Luke ends the call and puts the phone in his pocket. 'I'll come with you - I like shopping.'

'Shit, no! There's no way you two can be seen together!' exclaims Rumble. 'Separately you'd be OK - together you're unforgettable. I can't think of anything more noticeable than a very pale-skinned little redhead and a big Chinese guy. Much better if Bella goes with you, Minli. And by the way, I'm surprised somebody who lives in this block hasn't told the media that you're living here. Best not to appear side by side anywhere for a while.'

'You're right – I'll have to go on my own.'

'I'll tell Bella you want to go shopping this week, I'm sure she would enjoy going with you,' says Rumble and opens the door.

The door shuts behind him and leaves them looking at each other with raised eyebrows. Luke speaks first, 'Watch this space?'

'Maybe.'

57

At Rumble's insistence Minnie and Luke continue to live in the flat even when the media interest slows down.

'Listen mate,' he says, when Luke mentions that they are thinking of moving to his flat. 'I know the press siege is letting up, but Broker is still an unknown factor. We discussed this already and nothing has changed, has it? There's no indication that they're any closer to identifying him, so don't give the bastard an opportunity to harm you. Nobody has found this place yet, which is a fucking miracle. Just stay for a while longer. You're comfortable here now, and I've ordered a bed. Should be here tomorrow.'

'You what?! Ordered a bed? You've got to stop buying furniture,' says Minnie. 'It's not as if ...'

'That's just what is, Petal – it **is** as if you're living here, you **are** living here. I can't bear to think of you both sleeping on the floor like you're camping. You need a place that's like a real home, not all this make-shift shit that we've used for so long.'

They are having breakfast very early; just one media appointment and then they are free for the rest of the day. With a bit more time on her hands Minnie managed to go shopping with Bella the day before, a welcome change that nearly resembled normality, but she is worried about Brendan, who is no longer comfortable with phone conversations and forgets whom he's talking to.

'Can I borrow your car to go and see Brendan? I must get his car out of the garage at home, so I have a car to use, but I don't know if it will start - it hasn't been used for months.'

'I'll take you to the resthome, and then we can go to your place on the way back and check out Brendan's car. If the battery is flat, we'll jump start it, so you can drive it back here. Have you got his car keys? When do you want to go?'

'I'm sure the keys are in the car. Sounds mad I know, but he always left them in the ignition and locked the garage, so he didn't have to search for them when he went to work. Let's go straight after that Zoom interview at half past eight.'

Minnie's phone pings with a text message from Jane, the first since the press conference. 'Very disappointed you did not trust us with the truth. Jordan and I both feel used. I thought we were friends.'

Minnie reads the terse message twice, her face pale and still. Luke looks up from his bowl of cereal and stops with the spoon halfway to his mouth. 'Is it about your dad?'

She pulls herself together and tries to smile. 'No, it's from Jane, she's angry – she says I've used them and lied. She must have been thinking about this since the story broke, and now she's really angry.'

She pauses and adds, 'And it's true, I did lie, but she could try to understand the reason.'

She hands him the phone, and he reads the message. 'How much does she matter to you?'

'Well, she's the only close friend I've made since I moved back here. We get along really well - and it's important to have a friend, a woman friend. I had lost touch with most of my old school friends. Why?'

He gives her a considering look. 'I am going to tell you my life philosophy. This is how I see it - life is not a rehearsal and time is limited. Pandering to people who don't love me or matter to me is not an option. If people misunderstand me or get hurt by what I say or do, then I apologize, and we move on. But if they get upset because they are reacting from an ego-driven point of view, then I do nothing. I particularly resist the urge to seek them out, to explain or to make them see my side of it and I *never* use the word 'sorry'- and that's that. If I meet them, I am perfectly pleasant and polite - and I never refer to their grudge in any way at all. But if you for example, or Bella or my mum, misunderstood my motives or got upset because I was unkind, then I would walk over burning coals to apologize and promise not to hurt you again.'

She laughs. 'You take the prize for honesty, you really do! Most people probably think more or less like that, but few would be able to carry it out.'

Now he smiles too. 'I think it would be a mistake to include the word sorry when you reply to Jane. Even if you mean you're sorry that she feels that way, she will think you are apologizing - and I don't think you need to. Even explaining or putting your point of view might make her think it's an apology.'

He puts the phone on the table between them, keeps his hand on it.

'She should be able to figure out that you had to do what you did to keep others safe - and you risked your own life to do it. Hers is a purely ego-driven accusation – she is only considering her feeling of having been left out or used - no thought for the bigger context or for what you have put yourself through.'

She picks up the phone, composes a text and sends it. He's waiting and she knows it, but she returns to her toast without comment and after a minute his curiosity gets the better of him.

'Well? Are you going to tell me?'

She hands him the phone and continues eating while he reads it aloud: 'When faced with a dangerous situation I made the decisions I thought best and safest for all concerned. As far as I am aware, I have not endangered anyone but myself - as demonstrated.'

'Wow - that's pretty succinct. You take no prisoners - perfect.' He puts the phone down and picks up his spoon. 'I was so right about your new name.'

A quarter of an hour later she gets a message from Jordan, much the same sentiments as Jane's, but expressed with more force and many more words. He feels used and upset that they didn't trust him enough to ask him direct questions and accuses them of being devious and putting him in danger of losing his job for their own purposes.

She gives Luke the phone and watches as he types a reply and hands the phone back,

'Delete it or send it,' he says, and she reads it twice: "We trusted nobody and used the means available to unmask as much as possible without endangering others."

'Talk about succinct!' She pushes Send.

. . .

'Hello, Morgan,' says Minnie after breakfast, leaning against the windowsill in the living room with the autumn sun warm on her back. 'I must apologize for lying to you and to the headmaster - I sent a message saying I had measles and that obviously wasn't true, but as you already know, I had to go into hiding.'

There is a long pause while she listens to Morgan's reply while Luke tries to look as if he is not paying attention.

'Yes, it was very scary – and it still is in a way. Obviously the most dangerous thing I've ever done.'

Silence while she listens and then she smiles. 'You are very kind to say so, but it wasn't just me, very far from it. Without these amazing guys to help me I would be dead now and nothing would have been achieved. I had no idea how to handle it alone. I would have made fatal errors if I had tried.'

She listens, smiles. 'Yes, the headmaster said the same thing, he was very forgiving. I'll be in touch and if not before, then I'll see you in term three.'

She puts the phone down and sees Luke's eyes asking a question. 'Yes, I did. I asked for a term's leave of absence. The headmaster said he quite understood, and he hoped the formalities wouldn't be too tiresome. He's quite reserved and hardly ever says anything personal. He and Morgan have been very understanding.'

She comes to sit opposite him, looking down at the phone in her hand. 'I've heard nothing back from Jane. It's strange, Luke – if you hadn't given me the philosophy talk, I would be fretting and fuming about her message and feeling that I must explain it to her in detail and get her to understand my reasoning. But instead, I feel really calm and sort of detached instead of worried or tormented.'

'That's good,' says Luke calmly and turns back to his task, but she knows he is pleased. She is intrigued by the simplicity of his philosophy, and how effective it is when applied. Like a magic potion, she thinks, and watches him absorbed in what he is doing, and now I've used it once I can apply it to any situation and avoid stress and self-torment. I wish I had worked it out years ago, it would have saved a lot of agonizing.

58

Minnie's visit to Brendan is confusing. At first, she thinks his mind has tipped right over the edge, but after a few minutes, realization dawns.

Good Lord, he thinks I'm Mum! What do I do now? Carry on and kind of agree with everything he says, or do I put him right and maybe upset him or confuse him even more?

She does nothing and fifteen minutes later, after long pauses while he gazes absently at the fishes in the aquarium, he falls asleep.

She gets up, touches his cheek lightly and goes to find the nurse. But she is prosaic when Minnie tells her what happened. 'That's very common, happens all the time. They get to a point, when they confuse generations and can't tell people apart. Next time he might think you're his mother.'

Not very comforting, thinks Minnie, as she goes out into the cool autumn day and gets into Luke's car.

'God, this dementia thing is awful - I hope you never have to deal with it.'

She tells him the story and feels better having shared it, but she knows that things will only get worse, and each time her father loses another piece of himself it will make her just as sad as it did today.

While Luke parks just down the street from Brendan's garage, Minnie looks at the house and frowns. There is police crime scene tape blocking the path from the garage to the house and a notice saying it is a crime scene,

'They're taking far too long! I can't believe they won't let me back into the house – I wonder if they just forgot to take the tape down, maybe I should call and ask.'

'I hope the garage key isn't inside.' Luke follows her towards the garage, and she replies, 'No, it's in my hand' over her shoulder and puts the key in the garage lock, but the key jams, and when she tries to pull it out there is a little click. She pushes harder and Luke shouts 'no!' and shoves her hard to one side, as a deafening blast lifts her off her feet and throws her to the ground. She lands hard on her side with her ears ringing. Luke is lying half across her body with his head on the sidewalk, not moving. Terrified she twists and squirms out from under him and gets unsteadily to her feet.

Pieces of splintered wood, parts of the car and debris she can't identify are spread across the sidewalk and the street. The front of the garage is a gaping ruin, everything inside is covered in patches of flame and the garage itself is on fire. Coughing and choking from the smoke and fumes she kneels beside Luke and rolls him onto his back, but she can see no injuries apart from a gash on his cheek. She puts her hand on his chest and feels his heart beating steadily, and when she touches his face, he moans. but his eyes stay closed.

People are coming out of houses and approaching with shocked faces. Two elderly neighbours lift and drag Luke further away, and Mrs Beattie from the corner house takes Minnie's hand and pulls her along the footpath saying something she can't hear. She is looking back at the garage when there are two more explosions in quick succession. Her impaired hearing registers the violence of the first and the muted whoompf of the second. They are just far enough away from the garage to avoid being enveloped in the bright orange fireball, but the pressure wave is like a physical blow that rocks her on her feet. A few moments later thick black smoke obscures the scene.

She sits patiently on the edge of the sidewalk holding Luke's hand and waits for help. He is conscious and his eyes open a couple of times, look blankly at the sky and close again. And Minnie watches the black smoke that rises in a tall column before spreading northwards in a dark smudge against the clear sky and waits. An ambulance and two police cars arrive, and Mrs Beattie walks away towards her house. Paramedics kneel beside Luke and two fire trucks come around the corner, but her sense of unreality and detachment continues throughout the confusion. Sounds are muffled and distant, and she can only just hear people's voices over the whistling noise in her ears. Her throat feels scorched and she keeps coughing, but gradually she begins to think instead of just reacting. She brushes off the man who wants to guide her to an ambulance and walks back along the street on the far side from the burning garage, gingerly stepping over fire hoses, pieces of charred wood, glass and metal.

My God, those last explosions, she thinks, must have been mum's oxygen tank that was still sitting in the garage and then the petrol tank in the car and maybe the can of petrol for the mower - that smoke tastes toxic.

She walks slowly around Luke's car and looks at it from all sides, whispering to herself. 'The car is OK, the windscreen's chipped, his keys are in the ignition, it's too close to the fire, I think I'll move it a bit further away.'

She gets in and reverses into a driveway on the other side of the street, turns in the opposite direction and finds a safe spot to park just before the corner, away from the emergency vehicles and the fire. She gets out and searches the car still talking quietly to herself. 'I'll take Luke's satchel and my bag, check the glove box, check the boot, take his jacket and his cell phone, put the stuff in the satchel, lock the car.'

She walks away, stops and looks back at the car to make sure it is far enough from the corner and turns to see a policeman coming towards her; his mouth moves, but she can't hear him. When he reaches her, she holds up her hand, and her voice sounds strange and far away inside her head.

'I can't hear anything, or not very much. Please speak really loudly.'

He was stares at her with a strange expression. 'You're Minnie, aren't you? Is that your garage?'

Her sense of detachment is so profound that she doesn't even register the fact that she is now public property, and strangers know her first name.

'Yes. The car in the garage is my father's, that's his house. I usually live here too, but I haven't been here for a while and he's in a resthome.'

She pauses, but when he says nothing, she continues. 'The car I moved belongs to my friend Luke. I must go back to him – he's injured.'

She walks away without waiting for an answer. People have been herded away from the fire to the far side of the street. The firemen have manoeuvred their trucks closer; smoke and steam create a dense spreading cloud around the garage, white foam and black water overflow the gutter and run down the slope of the street. Suddenly she is frantic and runs along the sidewalk hardly glancing at the garage on the other side, past the fire engines towards the ambulance. Another police officer intercepts her. 'Where are you going?'

She gestures to her ears, and he says just loud enough for her to hear. 'My God, it's you! Is that your friend in the ambulance?'

She nods and starts running again, and he follows. The doors at the back of the ambulance are open and she can see Luke on a stretcher with a man bending over him. Without ceremony she climbs in, pushes past the paramedic and looks down at Luke. His eyes are open, and he smiles and for the first time since the garage door blew out, she feels like herself again. She kneels beside the stretcher and puts her hand on his chest.

'I'm a bit deaf – are you OK?'

He says 'yes' and points to his own ear – and suddenly she laughs, the relief is overwhelming.

'God, what a pair we are – deaf and dusty.'

She has no idea if she is speaking loudly enough for him to hear. 'I checked your car, took some things out and locked it.'

She gestures towards the floor, where she has dropped his satchel. He says something she can't hear, and the ambulance man touches her shoulder, speaking loudly. 'Please sit down over here and strap yourself in.'

He gestures to a seat and she sits down; tries to think what she ought to do now. She must tell Rumble and Bella about Luke, and Bella can let Ling know. Should she get in touch with Paul Morris? No, that can wait.

Relieved to find that her phone wasn't smashed when she fell, she starts writing her text message with clumsy fingers and notes absently that her coordination is not what it should be, and the movement of the ambulance weaving through the traffic makes it harder still. They are nearly at the hospital before she has composed her message.

59

Rumble and Bella arrive while Minnie waits for Luke to come back to ED from a scan. She herself has only bruises and a skinned elbow and hastens to reassure Rumble, who seems convinced that she must be more seriously damaged.

'Are you really sure?' he says and looks her carefully up and down. 'You were bloody lucky then – I hope Luke's OK.'

Her hearing is slowly coming back. Background noises are muffled, and the whistling sound continues, but she can hear Rumble's deep voice quite well. She starts telling them what happened, but something filters into her mind; Rumble is worried and she stops mid-sentence and looks hard at him.

'What is it Rumble? Something is wrong, something else – tell me!'

He takes her hand. 'Sorry Minnie, but the house is on fire too – they think the whole place is going to be lost.'

Her mind finds it hard to process the additional stress – she is about to lose control, to scream or cry. She clutches his hand hard and suppresses the feeling with a huge effort.

'What!? There were two fire engines there already - can't they put it out?'

'I don't know exactly. We heard it on the radio on the way here - they think the fire spread by burning debris that was flung from the explosion. But it's turned into a huge blaze – very quickly. Your neighbours have been evacuated.'

He studies her face for a moment and then he reaches over and takes her hand in both his. 'I'm sorry, Petal. Your life is being torn apart and I can't do anything about it.'

She liberates her hand, gets up and walks to the far end of the waiting room and stands in front of a large notice board, as if she is reading the poster about multi-flu vaccinations, her mind in turmoil. It's all gone, she thinks, all the things that link me to the past, the house where we lived when Sander was alive and everything in it. I'm the only one left who can remember my family's life, and now I'm in a vacuum with nothing to look at or hold to remind me, apart from the photos in those boxes.

Random images of what has been obliterated appear in her mind; Brendan's books, her mother's collection of glass paperweights, the oval portrait of her great-grandmother in the dining room, her own possessions – the list is endless. She feels dispossessed, like a refugee; adrift with nothing to anchor her to her past.

A whisper appears in her mind, 'don't panic, be strong' and gradually rational thought returns. She turns and sees Rumble and Bella looking at her from the far side of the waiting room, apprehensive and unhappy.

Poor things, she thinks, they're worried about Luke and sorry for me, and they feel so helpless – I can see from here how traumatized Bella is.

She returns and sits down beside Rumble again. 'I think the insurance company will ban me forever – two cars and a house! My risk rating will go through the roof,' she says, her voice unsteady.

They laugh, slightly out of control, and talk about other things until a nurse comes to say that Luke is back and takes them to a cubicle behind the scenes.

Bella bends over Luke and he lifts an arm and holds her tight. They stay like that for a long time, while Rumble and Minnie stand silently watching. Bella straightens up and wipes her hand across her wet cheeks. 'Thank God you're all right!'

Minnie thinks of Sander and how she never had the opportunity to know him as an adult. She wonders if she would have had this kind of close relationship with him, but perhaps it's unusual that a brother and sister are so close. She remembers Luke telling her how he could feel Bella's pain even as a child and thinks that they probably have a bond beyond normal sibling affection.

• • •

Eventually they get back to the flat, tired and battered, relieved that the day is over.

'Normality is what we need, 'says Rumble. 'No more drama – particularly not for you, Minli. You've used up your quota.'

'God, I hope it's over and done with,' she says tiredly. 'Mind you, none of our lives have been normal for a couple of months, not since I unlocked that phone - we have a new normal.'

'Yeah, right,' says Rumble. 'With some added dimensions for you, like slight deafness, no house and a headache. Anyone else would be in a screaming heap on the floor.'

She shakes her head and thinks that he will never know how hard it is to hide her inner turmoil, to make it less traumatic for the rest of them; acutely aware that their focus is on her and her multiple losses.

Bella, who left them outside the hospital, arrives at the flat laden down with the ingredients for a Chinese meal.

'Christ, Bella!' says Luke. 'It's a long time since I saw you cooking anything Chinese. Ling would be delighted.'

'She was! I went home and she gave me all the stuff I need to make some of the dishes I know how to do. She says you have to be careful with your concussion, and I am not to let you cook or stand up for too long.'

She puts her bags on the little kitchen counter and starts unpacking pots and a jumble of packets and canisters.

'So that's why you kept postponing any discussion about dinner,' says Minnie to Rumble as they sit at the table watching Bella and Luke working together. 'I thought it was unusual that you were suddenly uninterested in food.'

Rumble turns to her and says quietly, 'They're very close those two – more than most, I think. Not that I know, of course - not having any brothers or sisters, apart from you.'

'I think what we have is better than most people who have blood ties. And I must tell you – today when the garage was on fire, I didn't panic and try and get as far away from the flames as possible. I stayed with Luke, and I did what I had to do. Perhaps I've finally outgrown my phobia about flames.'

She gets up to see what they are doing at the kitchen bench. 'Lovely smells, Bella. You can't imagine how nice this is after a day like today. You should have asked Ling to join us.'

Bella turns around, pink cheeked and busy. 'I did ask her - I knew you wouldn't mind, because she already knows where this place is, but she said you can come and see her, when you feel better. She just needed to know you're both OK and she said to tell you she's very sorry about your house, Minli.'

By the time they are ready to eat, Minnie feels exhausted. She looks at Luke's pale face and knows they were lucky to get away with no serious injuries in that blizzard of flying debris, that it could have been much worse, but the emotional toll is like a heavy weight. Luke is concussed, of course, but nothing that time won't mend, she tells herself, and her own tiredness is more mental than physical, the entire day has been traumatic from beginning to end. It seems like a week since they sat here peacefully having breakfast, but she will put on a brave face, because the others will feel a lot better if there is no more emotional drama. By morning, the explosion will have regenerated media interest, and the demands for interviews will ramp up again. She steels herself for what is to come and the need to strike a balance, to be factual and reasoned, without giving the impression that events have not deeply affected her on a personal level.

60

After dinner Bella says. 'Hey, would you like me to take you up to your house tomorrow, just so you can have a look?'

Minnie restrains herself with a nearly physical effort. 'No, thanks, I don't think I could bear it just now. I'll wait until they tell me the place is safe.'

The police called just before dinner and told her that the house is completely burnt down, nothing has been rescued, and the site will be cordoned off until an investigation is completed. Now, Rumble turns to her: 'What else did they tell you? Do they actually know anything specific?'

'No, they just said everything is still too hot for anyone to start poking around, but they believe the house was booby-trapped. I can't believe they hadn't even been inside yet. But I suppose it's a good thing some poor police officers didn't get blown up.' She tries to remember the exact conversation. 'They think the house was set up with something, possibly explosives as well, because it went up like a bomb. So, I think you were right, guys - Dustman did go back that night, after he had dumped me. He might have noticed someone had been there in the meantime, and perhaps he thought if you came back again, he could kill you too. They are ruthless monsters, and they don't care what they do. People's lives don't matter - it's all about money and power.'

Luke is absent-mindedly twirling a chopstick between his fingers. 'I wonder what he used to make that explosion in the garage and how he knew how to do it? It was certainly effective.'

Minnie smiles. 'Oh, I could have done that. And so can lots of people, if they read up on it – no need to have a science degree. It could have been something like mercury fulminate, that's what I would use anyway. Possibly silver fulminate, but that's a lot more dangerous to handle.'

She picks up her glass, and Bella says indignantly, 'You can't stop there. Tell us more – we don't know the things you do. Could you really have set it up to explode like that?'

'I could make mercury fulminate here at the kitchen bench - and then I would take it very carefully to the site and insert a little capsule of it into the keyhole, so that when the key was turned, the capsule would squash or break, and the powder would explode. An old-fashioned lock like that, with a big open keyhole for a big key, is perfect. A contained space so the capsule ruptures when enough pressure is applied – it wouldn't work in a modern lock. And now that I think about it – did he really booby-trap the house that awful night? Or did he just force the door that you two had locked, so he could search the house or whatever he wanted to do? He wouldn't have had the mercury fulminate ready at that stage – he must have set the explosions up later, hoping to kill any of us who came back.'

Their eyes are still riveted on her face, and she smiles. 'I wish all my students were as keen to learn as you are! OK, then, here's the complete chemistry lecture. Once you've made your mercury fulminate, you must be very careful, because it's extremely unstable and it can go off for several reasons – friction or impact or just pressure. Say that Dustman made an oblong capsule from a little bit of very thin copper or aluminium, or even aluminium foil - he flexed and folded it and put the powder into it. Then he inserted it very carefully into the keyhole, without putting any pressure on it – quite risky. And then I came along and put the key in and turned it, which compressed it and it exploded - a great little bomb.'

'And then?' asks Bella and leans forward over the table.

'Let's say that he had already broken into the garage through the window at the rear and attached a much bigger parcel of mercury fulminate to the inside of the door with duct tape - right across the keyhole, and perhaps he attached a glass bottle of petrol over that with more duct tape. Now he has the makings of an explosion plus a fire scenario that will go off with a bang – sorry! You can see how this would work? A smallish explosion in the keyhole when the key is turned causes a bigger dose of powder to blow up and the bottle shatters and sprays burning fuel over everything inside a wooden garage. The bigger explosion also blows the wooden door out and fragments of burning wood fly around in all directions and the whole place is covered in burning fuel.'

'Shit, Minnie!' says Rumble, deeply impressed. 'When did you think all this up? I didn't know you were such an expert.'

'Oh, don't be silly – it's just basic chemistry. I saw that the inside of the garage was burning in patches, so I knew burning fuel had been flung around. And that click, when I put the key in – that was the capsule moving, and then I compressed it more by forcing the key to turn. And it caused the small charge to explode, which in turn made the bigger bomb go off - and when it did, the effect would have been instant, *nobody* could have reacted in time, but somehow Luke did, which is incredible, now that I think about it. He saved both of us from terrible injury – he flung himself at me and threw us both to the side or we would have been right where the big blast hit. I have no idea how you sensed danger just in that split second? I'm sure my hand was turning the key even as you pushed me.'

She looks at Luke and he shrugs. 'I've no idea - I just knew something was about to happen,' says Luke. 'Like a flash of panic.'

'You must tell the cops, Minnie,' says Rumble, but she shakes her head. 'They'll work it out – they have arson experts and all sorts of forensic people.'

'No really, Minnie - you have to tell them what you think, even if it's only a theory. You figured it out right away, but you're very smart and it might take them longer. Just give them a call and talk to them.'

He sees her look of stubborn reluctance and shakes his head in frustration. 'It's not like telling people how to do their job, but it might make the investigation a bit quicker. They might know what kind of person would have access to the recipe or whatever you call it, and the ingredients.'

'OK, I will. But everyone who's interested in early weapons for example, would know about it – mercury fulminate was used a long time ago to trigger the gunpowder explosion in firearms to propel the bullet – you know, instead of the old flint technique. And here's a fun fact, but unrelated to this explosion. You know that TV series Breaking Bad from years ago? The one that was replayed on Freeview just recently – for the umpteenth time.'

They nod, expectant faces watching her intently.

'There's an episode where the science teacher goes to see some drug king and he has a little plastic bag that he pretends is crystal methamphetamine, but it's really mercury fulminate. They have an argument about money, so he throws the bag at the window and causes a huge explosion that blows the air conditioning unit out into the parking lot. Well, here's the truth – the TV people put some bath salt crystals or something in the bag, to look like methamphetamine – but mercury fulminate doesn't form crystals that size, it's more like powder.'

'Typical bloody Hollywood – spreading misinformation as usual,' says Rumble.

Luke's phone buzzes, and he answers, then retreats to the bedroom. He returns ten minutes later excited by the news he just heard.

'The cops are releasing the media update about Dustman in an hour. They know who he is, but they kept it quiet until they figured out a bit more about the gun and the rubbish truck and all that. His car is registered under a fictitious name, and he had no ID on him, just an EFTPOS card and keys and a phone, anonymous again. I don't know how they found out who he really was, maybe fingerprints. Once we gave them the flash drive, they put two and two together and knew he was the one who attacked us in Hanson Street. He was an ex-soldier, and he'd been a mercenary in a couple of African countries. He had also worked as a so-called security guard in the Middle East – possibly meaning someone's private army. He lived in a flat in Newtown, so he would have done his shopping at that supermarket - it all fits. They don't know why he was in the rubbish truck.'

'Snap!' says Bella. 'If he was a soldier, he might have known about mercury fulminate. I love science. I wish you would tell me something new every time we meet, Minnie. And you never told us about the silver version, you said there was something similar, but made with silver?'

'Don't even think about it – you could easily blow your hand off, or your face. It is so unstable that if you pile a bit too much up in one heap, the weight of it on itself, so to speak, will cause an explosion.'

'Cool!' says Bella.

61

Two days after the explosion Paul Morris calls and tells them the police want to interview Minnie and Luke that afternoon if possible.

'I hope they're not going to argue about the video camera,' says Minnie. 'Did anyone mention it?'

'Paul told them we're bringing our own camera. Rumble left the camera and the tripod in the wardrobe a couple of days ago. It will be interesting to see if they'll try to separate things into two boxes – one for what was done to you and the other for how things relate to Broker. Until a commission is appointed it's all up to the police.'

'So now is the crunch point about the rubbish truck,' says Minnie slowly, 'and God knows what else – I took for granted the Te Papa incident and the night Dustman invaded the house would be on the agenda.'

Talking about what Dustman did to her will be like telling intimate personal details to strangers. In the material released to the media, her abduction was dealt with from the perspective of others; what Luke and Rumble discovered at the house, and how they found her. Luke is the only person she has told exactly what happened that evening, and she asked him to tell Rumble. The media have taken the statement on the flash drive at face value and accepted as fact that she has no memory of the attack either due to concussion or to the alcohol and drugs they assume Dustman forced down her throat.

But with an interview imminent she suddenly feels threatened and anxious. Can she pretend she still has no recollection of it? Can she cope sitting face to face with people she doesn't know, telling them about the terror and panic, how she felt she was drowning? That her only consistent thought was that she must keep silent until he killed her, and how the thought that she could offer passive resistance and foil him, had infused her with a perverse sense of power. Can she sift through all those ghastly memories again and tell them only what is important for them to know? Will she get away with lying by omission about Luke refusing to save Dustman from the compacting blade in the rubbish truck by pretending they didn't see it happen?

Luke watches her face in silence as anxious thoughts tumble through her mind and says, 'You'll cope, Minli. Remember that you are strong and clever.'

And she hopes he is right; she will never forgive herself if she gives anyone reason to cast doubt on their evidence.

The interview room is brighter and larger than Minnie has expected, not unpleasant, but not comfortable enough to want to stay longer than necessary. They spend two hours on hard chairs answering a wide range of questions from two detectives with Paul Morris silent on the far side of Luke, ready to intervene if necessary. Every now and then Minnie glances across at him, as if to reassure herself that he's still there, but nothing they ask implies blame or doubt. It is mostly questions about how much more detail they can supply about Dustman and his attacks on them, and the two cell phones.

'Could you identify the type of gun if we show you pictures?' asks one of the police officers, when they discuss the attack outside the museum. 'Obviously a handgun?'

'Some kind of handgun, but it was dark and it was jammed into the side of my ribcage. I never really saw it properly.'

She looks at Luke, but he shakes his head. 'I can't either. When he went down the first time and dropped it, I just kicked it over the edge of the quay to put it out of his reach, before he got back on his feet again. I've no idea what it was, just a pistol. Perhaps you could dive for it? I think I could tell you pretty exactly where we were.'

'He seems to have had a supply of guns,' says the officer. 'One's in the harbour, one was delivered to Parliament and one we found in Hanson Street. And while we're talking about the Hanson Street attack – we have some questions about that too.'

Oh God, here it comes, thinks Minnie and tries to keep her face neutral. This is the serious stuff. I wonder if that's why we're really here. But much to her surprise, it passes very easily.

'I'd like to hear it directly from you,' says one of the detectives. 'He caught up with you and accosted you - and then? We've read the story but tell us anyway. Something new might crop up.'

Minnie mentally crosses her fingers and listens to Luke telling them how it happened, the way they had agreed he should.

'He must have followed us, but we don't know for how long, maybe from the supermarket car park where we stopped, as you know. Then we got held up by the rubbish truck near the top end of Hanson Street and sat behind it for a couple of minutes - and then suddenly Minnie screamed something and smashed her door open with her feet and I saw the gun. So, I leapt out of the car to divert him away from Minli, and as soon as he saw me, he took a couple of steps along the side of the car and kind of vaulted up on the bonnet, one hand on the bonnet and the gun in the other. My God, he was fast! He pointed the gun straight down at me and there was no way he could miss. And then he would have got Minnie too - he had the perfect vantage point up there. Running would have been useless.'

He pauses and one of the detectives says, 'And then?'

'The only idea that flashed through my mind was to unbalance him somehow, more or less instinctive. I had no weapon, and I was at a disadvantage standing below him, so I grabbed his ankles and kind of lifted and pushed at the same time. And he toppled.'

One of the officers says, 'Minnie, did you see this?'

In the back of her mind, she notes that everyone she meets calls her Minnie now.

'Oh, yes - I couldn't have looked away if I'd tried to. He pointed the gun straight dawn at Luke and Luke's hands just shot out and grabbed his ankles and wham! - he fell sideways. We seemed to be very close to the truck suddenly. Maybe it rolled back a bit when the driver took the brakes off? Dustman fell onto the edge of that low lip at the back, where they toss the rubbish in – he kind of lay along the top edge, waving his arms for balance. He nearly rolled down the outside, but then he fell into the back of the truck.'

She looks at Luke and then back at the man she is talking to. 'It all happened so fast - it was over in a couple of seconds. The truck drove off and I was expecting Dustman to appear, ready to climb out next time it stopped. But at the Adelaide Road T-junction, the truck turned left, and we went right, so we never saw it again.'

Apart from omitting that they had seen the compacting blade compressing the load, she has told the truth, but lying by omission, she thinks, is just as bad.

'And the gun? Did you see it fall?'

'It didn't fall, it literally flew to one side, quite high and quite a distance. We never thought of it until we got home, so then we went back to find it - to make sure no kids got hold of it, but by the time we got there, the police were all over the place.'

She looks seriously at the two detectives. 'And as you know, at that stage we couldn't say anything about what had happened– it simply wasn't safe.'

A few more questions follow, but nothing like the interrogation she feared. Ten minutes later they are talking about the Remutaka road incident.

'I know you can't remember much,' says one of the officers,' and we can't charge this guy you call Dustman - but anything you can tell us will flesh out the file we've been asked to compile for the Government investigation.'

She knows it's important that someone documents the extreme measures Broker and Dustman were prepared to take, so she must tell them the full story, and Broker is of course still to be held accountable at some future date. When she tells them that despite what was implied in the material released to the media, she can remember what happened, the two men on the other side of the table glance at each other, and one of them asks, 'Why wasn't it included?'

'She had no recall for ages, she was too traumatized, not to mention concussed,' says Luke. 'I've only just heard the details myself the other day and it's a brutal story.'

Throughout she keeps her gaze on the table-top, halfway between herself and the men opposite. She keeps it minimal and factual and tells it chronologically, from the knock on the door until she blacked out. Last of all she describes how she came to, feeling cold and sick, and what she heard the men say as they pushed her car over the edge of the abyss.

'Two men?' says one of the officers. 'So, Dustman had an accomplice?'

'He must have had,' says Luke reasonably. 'One drove Minli's car and the other followed and drove them both back. Rumble, I mean Peter Smith, put the GPS location of where we found Minli's car on the flash drive - you can go up there and have a look at it if you want to. It's way down the slope, burned out and completely wrecked. I hope you noticed the photo of the gear shift in neutral.'

The last item to be discussed is the explosion at Brendan's house, and ten minutes later it's over.

'Thank you very much for coming in,' says the officer who has asked most of the questions, and finally he smiles. 'Now it's your turn. Anything you would like to ask us?'

'Have you found out what caused the explosion?'

He looks surprised at Luke's question and turns to his colleague. 'Did we get a report yet? I can't remember seeing it.'

His partner nods. 'Yep - I'll just go and check what it was. It came in this morning, but I haven't read it yet.'

He returns a couple of minutes later with a sheet of paper in his hand. 'I've printed off the summary page,' he says and stops just inside the door scanning the page.

'Here it is – mercury fulminate and petrol.'

Luke laughs out loud and looks at Minnie. 'Perfect score, Minli, exactly what you said!'

Both detectives are looking at Minnie now. 'How did you guess?'

She says nothing and Luke replies. 'She's a scientist – chemistry is her subject. She told me it could have been mercury fulminate in the keyhole – even explained about how they could have made it more effective with some more of the stuff plus a bottle of petrol taped on the inside of the door over the lock.'

'That's impressive. Taped inside the door, ha? I must remember to trot that out when I speak to the forensics guys next. Anything else you want to know?'

'Yes, what did you find in Dustman's flat and in his car? Anything that might reveal who Broker is? Or can't you tell us?'

The detectives exchange a glance and then the senior one nods.

'They're working on his phones. You know how the one you picked up after the attack at Te Papa had a huge number of text messages? Well, there were two more phones in his car, and I expect there's a lot more stuff to be sifted through. But it's out of our hands, the high-tech crimes unit is dealing with that side. There was nothing in his flat apart from anonymous stuff like clothes and food, nothing that helps us. No computer or papers. We identified him from his fingerprints – the army had them. He was discharged 'dishonourably' as they say – for violence. We think he might have another flat or perhaps a storage unit for his personal things. Very risk averse, that guy.'

'Maybe something like a storage locker at boxing gym or whatever,' says Minnie, 'where he keeps things that he doesn't want anyone to find?'

The officer's eyes are suddenly sharp and alert, and she knows why, so she answers before he asks.

'My cousin was in the police, and he was in Hawke's Bay tracking down some drug villain a few years ago. And a key person in that case had stashed a lot of valuable evidence in a locker in a boxing gym in an Auckland suburb – it was in all the papers when they finally found it.'

'Andy Black! So, he's your cousin, is he? He and I went through the Police College together. What an investigation that was, first class drama. How is he these days? Did you say he was in the force – has he left?'

'He resigned not long ago. He is thinking of buying a business.'

'Please give him my regards when you see him.'

Back in the car Minnie leans back, relieved it is over. Luke reaches over and puts his hand on hers, 'Done! You'll never have to talk about it again.'

62

On Tuesday morning, when Minnie is alone in the apartment, Rumble calls. 'Check the news online. They've just announced the Royal Commission: two retired supreme court judges, a former police commissioner and an Australian Professor of Constitutional law. Luke got it right. The terms of reference will be made public later.'

And she puts the phone down and thinks with dismay of the time ahead; more meetings and giving evidence, possibly being a witness in court cases. A timeline stretching into her future for months or maybe years. She feels as if something she did for the common good has turned on her and imprisoned her, an indefinite sentence.

She is still sitting there, gazing at the shopping list in front of her, when her phone buzzes again. 'Luke, hi! You're not anywhere near the supermarket, are you?'

'I am, but I rang to say that I just heard from a friend at TV One, that a Cabinet minister has resigned. It's not been officially released yet, but it will be at midday and he thinks it is Guthrie, Department of Conservation. There is also a rumour that two police personnel in high positions have taken early retirement – but nothing confirmed yet. Not that leaving will protect them.'

'Wow - the first resignation of a Cabinet minister. I presume it will be for so-called family reasons? I wonder if the Prime Minister will risk sticking his neck out and make a comment?'

Luke's voice is cheerfully cynical. 'Of course not. And if he does, he'll use words like appalled, disappointed and shocked. And then there will be another one or two leaving the sinking ship, I'm sure. What do we need from the supermarket?'

Rumble is working from his own place that evening, and the flat is quiet and tidy after they spent the afternoon tidying and sorting the debris left from weeks of using the flat as an office as well as a place to live. Now Luke turns the TV off after the news and reaches for his book, and Minnie says, 'I must look up Royal Commissions and what they do - I suppose you know all about it already?'

'It's the most powerful tool to investigate we have, and it can only be appointed for a specific purpose, by the Government, and once it's been set up nobody can disband it, not even the Government who set it up. The Commission has a totally independent existence – sometimes they take years to finish investigating. In which case it's up to some subsequent Government to act on the recommendations they make.'

He puts the book back on the table. 'Remember when I said I could guess who would be appointed to sit on a Royal Commission if there was one? It's nearly always a retired judge or two, hopefully with no political bias. Sometimes they include an academic with some special knowledge, like the one today.'

'And they can demand answers and information?'

'Oh yes, they can access everything - classified documents, information that people have tried to hide, bank and taxation records, literally anything.'

Minnie frowned. 'If that's the case it will take forever before they produce a report or a conclusion or whatever it's called.'

'Sure – it will take time, but in the meantime all these people will be called to testify under oath. A Royal Commission has the same powers as a court – people testify under oath and if they lie, it's perjury. And masses of information will become publicly known - things that we could never have unearthed. And bit by bit Broker's network will be revealed. Of course, they can only investigate according to the terms of reference that the Government draws up, but it's the best thing that could have happened. They've had to get retired judges, of course, so they knew they hadn't been involved with Broker.'

'I hope they find out who Broker is at an early stage, so we can relax. It won't be over until they get him – or her.'

• • •

The following day a massive demonstration takes place after word spreads via social media. Luke hears about it from Bella, and they watch mesmerized as hundreds of comments stream in on Twitter and Face Book, soon growing to thousands. It is livestreamed on social media and YouTube from drones flying illegally low over the CBD. People leave offices and shops, drive in from the suburbs and gather at Parliament. Surprisingly quickly the crowd grows to thousands, then tens of thousands. At an early stage the police try to throw a cordon around Parliament and the High Court, but it is too late, and the crowd continues to swell all afternoon; city traffic is at a standstill. The mass of people spreads further out in all directions until it totally fills the streets and open areas around Parliament, and shops and businesses close their doors; the city centre is paralyzed.

By five o'clock the city centre is full of chanting protestors, and still people continue to flow in. Cars are parked illegally on the sides of the motorway and in every available place as people abandon them and continue on foot into the centre of town. The crowd spreads further and backs up along Lambton Quay and The Terrace, and down along the waterfront.

Police efforts to block newcomers from joining the protest fail. Peaceful crowds simply link arms and push aside police in riot gear by sheer force of numbers and continue towards the centre of the vortex. Police helicopters circle overhead, protest speakers mount the steps of Parliament with loudhailers and the crowd chants and roars. It is not until mid-morning the next day that the last protesters disperse, after immense problems clearing the thousands of cars blocking arterial roads and the motorway. To everyone's amazement there is no violence and no arrests.

Minnie and Luke alternate between watching it live-streamed on the Internet and on TV, unable to take their eyes off the action. Continuous footage from drones and surrounding high rise buildings show the enormity of the crowd seen from different angles.

'It's like some kind of slow-moving liquid,' says Luke. 'It flows out in all directions, changes its shape and fills every available space. There's no way they can stop it, they just have to wait. It's interesting that they aren't using water-canon or teargas or anything like that. Must be orders from above to keep it peaceful.'

The Government and security forces issue statements about the size of the crowd, downplaying the numbers to minimize the impact. Within hours social media and TV news show material from drones with artificial intelligence estimates of the crowd numbers in white text on images from streets and open places, making nonsense of the official figures. The next morning someone flies a drone low over the grounds of Parliament before any attempt to clean up the resulting mess has been made. A carpet of placards has been left lying face up on the ground and images of signs demanding honesty, open debate and an end to corruption appear in global news media and on social media.

'It's extraordinary,' says Luke at lunchtime, after they have watched the nearly continuous news coverage on TV for a second day. 'We've triggered something in the general population that I really wasn't expecting – it's become a movement and taken on a life of its own. God knows what might happen next – I can't wait.'

Early that evening the Minister of Primary Industries is reported to have 'died peacefully in hospital surrounded by his family', and it's rumoured that he never regained consciousness after his collapse in the Debating Chamber. Luke and Minnie are in the car on the way to Bella's flat when they hear it and look at each other without comment. There is nothing left to say, it's too late and all possible comments have been made already. They drive on and talk about other things.

This is the first time we've managed to mentally stand to one side, thinks Minnie, maybe we *will* learn to just let it go, and not feel it is our issue any longer, that the world has taken over the campaign and we can do nothing to influence it.

The first consequence that makes it feel personal is the suicide of the civil servant they identified on the bistro's security video. The news item simply states that a civil servant put under scrutiny by the corruption evidence has been found dead, and that police are not looking for anyone else in connection with his death.

Minnie and Rumble hear the news as they drive back from visiting Brendan at the rest home.

'It's weird that I'm always in the car when I hear these things,' says Minnie and calls Luke. 'Did you hear it, Luke?' She is struggling to come to terms with the fact that she has contributed to someone committing suicide. She listens without saying anything for a couple of minutes, looking absently at the traffic.

'OK, I'll try. See you later.'

'Did Luke know anything more?'

'Someone from the TV One news team told him that his wife found him this morning - he'd taken an overdose of sleeping pills and drowned in the bath during the night.'

Rumble glances at her. 'And what is it you'll try? You said OK to something.'

She hesitates for a moment then decides to be honest. 'Luke says I have to remember that we didn't kill him, we told the world he was a thief and a cheat, and he killed himself.'

'Too true!' says Rumble and goes around a corner too fast. 'I know you have an issue with some of Luke's attitudes. He's bloody radical when it comes to punishment, I agree with you there. But you must admit that if it hadn't been for him, you wouldn't be alive - and he didn't actually kill Dustman, though he did let him die by doing nothing to stop it.'

'I know, Rumble, but to me there's no moral difference. To me it's still killing – if the intent is that someone will die. But I'm learning to live with this ongoing conflict between what I feel for him and some of his attitudes.'

63

As soon as the apartment door closes behind them, Rumble returns to the conversation they had in the car. 'Sit down Petal, have a cup of tea or some grapefruit juice. I'm going to have a beer and tell you something you ought to know.' He sounds troubled in a way she doesn't associate with Rumble, troubled and hesitant.

'God Rumble, you make it sound scary. Tell me now!'

'No, let's get ourselves a drink each and sit down, this might take a bit of time to explain.'

Minnie knows it must be about Luke and seeing Rumble look so serious it frightens her. What does he know about Luke, that he hasn't told her? Has he found out that Luke has actually killed someone? Her mind is full of frightening possibilities, each one worse than the last.

Rumble drinks some of his beer, looks thoughtfully at the floor and says nothing for what seems like an eternity before he shifts his focus to her.

'This is going to sound crazy, and I'm not sure if I've blown it up out of all proportion, but I must tell you. It's been on my mind ever since you were abducted, and I can't stop thinking about it. Every now and then, when I'm with you and Luke, I remember and start worrying about you again.'

He takes a deep breath, his gaze just to one side of her face, as if he is reluctant to see her reaction to what he is about to say.

'When Luke called from your house that night he was like a madman. Not ranting and raving, but he was tight and closed-up somehow, as if his focus was so pin-pointed he couldn't bear to waste time on talking to me. He did talk, of course he did - we discussed options, plans and what-have-you, but only half his attention was on me.'

Minnie can see how uncomfortable he is - reluctant to tell her and struggling with how to say it, and she herself is so tense that it's hard to breathe.

'And then the next morning, suddenly, for no obvious reason, he was back. I mean his mind, his attention. And he said the weirdest bloody thing, he looked straight at me and he said, "thank God - she's alive, she's in pain and she's scared, but she is alive". It was the strangest thing, as if he'd had a vision. I thought it was just something his brain had produced, and if it made him feel better – well, fine. I was still beside myself, sure you were dead.'

This soothes her worry that something Rumble knows will force her to end her relationship with Luke, because living without him is not an option she can bear to think about. 'And then? Did he explain?'

'No, I didn't ask - he said nothing more and we carried on searching. And as I said before, he was like some bloody superhero, climbing up and down those nearly vertical slopes looking for you, determined to find you. There was one other moment with the same kind of weird thing – he shouted, "No!" and something I couldn't catch. And then he said "sorry, I can't bear it, she thinks she's going to die alone down there". And then he changed the subject.'

Minnie, her mind suffused with relief, puts her hand on his. 'Poor you – as if he was losing his mind and you were stressed out yourself.'

'Minnie, listen, I think he can hack into your head somehow. I know it sounds like science fiction and it scares the shit out of me. It's like he has some kind awareness of what's going on in your mind, ESP or whatever they call it. I've thought a lot about it – can't get it out of my mind. I never thought that kind of stuff was real, but now I think it might be. And you should know about it – I'm certain he does it.'

She smiles at his worried face.

'I know about it Rumble – it's true, he can do it, at least to some extent. He knows when I'm in pain or in trouble. He thought I was dead while I was unconscious, but when I woke up, he knew I was alive. It's happened several times and I can't dispute it. And he can tell anger and fear from pain. But don't worry, he can't read my actual thoughts, just the effect things have on me.'

She watches his face to see how he reacts, but he still looks worried. 'But isn't that like he's invading your privacy, don't you mind?'

'God, Rumble - it's the strangest thing that ever happened to me, and at first I was really upset. It turned all my ideas of what is possible and not possible upside-down. But I must tell you the rest of it - it's better that you know it all. I don't want you to worry about it.'

She thinks fast; how much will she tell him and how will she put it? And she will have to tell Luke that Rumble knows both sides of it, but it's for the best.

'When I discovered that Luke can literally feel my distress, something else became clear, something I'd been wondering about for a while. You see, his reactions to my feelings feed back to me – it's like we're in a loop. You know how you sometimes talk to yourself inside your head – like you're talking out loud, but you just think the words, different from ordinary thoughts - more deliberate? When Dustman grabbed me outside Te Papa that night and pushed the gun into my ribs, I was so scared, Rumble - I thought he might shoot me. But I had this little whisper in my head, very quiet, saying "be calm, don't panic, be strong". And it made me calmer, and I felt more in control. I can't remember it from when Dustman invaded the house. Perhaps because that's not a direct memory, I kind of recovered it afterwards, so maybe there was a whisper at the time. I'm sure there must have been, because Luke got such a strong signal of fear and pain from me. But during those days in the Remutakas it happened several times. Always encouraging me to be strong, to not give up - it was very comforting. At the time I had no idea it was coming from Luke.'

She tries to think of a way to explain what it was like. 'Imagine that I'm standing right behind you, and you don't know that I'm there, and I whisper as quietly as I possibly can – you'll hear it, but only just, and you won't know who it is. That's how it feels.'

Rumble looks more conflicted than ever; she must make him more comfortable about what he sees as either threatening to her or impossible to believe.

'Please don't worry about it. It is weird, but it *is* real. Luke didn't know I can hear what I call the whisper – he wasn't trying to say anything to me. And he has this strange mental connection with

Bella too – but without the feedback loop. I've asked him why he thinks that is and all he could say was "don't ask me, I've no idea" - but it is definitely real. It's not something he or I have any control over.'

Is this the day for baring her soul completely or should she wait to another day when Rumble has not already been drawn into her conflicting emotions? But the wish to have another opinion decides her.

'Rumble, there's something I want to ask you. Do you think you could love a killer? And I don't just mean romantic love – just love.'

If he is surprised by the sudden change of subject, he doesn't show it. 'I presume you're talking about Luke. He's the killer here?'

'Yes, but say it was me, and you discover I am capable of killing – or wanting to kill someone. Would you stop loving me? Or would you adapt to it? How do you think you would square it with your conscience?'

Her eyes are fixed on his face; she wants to catch every shade of emotion she can read there. If he is going to soften his stance so as not to hurt her, she wants to know what his first fleeting reaction is.

When Rumble answers, he speaks slowly, sifting through his thoughts, careful with the words he uses. 'Well for a start he's not a killer, as far as I know he's not killed anyone – yet. I know what you're thinking – first he was prepared to let Dustman drown, if he couldn't swim, and then he refused to let you stop the truck and save him.'

He pauses for a moment. 'OK, maybe that counts as being a killer, by omission rather than something he actively did. Like you said the day it happened, the intent was there. But don't forget that Luke knew that Dustman was completely ruthless, prepared to torture you and leave you to die. That's a pretty potent reason for being unforgiving. And neither could I forgive him, Minnie – but to kill him I would have to be in a situation where I acted in the heat of the moment. And who knows, maybe I would have refused to prevent him being crushed – impossible to know for sure.'

He pauses again, and she waits.

'OK, could I love a killer? Yes, I could - if you love a person, you love them and that's that. If I found out that you had killed to get someone's money or for some other selfish reason, to benefit from their death – I'd probably stop loving you right then. I'd just look at you and think "I don't love you anymore". Not like a decision, it would just happen. But if you killed someone, who had hurt and maimed me and left me to die, and you did it because you thought that person was going to avoid any consequences – or that they might try again or do it to someone else - well yes, I'm sure that I would still love you.'

Minnie says sadly, 'That's kind of what I feel too, but it has worried me so much. I tried to not love him, more or less on principle - but you're right. You can't decide to not love someone - either you love them or you don't. And then you have to make a decision if you can live with them or not, but that's another story.'

Rumble visibly hesitates before he speaks. 'I'll tell you what, Petal – you'll never find anyone who loves you like he does, I'm sure of it. When I came back with the medical supplies, that evening after we found you, he was kneeling on the floor beside you. He had finished washing you and he had wrapped you up in that rug – and he was untangling twigs and bits of rubbish out of your hair, piece by piece, very gently – I'll never forget the look on his face.'

She can only nod silently.

'God, Minnie – the things that have happened to us in the last couple of months - would we have started this if we'd known?' His face is troubled, and she has no answer.

64

Over the next couple of weeks there are signs of unrest both among politicians and the general public. Speculation is rife and the media hound ministers and state servants without mercy. The print media start a list that quickly acquires the name The Gone List, which is published whenever there is a new development. There are rumours about police staff and judges, but no names. The Gone List is a mixture of resignations and 'on paid leave pending investigation' or people moved sideways for unspecified reasons; and three deaths so far, two self-inflicted.

'What's the Gone List tally now, the unofficial one?' says Rumble one evening, when they are discussing a news item about resignation rumours in the Ministry of the Environment.

'Hang on,' says Luke and counts on his fingers. 'The media version is fourteen, but including rumours I get sixteen or seventeen, depends on what you regard as 'gone'. If it means dead or resigned or on garden leave, let's say seventeen. If you add the one who's been moved, for no apparent reason, to a position where she can do no harm, then it's eighteen. It will be interesting to see how long it takes before the system starts creaking under the strain. They're mostly linked to four Government departments.'

'I wondered about that last week,' says Minnie, 'when that guy Smith resigned on the same day as somebody else did. They're losing top people, both state servants and politicians. How many more before they reach critical mass or rather critical lack of mass? And then what?'

Luke grins. 'Nobody knows - perhaps there will be a vote of no confidence and the Government will fall. The state services will be OK for a long time – they have career people and a built-in succession plan, people ready to step up to the next level. It's damn interesting though – my press gallery friends are laying bets on the outcome. It's like a real-life political science experiment. And it's spreading - to start with it was just questions being asked in other countries, but now it is moving up a level everywhere. Look at the UK - demonstrations demanding investigations, the media have taken it up – the same in France and Germany. It's an international movement now.'

Rumble nods. 'Bloody incredible when you think of how it started. We thought it was just a couple of corrupt officials, we had no idea it would turn into this monster of dishonesty being revealed. I suppose this sort of thing has become more common since big business took over running the Western world, not to mention those fucking Russians - funding stuff on the sly and manipulating things all over the globe. This deepfake stuff is pure evil.'

'There's a lot of speculation about who helped Broker move money around to clean it up,' says Luke. 'Even with Bitcoin and the other currencies they can still do some tracing these days. So, it's the same sort of issues as in the Panama papers case years ago and then the Pandora papers, layers of deceit and corruption coming to light. Very interesting, but hard to untangle.'

Minnie shakes her head, dismayed at the deviousness of the world. 'I don't want to think of it – it's ruined my faith in human decency.'

As the days pass there are fewer demands on their time, and they exist in a state of limbo, removed from the action with their lives partially on hold.

'We're in a bubble,' says Luke one evening, when Rumble has come over for a visit. 'Minli and I don't go out to work, we can't go and live in my flat yet and now we have very little to do. It's very strange and a bit boring, and we still don't know who Broker is. I wish they'd find him, so we can have normal lives again. Perhaps we should go on a holiday to some tropical place and pretend we have regular lives? And I must start looking for a new job.'

Rumble nods. 'Yeah, I know, I'm lucky compared to you. At least I can continue working. To tell you the truth, I've been asked to take on so many jobs that I've had to turn people down – from all over the place. But I know what you mean about a bubble. What is it people call that calm patch? You know, between the tide coming in and going out again?'

'Slack water,' says Minnie. 'And that's it – perfect description. We worked like mad and lived on fear and adrenalin, and then everything went crazy after the press conference and, now it's boringly calm. And then it will ramp up again when the Commission gets going. And I'm living on my savings.'

'Yeah, – suddenly they'll get into gear and we'll be questioned and interviewed and have to make statements,' says Luke. 'I've nearly forgotten what normal is like – going to work, coming home, only thinking of my own life.'

'At least we don't get asked for comments all the time now. It was like being in a loop, same questions and same answers.' Minnie looks accusingly at Rumble. 'How come you got so few of those jobs, Rumble? Was it just your famous talent for avoiding talking to strangers, or did you bribe Luke not to schedule you for any?'

Luke is opening his mouth to reply when Minnie's phone buzzes. She answers, listens for a moment and disappears into the bedroom, closing the door behind her. Rumble looks at Luke with raised eyebrows. Luke is silent for a moment, then he says baldly, 'Bad news.'

The Emergency Department seems very low-key with just a few people waiting and talking quietly.

'I've come to see my father - Brendan Porter,' says Minnie to the woman at the desk. 'He came in by ambulance from a rest home a short while ago.'

The woman gets up and comes around to their side of the glass screen, her face blandly professional, but Minnie notices that she avoids eye-contact.

'Yes, of course, come with me please.'

They follow her across the waiting area and along a corridor with curtained cubicles. She stops by an open door, motions for them to enter. 'Please go in. Dr Walker has been looking after your father.'

At that moment Minnie knows without any doubt that Brendan is dead. She stops outside the open door for a moment and Luke puts his hand on her back and gently pushes her forward.

'I am so sorry,' says the incredibly young-looking Dr Walker, who is chubby and pretty, with a face better suited to laughter than seriousness. 'He was brought in unconscious, and he died about ten minutes after he arrived. I believe he slipped on a wet bathroom floor and hit his head very hard. The fall probably fractured his skull, but as yet we can't say for sure.'

Luke looks at Minnie, who remains silent, and asks, 'Was he alone when it happened?'

The doctor seems relieved that someone is responding and looks at her computer screen. 'It says here that he was in the bathroom having a shower, while a caregiver was tidying his room, ready for him to go to bed. She heard him fall and thinks he hit his head on the edge of the toilet.'

She looks at the silent Minnie and says kindly. 'Would you like to see him?'

Minnie gets up and says calmly. 'Yes, thank you, I would.'

Twenty minutes later they walk through the suddenly busy waiting area and out into the damp night air. As they cross the parking lot, they meet a man carrying a baby wrapped in a rug, followed by two small children in pyjamas and dressing gowns. People always say that life goes on, thinks Minnie, and of course it does, but right now I feel as if everything is on hold and I'm not sure I know how to start it up again. She pauses with her hand on the car door and looks up at the night sky, and everything feels unreal and distant. She remembers the sensation of ultimate loneliness, when she realised there would be nobody after her to be interested in the family photos.

'I can't believe it,' she says to nobody in particular and gets into the car. They don't speak during the drive back to the apartment, where the lights are on, but Rumble has left. When Luke closes the door behind them, Minnie leans her face against his shoulder and says in a voice muffled by his jacket, 'There's nobody left now, just me. I knew it would happen one day, but now it's real. It feels very strange.'

'Wrong,' he says. 'As long as my heart is beating you will never be alone.'

65

The day of the funeral is a typical Wellington late autumn day, cold and blustery, with a threat of rain hanging in the air. Luke has gone back to his flat to get changed, and Minnie is in the bathroom looking at herself in the mirror.

She went shopping with Bella the day before and decided that black was too much. 'I don't want black,' she said to Bella. 'I never wear black. What do you think - grey?'

Bella said decisively, 'God no, you should *never* wear grey. And you must stop wearing camouflage, trying to go unnoticed. Let's look for aubergine. I don't mean purple, but deep, dark aubergine, just like the vegetable.'

Now Minnie looks at herself in the mirror with a sense of awe and thinks how clever Bella is. The colour makes her pale skin look luminous and emphasizes the red of her hair, which Bella insists is her best point and which Minnie has disliked since childhood.

'You're just stuck in this negative thing from primary school when you got teased. I think you look like some fairy tale creature with red curls – like a cartoon princess or some manga character. So, you've got to pick the right colours. Thank God you don't do mad things to your hair and try to look like everyone else. You know what they say – if you've got it, flaunt it.'

Now the sound of a key in the door makes her turn. 'Luke – wow!' she says. 'You look extremely ...'

'Extremely ... what?'

She contemplates him for a moment, and then she starts to

laugh. 'Extremely everything. I don't know, maybe impressive is the word? I've never seen you in a suit apart from on TV. You've turned into a different person somehow.'

'Still the same old me,' he says. 'What time do we leave?'

'Quarter past eleven. Bella is bringing Ling and Rumble, and Andy and Cara will come straight from the airport.'

'Is Jane coming?'

'I don't know. The notice was in the paper, but I haven't heard from her since that angry text message.'

A caregiver from the rest home is the only person at the funeral chapel when they arrive. She stands by the door like a lonely sentinel and greets them with relief. 'I got here far too early,' she says. 'I must have got the time wrong - I had to go inside and check I had the right day.'

Minnie is touched that she has come in her time off and takes her hand. 'It's very kind of you to give up your free time.'

The woman smiles then. 'I really liked Brendan,' she says. 'He was always telling me about interesting things, stuff that I'd never heard of - stories about gods from long ago and big battles and the man who ran from Marathon. And my name is Helen, so he told me about Helen of Troy. He always had a new story for me.'

'That's what it was like when I was a child - he loved telling the ancient stories and he would have been so pleased that someone had time to listen to him.'

Over Helen's shoulder she sees Jane approaching in a small group of people and steels herself for something potentially hurtful, but Jane just kisses her cheek and looks genuinely sad.

'God, Minnie, as if you haven't had enough to cope with already. I'm so sorry.'

Then she stands back, looks Minnie up and down and smiles. 'You look fantastic in that colour!'

When they finally take their seats inside the chapel, Luke leans close and says quietly, 'Jane is right. You look amazing, like a fairy – one with a mind like a steel trap.'

Minnie has chosen a restaurant on Oriental Parade for lunch, because her family used to go for weekend walks along the waterfront there, stopping for coffee or ice cream along the way. It's a typical Wellington late autumn day with racing clouds and waves on the harbour. The view through the restaurant windows is dramatic with occasional glints of sun on the water and seagulls riding the blustery wind.

At the end of the afternoon Minnie and Luke drive Andy and Cara to the airport and Luke says, 'We'll wait with you till the plane leaves. Let's find somewhere comfortable to sit, so you can spend a bit longer together. You go on inside and I'll park the car.'

They sit beside a window in the airport bar, and Andy and Minnie talk about their shared childhood summers and their memories of Brendan.

'He would have approved of today,' says Minnie. 'A very low-key funeral and then a great lunch in a part of town he loved. What a pity your parents are overseas and your sisters so far away - it could have been a bit of a family reunion.'

'We'll do it next summer,' says Andy, 'like we used to - all of us together at the beach. I think my sisters are all having an our-side-of-the-family Christmas this year. They have it with their various in-laws every second year – they try really hard to be fair to everyone.'

66

Life in the flat develops a rhythm of its own. Luke is contracted to write a weekly political column in The Dominion and spends a lot of time making notes for a book. His old boss gets in touch and offers him his presenter job back at higher pay, and he turns it down. Cartwell gets in touch about a 'roving project' job, but Luke says, 'no thank you'.

'I'll hold off for a while - I need a complete change.'

Minnie is sorting out Brendan's estate, nearly overwhelmed by the number of insurance forms and paperwork. Rumble comes and goes, shares their meals and discusses what develops in the public arena. Occasionally Bella comes for a meal and they play Scrabble with a set she has donated for their amusement, and twice they all have dinner at Ling's house.

'Are you finished with these?'

Minnie is filling in yet another form and looks up to see what Luke is holding. 'Yes, those are done, I'm taking them to the lawyer today, and the claim forms for the cars too. I finally have copies of all the police and fire reports.'

She has spent days getting everything completed, claim forms for three different insurance companies and various police reports to back them up. The process has been complicated by the fact that Brendan's estate has not been finalized.

'That poor lawyer, I think she's really over it. Everything about this has a snag in it. The claim on my car is irregular, because it hasn't been recovered and inspected and no police report was made at the time. And then Brendan's house and car were destroyed – which we could have processed easily while he was alive, but he died, so now it's complicated by having an estate making the claims for something that happened before it was an estate. And on top of that I found a small life insurance policy he'd kept for some obscure reason– I've never seen so much paperwork.'

'Have you got all the details you need - car ownership papers and that sort of thing?'

'Yes, most of them. Remember those boxes you and Rumble took away that night, the ones beside the front door? Those were the important things I found when I sorted Brendan's papers - all sorts of things including photos, and I put the boxes in the hall, because I hadn't decided where to keep them.'

Luke smiles. 'It seems incredible now. It was pure chance that we took them with us. We didn't know what was in them, but Rumble had a quick look and saw family photos, so he said, 'let's grab these in case that fucker comes back'. The way they were sitting there in the hall, it kind of looked as if you planned to take them somewhere. We never dreamt that the whole house would be destroyed.'

When Minnie returns late in the day from a long meeting with the lawyer, Luke is standing at the balcony door looking out into the early evening dusk. He doesn't immediately turn around when she opens the door, and a shiver of apprehension creeps down her spine. When he turns to face her his dark eyes are strained. 'Broker called.'

'What!'

'Just after you left. I've talked to the chairman of the Royal Commission, told him all the details. I'll go and make a statement under oath tomorrow. And I've given them, I mean the Commission and the police, the number he called from - but I'm sure Broker has a stack of disposable phones that can't be traced.'

'What did he say?'

Luke hesitates.

'Let's sit down. I think I need a drink and I'm sure you could do with a cup of something after that endless insurance meeting,'

Minnie holds her mug between both hands; suddenly she feels cold. The thought that Broker has made contact has shaken her, because somehow over time he has become less real in her mind, more like a concept than an actual person.

'Tell me, please! What did Broker say?'

'He said he knows that I started investigating him because of things I found out when I was in the press gallery. He's sure that I know who he is - there's no doubt in his mind.'

He shakes his head and drinks some of his beer. 'I told him I have no idea who he is. I said the information we gave the media is exactly and completely all we found – there's nothing more. But he thinks I'm planning to expose him in some sort of personal news scoop. He's furious we got hold of Dustman's phone and that Rumble broke into it – that really riles him. He asked if I wanted money, offered me a fortune not to publish my so-called scoop. He was raving, Minli, foaming at the mouth. In the end he completely lost his cool and said he'll find me and torture me and bury me alive. He's obsessed with revenge; his empire is in ruins, and he's under siege – and he needs to punish someone.'

'God, that's terrible!' Minnie's mind is in turmoil. 'Did you recognize his voice? *Do* you think you know who he is?'

'No, I don't. I told the Commissioner that I thought at first there was something familiar about the voice, but I couldn't put my finger on it. Maybe a phrase he used, I don't know - but I didn't get that vibe again. Broker is totally discounting the fact that it started with the phone Jane found, and I got involved later. When he found out I was part of this, he leapt to the conclusion that I've been working on it for a long time, since they warned me off last year. I told the Commissioner all this and he asked if I wanted protection.'

'You should have protection! If Broker is losing the plot, he could do anything.'

'But he doesn't know where we are, does he - or he would have sent someone here already. Thank God we didn't move back to my flat. Even with all this attention nobody has found us here - which seems incredible really, seeing how many times we've been out in the open lately. I'll stay here till we decide on a plan.'

There is no answer, when Minnie calls Rumble, so she sends him a message: 'We need to see you. Please come asap.'

He walks in an hour later, concerned and confused. 'What's going on? I could tell you didn't think a phone call would do the trick - what's the emergency?'

The news about Broker's call stops him dead in his tracks, stunned.

'Holy shit, that's incredible! Which phone did he call - your own or the media phone?'

'My own. The cops will trace which cell the caller was in when he made the call, but his phone was set to show no number.'

Rumble listens intently to Luke's description of what Broker said with a grim face. 'So that bastard is off on a tangent now, blaming everything on you. Sorry to sound so dire, but it seems to have become a personal vendetta. You've got to be bloody careful.'

Luke glances at Minnie before he replies. 'I'll be very careful. I'll stay here for a couple of days longer, so I can sort out some place to go.'

Does he mean to go off on his own, she thinks, without me? Surely the police have a witness protection system. Why not use that? I'll wait until he tells me what he's thinking – he probably needs time. Questions won't be helpful.

She braces herself to be patient and lives through forty-eight hours of torment. On the third day she goes to sign papers at her lawyer's office and returns to an empty flat. Her heart misses a beat; he didn't say he was going out. Has he left without telling her where he is going? But there is a note on the table, 'I might be late, will bring dinner. L'

67

When Luke finally returns, it's early evening and he brings Italian take-away food, a bottle of wine for himself and a carton of her favourite pink grapefruit juice. Their forced attempt to have a normal conversation fails and they finish the meal in silence. Minnie gets up, overwhelmed by a sense of dread and says in a voice that comes out like a cry for help, 'This is driving me crazy, Luke. Please tell me what is going on!'

His expression is one of tight control and restraint; she knows he is going to say that he is leaving. For the last two days she has walked a tightrope of indecision; asking and being told something that will change her life, or not asking and imagining the worst.

She says flatly, 'You are leaving.' A statement, not a question.

'I have to. Broker will get me one way or the other if I stay. I can't hide – there's nowhere in this country that would be far enough. He'll stop at nothing – I think he's half mad.'

He gets his phone out, opens a text message and holds it up.

"This came yesterday. It's from yet another unknown number, but it's Broker.'

The message reads, 'You are a dead man walking. I will track you down. You can't hide from me.'

"Oh, my God – he *is* mad!'

'Yeah, I think he is. And we don't know what resources he still has. I've discussed it with Paul Morris and Rumble – we all agree that the best thing is to issue a press statement to say that I'm leaving the country and why I'm doing it, make all the details public, including that I'll tell nobody where I am going, not one single person, not you or the Commission or my family. I'll assume another name and live somewhere, where nobody would think to look for me. No communication with anyone at all for some time. I hope that if I disappear, he will give up or he'll be identified. If I stay, he'll try to get to me through you, or Ling or Bella. I really think he's insane – and very dangerous. I have to wait until they work out who he is.'

'When are you going?'

'Tomorrow.'

The blood drains from her heart and she stumbles, nearly falls and Luke steadies her. They lie close together all night, occasionally talking, sometimes sleeping lightly, then waking up and talking again.

At one point he says, 'Thank you for not trying to talk me out of this - it's hard enough as it is. I can't imagine life without you.'

She puts her hand on his face. 'It's better this way because I want you to be safe. The world would be a dark place without you. Better to know you are alive somewhere else than having you risk being killed here.'

Later he says, 'I could trick him into the open and kill him, but then I would lose you - and I'd end up in prison. But remember what I said – I'll kill anyone who harms you. If he harms you, I will hear about it, and I'll come back and kill him. Right now, the best option for us all is for me to disappear and protect you by my absence.'

'How will you live? Have you got enough money? It could be a long time.'

'I've given Power of Attorney to Rumble. He's buying my flat and Bella is going to live there. I need the money, so I asked him to organize a real estate firm to sell it, but he thinks this is a better idea. Bella doesn't know yet. And he'll sell my car, when I get it back from my mate, and some shares I have. The money will sit in an account here and I can transfer money to an account I've set up in Switzerland. I've put some things I want you to keep for me into a suitcase – it's in the other bedroom.'

Numb with misery she listens without comment, there is nothing she can say.

'Rumble has access to the bank account through the power of attorney - he'll be able to check it and let you all know that I am alive and well and using money – somewhere. And I know that you and he will keep an eye on Bella for me. Maybe I haven't done this the right way, but I had to act fast. I didn't involve you – it would have been too hard on both of us, discussing things and planning.'

Just before dawn he says, 'I'll go and say goodbye to Bella and Ling first thing - my flight leaves at midday. I'll tell them what I told you, nothing more. I said goodbye to Rumble yesterday. He's sending out a press release I wrote - the fact that I have left and why, so that will be big news for the next couple of days. You'll be asked for comments – I'm sorry, but there is nothing I can do about that. I'll use my own passport to exit New Zealand, so Broker can check that I really left – I'm sure he knows how to get that done even now.'

She doesn't ask where he is going or if he plans to get a false passport somewhere else. She knows he wouldn't tell her, maybe he doesn't know himself. And she knows that when he has left, her heart will break and he will feel her pain and know that she is inconsolable without him, but there is no help for either of them.

When he is leaving, she says, 'Just one thing, Luke – wherever you are I will always belong to you.'

68

eight weeks later

Ling opens the door and hugs her tight. 'How are you, Minli? I'm so pleased you decided to come to see me. Come into the kitchen while I cook.'

Minnie puts her coat on a stool by the breakfast bar and perches on another. The kitchen is bright and warm after the chill of the winter evening. Ling is chopping vegetables into tiny pieces and adding them to a heap of ingredients in a large bowl. Jars and bags of mysterious ingredients are spread over the bench and the air is scented by spices.

'Would you like a cup of tea? Dinner won't be ready for an hour at least. I hope you don't mind, but I invited Bella and Rumble too. It cheered me up when you called and said you would come and see me, so I thought a little dinner party would be nice.'

Minnie sips her tea and re-considers how to start. Now she must say what she has come to say before the others arrive, instead of introducing the subject gradually over dinner, because Ling must hear it first.

'I am going to send a message to Luke.'

Ling's knife stops mid-air and she stares at Minnie. 'Has he been in touch? Do you know where he is?'

'No, I don't. You know how he said he wouldn't communicate via any social media or in any way that could be traced? And whether he stays away for one year or three years, there must be a complete separation, no contact at all?'

Ling nods, her hand with the knife still suspended just above the chopping board, waiting.

'I think I've found the perfect way to send short messages to him. Rumble is going to help me, but he doesn't know it yet – I'll tell him when he arrives. My message can only be thirty-six letters long, but I can do it more than once - it's a new way of communicating.'

'How on earth are you doing to do it? Or would you rather not tell me?'

Minnie smiles affectionately at Ling, pleased to give her some comfort as well as news. 'Of course, I'll tell you. You know how all Luke's money is in a bank account here, and when he needs some, he goes online and transfers a sum to his Swiss account – and from there to wherever he is. He gave Rumble access to the New Zealand account for the sale of the flat and the car – but also so Rumble can check it now and then and see that Luke is alive and well and using money somewhere in the world.'

'And? I don't see what you're getting at.'

'Now and then I will ask Rumble to deposit $10 into Luke's New Zealand bank account and to type my message into the fields where you can put comments and references. You know, like an invoice number or whatever the person you are paying needs to know. My first message is a tight fit. It will say 'Loveu.besafe.yoursonduefeb.Ihearu.M' – all thirty-six spaces used.'

The sensation she thinks of as a whisper in her head still happens at intervals, sometimes not for a couple of weeks. It is just the slightest sensation, ghosts of whispered words from far away.

This book is dedicated to all those who contributed to it.

To my husband, Brett Clough,
for his endless patience
and understanding.

To Andrene Low for the
book and cover design
and much appreciated advice.

To Annika Bennett
for believing in me.

To Camilla Koutsos,
who loved this book before
it was more than an idea
in my mind

MANY THANKS

We hope you've enjoyed reading this story and would consider leaving a review on your favourite review site, or with the retailer you purchased from.

These are not only much appreciated, they also help other readers discover new authors.

For more about other titles in this series, please read on.

ALSO BY TINA CLOUGH

THE GIRL WHO LIVED TWICE

What would you do if you woke up one morning and found that time had rewound exactly a year? Would you revisit your past mistakes and try to do better? Would you try to get revenge on those who had wronged you? Or would you use what you knew to get rich? When Mia finds herself in her own past, she must decide how best to use her pre-knowledge of one year's worth of events and personal issues.

RUNNING TOWARDS DANGER

When Karen's flat-mate Nick is gunned down in front of her in the street her life is turned upside-down. Everything she thought she knew about him turns out to be a lie. She becomes a suspect in the police investigation and drug bosses think she knows where Nick has hidden a large sum of money. When her life is threatened, she decides to leave town and disappear.

Karen becomes Cara and creates an anonymous existence, severs all links to her past and adopts a cash-based way of life that leaves no electronic traces. But despite her careful planning danger still stalks her and she is forced to make dramatic choices in the face of threats and brutal violence.

Can she trust the man she is attracted to, or has he been sent by the killers to gain her confidence and find the money they believe she has?

THE CHINESE PROVERB

Book 1 - Hunter Grant Series

Army veteran Hunter Grant thought he had left war behind in Afghanistan – a conflict that left him with physical and psychological scars.

But finding an unconscious girl in the Northland bush and gradually untangling her story involves him in warfare of a different kind in his own country.

Hunter sets out to find and punish the man Dao calls Master, but he soon finds there is more to this story than enslavement. Before long he himself is being hunted by the overlord of a drug empire whose sole objective is to kill Dao because she knows too much.

Protecting her and waging war while trying to keep the police from stifling his enterprise takes all Hunter's ingenuity and determination and puts him in deadly jeopardy.

ONE SINGLE THING

Book 2 - Hunter Grant Series

Journalist Hope Barber disappears two weeks after returning to New Zealand from an assignment in Pakistan, leaving her front door open and her bag and phone inside. The police are tight-lipped about their reluctance to act, and Hunter Grant and Dao agree to help Hope's brother Noah find her. Details about Hope's time in Pakistan gradually emerge but only raise more questions.

Was Hope under surveillance?
Was she linked to terrorists?
And who is the man Hope called 'my stalker'?

FOLDED

Book 3 - Hunter Grant Series

First notes asking for help and folded into tiny origami shapes are found outside a city apartment building, then a physics textbook with tiny writing between the lines and then the woman who found them abruptly resigns and disappears. Are the notes asking for help real or is it a game? Hunter Grant, ex-army and with a pragmatic view of justice, reluctantly agrees to help find the missing woman.

Things get complicated when a high-powered lawyer arrives form the US, and shortly after his meeting with Hunter and Dao, a "cease and desist" letter arrives from the Cayman Islands. Inspector Bakker - a woman, who in Hunter's words "looks as if she would be useful in a brawl, provided she was on your side" - takes instant exception to his involvement and threatens to arrest him for interfering in an investigation.

Dao sets out alone on a dangerous mission, driven by a compulsive need to find out what has happened to the girl who wrote the notes, and Hunter looks death in the face when he decides to risk everything to put an end to the Darknet forces that threaten their lives.

THE SHADOW BROKER

It is 2026 and individual freedoms are severely curtailed, with state surveillance everywhere. State Security has a Watch List, and being on it means that nothing you do or say escapes the authorities, but does the Kill List really exist? And if it does, how would you know if you were on it?

Coded messages on a found burner phone, top-level government corruption and a shadowy mastermind who calls himself The Broker. In this climate of state control, three unlikely friends start quietly looking for connections and set in motion a deadly game of hide and seek that will change their lives forever.

Trying to uncover the truth means risking your life, and nothing is more dangerous than searching for evidence of government corruption.

LETTERS FROM THE PAST

Letters from the Past is a series of stand-alone novels where a letter from or about the past reveals something that changes a woman's perceptions of herself or of her family, and that affects her outlook on life.

These books are such fun to write, and I am always working on the next title in this series. I hope you will enjoy reading them as much as I enjoy writing them!

Tina

Having had nobody in her life since her husband died, Lara unexpectedly finds herself involved with three men. One is planning to use her, one she plans to use for her own ends, and one becomes a "friend-with-benefits" with surprising results. Sometimes a quiet schoolteacher is not all she seems at first glance.

Callista experiences an event of apparent ESP at the Okehampton Castle ruins and becomes a media sensation, but the effect it has on her life is dramatic. How do two people, one calm. one seriously claustrophobic, who feel they are poles apart, cope for an hour and a half in total darkness in a stalled lift? And can they handle the consequences?

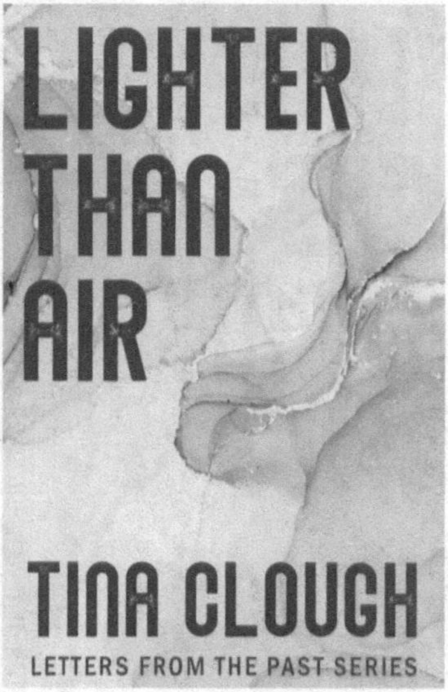

Sofia's life is in turmoil: a difficult diva mother, a letter with a confession about a family killing and having to accept help from a man she loathes when she is injured. Can reluctant attraction turn into love?

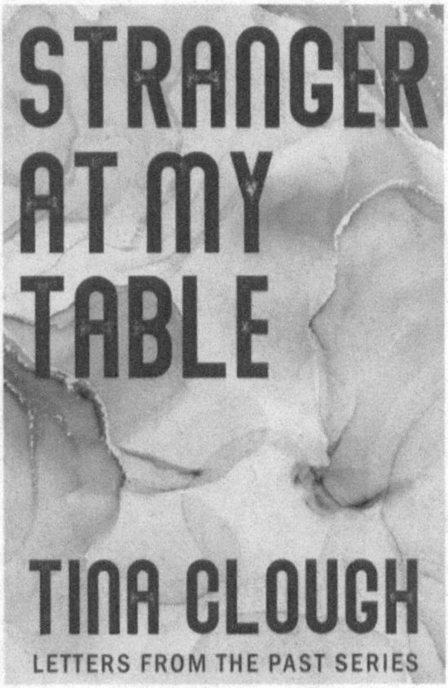

Who is the stranger living in the empty house Miranda inherited from her grandmother? Why is he living like a secretive recluse in someone else's house? Reckless Miranda decides to confront him, and what she discovers prompts her to set out on a fearless quest to bring justice to a man who has given up hope. But is the gamble too great or a risk worth taking?

When Emma finds an old letter in a library book she is instantly intrigued, but by researching the origin of the letter she unwittingly opens the door to danger and becomes the target for threats and harassment. Nearly desperate, she takes a leap of blind faith into the unknown and accepts an offer of help from a stranger - but can she trust him?

Jamie, an ardent protester against the gigantic Vista Resort development and Leo Masters, the high-powered developer, seem unlikely to ever agree on anything. But unexpected coincidences and chance brings them together in a fragile state of mutual respect. Will courage and kindness resolve the situation, or do they need help?

After a bizarre accident with ESP overtones, the media haunt Arapera. But can she trust an offer of help from a man she has only met once? Or will she regret it for the rest of her life if she doesn't take the chance? Sometimes life is a knife-edge balance between staying safe and taking risks, and there is no way of predicting if the gamble is worth it.

When crime-writer Saskia finds an unconscious stranger, she has a strange and strong emotional connection. Pretending to be his cousin and with no thought for the consequences, she spends weeks at his hospital bedside. But what will happen when he wakes and discovers she has invaded his life, breached his privacy and made crucial decisions on his behalf?

ABOUT THE AUTHOR

Tina Clough grew up in Sweden and now lives in New Zealand; dividing her time between writing fiction and translating and editing medical research papers.

Between working and writing she looks after an acre of fruit trees, vegetable gardens and roaming hens.

Apart from reading her interests include photography, wine, growing organic vegetables, making jam and kayaking.

https://lightpoolpublishing.com

www.ingramcontent.com/pod-product-compliance
Lightning Source LLC
Chambersburg PA
CBHW011129190726
48289CB00012B/2972
9781738627233